CONSPIRACY
OF
RAVENS

Funny, how he'd started out with nothing but a one-eyed mule and a pair of boots, had gotten pretty much everything he'd ever wanted, had lost it in one night, and was now burdened with one eye of his own, a surly donkey, and an even worse-fitting pair of boots.

But he wasn't anywhere close to quitting. He'd get it all back. And soon.

He fell asleep counting all the shit he was gonna take back.

Deep in the night, possibly on the edge of morning, something jolted Rhett from untidy dreams. He opened his eye and sat up, muttering, "What the Sam Hill—?"

And that's when a hand landed on his shoulder and a knife stuck deep in his side.

By Lila Bowen

The Shadow

Wake of Vultures
Conspiracy of Ravens

CONSPIRACY OF RAVENS

THE SHADOW: BOOK TWO

LILA BOWEN

orbit

www.orbitbooks.net

ORBIT

First published in Great Britain in 2016 by Orbit

1 3 5 7 9 10 8 6 4 2

Copyright © 2016 by D. S. Dawson

Map illustration by Tim Paul

Excerpt from *Speak* by Louisa Hall
Copyright © 2015 by Louisa Hall

A CIP catalogue record for this book
is available from the British Library.

ISBN 978-0-356-50658-6

Printed and bound by CPI Group (UK) Ltd, Croydon, CR0 4YY

Papers used by Orbit are from well-managed forests
and other responsible sources.

 MIX
Paper from
responsible sources
FSC
www.fsc.org FSC® C104740

Orbit
An imprint of
Little, Brown Book Group
Carmelite House
50 Victoria Embankment
London EC4Y 0DZ

An Hachette UK Company
www.hachette.co.uk

www.orbitbooks.net

For my favorite lich, because all my books are, really.

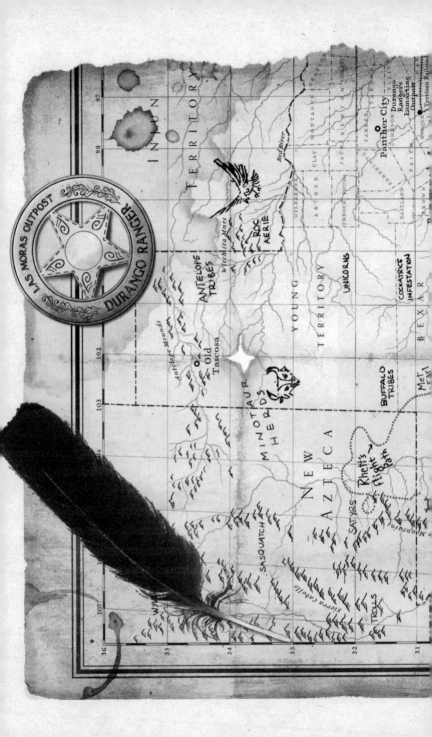

MAP of
DURANGO TERRITORY
of THE FEDERAL REPUBLIC *of*
AMERICA

According to the Newest and most exact observations of
Timothy dePaul, Geographer

GIANT GILA
MONSTERS

A Z T E C A

PRESIDIO
TERRITORY

BRACKVILLE (DWARFS)

GORGON
NEST

JAVELI
TRIBES

Reveille

Durango
Rangers
Las Moras
Outpost

CHUPACABRA
TERRITORY

JAUN
de BLANCO's
LAND

Gloomy
Bluebird

Rio Bravo R.

SAND
WYRMS

Buckhead

Prosperas
Camp

Waterloo

San
Anton

Kinney

MERMAID
COLONY

CAMERON

0 10 20   40   60   80   100

© Tim Paul 2016

24 Published by Mssres. Howard & dePaul

CHAPTER 1

Nettie Lonesome was falling fast, and she didn't need two eyes to see that the ground looked right glad to meet her. Maybe she'd been wrong. Maybe Dan was right and she wasn't a skinwalker at all. Maybe she was about to do the Cannibal Owl's work on her own and paint the valley of bones a new shade of red. What had Winifred's song said? Find the golden string in your gullet and yank it? The only thing in her belly right now was a scream, high and terrified. She closed her eyes and accepted that she'd made her last mistake.

And damn if it didn't hurt, when it happened.

Not the splattering on rocks part.

The changing into . . . whatever it was.

Like being turned inside out in fry butter, wet and hot.

And then she was skimming inches above the hard brown dirt, wings spread wide and a sense of joy and freedom she'd never known singing in her heart. A sense of rightness. And then she wasn't Nettie anymore. Not Nettie or Nat or Rhett. What she was had no name and belonged to the sky. If she didn't think about it too much, her body did what it was supposed to, naturally, and she twitched her wings to send herself up into the clouds. After a few near falls, she gave it up altogether, being human. Too much work by half, all that caring about things.

Riding the thermals through the mountains and out over the plains, she forgot about the Cannibal Owl, about the Rangers, about the Shadow, about her friends. Even about Samuel Hennessy. She focused on one thing and one thing only: finding something nice and dead to eat.

Days passed. Nights, too. She was a solitary creature mastering a new world, and she was mercifully free of foolish human encumbrances. She learned the taste of the air as the sun rose, flipping from a small red disk to a burning white one. She gathered dust and smoke and grit in the corner of her one sharp eye. She was attacked, or maybe the other bird-thing was trying to mate with her, but it didn't matter. She killed him. And ate him. She tasted delicacies ranging from beeves to buffalo to rabbits to a tender baby goat kid she plucked from the ground and dropped to splatter open on the rocks, wiping her beak delicately afterward to clean it—and to sharpen it for the next gift of nature's bounty. She understood, finally, that a little time and rot only made things sweeter.

Through it all, day after day, she knew she was alone. The other creatures she encountered in flight and hunkered down in trees blinked at her distrustfully and scattered, aware that she was different somehow. When she landed, wings outspread in a puff of dust, the vultures and coyotes edged away to give her room. Laughing, she spread her wings wider to block any newcomers and got down to business. The scrape of beak on bone reminded her, strangely, of a spoon fetching up against metal in an empty bowl of beans, but she put that thought from her mind. It hurt too much, brought back downright uncomfortable feelings. Better to hop along and pump back into the sky, where such petty things as feelings and memories were forgotten.

One day, something caught her eye. A familiar shape drew a long shadow deep in the desert where upright things, besides cacti, did not belong. She circled lazily lower. Might it die soon? As lovely as aged meat might be, being the first to rip into a belly also offered its advantages.

And yet...

She knew this thing. Knew what it was. Had mixed feelings on the matter.

When it cried out and toppled over in the sand, she was drawn to it, whether for good or ill. Landing lightly, she hopped sideways toward it, wings outstretched menacingly and beak open and hissing. The thing turned its head to stare at her, sand stuck to red scruff on its face.

"I suppose you're thinkin' it's me time to die, then," it muttered.

He muttered.

She ruffled her feathers. Maybe yes, maybe no.

"I got a trick, though, see?"

She cocked her head. This close to him, it, her prey, she felt a bit sickly, her belly writhing as if she might vomit up the bits of sun-blackened beef she'd swallowed down earlier that morning. With another hiss, she lolloped backward a few steps, waiting for her proper hunger to return.

"You like tricks, you ugly son of a whore?"

That made her squawk, and he laughed and heaved up onto his hands and knees, shucking his drab brown-and-rust-red skin into a puddle on the ground. He did some other things she didn't understand, but the end result was that the talkative creature was now stark nekkid and tender as the morning, pale white with red-burned edges and hair like fire.

She raised her wings to rush him, and he...

Changed.

On hands and knees, he rippled and bellowed and became just about the least appetizing thing she could think of: an ass.

She blinked and remembered—everything. It all came rushing back in a series of terrifying images that flashed inside her tiny brain. What he was—she was that, too. She had things to do. People who needed her. People she cared about. She just had to remember...something about a golden string...

It was like swallowing backward, and everything rippled and hurt, and then the hot sand burned her skin as she lay there on her knees, coughing and human.

The donkey had galloped away a bit and stood, watching her warily. He was small and dusty and almost obscene in his ugliness. His lips pulled back over long yellow teeth, and he brayed a laugh.

"I'll teach you to laugh," Nettie muttered.

She stood, stepped into his pants, shoved her feet into his boots, yanked his hat down over her grown-out hair, grabbed his beat-up leather saddlebags, pulled on his shirt, and, without buttoning it, ran for the hills.

Unfortunately, the hills were farther away than Nettie would've liked, and the stranger's boots were too big. Sand spilled into the cracked leather with every step, rubbing her feet raw. However long she'd spent as—whatever she was—she'd lost her human stamina. Days, definitely. Weeks or months? There was no way to know until she got back to the Rangers and asked. And she had no idea where the Rangers were. Or where she was. All she knew was that the hills in the distance were wavering with heat, and there was no telltale smudge of green on the horizon to promise the water she so desperately needed. She'd once cursed herself for running out into the night like a fool, but this was a goddamn desert, and running off in the full heat of the sun was about as stupid as a creature could get.

She slowed down, panting, and looked over her shoulder. That damn donkey was following her at a jaunty trot like he knew something she didn't. After a few hours had passed, she understood why: Donkeys could keep on going forever in just such a hellscape, but humans most definitely could not. Her mouth was parched beyond all fool reason, and her feet were slick with blood and sweat and blister juice inside the boots. The clothes weren't much better, crusted with the donkey feller's sweat and probably piss, if the smell was any indication. The hills were no closer, and Nettie was pretty goddamn near to becoming exactly the sort of morsel she would've relished just yesterday. She looked up and watched the vultures circle. Was she one of them? Or something else? She'd felt...bigger. But she fed as they fed and shunned their company, so maybe, like always, she was just plain different. It didn't matter what she'd been. Right now, she was on her way to becoming lunch.

There was no way she could reach safety, shade, or water before this stupidly fragile human body wore out. She knew that, and the donkey knew that, too. Maybe a bullet couldn't kill her, but lying on the ground like a strip of jerky, barely breathing, didn't much appeal. Every now and then, she'd stumble, and he'd let out one of those braying laughs. Annoying as he was, she figured he'd get on good with Coyote Dan. It was a grand accomplishment to make someone feel dumb as hell when you couldn't even speak their language. She needed these clothes, though, if she was going to wander back into Ranger camp, or into any human settlement. Everything she valued in life currently hinged on folks taking her for a man, and she'd rather die and get danced on by a rude donkey than see Jiddy's face once he found out the tracker who'd bested him was a skinwalker and a girl to boot.

So what she needed was to turn back into a bird—and somehow keep the clothes. If she could just get to someplace safe, somewhere the donkey couldn't get to, she'd maybe have a hope of taking back her former life. Putting on a fierce burst of speed, she ran as far as she could and stripped off the clothes. The shirt was most important, as it was long enough to cover everything she needed to keep hidden. She tied it around her bare ankle as the donkey galloped toward her, bucking as he came. Then she took off running again, focused on that golden thread inside, and leaped into the air.

But instead of elegantly morphing into a bird and flying away, she tumbled to the ground in a heap of feathers and claws. Something clung to her leg, holding her back. Stupid scrap of nothing. Righting herself, she hopped around, wings spread wide, shaking her foot until the damn thing came off. She didn't have time to take off before the donkey had spun around to kick her with sharp black hooves, and she hissed and hopped back. The animal she faced off against was not good for fighting and no good for eating until it was dead. Even then, the taste was not appealing. So why was she here? What she needed to do was escape. And yet every time she looked at the pile of brownish-red trash on the ground, something tugged at her. She needed that…thing. Not for eating. For another reason.

Clothes. That was it.

She needed clothes.

When the donkey turned around to snap at her with clacking teeth, she flew at his face, claws out, forcing him to dance back. Clutching the shirt in her claws, she awkwardly launched herself into the air and flapped toward the buttes.

Far below, something rippled, making her gullet twist. A figure chased her, shaking a fist.

"I'll find you, buzzard," it called. "That's my favorite bleedin' shirt!"

From the air, the mountains were close, and that was good. There was a hollowed-out cow on the way there, and that was better. As she hit the scrub that cozied up to the rocks, it rained for a bit, and she huddled on an old dead tree, blinking at the lightning as rain pearled up on her feathers. She didn't know why she clutched it still, but there was a wad of something under her talons, and she wasn't going to let go of it. All the while, in her wake, trotted an ugly little donkey. He never seemed to tire, although he did occasionally kick up his heels at a fly. He made her downright irritable, and she kept a sharp eye out for wolves or a rattler or any other predator that might do her the favor of ending him. Nature, unfortunately, was not so kind.

The donkey drooped under her tree, just as miserable in the punishing rain as she was. He had something slung around his neck—some human thing like the scrap she carried with her. Everything was wretched, and he wouldn't go away, even when she lifted her tail and dropped a runny plop on his sodden back. His ear barely twitched; that was all.

She forgot about him by morning, but she kept the scrap clutched tight.

That afternoon, she was playing tug-o-war with a snake, and damned if some upstart donkey didn't show up and try to drive her away. From her own snake! The donkey was vaguely familiar, like a tick she'd already picked off and spat out. They tussled for a moment in a tornado of hooves and claws and drizzle, and she flapped up into the tree, and the donkey was suddenly upright and shouting on two legs.

"Just give me back the blasted shirt, woman, and I'll leave you be!"

She ruffled her feathers and looked away.

"Oh, you don't like hearing speech, hey? You runnin' away from something? Or don't like being called a thief?" He punctuated this last bit with a thrown rock, which pinged painfully off her wing. She hopped a few branches higher up and sighed in disgust.

"Listen here, then. You're a thief, and you're costin' me valuable time on this wild goose chase. People are dying while we play fetch. I don't even know if I'm on the right track to the Rangers anymore. Why on heaven and earth were you sent to torment me? Buggerin' harpy!"

Her head snapped toward him, her eye bright. Three words in that last garbled bit had struck home more firmly than the rock. She considered her options: Fly away forever, or . . .

She flapped to the ground, talons still curled around the shirt, and changed.

"Not a harpy," she muttered, tasting old blood on her tongue. Her fingers unclenched from around the sodden fabric. She rolled over to sitting and shrugged it on. "Not really a woman. And what about the Rangers?"

"Oh, you want to talk now? Fine then." He turned his back on her as he pulled pants out of a bag and stepped into them, and Nettie went cold to her toes—well, colder, considering she was soaked to the damn bone. The man, and he was more of a boy, to be honest . . . well, for a pasty white feller with fire-red hair, his back bore a striking resemblance to Nettie's own. Painfully thin and painted with twisted old scars. She pulled her knees to her chest under the shirt and leaned back against a rock.

"Who beat you?" she asked, voice low.

"That's how you start a conversation? Stealin' my favorite shirt, dragging me out here, shittin' on my back, and then asking the most personal question a body can ask?" He turned to face her, holding up his oversized pants with one hand. "I might as well be askin' you who took your eye."

She blinked slowly. "You ask a lot of questions yourself."

"Oh, well, now, that would be because I've been schooled in the conversational graces, Your Majesty." He cut a clumsy bow. "And the answer is the only answer there is for such a question: The person who beat me was somebody who had no damn right." He stared at her, shivering. "But considering as how I've seen the scars on your back, too, I'm forced to ask me own personal question: How'd you escape the camp?"

"What camp?"

He cocked his head at her like she was dumb as a damn post, and Nettie's temper flared up, reminding her of why she didn't much prefer being human.

"The railroad camp. Were you dropped on yer head? What other camp is there?"

She grunted and shook her head. "No railroads around here. All that's back east."

He pulled his boots out of his bag and winced as he shoved wet, sandy feet into the crusted leather. "So you are dumb, then. The railroads are coming, missy, and they're coming fast. I escaped one quite recently, in fact, run by an evil son of a whore who goes by the fancified name of Bernard Trevisan, and I tell you now that he's single-handedly driving that engine clear to Calafia."

"Stranger, the desert has clearly gone to your head. You can't talk straight, and you're imagining railroads in a land that would swaller them up and spit out spikes. So you go on your way and I'll go on mine, and we'll call it a draw."

"Like hell we will. Now give me back my shirt!" He spun around to face her, holding up a large, well-used knife. Panic brushed up against her like a hissing cat, but then she remembered that wounds were more annoyance than doom, now. His stance suggested he knew how to use the scarred blade, but the trembling of his mouth suggested he wouldn't.

Nettie stood, spread her bare feet, and put her hands on her hips, wishing like hell she still had her pants and gun belt. There was nothing in the area that even vaguely resembled a weapon, and without wings, even the lowest branches of the half-dead tree were out of reach. She put her hands up, as she figured it might make the feller feel like he was doing good.

"I'm keeping this shirt, and you won't stick that knife in me," she said calmly as rain sluiced down her face. "So let's just forget it all and go our separate ways."

"You know where we are?" he asked.

She shook her head. "No idea."

"But you can turn into whatever the hell you are and fly around. You can see for miles!"

"Mister, you know as good as I do that we can't remember shit when we're critters."

The knife dropped, just a little. "But that's nowhere near true."

He sounded surprised.

And she felt cheated. "You mean...you can? You can remember?"

"I can always remember. It's just like lookin' out through a different window."

Hearing him say it, all casual, like she was the dumb one... well, it made her wish for his knife and the aim two good eyes would've given her to throw it at him. "Bullshit."

Now he shook his head, red hair swinging across his eyes.

10

"You're not playin'? You really can't remember? Then why'd you keep that shirt with you, all this time?"

She shrugged and crossed her arms. "I guess I'm angry enough in both forms not to let go."

"And how is it you're missing an eye?"

"Silver bullet." She chewed her lip. "And how come you got such deep scars?"

He raised an eyebrow. "Silver points on a cat-o'-nine tails. When Mr. Trevisan wants to scare somebody, he knows his business." The knife's tip dropped as he considered her. "We could do well, traveling together. Maybe when we get where we're goin', you'll be giving me shirt back. Me mother made it, back in Ireland. Sentimental value, see."

Nettie shook her head. "I do better alone."

"Where are you going then?"

"I've been wandering."

"With an *a* or an *o*?"

"With no goddamn thing. Aimless."

"Running to something or running away?"

"Hellfire, donkey-boy. I got a talkative friend named Dan you'd like just fine. You could just talk each other's furry damn ears off. I been wandering, with my wings and my feet, and the only thing I found so far is you, and that's turning out to be one hell of a disappointment."

He cocked his head. "You've got friends, then? Where?"

She surveyed the land, hunting for anything vaguely familiar, but it was all just the same brown dirt and gnarled trees and scrubby mountains perpetually arguing with the sky, which was currently stone-gray and drizzling. "I got no rightly idea."

"Well then." The man dropped his knife and held out his hand—a sand-dusted, callus-hard, sunburned hand lightly furred on the back in orange. "The name's Earl O'Bannon.

Once out of Galway, most recent out of the Trevisan Railroad labor camp. I could use some friends, meself, and I could do a lot worse than you."

Her eye narrowed. "You trying to butter me up?"

He chuckled but didn't let his hand fall. "Oh, for certain. You've so many charms, lass."

That got her hackles up. She stepped forward, hands in fists. "Don't call me a girl."

"But aren't you one, then? You've got all the requisite parts—"

Instead of shaking his hand, she punched the Irishman in the face. He wasn't ready for it and stumbled back, landing hard on his rump and staring up at her in surprise that quickly gave way to anger. His face went red to the roots of his hair. Nettie was pleased that she'd finally managed to punch someone without hurting herself, and she gazed at her own rain-slick knuckles in admiration. She'd missed punching people, and her foul mood lightened considerably.

"Now, as a rule, I don't hit women, but you seem to be saying—"

"The name's Rhett Hennessy, and I'm a Durango Ranger, so if you want to get in a fight, you'd best prepare to die."

Apparently, he'd missed the bit about dying, as he popped upright and surged toward her with a franticness that spoke of desperation. "You're a Ranger? You know where the Rangers are? Then you can help me! Oh, thank the gods that be you stole my bleedin' shirt, la—" He cleared his throat. "Laddie," he finished carefully.

Nettie gave him a nod so he'd know he'd done right. And then she realized that in her pride, she'd managed to give him all the more reason to continue annoying the hell out of her. She shook her head and spit on the ground at his feet, although it was a sad little glob, for lack of water.

12

"Don't know where the Rangers are. Don't know when I last saw 'em. Don't know how to find 'em."

"Oh, yes, well, aside from your ability to turn into a great bleedin' bird and view the world from up high, I'm sure you're utterly without resources."

"Hellfire, you don't give up, do you? You cluck like a hen that wants a wrung neck."

"I come by my stubbornness honest. Now, these here are the Aspero mountains, are they no? I was headed west, on the hunt for the Las Moras Outpost of the Durango Rangers."

She shook her head. "I ain't been here before, but I been there, and this ain't it."

"Would that be the Pecana River, do you think?" He pointed to a smudge of green on the dreary horizon.

"What part of *I don't know* sounded like *keep on asking*?"

He scratched the orange stubble on his chin. "Anyone ever told you you're a people person?"

She growled and began to walk off to a spray of shrubs where she could transform back into a bird with some privacy. If she had to listen to him, she'd rather not have to understand what he said.

With a squeak, he stumbled along behind her. "Look, lad. I'm sorry. I've the gift of gab and I've been alone for too long and if I don't find your friends, the Rangers, over a hundred souls including me own brother will continue to suffer. They're being tortured. Having fingers and toes lopped off willy-nilly by Trevisan and fixed by Grandpa Z and sent right back out to cut the lines and lay the rails."

"Don't lie to me."

When she didn't stop walking, he put a hand on her shoulder and yanked hard, dancing back to avoid the haymaker that they both knew would follow such a trespass. As she advanced on him, hands in fists, he yanked off a boot and hopped around on one leg as he held up a much-abused foot missing two toes.

That got Nettie's attention and made her step closer despite her dislike of the strange feller. He was a monster, a skin-walker, and that meant the stubs of his toes should've been open wounds, like Winifred's ankle and the child's foot they'd found in the desert, left behind by the Cannibal Owl. In Nettie's experience, the peculiar healing power of monsters meant that flesh wounds grew over while open bones refused to heal. But this feller—and he was a monster, to be sure—his toes were neatly sealed over, covered with stretched, whole skin.

Nettie grunted her interest. "How'd you do that?"

Exasperated, he stuck his foot back in his boot. "Told you. Trevisan needs monster bones, so he takes toes and fingers, wherever they can be spared. Grandpa Z uses his mysterious Chine medicine to fix 'em so we can still work."

"What medicine?"

He put his hands on his hips and looked at her like she was a damn fool. "You think he told us? Handed out a hymnal on Chine magic? They knock you out so you can't see. You wake up, and it's all healed. Grandpa Z and his girl won't tell nobody, as then Trevisan might start lopping off bits of them, too, far as I can figure it. Those as has secrets in the camp hold 'em close."

Nettie worried at her lip, considering how to get what she needed with minimal annoyance. "Maybe we can help each other. You want to get to the Rangers, right?" Earl nodded, the eagerness and hope in his eyes making him seem barely a boy grown. "Well, I want two things: I want you to teach me how to remember what I see when I'm..." She wasn't sure of the right word. What was she, really? "Flying. And if my friend's still missing her foot, take us to this camp and get me to the old feller who knows how to heal lost limbs."

Earl pulled at his bedraggled mustache. "I can't promise you either thing. I don't know how to do something that comes natural, and there's no oath on this earth that could compel me back to that hellforsaken camp."

"Promise me you'll try to teach me, then. And tell me how to find the camp."

"I'll do that anyway. Whole reason I need the Rangers is to convince 'em to go destroy Trevisan. He's a demon. Or something. Never seen a creature like him, in his fine dandy coat and shiny shoes, but he does the devil's work for sure."

Nettie stared hard into his eyes and held out her hand. When he quickly reached to grasp it, she tightened her larger hand around his. "Mark my words, donkey-boy. You cross me, and I'll slit your throat and eat your guts before I ever find your heart. I don't trust easy, and I'm not a kind person."

"Never would've guessed," he muttered, but his hand only squeezed tighter. "When you're alone in the desert, you'll be needing strength more than kindness, don't you think?"

"Welcome to Durango, Earl O'Bannon." She dropped his hand and rubbed her palm off on the red fabric. "I'm keeping your damn shirt."

She started walking toward the river, and he picked up his knife and bag and followed at a respectful distance. The drizzle had stopped, and the very land sizzled under the sun thus revealed by broken clouds.

The desert was a great and silent place, but everyone within fifty miles must've heard Earl's growled whisper, "Like hell you will, lad. Like hell you will."

Nettie smiled.

CHAPTER 2

They didn't speak again until they'd drunk from the creek and set up camp. When Nettie began yanking already-dry twigs from the scumble of greenery, Earl followed suit until they had a respectable pile. He was completely hopeless, and after watching him rub two sticks together like a dumb child playing a broken fiddle, Nettie gave in and did all the work. He soon began singing off-key as he dried his hands over her crackling fire, and Nettie gladly snatched his knife and went out of hearing range to find something small and edible to kill. Rattlers were plentiful under the flat stones, and it wasn't long before she had one skinned and roasting over the fire.

"You afraid to eat snake?" she asked, watching the meat drip and sizzle.

He shook his head. "I'll eat anything as won't bite back. Ate some bugs when it got bad. Bit before I found you." He ran a thumb down his chest. "Never was a brawny lad, but I'll take whatever meat I can get for these bones. Food's not bad at the camp, you'll understand, but it's not plentiful for the workers, neither. Wasn't good in Ireland, but at least then we all starved together."

Nettie said nothing, just poked the snake with a twig. She'd had some deathly belches since returning to this form and was looking forward to something fresh that wouldn't disagree with her human guts.

"So where are you from, then?" Earl asked, settling back on his elbows.

She shot him a dark look. "Nowhere town you never heard of."

"You got family?"

That earned a snort. "Do I look like anybody ever loved me?"

He squinted as if looking for the right line to crack a nut. "If you're alive, somebody must've, sometime. Me, I got a big family back home. Eight brothers and sisters, all smaller and hungrier than me. Mostly sisters. Mam could barely keep up. Me and me brother Shaunie thought we'd come over here, find some gold, and send back lace and velvet by the boatload. Ha!" He flung a rock out into the night. "No jobs for the Irish, back east. No way to get west for the free gold. Railroad lad said they paid well and kept you healthy and strong as you rode across the prairie to the land of milk and goddamn honey. If I ever see him again, I'll bash his bleedin' head in."

Nettie grunted and reached for the snake. It wasn't quite cooked yet, but maybe he'd shut up if he had some half-raw meat in his open mouth. When she held it out and jerked her chin at his knife, lying between them on the ground, he picked it up and sliced off half for himself. She nodded; for a starving feller, he could've been more of a greedy sort for certain.

For a while there, they just blew the night's cooling air on their steaming chunks of charred meat. Nettie's heart ached, a dull tug she recognized as missing Sam. Many a night they'd laid their bedrolls by a fire just like this, chatting in a friendly fashion side by side as they drifted off to sleep under the stars. Those days were the best ones of Nettie's life. A job, the respect of men she respected. Cash money for breaking broncs or killing sirens. Something like hope. When she glanced across the flames and saw not Sam's sunny smile and bright eyes but instead only a slight, vexful Irishman juggling half-cooked meat and chewing with his greasy gob open, she felt like she'd lost everything she'd ever had.

She didn't like anybody, not really. But she liked Sam.

"Are your ears full of rocks, lad?"

Her head jerked up, her eye slitted in anger. "More like muck, if you can call your constant yapping muck, but yeah."

"I asked you when you started changing."

She snorted and took a big bite of snake, considering. Might as well tell the truth. No point in lying, really. He was just a damn donkey. "Not sure. Might be days ago, might be weeks."

"But you're..."

"Go on and finish that damn sentence."

"Not a child," he said carefully. "It usually begins around age five, say. If it's going to. I still remember my first time. Gave me mum a merry chase about the garden. Me younger brother Shaunie, too. You're clearly older than that."

"I'm different."

He looked her up and down. "Obviously."

Before she knew she was doing it, she'd leaped across the fire and had a finger poking into his bony chest. "Don't test me, son."

Earl's hands were up. "Christ, but you take offense easy. All I meant was that you're some giant bird I never seen before, and you changed late. You got to stop going through life thinkin' a person's got ill intentions toward you."

She sat back on her haunches and glared at him. "Most folks take offense to me."

The wee man nodded. "And so you take offense first. Beat 'em at their own game."

"You go on and tell yourself whatever you want, donkey-boy. It don't change the taste of beans."

He settled back, just to prove he could. "Well, then. If you'll back the hell off, I'll tell you the first rule of changing, if you'll promise not to poke me or hit me again. But you're not gonna like it."

Nettie returned to her side of the fire and brushed the sand off her dropped meat. "Go on, then."

"The first rule is that you got to know what you are." He held up a hand when she opened her mouth. "Shut up and learn something, will you now? If you switch from one thing to another and don't know what either one is, of course you're bound to get lost. Like taking a wrong turn from a wrong turn. You got to know, to your bones, who and what you are."

As his words echoed in the night, gooseflesh pearled up on Nettie's bare legs. Winifred had sung her a song, back in the Cannibal Owl's lair. "Little one that I love, you are two creatures with one spirit. Reach down inside, deep inside, and find the golden core of you, connecting you to the earth and sky, the trail the moon leaves on water. Pull it like a rope, inside out, and know that you are perfect in either skin."

Without meaning to, she'd muttered the last line, barely more than a whisper, but Earl was smiling and nodding. "That's about right, yeah. I figure it's like...well, say, me own house and me grandmam's house. I know 'em both, inside and out, and I know the way between 'em. I never get lost, and whichever I'm in, I know where I am."

Nettie's chest constricted, her throat uncomfortably blocked. "I..."

"Don't know either skin too well, eh? Well, let me explain it to you, as I see it, from an impartial perspective, as they say. Me pap was a newspaperman before he passed, so excuse all the

19

big words." He set down what little was left of his snake, mostly the raw bits on a tail of bone, and gestured to her. "Right now, you say you're a man named Rhett Hennessy, but do you really believe it?"

Rage hit her first, but then a peculiar feeling tamped it back down. She'd punch a feller for calling her a girl, but she still thought of herself as a girl, didn't she? And that was her own damn fault. Whatever her vision had shown her, when she was wandering the desert for four days with mesquite poisoning, in the end, it had told her that she was now a man, and she'd believed it. Agreed with it. She'd felt the rightness of it settle over her shoulders like a winter coat. So why'd she still think of herself as a she, a her? As what used to be Nettie Lonesome?

"My name is Rhett Hennessy, and I'm a man," she said.

No.

He said.

He.

"I'm a man." That time, it was a little louder, a little deeper and he felt it down to his very bones.

"You been fightin' it the way you fight everything, haven't you?"

Rhett's smile was a grim thing. "Fighting's the only way I get anything I want."

Earl nodded. "Good for you, lad. Fight for this, then. Fight for yourself. And the other thing you are is..." A shrug. "Hell, a great big bird. Not a vulture, but close. Bigger. Not particularly pretty. More scary, to be honest. I don't know what it's called. But it's the most dangerous-looking thing I've ever seen in the air, if that makes you feel any better."

Rhett nodded and held out his hand, fanning his fingers like feathers. "When I'm...it...I feel powerful. Like cracking bones. Like I always get to go first. Like I'm different."

"Sounds like you've got a good feel for it, then. So I guess you might wish to transform while thinkin' hard on what you are when you're human. Think about something that ties you to this body and this earth. The first time I did it, I was thinkin' about how me mam was going to tan me hide for mucking up the laundry. And I wanted so badly to be something else so's I could hide. And then I was suddenly shorter and on four legs, giving her a scare and a chase and stomping her clean white sheets into the mud with me trotters. But I was focused on her, scared of her and then excited to trouble her with me newfound mischief. So think about how much I annoy you, or think of someone you actually like. Tie this body to that and that to this, eh?" He cocked his head. "Might explain why you keep hangin' on to my shirt, even though you don't understand much else as a bird. Because this form wants a shirt with a great yearning, you see. What else do you yearn for—in both bodies?"

Rhett took a deep breath and considered. "Every million words or so, you make some good sense."

Stepping away, he turned his back to Earl and the fire and slipped the shirt over his head, placing it on the ground and stepping on it firmly. He reached inside for the golden cord and pulled, thinking about the shirt and Earl and how much he wanted to find Sam again. Every time, the change hurt a little less, and soon he was ruffling his feathers and opening and closing great claws on the rust-red shirt.

"Hey, Rhett! Hey, lad! Looky here!"

The bird made a hobbling turn on his talons and blinked irritably. It was that vexful man again, waving his featherless arms like a damn idiot.

"Remember this: *There was an old lady from Wheeling who had a remarkable feeling.*"

Rhett opened his mouth to tell the feller to shut up, but all that came out was an annoyed squawk.

"Good! Good, Rhett. Now turn back."

With a deep sigh, Rhett turned. It was colder, without feathers, and he quickly tossed the shirt over his head and settled it over breasts that no longer felt like they belonged on his body at all. When he turned around, Earl was grinning like a fool.

"What the hell is Wheeling?" Rhett said, "And why would I give two turds in a bucket about some old lady?"

Earl laughed, a remarkably catchy sound, and rocked back. "You did it, lad! You remembered! That, me boy, is the beginning of a dirty poem, and the fact that you remembered it at all means you're starting to understand. It's working."

Rhett sat back down by the fire and shoved his last bit of snake into the flames. The little bastard was right—finally, it was working. But now he was tired and sleepy and mostly full. Coming to terms with such great truths was exhausting. He was a man of action, not...chewing thoughts like cud. And it made his head ache.

"I reckon it is working, now that you mention it. I'm going to sleep now, and if you touch me or try to take back this shirt, I'll—"

"Kill me with one body and eat me with the other. Oh, I do so certainly get it. Look, I'm an Irishman freshly come from a railroad camp. Even your threats are a pleasant chorus by comparison. So let's just sleep like friends and wake up alive and uneaten, if you please. You did good, laddie."

Rhett wanted to shoot back something smart about how he didn't need the opinion of some goddamn donkey, but the feller had taught him something valuable. And, as much as he hated to admit it, even to himself, Rhett felt better in mind and body than he ever had before. The feller had given him a gift, damn him. Rhett felt the heavy weight of owing settle around his neck like a chain. This was what bound him to Sam and Dan and Winifred and Chuck and Monty and the Rangers. This is what tied lives together and made folks worth dying for.

Rhett didn't like Earl. He didn't trust Earl. But he was goddamned if Earl wasn't turning out to be a good friend.

The bastard.

Rhett slept harder and longer than usual and awoke with a start to find the sun already installed in the sky like a crisp fried egg. Earl was still sleeping, flopped out like a fool with a curious scorpion just about to explore the boy's open hand. With a heavy sigh, Rhett grabbed a rock and crunched the creature with a satisfying thump that also did the work of waking his companion.

"What the bloody hell?" Earl mumbled, snatching his hand back.

Rhett lifted the rock to show him a mess of guts. "Looks like you owe me again, donkey-boy. You ever been stung by a scorpion? Human feller can lose an arm that way. And there's no sawbones for miles."

"Oh, I suspect I've lived through worse." Earl inspected his hand before using it to scratch his nethers. "What's for breakfast?" Turning his back to the remains of the fire, he unleashed a pathetic stream of piss.

Rhett turned and walked away in disgust. He was accustomed to waking among the Rangers, each feller doing his part to keep camp harmonious. But Earl was undisciplined and untaught, which meant Rhett had to do everything himself. Hunting down breakfast, smothering what was left of the fire, all while avoiding the quickly drying puddle of piss. A damn inconvenience, traveling with a green feller. Of course, Rhett himself had been green just a few short weeks ago, settling in at the Las Moras Outpost, but most of the fellers had been glad to teach Rhett the necessary skills, if only so they had someone lower on the fence to do the work.

Seeing nothing all the way out to the horizon, Rhett spat what little moisture he had. "How the Sam Hill'd you get this far without a damn skill to your hand?"

"Took the easy way out when things got hard," Earl said. Rhett heard the sound of fabric hitting the sand. "Gonna do it again, too. A donkey can live damn near forever on nothing. Couple of little scrub trees, few slurps of water. Hard little black trotters just keep on trotting. You'd best be doin' the same. There's nothing much alive out here, if you can't tell. And I'm guessing that little rain-creek's already dried up like me mam's tit. At least as a—whatever you turn into—blood's easy to come by."

"We need a plan, then. Can't be two dumb animals, moseying around and fighting over a damn shirt."

Earl was busy stuffing his britches in his bag, and Rhett looked anywhere but at his lily-white buttocks. "What we need is you in the air, trying to figure out where we are and where we're going. Look here."

He turned around, and Rhett shielded his eyes. "I ain't here to look at your parts, donkey. Put on your damn drawers."

"You're a delicate lad, you know." Earl grinned and held his bag over his danglies. "Sorry. See, when I get thirsty, I just change and let the donkey take over, but I suppose I can wait a bit. This is what I want you to see, though." He stood and pulled a scrap of fabric from his bag.

Rhett stepped forward and took the filthy, worn canvas. Brown lines scrabbled all over it, wiggly and lumpy. When he turned it around a few times, he recognized a rough map.

On the right was a ladder-type design that must've stood for the railroad, and on the left was a little house shape with a star-badge smudged beside it. In between them, there were mountains and creeks and a few blobby dots that might've been cities. What he didn't see was any way to make sense of it when you were in the middle of it.

"This is San Anton." Earl pointed to one of the blobs, as if that helped.

"Ain't much of a map. How are you supposed to know if you're even on the right track? These mountains are just little lumps. Now over here's where Bandera Pass would be. But I don't know how to tell where we are from where this is."

"Fly, then, fool. That's the whole point."

"How the hell do you know I won't just take off and keep flying?"

Earl grinned. "You're gonna give me back that shirt, and I'll tie it around a stick and wave it at you while you're flying about. That should get your bleedin' attention."

Rhett's filthy fingers curled into the rust-red fabric. He didn't want to give up the shirt. And he didn't know if Earl would give it back. But he had to trust someone sometime, didn't he? Earl hadn't tried anything yet and seemed mostly useless in human form. Between the map and the bird's-eye view, maybe they could pull it off. He nodded.

"Can't believe I'm saying it, but your plan ain't horrible, donkey."

"So let's turn about, change, eat, and get on with it. You remember how to stay focused, do you then?"

Rhett nodded. "I reckon I know my business."

"Then I'll be seein' you on the other side, brother."

Once Rhett heard a right peculiar, ripply noise, he turned to confirm that the donkey, bag slung around its neck, was trotting toward what was left of the creek. He slipped the shirt over his head, recalled that line about some old lady from Wheeling, and transformed. It seemed easier now, somehow. Less like being pulled inside out and more like pulling on suspenders. In bird form, he shivered to get his feathers in place, took a few hopping steps away from the shirt, and launched into the sky. His thoughts were simple: dead things, red shirt, Wheeling.

Up in the air, soaring on thermals, the bird looked down. There: A man stuffed his red shirt into a bag and turned back into a donkey. Not good prey. Too tough to die easy. Annoying, but... a friend? The bird headed toward the rocky cliffs, noting the shape of the mountains. Nothing familiar here. He had to range farther. Flicking feathers, he wheeled... like Wheeling. His thoughts began to shift like that, human to animal.

The body's desires pressed against the heart's needs and memories that were too strong to die. The shadows of trees far below wavered and became Sam, Dan, Winifred. A black splotch of vultures feeding became harpies. Burning with fear and hunger, he dive-bombed the wake, forcing the birds to flee in terror. The horse they'd emptied out seemed small and fat with rot, but there was plenty of clinging flesh, a multitude of delicious bones ripe for cracking in his sharp, curved gray beak. Back in the air, sated, he looked around with his one good eye. These mountains were familiar—almost. He just had to range a little farther.

More flying. There. Boxes of wood, fabric flapping on lines. Squat creatures with peculiar shocks of hair. *Dwarves,* the bird thought. Possibly edible. He remembered them, in any case. Using some interior bird-sense, he retraced his flight path and scanned the ground for that donkey, that shirt. It wasn't where he'd left it, and he screeched his rage from high overhead.

My shirt!

"Hey! Hey, bird! Looky here! I got what you want!"

Down below, a figure shook a rust-red thing, and the bird circled lower and lower, claws subtly clicking with a peculiar combination of annoyance and triumph. When he landed and hopped toward the man, his beak open and screeching, the man untied the shirt and threw it at the bird's feet.

"I'm turning around now," he said.

When the feller was facing the other way, the bird chuckled in satisfaction and changed into a man who scrambled back into the shirt. His belly was full, rounding against the shirt's rough fabric, and Rhett remembered exactly what he needed to know, much to his surprise.

He spun and pointed toward civilization. "That way. We go that way. There's a town called Burlesville. On the way to Las Moras, and they're friendly enough fellers."

Earl shot him a suspicious look. "What kind of fellers?"

"They call themselves dwarves. That suit you?"

Earl's freckled nose wrinkled up. "It's more whether I suit folks than if they suit me, if you get what I'm saying."

Rhett snorted. "Son, if you think they'd look down on you more than they'd look down on me, then you're looking to get punched again. Just go on and be a donkey, if you're so worried."

"But you'll steal me clothes! And if they're monsters, they'll know something's up. Best to just let them be disappointed from the start."

"We can get more clothes in Burlesville, fool. And find out if the Rangers have been through on their way back home. And who cares if they're disappointed? They're just dwarves."

Rhett didn't mention everything else he needed to know. How were Sam and Dan and Winifred? Was somebody taking good care of Ragdoll and Puddin'? Where were his goddamn

27

guns and his Ranger badge? And would the Rangers still take him, considering he was a big damn bird? With the Cannibal Owl dead and gone, was he still the Shadow? And that was all before the donkey-boy started making his demands about this godforsaken railroad camp. Just when things seemed like they were getting easy, they went and got all tangled up again.

"I'll be a donkey until we're near," Earl said. "Keep me feet soft."

Rhett looked him up and down. "Say, don't folks ride donkeys?"

Earl gave him a dirty look. "Only folks as want to get bitten. I'm not that kind of donkey. You'd be better off flying, yourself." He dropped his britches defiantly, stuffed everything in his bag, and handed it to Rhett, who wasn't even vaguely interested in the boy's body. As fascinated as he'd been by Sam's various bits and pieces and as unexplainably riled as he'd been by Winifred's curves and bumps, he didn't find Earl intriguing in the slightest, and the sight of the man's giblets just made Rhett feel awkward.

He was much more comfortable altogether when the feller became a donkey.

Rhett slung the bag over his shoulder and stared at the furry critter. The donkey stared at Rhett for a moment before letting out a long, impatient bray.

"Oh, right. I'm the only one who knows where we're going. Shut your fool mouth and come on. It's gonna be a hell of a hike."

The donkey nudged Rhett with his long, sharp nose, and Rhett shoved him away and paused to stretch before walking. "Give me a minute to gather my thoughts, you testy thing."

He acted like it was nothing, going back to Burlesville, but in truth, he was dreading it. Of all the towns to walk into half-naked, why did it have to be this one? The last time he'd trotted down the dusty road, he'd been on horseback, fully armed and surrounded by the most dangerous and righteous men in Durango, and still the fools had shot at him. Now, half-dressed and accompanied by a complete ass, would they still be shooting? And did it matter as much, considering Rhett knew for sure now that he was a monster? Would they even recognize him?

As his fingers gently prodded the twisted scars of what used to be his right eye, he had to wonder...these days, would he even recognize himself? On the inside, the answer was yes, and that was what really mattered. Inside, he knew himself better than ever, and that was a hell of a thing.

Feeling the heat of the sun set in for good, he stripped off the shirt, stuffed it in the bag, and slung it around the donkey's neck.

"Come on, donkey-boy," he muttered. "Let's go vex some damn dwarves."

And then he took to the sky.

CHAPTER 3

Burlesville appeared like a shimmering mirage in hell. The sun was headed down more slowly than usual, a dark orange disk going to ground among stark black buttes. The bird's eye was drawn to a dusty man waving a red shirt, and it glided down to an ungainly landing and changed.

Slipping on the shirt, Rhett recognized the church tower, where a shooter had been positioned last time, nearly blind though he was considered the most sharp-eyed of dwarves. In anticipation of such repeated rudeness, Rhett figured they'd wait until the innocent light of morning and tie Earl's map to a stick to wave once they were in view. The bit of frayed canvas was nowhere close to white, but it was the closest thing they had. As he made the knot, Rhett realized that the crusted brown lines and squiggles were drawn in blood. Earl silently pulled on his pants.

"You find enough food, while you were a donkey?" Rhett asked.

Earl nodded. "Something green, I reckon."

"Then let's just sleep here. No fire. No point in sneaking up on blind fellers with itchy triggy fingers after dark."

"Mind if I sing a bit?"

Rhett threw him a dark look. "I most assuredly do."

They turned, back to back, equally annoyed, and slept. At some point in the night, they must've grown cold enough to change, as they both woke as creatures. The bird blinked, ruffled his feathers, and became a man with a purpose.

They walked into town, side by side, one pair of clothes between them. Rhett waved his pathetic excuse for a flag of truce. As they entered shooting range, Rhett braced himself for the discomfort of a bullet in a tender place, but no bullets were forthcoming. The bell tower, for all he could see with one eye, was empty. Still, the town seemed unchanged. Steady clangs suggested that maybe somebody was busy in the mine or working on the half-finished schoolhouse where he'd once bedded down beside Sam Hennessy, innocent and smitten like a damn fool. It was strange, he realized, coming back to a place you'd already been to after you'd learned a little something about the world. Now that he'd tasted the sky, Burlesville seemed a small, still thing.

"What, no welcome wagon?" Earl asked.

If Rhett had been a horse, he'd have pinned his ears and stuck out his teeth. "Not everybody in the world is glad to see me, donkey-boy. You neither. Only reason they were on the lookout last time I passed through was because somebody was stealing their children, and it wasn't the sort of lookout that comes with a welcome wagon."

As they entered the town proper, squat bearded women looked up from gardens and clotheslines to ogle them suspiciously with gem-bright eyes. Cats halted their washing on porches, and finally a man appeared, slamming the door of the general store behind him and standing before it with huge arms crossed over a tidy apron. The dwarf had the height of a feller who'd get ribbed for being short but made up for it by being twice as wide and made of stone-hard muscle.

"Well, if it is not the prodigal Ranger," he said.

"Hello to you, too, Jasper. I take it that means you saw my people recently?"

Jasper strode forward, his hand outstretched. Rhett just stared at it like a fool for a moment before realizing that he was expected to shake. It was an odd feeling, a feller reaching for him on purpose, and the dwarf's rock-hard hand crunched around Rhett's fingers. He didn't flinch, though—he outright refused to show the dwarf any weakness. Broken bones would mend, but a man's reputation took longer to heal.

"Came through a few days back. Headed on to Las Moras. Had two Injuns with them, including the girl we shot. Your Captain said you boys took care of our problem."

"I reckon we did," Rhett said, running the tallies on what *we* meant as compared to *you*.

"Then we owe you our thanks." Jasper's beard twitched with a grin. "And if that thanks was to come in the form of a pair of pants and some old boots, I suppose you wouldn't complain, *ja*?"

"We'd be much obliged."

With a nod, Jasper led them inside the general store. Earl followed, radiating anger. His face was plum-red, shining through his freckles and lighting up his hair. And why shouldn't he be angry? The damn dwarf hadn't even nodded at the feller. Rhett was right fascinated by all the different kinds of hate folks could hold in their hearts. A white man, unwelcome where a mutt like Rhett was greeted warmly? The world was truly upside down. At least Jasper still viewed Rhett as a man, even with his legs on display for all the world to see.

The shop was just as he remembered it, sparkling fresh wood swept clean with nicely stacked goods around the edges. One corner held a selection of used clothes, and Rhett's heart ached uncomfortably to note that a good deal of it was not in adult sizes. Just as before, the town didn't feel right without a single child causing a ruckus. They'd all been stolen away by the Cannibal Owl, their neatly folded clothes now useless. Jasper picked out a pair of used boots, comically wide, some hand-knitted socks, and a pair of pants with attached suspenders. Rhett took them with a nod and scooted behind a shelf of goods to step in. Whoever had worn these things must've been the size of two Rhett Hennessys plastered together side by side, and the legs ended abruptly above his ankles, but damn if it didn't feel fine to have something between his tender feet and the ground, something he wouldn't have to share. If it couldn't be blue sky under his toes, it might as well be thickly made dwarf socks, leather soles, and hobnails.

"Some food wouldn't go amiss, neither," Rhett added, eyeing a pyramid of sardines.

"Go see one of the widow women with all the cats, then. They like lost things."

"Might we trouble you for a shirt?" Earl asked.

Jasper's eyes went colder—which was quite a feat for stone. "All out of shirts."

It was a lie, and they all knew it.

"Gratefulness runs pretty slim out here, seems like," Rhett muttered.

A snort from Jasper. "With some more than others. We're a choosy people with long memories of fair-skinned shapeshifters raiding our settlements back home. You've been compensated now, Ranger. The debt is paid. Not everyone here is grateful for your part in our tragedy."

"Seems odd, not being grateful to the man who killed the thing that plagued you."

Jasper's eyes went flat. "The man who killed it too late."

Rhett's eye went flatter, and his fist started itching. "Then I'll just ask you when my people left and in which direction and be on my way."

"Last week. They were headed back to Las Moras when they walked right out the front of town, just as they walked in. Good day, Ranger."

Picking up a push broom, Jasper made as if to sweep the two visitors out the goddamn door, and Rhett hurried onto the porch before he had to break a fist on the dwarf's damn nose. As long as he lived, Rhett couldn't conceive of a day when he would gladly abide rudeness in a man. But he had what he needed, and supplies and information were more valuable than genuine thanks, in the long run.

"What the Sam Hill was that?" he said as they landed on dirt again.

"I told you, lad. Nobody likes the Irish. Especially not Germanic dwarves."

"Damn what they like. We need food, and we need another shirt, and then we're getting the hell out of this fool town. Come on, now."

Rhett remembered well the house where Winifred had gone for rose-smelling soap and a dress that swished becomingly around the girl's well-formed calves. If the lady dwarves wouldn't turn away a damn coyote-girl, surely they'd tolerate a redheaded feller who was being, for once, mercifully quiet. Dust swirled down the street as they hurried to the right house, and Rhett wished for a mirror, a bucket of water, anything to help make him seem more like a down-on-his-luck feller who needed a rare bit of help than a begging girl who couldn't keep clean.

The door opened after one knock, revealing a dwarf lady who looked, to Rhett, about like all other dwarf ladies, which is to say she looked like a dwarf feller wearing a flower-sprigged dress under a curly gray beard. She said nothing, just stared at them in inquiry.

"Sorry for the intrusion, ma'am," Rhett said, "but Jasper said as you might have some spare food. I'm a Ranger, and I been separated from my people for a long damn time. I mean, a long time, excusing your pardon." If he'd had a hat, he would've held it against his chest with both hands, affecting bedragglement. He wasn't a feller who liked to ask for anything or admit any weakness, but after several weeks of wandering the desert with nothing to eat but dead vermin, he was ready to try.

The dwarf woman looked them up and down, her shiny gray eyes narrowed suspiciously. "You're one of Winifred's people, are you not?" she asked with a clipped accent.

"Yes, ma'am," Rhett said, although it tasted strange in his mouth to say it.

She jabbed a thumb at Earl. "And who is this creature?"

"One of my people."

The dwarf lady stared at them as if testing the hardness of her heart, and lucky for Rhett, his stomach grumbled audibly, just then. If stony eyes could go soft, hers did. Sticking her head out the door, she scanned the street up and down before opening the door wider to admit them.

"Just don't tell anyone," she muttered.

Inside, her house was a riot of femininity. Not a single surface was spared a doily, a plate, a teacup, a carven figurine. The wallpaper was pink and hectic with flowers, and the chairs all had matching cushions. The scent of roses pressed down aggressively, and Rhett wanted to go roll around in some nice, clean dirt just to clear his senses.

"Thanks kindly, ma'am. And if you might have an extra shirt, my friend here was gracious enough to let me borrow his."

She stared Rhett up and down and nodded. "Don't sit. Go on out to the lean-to, and I'll see you fed. But I'll expect you to earn your keep. Got a coop that needs fixing, and the cow likes a gentle hand for milking."

Rhett nodded. "As you see fit."

Not that he had any idea how to milk a cow or fix a coop, but he wasn't about to say that. Had she been this tightfisted with Winifred, though? Rhett seemed to recall them laughing, and the coyote-girl never said anything about being put to work. Or maybe folks just didn't expect much use out of a girl on her lone in the world, whereas a man was expected to pull his share. Rhett would rather work than flutter around like a fool, giggling. To that effect, he nodded and headed in the direction the dwarf indicated, through a door in the kitchen that led to a rough lean-to outside with blue sky peeking between its boards. Earl followed him like a ghost, his bare, sunburned shoulders hunched and one hand ever holding up his britches.

When the woman nodded at a toolbox and shut the door on them, Earl finally seemed to come back to himself. Hefting the box, he jutted his chin toward the backyard. "Come on, then. Might as well be useful."

"I thought you weren't good for much."

"Not at roughin' it on the prairie, but I'm just fine for fixin' a coop. Grew up in a town a little like this, for all it was older than dirt. Lads as can't fix a coop or milk a cow don't get breakfast at me mam's house."

Soon Rhett was holding chunks of wood while Earl pounded nails with angry hammer strokes that, Rhett imagined, involved imagining Jasper's face on each nailhead. The chickens pecked around, the pigs grunted contentedly, and the single cow swished her tail and chewed her cud. It was right comfortable, which made Rhett a little itchy. This was what

Pap's place could've been, if anyone had given a damn. Fat animals, well-patched fences. No horses, though, which was unthinkable. When Earl seemed to have the coop under control, Rhett went to check out a bit of shingle that had fallen off the house and shimmied up to the roof to take care of that. For all that he couldn't build things, Rhett was right good at hammering down broken chunks that had fallen off, thanks to Pap.

Then Earl showed him how to pull up a stool and coax the milk out of the cow. It felt downright personal, yanking a creature like that, his cheek pressed up against her smooth, warm flank. Earl carried in the milk while Rhett gathered eggs in the apron of his shirt, glad for the ill-fitting pants and suspenders that didn't make it an embarrassment. Aside from the persistent growling of his stomach, it was actually a pleasant afternoon, and it only made him long the more for a milling herd of fresh horses and a white-board corral in which to break them. It was peculiar, yearning for freedom and a cage at the same time.

They met on the doorstep, and Earl set the toolbox on the lean-to floor with a clank loud enough to rouse the chickens. The dwarf lady opened the door and inspected the milk pail.

"You're done?"

"Yes'm." Rhett held out his shirt, and she took the eggs, one by one, in stubby hands.

"Did I hear you on the roof, too?"

"Yes'm."

She nodded and gave the hint of a smile. "Then I suppose you'd best come in and put some meat on those sorrowful bones."

Aside from some horrible green shit she called *collards*, it was possibly the best meal of Rhett's life, sticking to his ribs with an extraordinarily pleasant heft. Cold as the Widow Helen had been before, feeding them seemed to loosen her mouth to talk and smile, both. After they'd eaten, she handed Rhett an old shirt, well-patched and far too wide, which he took to the lean-to to change into in some privacy before handing the crusty rust-red shirt back to a relieved Earl.

"You boys don't want to wash first?" Helen asked.

"Lord, no, ma'am," Rhett answered. "We're just getting right back on the trail. No need to waste perfectly good water on the likes of us."

"Your friend Winifred was in a poorly way, last I saw her," Helen said, one eyebrow raised.

Rhett couldn't even feign inattention. "In what way, ma'am?"

"Poor girl was all bruised up. Arm in a sling. And her foot..." She trailed off and shook her head.

"Couldn't your horse doc, I don't know. Stick it back on?"

Helen gave him a pitying sort of look. "You can't just stick a foot back on. Can't even sew it on, considering the way it was done. They said it was the Cannibal Owl his very self. Did you see it?"

"I did."

"Then you know that the damage that monster has done can never be undone. We must hunt out these monsters as soon as we can, before they can do such damage, *ja*?"

Rhett glanced at Earl, whose jaw was tight as he shook his head angrily. Rhett figured he didn't want Helen to know about either his patched-up missing toes or the railroad. In any case, Rhett knew well enough when a feller wanted him to keep his own mouth shut, so he did that.

"It's a damn shame," he finally muttered.

"Like your eye. Some things can't be fixed."

Rhett's teeth ground. Like he needed a goddamn reminder. If he went long enough between mentions, he was able to forget that he could only see half the world now.

"Anything else you need done, ma'am?"

"I've upset you, and I'm sorry for that. I hope you boys find what you are looking for. And I hope someone can do something for that poor girl. Oh, and we've got a basket packed for you. Hate to send you out on foot to Las Moras without food. Regina?"

Rhett went on point, hearing that name again. But it had to be her, didn't it? The figure that flitted out of the pantry was noticeably smaller than the heaving-bellied pregnant woman the Rangers had left among the dwarves on their way to the Cannibal Owl's lair, and Regina's entire mien had changed completely. She'd seemed dreamy and complacent then, swelling with hope for her child and the return of her husband, dead though the feller surely was. Now she was whip-thin, her sprigged dress a dragging sack, her face as pinched as a mountain ridge plagued by eroding winds. Her eyes stayed on the ground, and she held out the basket with near-skeletal hands. "Good journey," she muttered.

"How are you, Miss Regina?" Rhett asked, taking the pail and wishing he had a hat to doff, as that was what a gentleman would do. It was what the Captain would have done, at least.

Her head jerked up, her eyes met his, and her chin quivered. "You."

Rhett shuffled his feet and fidgeted with the basket, feeling lost for words. He'd never much understood the ways of the female mind, even though he supposedly possessed one. "I'm mighty sorry about your loss, ma'am. I wasn't expecting to see you again. I heard you'd...done yourself some harm."

"I tried to join my sweet Marjorie, and they cut me down and brought me back to this hateful world. To suffer." He could hear a strangled sort of quiver in her voice now, like she still felt the noose she'd made and worn as a necklace.

"Well I'm...I'm just sorry. About everything." Because what's a man supposed to say to a woman who wants nothing but to be dead and was denied even that most personal of choices? What he wanted to say was that life was never fair, and he understood her completely. But she'd hate him even more for that.

"It was you, wasn't it? That killed the...monster?"

Her voice shook like the last leaf of November. Rhett looked down and shuffled his new boots.

"Yes, ma'am."

"That's what they said. The other Rangers did. That you finished it. Not soon enough, though."

He glanced up through his lashes, unsure of the next step. What she was saying sounded like it was thanks, but that wasn't what Rhett felt rolling off her.

Regina made a noise halfway between a sneeze and a sob. "Well, best go on and kill some more monsters, then, shouldn't you? They don't keep."

Rhett nodded and jerked his chin at Earl, who seemed just as perplexed by the whole interaction.

"Guess we will, then. Many thanks to you both for the hospitality."

With one last glance back at the sorrowful woman, Rhett threw his shoulders back and sauntered out the door and into the dusty evening.

"Let's get the hell out of this town and change. We'll find the Rangers faster if we ain't encumbered by..."

"All this goddamn humanity?" Earl said wryly.

"That."

They ducked into an alley and transferred the widow's meager food to Earl's bag, leaving her basket near the porch. It was just a bit of cheese, a heel of bread, an old skin full of water, and a few tins of peaches, but it would be good enough to chase the taste of death out of Rhett's mouth come morning. Hurrying along the road back out of town, Rhett couldn't help checking for a flash of silver in the tower. But, really, what did the dwarves have left to defend? The town was peaceful, and the buildings and the people and their peculiar feelings about Rhett were soon blanketed in starlight. Once they were so far out that even the most farsighted dwarf couldn't aim for them, Earl silently dropped his bag and began stripping. Rhett looked away and didn't turn back around until he heard the click of hooves.

"Take your bag, then, ass," he muttered.

As he hung the bags around the donkey's neck, Earl sighed in relief and snapped at him with yellow teeth, but not like he meant to do any damage. Rhett knew how he felt. It was easier to be a simple animal than to try to puzzle out the queer meanings of what folks said and didn't say. Burlesville should've considered Rhett a goddamn hero, but he'd been treated like the town drunk. And what the Sam Hill was Regina's problem? She didn't have to be glad to be alive, but she'd treated Rhett like he'd personally trussed her baby up for the Cannibal Owl himself instead of dedicating his life to killing the monster so it couldn't happen again.

Before he realized he was doing it, his fingers were already shucking clothes and stuffing them into the donkey's saddlebags. Both sides were full now, considering they each had a full kit. Right handy, having a built-in beast of burden—at least when Earl was feeling cooperative. As soon as Rhett's pants were off and in the bag, he was already reaching inside and trading shivering, embarrassed skin for proud feathers. The dust felt good under his claws, and the night air felt even better under his wings. He kept enough of Rhett about him now to fly lower and keep the donkey in his sights. It wouldn't be long now. They were on the Rangers' trail, and they had the single-mindedness of dumb creatures on their side.

Coyote Dan had once told Rhett that he had a friend who turned into a hawk, and that that feller couldn't think human thoughts while in bird form or he'd falter. Rhett found that if he tried to think in words, his feathers flicked carelessly and sent him wobbling. But if he thought only in pictures, he could stay aloft.

The main picture he saw? Sam Hennessy.

Whatever Rhett was now, whatever folks thought of him, he had to find Sam to make it right.

They traveled until the moon was high. The donkey brayed like Satan's trumpet, and Rhett came back to himself, mostly, and made an ungainly landing right as the donkey became a man.

"I'm sleepy, lad. Let's rest, then."

"To hell with sleepy, donkey-boy. Better to travel at night and sleep when the sun is hottest. We'll catch the Rangers faster. They're bedded down now, so we keep going."

Earl snorted and dug in his bags, tossing out clothes into two piles. "And you'll be forgetting that it's easier to fly than to trot, won't you? Hooves are delicate things, man. And mine ache." He handed Rhett a ball of cheese in partial apology.

Rhett took a bite, relished the richness, and handed it back. "Look, you got to learn how to live. A man's got to know how to rough it, in Durango. So you're gonna build this fire. Now start collecting little sticks."

They turned their backs to one another and dressed by moonlight. Earl made a damn mess of selecting kindling, and

Rhett realized how bone-tired he was as he tried to explain the many ways the donkey was an idiot. By the time they had the fire going, Earl's hands were a wreck from thorns and cacti, Rhett was out of patience, and both fellers were glad of the widow's provisions and too tired to poke around under rocks for something meatier. They curled up on the bare ground on either side of the fire, and Rhett's human thoughts came flooding back with a vengeance. He missed the Captain's tidy camp. He missed the snoring, farting knot of Rangers and the night sounds of the horse herd, just a bit away. He even missed Dan and Winifred, a little. They made things more lively, at least, and arguing with 'em took his mind off darker things. Most of all, of course, he missed Sam. And the feel of a gun at his hip.

Funny, how he'd started out with nothing but a one-eyed mule and a pair of boots, had gotten pretty much everything he'd ever wanted, had lost it in one night, and was now burdened with one eye of his own, a surly donkey, and an even worse-fitting pair of boots.

But he wasn't anywhere close to quitting. He'd get it all back. And soon.

He fell asleep counting all the shit he was gonna take back.

Deep in the night, possibly on the edge of morning, something jolted Rhett from untidy dreams. He opened his eye and sat up, muttering, "What the Sam Hill—?"

And that's when a hand landed on his shoulder and a knife stuck deep in his side.

CHAPTER 4

With a shriek of ever-loving rage, Rhett struck out blindly, knocking a body toward the hot embers of the fire. His vision dancing in red and black, he yanked the knife out of the soft spot below his ribs and stared down at it, expecting treachery by Earl's hand. But it was just a kitchen knife. A big one, to be sure, but nothing any self-respecting man would be seen carrying on the trail.

And not silver, either—thank goodness.

"What the hell?" he shouted, bolting to his feet and brandishing the knife toward the figure rolling out of the fire, coughing and moaning.

"What? What is it?" Earl was up, sleepy as an owl, hopping back and forth with his knife out, too, although he was pointed in entirely the wrong direction.

Rhett's eyes flicked up irritably. "Whoever it is, they're over there, on fire, and they're a damn fool." He rubbed the knife wound, already feeling his monster skin knitting it closed. If he'd been human, he might've lost a kidney, he figured. Instead, he just had an unsightly hole in his too-large shirt, damn it all. He stepped around the fire and kicked over the smoking, cloaked form. It landed on its back with a wheeze, and he toed

it apart like he was fussing with a bug that wouldn't unfold
its legs.

"Regina?"

The woman's pinched face was all filled up with hate, her
hands clutched in fists. She kicked at his leg, and he stepped
back and tried not to laugh at her pathetic clumsiness.

"At least roll the damn fire out before you try to kill me
again, woman."

She shook her head, stood, and tossed the smoking cloak
down to the dust.

"You deserve to die. Why won't you die?"

"Monsters like me don't die as easy as we'd like," Rhett
answered. "A problem you know a bit about yourself."

Regina said nothing, just glared her rage. The night went
suddenly cold and still. The three figures stood in the valley,
the world frozen around them, the dark withstanding even the
calls of locusts or birds.

Rhett spit in the dust and settled hands on his hips. "Why
do you want me dead, anyway? I saved your life at Reveille. I
killed the Cannibal Owl, gave you your revenge. You should be
saying thanks, not sneaking up at night with a knife."

The woman fumbled with her bodice, and Rhett sensed she
was hunting for her next weapon of choice, pitiful but determined as she was. His instinct was to punch her like he would
a man, but she was such a sad, broken, blundering thing. She'd
probably shatter at the touch of his fist. Instead, he watched her
carefully, muscles tense to repel whatever she next brought to
bear against him.

What she pulled out wasn't a knife or a gun. It was a locket.

She shoved it at Rhett, forcing him to take it or drop it. There
wasn't much light, but there was enough to see a man's silhouette
on one side, a roughly penciled drawing of a baby on the other.

"They were mine, and now they're both gone. And you're still here. And I don't want to be, anymore," Regina said, deflating and hanging her head. "If you'd just been a little faster. Just a few days earlier. You could've saved them both. But instead, you took your damn time, and now I got nothing. We were going to San Anton. I was to be a rancher's wife. That baby never even got to see the sunshine. My sweet Marjorie. Born under clouds, stolen in the night. I tried to find my peace. And then one day you walk back into town, expecting thanks?" The woman spit on Rhett's cheek, and he wiped it away with his sleeve.

"I can't see the damn future, woman. I ain't a god. I'm doing the best I can, just like you. Just like anyone. I'm just trying to find my way."

She swallowed hard and breathed out a sob. "Then take me with you. I don't want to be here no more. House servant to a . . ." She shook her head. "Rocks for eyes and a beard. Not a proper Christian woman at all. Take me back to my people. It's the least you owe me. I just want . . . I just want to be ordinary again."

Rhett looked at Earl, who shook his head.

"Look here, now," Rhett said softly, like he was coaxing a spooky mare. "You can't go with us. You can't keep up. We got no horses for you to ride."

Regina latched on to that like it was something close to hope. "You can walk. I can walk, too. I won't slow you down none."

Rhett glared skeptically from her cavernous cheeks to her high-heeled boots. "We don't walk. And we ain't the sort of ordinary you're looking for."

The scrawny creature stood up straighter, and her eyes took on a mad gleam. "You don't take me with you, I'll just keep walking. I'll die in the desert, and it'll be your fault. I'll haunt you."

Rhett chuckled darkly. "For one thing, threats don't work on me. For another, I been haunted, and I know damn well you can't do it. So you go on and do with yourself what you will, but know that it's on you. I saved your life once. That don't mean I owe you a second time. If you ain't got the good sense to stay in a safe place, living a safe life, then you'll get what's coming to you. And I'm keeping your knife." He glanced at Earl, who stood, feet planted and face hard, waiting. "You ready to move on, Earl?"

"That I am." Earl reached into his bag and pulled out the cans of peaches. "No offense, miss, but we're on a mission and can't be slowed down. Head back home now. Better safety than glory, eh?"

Regina wouldn't take the peaches. She leaned over, dusted off her cloak, checked that it was no longer smoldering, and put it on. "If I can't haunt you dead, I'll haunt you alive. So go on, then. Your guilt will dog your every step until I collapse."

Rhett shook his head. "I liked you better when you was in a family way."

"You're not alone in that. I had hope, then."

She sounded enough like a ghost, damn her. Rhett kicked dirt over the fire and started walking. Earl was right behind him, and Regina trailed in their wake, sobbing softly.

By midmorning, Regina was just a smudge on the prairie, long behind them and fading fast, and Rhett was heavy with what might've been guilt.

"Oh, hellfire," he muttered. Stripping off his clothes, he tossed them and Regina's knife at Earl, took a running start, and leaped into the sky. Wheeling around, his eye scraped over the scrawny figure stumbling over rocks in long skirts and a broken boot. But he was something else now, something that didn't care about the woman's plight.

Or, to put it more accurately, he only cared that she might die in a convenient place, and that he'd be the first one there to find her.

At least, that's what the great bird told himself.

Days later, when he next heard a donkey's bray, Rhett spiraled down gently and landed in a pretty green copse around a sweet little creek at sunset. The area was familiar in a menacing sort of way, and he spun around until he got his human bearings. That blackened stain over yonder had once been the siren's town, Reveille. His time there had been brief and victorious, if you considered killing a siren, having first cut of spoils, and saving an ungrateful pregnant woman's life victory. Now it was just a reminder of what he was trying to get back to: life among the Rangers, fighting things that had the good sense to wear their evil on the outside. He sighed. If only the Rangers weren't so hell-bent on burning every place they left behind, he and Earl would have had more than enough food and supplies to continue their journey in slightly more human comfort.

"It all burned down to nothing."

Rhett spun in surprise to stare at Regina, who was studying what was left of Reveille. Her back was to him, her thin arms crossed over her bony chest. Earl struggled into his clothes, and Rhett hurried to join him, suddenly embarrassed to be nekkid in front of Regina. Strangely, being bare in front of Earl no longer bothered him. In accepting Rhett as Rhett from the start and helping him better understand how to shift, Earl had earned an unusual sort of respect in Rhett's estimation, and Rhett didn't so much care if the Irishman saw the lady parts he wished to hell he didn't possess. But Regina . . .

Well, if Regina considered Rhett a man, he didn't want that to change when the woman saw what he kept hidden under his clothes.

"Captain burns everything," he said, once he was properly covered. "Helps keep the other monsters in line. A warning, like."

"Monsters?"

Rhett exhaled in a huff and stood beside her. "Don't be a fool, woman. You been living with dwarves, and you watched me change. You know we ain't human. Might as well call us monsters as anything else. The thing that built this town— well, it was more monster than most, I reckon. I watched it eat my friend's face off."

"My time here felt like a dream. Maybe a nightmare. They were good to me, though. Kept me fed. Treated me like a queen."

"And how'd that work out for you?"

In response, she wobbled and swooned. Earl caught her but couldn't hold her up and had to guide her to the ground like a spilling sack of potatoes.

"I reckon she needs water," he said. "She got to mumbling nonsense."

"She does tend to do that, water or no."

Earl tipped the last drops out of the water skin and into Regina's mouth, but there was barely enough to wet her tongue. Cussing in his own language, the Irishman used his knife to tear holes in the peach can. He scooped out a handful of slimy orange fruit and motioned for Rhett to hold out his hands. Without much choice, Rhett slurped down the overly sweet slivers as Earl tried to force the juice from the can directly into Regina's mouth. She spluttered at first but then figured it out. Earl ate some peaches, too, then jerked his chin at the creek. Rhett shrugged and picked up the skin and the empty can for more water.

Before walking away, he stopped, hands on his hips, and stared at the two of them splayed on the ground. "How'd she get this far, donkey-boy? She was half-dead, last time I was on two legs. It's been days since Burlesville, ain't it?"

Earl shook his head, looking mournful. "I carried her, if you must know. Don't weigh nothing, the poor thing." He looked up, eyes pleading. "I got sisters, lad. This woman...she stinks of tragedy, does she not? If the Rangers will help me, maybe they can help her."

Rhett snorted and took off for the creek. "Tender heart like yours is bound to get broken. Rangers kill what needs to die. They don't carry what's not willing to live and fight."

The walk to the creek was quiet and pretty, at least until the stench from Reveille caught up with him. The siren and her husband had taken what they'd liked from their victims and dumped their bodies into a trench out back. The Captain had set the trench on fire, along with the rest of the town, but there was enough unburned meat left to raise a hell of a stink. After he'd wordlessly delivered what he could of the silty water to Earl and the near-dying girl, he moseyed toward the death-black boards poking up out of the prairie like rotten teeth and shifting in a downright unnatural way as the harsh wind shuddered through.

Set against the hot haze of sunset, the town's dark bones seemed to squirm. Rhett's footsteps slowed at first, and he cocked his head, willing his good eye to focus and stop telling him lies. Hellfire, how he wished for a gun belt hanging loose on his hips, his trusty pistol heavy in his grip. Because what he was seeing couldn't be the truth.

Mist wavered off the ground, and the town swayed back and forth as if breathing. A strange rustling quickened his steps until he was running, flailing his arms and shouting.

It was crows. More crows than he'd ever seen. Bigger crows than he'd ever seen.

As he approached, they took off as one, a violent tornado of cawing and wings and feathers that swirled up from the ruined town, hurtling out of the death pit and up from the skeletal trees to fill the sky, almost as dark as midnight but not nearly as friendly.

"Get on with you!" he shouted.

The cloud of crows made strange patterns in the sky, heaving apart and surging together as if of one mind and aiming for Rhett, skimming so close overhead that he felt his hair ruffled by clutching claws. He longed to shift into what now felt like his true form and cut a swath of murder through the lesser birds, but something held him back. They couldn't hurt him. They weren't people armed with silver. They were just crows, carrion birds in funeral black without the patience and dignity of vultures. The sleek bastards churned and whirled and wheeled and shimmered toward the dark edge of the sky, diving into the horizon and disappearing, far away.

All around Rhett, the prairie went quiet. He reached for his hair, certain he'd find it stuck full of oily black feathers after such a ruckus. And yet…there were no feathers to be found anywhere. Not on the ground, even. Nor the white splatters he'd expect from what had to be hundreds of the damn things. The trench had been cleaned down to fire-blackened bones.

Walking toward the remains of the saloon, he felt as if he were being watched, as if something savage still lurked among the charred timbers. The Rangers had set the fire in the back room, where the siren and her man had neatly stored all the loot stolen from the bodies of the cowpokes and tinkers drawn to her foul song. Rhett's sensible heart ached for the tidy piles of fine saddles, warm cloaks, and boots cobbled to fit folks who weren't dwarf-sized. Nothing was left but ashes.

Except—there. In the corner where the pocket watches and such fripperies had been. Was that a wink of metal? Rhett's fingers tightened on Regina's little poke knife as he edged into the murky shadows. Something moved, right where he was looking, and a bit of darkness detached and took to the sky with a sudden violent flapping. Another crow, clutching something in its beak. A chunk of molten gold or chain, maybe? But such creatures always coveted shiny baubles. Rhett scooped up a lump of charred wood and aimed it at the bird, which dodged the throw neatly and fled into the clouds, cawing its displeasure.

"Smug bastard," Rhett grumbled.

He picked through what was left of the saloon and found nothing of any value, just twisted clumps of junk and charred boards. After a violent kick that sent black wood skittering, he headed back to fix whatever abomination of a fire Earl had managed to scrape together.

The damn crows could have what was left of Reveille, and be welcome.

After an uneasy sleep around a poorly made fire, Rhett woke up hungry. He gladly took his knife out onto the prairie, alone, cut his finger as bait, and caught two fanged jackrabbits. Upon returning, he had no choice but to share his kill with what he considered a ball and a chain: a starving, heartsick woman and the foolish, stubborn Irishman who'd brought her into their uneasy truce. The widow's food was gone, and the rabbits were thin and gristly. The water was clean, at least, and the crows had the good sense not to return. The next day, Rhett waited until Regina was off to squat in the bushes before he shoved his clothes at Earl and took to the sky, glad to be unburdened by so many cumbersome feelings.

He lost track of the days that went by like that, soaring over-head and keeping pace with a steadfast donkey slowed down by the dead-eyed woman clinging to its sweaty back. In the rare moments Rhett walked on two legs, hunting for food to keep them alive, the sorry pair forced remembrance of another woman riding a wet black steed, dogging Rhett's every step. The Injun woman's ghost was gone, but the weight of responsi-bility remained. Coyote Dan had told him he couldn't outrun his destiny, that no matter how much he'd like to pursue a nor-mal life, Rhett would be compelled to end the monsters that wrought havoc. Even out here, in the middle of nowhere, he'd managed to find the two most pathetic, helpless critters alive. Soon, at least, the Rangers would share this burden.

It was a fine afternoon when he finally spotted a curl of white smoke and flapped ahead to note the familiar ranch house swarming with men. Returning to the donkey, the bird that was Rhett let out a horrific squawk and jerked his head toward their shared goal.

The Durango Rangers Las Moras Outpost.

Uncertainty made his flight path erratic. He had a powerful yearning to be there, but not as he was. Not as…this. But the donkey had his clothes in his saddlebags, and the Rangers still didn't know what he looked like as a human in his altogether, and he wanted to keep it that way for as long as possible. He set-tled for gliding in wide circles, stopping once to snatch a pigeon out of the air and swallow it whole just to quiet his nerves.

When he heard braying, he hurried to the ground beside Earl with an inelegant, lolloping landing. He hastily changed into a human, and then into a clothed human, careful to keep his back to Regina, who was all aquiver with worry and of too sensitive a constitution to look anyway.

"This isn't a city," she said.

"Nobody promised you San Anton, woman," Rhett said gruffly. "Our aim was the Rangers, and that's what we found. You're their problem now." He turned to Earl, who was shaking in his damn boots. "You going to piss yourself, donkey-boy?" he asked, not unkindly.

Earl shook his head and mopped sweat off his face. "It's one thing to seek and another thing entirely to find. You got to understand, lad. The Rangers are the only ones who can help me, but I'm scared to death of 'em. Not so kind to monsters, are they? And not terribly big fans of the Irish I'll bet, neither."

"They accepted me."

Earl's smile was wry, his cussedness shining through his fear. "And then they left you behind, didn't they? I saw that town. Burned to the ground, monsters and innocents alike. I can only hope they're feeling charitable today, eh?"

"All you can do is tell the Captain the honest truth and hope he sees it the same way you do."

"Then lead on. At the very least, I could use a damn drink."

As they walked on, Rhett was painfully aware of the picture he presented. Hatless, filthy, wearing too-wide dwarf clothes stained with his own blood, dragging along a woman the Captain had already scraped off once and a donkey feller who could drive anyone crazy with his yammering. He might've slowed down if he hadn't been desperately hoping that Sam was just around the bend, not to mention maybe Dan and Winifred. The three of them balanced out the annoyance of Jiddy and some of the other, less friendly Rangers. Well, and at least Delgado was gone. The son of a bitch had taken Rhett's right eye, but Rhett had taken his life, so that weighed ever so slightly in Rhett's favor. Hell, maybe the Rangers had a new cook who wouldn't shoot anybody.

As they topped the last hill, the ranch house came into view, pretty as a picture under the hot afternoon sun. Two familiar figures stood on the porch: the Captain, his rifle slung over his shoulder, and the tracker, Jiddy, who resembled the bear he occasionally shifted into when the occasion warranted it—although Rhett had never witnessed that act personally and had only heard rumors. And thinking back, there were plenty of moments among the Rangers when it would've been right helpful, having a bear along. Say, when they'd been circled by murderous werewolves. But that was a problem for another time. As for now...

"Rhett Hennessy. I'll admit to a bit of curiosity regarding whether I'd ever see you again, son," the Captain called, all friendly-like.

Rhett inclined his head. "I'm a Durango Ranger, Captain. I reckon as long as there's something out there that needs killing, you might have a use for me."

"For you, but not for them. I recognize the woman, but who's your other friend, Rhett? Jiddy tells me he's more than he seems."

The bearlike scout nodded sternly, doing his best to look tough despite the tobacco stains dribbling down his gray shirt.

"This here is Earl O'Bannon, Captain, I'll leave him to tell you his personal reasons for being here. There's trouble east a bit, the sort of thing only Rangers can handle."

The Captain nodded slowly. "And the woman?"

Rhett held out the bloodstained hole in the side of his shirt. "Tried to kill me and followed us on foot out of Burlesville. I've washed my damn hands of her. Says she wants to be among people again."

"We ain't people."

"I told her that. I'd recommend keeping her away from knives, if you catch my meaning." He tucked his shirt back in to signal he was done with Regina. "What I'd like to know—"

He was interrupted by a whoop of joy, and his heart just about jumped out of his chest. Soon Sam had barreled into him, and they were pounding each other on the back as only the manliest men did when being reunited after near death. For that brief span of time, every goddamn worry fled Rhett's brain, and he was as happy as a pig in slop and grinning like a fool. Then Jiddy spat in disgust, and they pulled away for a more formal, punishing handshake.

"I figured you for dead, Rhett."

"Kind of you to worry for me, Sam."

"Didn't say I was worried. Guess I don't get to keep your watch now."

"Well, if there's one thing I've been missing while I wandered the desert in a state of near death, it's the goddamn time."

"Rhett!"

A flutter of skirts broke their banter, and then Winifred was hugging Rhett with one arm in a cloud of that damn rose soap she liked.

"Howdy, Winifred."

He pulled back and frowned. She had a crutch under one arm, which was what made her hug even more awkward than it should've been. Below her long skirts, only one foot was visible, clad in a man's boot. The other one ... flat out wasn't there. Which meant nobody had yet figured out how to reattach it.

"Where's Dan?"

"Where do you think? He's out looking for you, fool."

Rhett went red. "Nobody needs to worry for me. I've lived this long, haven't I?"

"You were alive, but we didn't know if you were you or if you'd gone full animal. When you jumped out of that cave, I ..." She pressed a hand to her chest and smiled. "It doesn't matter. I have your things."

Rhett wasn't fond of staring, but his eye was drawn to the girl's face, which still wore the faded greenish yellow of old bruises. Stepping away, he held her by the shoulders. One of her fingers was sitting funny, and she had the fretful look of a creature trying hard to ignore pain.

"What happened to you, Winifred? Why're you all beat up?"

The Captain cleared his throat from the porch to get their attention. "Get settled in, Rhett. We'll talk over supper. Keep the paddy with you. Woman, you can help out in the kitchen or hit the road to San Anton. This ain't a charity house. And you already owe us one chit."

Regina nodded, but her eyes burned with a familiar defiance that Rhett knew well. She headed for the steps, but the Captain held out his Henry to block her path. "Around back, if you please."

Regina looked like she wanted to spit on his boots, but she just turned on her heel and marched around the side of the building. Rhett figured she'd be looking for more knives.

The Captain inclined his head. "Go on, then. Can't have you fellers standing around like new pups in the yard. See to your horses. And get rid of that clown suit before you put on your badge, for Pete's sake." Rhett's head jerked up, and he wanted the Captain to repeat the bit about the badge, but Jiddy's scornful stare stopped him.

"Yes, Captain. Thank you, Captain."

The Captain gave the smallest smile and tipped his hat. "Glad you found your way home, son."

Rhett returned his nod and headed for the horse pens at a fast clip with Sam at his heels. It took a few beats before he realized that Winifred couldn't keep up, so he stopped to stretch and find a pace that suited her. The coyote-girl could be annoying, but she'd done her fair share to keep him alive and hold his secrets; it was the least he could do to keep the poor girl from causing herself further harm.

"I been seeing to your horses. That paint's got right fat without anyone to ride him, but the appy mare's been in a funk. I suspect she's missed you," Sam said.

They were walking side by side with Earl and Winifred trailing behind. Rhett figured he hadn't been this happy since his all-too-brief days with Monty at the Double TK. As the milling horses came in sight, he let out a long, high whistle. A host of curious ears perked up, but only one horse bugled a welcome, and that was the ugliest critter in the herd, a sand-colored appaloosa with a bottlebrush tail and bare black frizz of a mane. Ragdoll trotted to the fence with a black-and-white paint, fat little Puddin', in her wake like an agreeable dog.

Dashing tears out of his eyes with his wrist, Rhett ducked between the boards to rub velvety noses and subtly check on hooves and legs and the various things that could go wrong with a horse while a feller was flying around the prairie as a giant bird.

"I told you I took care of 'em," Sam said, and Rhett got the distinct impression he was being teased.

Sam was in the pen, too, sneaking a handful of grain to his dappled palomino and fending off the muzzle of an unfamiliar horse, a blue roan with the sort of chrome Sam couldn't resist.

"New horse?" Rhett asked, fighting down his emotions.

"Yep. Lost the black on the way home. Got all excitable, jumped the wrong way, and snapped a leg. This boy's name is Blue."

Rhett had to bury his face in Ragdoll's shoulder to keep his tears back.

"I used to have a mule named Blue. Only had one eye. Now I reckon I know why he was so ornery all the damn time."

Sam muttered, "Holy crow," and Winifred let out a chuckle.

Rhett looked from one to the other. "What?"

"You'd better come see what's in the second-string pen. I swear, you got the devil's own luck, other Hennessy."

Rhett followed Sam over to the pen where the Rangers kept the horses that didn't see much use, all the while feeling a strange shiver creeping up his neck. He heard the bray of welcome before he saw it and couldn't stop himself from running toward the bone-thin critter making the noise.

"That's your Blue, ain't it?" Sam asked, his sunny-fine face split in a glorious grin.

Rhett nodded, his arms strung around Blue's neck as the mule danced in place and nuzzled his back like it was a new bale of hay. "How'd…what…?"

"Feller just showed up one day, louder than life. Captain figured he'd pull a wagon fine, once we got some weight on his bones."

Rhett looked his ugly old mule in his good eye and shook his head in wonder. Everything he'd longed for in the desert, everything he'd lost, everything he needed to be happy—was back in his possession. "Pinch me, other Hennessy. I reckon I've got to be dreaming."

"Don't go being too happy. Jiddy's been hoping you wouldn't turn up and promising a fight if you did. Captain's been assigned to see to a sand wyrm problem down near Lareda and is ready to set off. Those things are nasty, and he's already warned us that we're likely to lose good men. Winifred's still hurt with no sign of improvement and Coyote Dan ain't back."

"Those sound like problems for tomorrow."

"Then do us all a favor and get cleaned up. Because today, I promise you that you smell worse than that mule," Winifred called.

Rhett looked up to where the girl leaned on the fence, smiling. Earl skulked a bit behind, looking sulky and out of place.

"Does he know?" Sam asked, tossing his chin at Earl. "About..." He paused, his face screwed up in puzzlement. "You?"

"We've been lost in the desert for a week. Of course he knows. We've been fighting over his shirt, most of the time."

"Damn, but it's good to have you back," Sam added.

Rhett figured he'd died and gone to heaven.

Of course, such feelings never lasted long.

CHAPTER
5

By the time the sun was moseying down, Rhett was a changed man. He'd washed and dressed in his own clean clothes, grateful beyond measure for a length of muslin to wrap his chest up properly. His old boots still fit, his socks were warm, and Winifred had found some salve for the quickly healing blisters and cuts that had hidden under all the dirt. She'd handed over his little leather bag of treasures, too, and the weight of it in his hand was a welcome comfort before he looped it around his neck. His too-long hair was crumpled under his hat, and Sam had offered him full run of his bandanna collection. The first thing Rhett did was roll one up and tie it around his gone eye, which made him a little less self-conscious about the face he showed the world. He'd thought himself ugly for so long that it was peculiar, now, to yearn for his old face, with both its eyes blinking back distrustfully.

And yet.

He liked what he saw a little better.

For once, he didn't want to smash a mirror when he saw his reflection. He looked like a dangerous young feller until you scanned down to the shiny Ranger badge pinned proudly to his collar. His hat snugly shaded his eye, his gun belt felt solid and sure around his hips, and he confirmed that his hands had indeed missed the grips of his pistols.

Sam grinned as he handed over Rhett's watch, still warm from the boy's body. Even though Rhett knew that they could ever only be friends, that Sam didn't feel the same pull he did, still he couldn't help the thrill that jerked over his body when he slid the watch securely into his vest pocket, knowing it had been nestling close against Sam's body all this time.

Rhett checked to make sure no one else but Earl was in the bunkhouse. Spreading his feet and throwing his shoulders back, he snarled at the mirror and let his fingers hover over his gun.

"You sure you want to mess with me, feller?" he snarled.

Quick as a blink, he pulled out his pistol and aimed it at the mirror, looking every bit the outlaw but knowing he was one of the good guys. A damn fine feeling, that. And yet he suffered a peculiar yearning to see his other self in the mirror, to know what skin he wore when he let his humanity fall away and soared into the skies. Not a vulture, Earl had said. But that left a damn lot of birds. Maybe, like his human body, knowing what he truly was, deep down, was more important than seeing it on the surface.

"You ready?" he asked Earl.

The Irishman had been quieter than Rhett had ever seen him, all through their shared ablutions. Now water glinted in the feller's redder-than-red hair as he tucked in his rust-red shirt and slung on some old, stretched-out suspenders and a pair of cast-off butternut pants that were still just a little too big. Earl's old pants were, as Winifred said, not fit to help birth a horse.

"Not looking forward to this talk," Earl grumbled. "I'd always heard the Rangers were heroes. Guess I figured they'd hear my story first off and ride off into the sunset to save me friends. Who knows how many men are losing fingers and toes and breakin' their backs while we fuss with our britches and wait for supper? I don't like it, Rhett. I don't like it a bit."

"It's not yours to like. Captain's not a man to work on another feller's timetable," Rhett said, bristling. "If he missed a meal every time somebody wanted to tell him a story, he'd be dead of starvation."

"What if he's not moved to my cause?"

Rhett wanted to bark in the Captain's defense, but truth be told, he didn't know the older man well enough to venture an explanation of his actions. "Captain's a fair man," was all he could say. "If it needs doing, I reckon he'll do it. So let's stop pussyfooting around and get on."

When he stepped onto the bunkhouse porch among his friends, he hooked his thumbs through his gun belt and heaved a mighty sigh. Winifred looked up from the steps and cocked her head.

"You need a haircut."

"I do not need any such thing."

Sam stood, yanked off Rhett's hat, and eyed him closely, making Rhett squirm. "You'd look right good with it cropped close."

Rhett exhaled and stared at his feet. "Reckon I'd better have it cropped close, then."

Winifred snorted and sent Sam to borrow some shears from wherever the Rangers kept such things while she shoved Rhett toward a low stool. He sat, hat in his hands, feeling ridiculous. Back in Gloomy Bluebird, the fine men of the town had gone to a barber to have their hair trimmed and their throats scraped raw, and of all his particular troubles, Rhett was glad he would never require a stranger's straight razor to his neck. Winifred pulled the bandanna from over his eye and slung an old serape around his neck.

"You've lost weight, Rhett. And you didn't have much to lose to start with."

"Yeah, well, I've been mostly eating dead things." He waited a beat, feeling awkward, before deciding to hell with it. "So who beat the shit out of you?"

Winifred chuckled and fussed with his hair a bit, running her fingers through it experimentally and making queer shivers run over Rhett's shoulders.

"The mountain, I suppose. You jumped and turned just in time, but then you were gone. I was left up there alone. We tried a dozen ways to get me down, but Dan couldn't find any harpies or rocs, and there was no rope long enough. In the end, I threw down all our things in a bundle and figured I'd have to do it myself. So I changed. I supposed my coyote bones were lighter, that I would heal more easily. But I couldn't jump."

"Too scared?"

She shoved his head playfully.

"No. Turns out coyotes have more sense than humans. I suppose we're the only species that gets suicidal. That body simply wouldn't jump, no matter how much this one willed it. So I turned back, tossed the spike out of the Cannibal Owl's basket, crawled into it, and…"

"Jumped?"

"Rolled, more like. Might as well have jumped, for all the damage I took on the way down."

Sam hopped onto the porch holding a sharp pair of silver shears and a puppy grin. "Beat to hell by the time she fetched up at our feet in a broken basket. Bruises, cuts, fingers pointing every which way. Dan was just about beside himself. Poor feller still figured he was going to find a miracle and get her down in one piece."

"None of us left that night untouched," Winifred said softly, and Rhett turned his head away before she could touch the cheek under his gone eye with pity.

"Well, get on with the cropping, then. Supper bell's ringing soon, and as long as it ain't Delgado's beans, I reckon I'll want to be there."

Sam and Earl watched as Winifred hobbled around, her crutch under her arm, snipping here and there. Tufty bits of frizzy black fell around the serape and rolled around Rhett's boots like tiny tumbleweeds. An unfamiliar breeze stirred around his ears, and he felt altogether too exposed for someone wearing a man's full complement of clothes.

"And what about your foot?"

The shears snipped in warning, brushing his ear and making him flinch. "Captain gave me a pretty box to keep it in. Nobody knows how to attach it. That doctor in Burlesville just laughed at me."

"We stopped there. Dwarves got a funny way of showing their thanks."

"It's that way with the Rangers, a lot of the time." Sam rubbed his own well-shined badge. "We do the best we can, and it's never enough for some folks."

The supper bell rang, a softer sound than when Delgado had been the one beating it with a stick. Rhett tried to stand, but Winifred held him down with one hand while she finished her work. He let her, mainly so he wouldn't knock her over, wobbly as she was.

"And we'll see the truth of it shortly," Earl added, standing to face the lantern-lit ranch house. "So tell me: Why does it feel like I'm walking to the gallows?"

"The Rangers only hang horse thieves," Sam said helpfully. "The human ones, at least."

"And who among us hasn't stolen a horse?" Earl shot back.

Sam cleared his throat and stood. "Well, don't go reminding him of that, first off."

"There." Winifred took a final snip with her shears and whipped the serape off Rhett's shoulders, shaking out the hair.

He stood, rubbed a hand through his short scruff, and replaced his eye kerchief and hat. When he hurried inside to check the mirror, what he saw matched what he felt like. A rough creature of harsh lines and edges, of dark skin and darker eye. The Shadow.

The Shadow wanted revenge, but more than that, just now, the Shadow wanted food.

The new cook was a grouchy thing named Conchita, a hunched and grandmotherly Aztecan woman in a fringed jacket with gray hair pulled back tight in a bun. When Rhett went to sniff the pot for evidence of Delgado's bean recipe, the old woman smacked him with a spoon.

"Get out of my kitchen or I stick you," she muttered.

And Rhett believed her, so he did.

Sam had saved him a place at the table—his old place. It raised his spirits, seeing that Sam hadn't taken up with any other Rangers in his absence. Of course, most of the newer fellers had met their fate on the way to the Cannibal Owl's lair, and the grizzled old fellers all had long friendships of their own to tend. Still, it felt good to slide onto the bench and wait in turn for the warm mess of beans and goat and tamales on a scarred tin plate. He was scooping food into his mouth before Conchita had moved on, and it was the complete opposite of the slop Delgado had served, which gave Conchita the glow of a goddamn angel, as far as Rhett was concerned. Regina distributed the tamales, and Rhett could feel the rage radiating off the woman.

Not that he could blame her. Demanding to live among citified people and being installed in the kitchen to tend to a ragtag bunch of Rangers was no one's idea of freedom.

Beside Rhett, Earl ate far more slowly. Whether it was because he was unnerved by the prospect of speaking to the Captain or because his soft Irish belly wasn't accustomed to Aztecan spices, Rhett could not have ventured a guess. He handed the sullen feller a tamale and elbowed him.

"Eat up, man. Fortify yourself."

Earl didn't say anything, but he did nibble the tamale, so that was something.

As the fellers' spoons scraped against tin, the Captain pushed back from his chair at the head of the table and rubbed his spare belly.

"Well, then. Welcome back, Rhett. Why don't you introduce your friend, and we'll see if his request falls within our jurisdiction."

Rhett burped and sat up straighter. "Thanks kindly, Captain. As I mentioned, this here's Earl O'Bannon, and he came from a railroad camp with a problem of sorts." Earl said nothing, so Rhett shoved his shoulder. "Go on, fool."

Earl stood suddenly, knocking his plate sideways. His face was as red as his hair, his eyes wide with terror and what Rhett suspected was a bit of defiance.

"Me name's Earl O'Bannon, formerly of Galway. If there were Irish among you, I'd regale you with me family history, but I can tell by the number of hands on pistols that you lads aren't much for gab."

"That we ain't," Jiddy growled.

"The short of it is that I've been for many months an employee of the Trevisan Railroad Camp, but as pleasant as it sounds, it surely isn't. I joined up with me brother Shaunie and some other Irish, as the bill didn't exclude our kind, but those lads didn't make the cut. Mr. Trevisan keeps a camp of what you lads call monsters. Most of the gangers and scouts are white, and the workers are a mixed bag, mostly immigrants. Many are Chine or Injun, but there's some from Afrika and the Caucasus lands among 'em. A few hundred men, working to lay the tracks for Mr. Trevisan's railroad. When I left, they were headed past Lamartine and toward San Anton."

The Captain leaned forward, one elbow on the table. "Forgive me, son, but I never heard of that railroad company, and that route ain't the most useful, if I know my map. Transcontinental's a good bit north of Durango."

"It's not a proper company, sir—not a public one. Mr. Trevisan owns it, runs it, and he decides where to lay the track according to some dark plan of his own. Far as I know, they're set to cut west from San Anton and aim for Calafia through Azteca, Queen-of-Angels being his ultimate goal."

"And what does this Trevisan plan to ship on his private railroad?"

"If he knows, he wasn't sharing it with the likes of me, sir."

The Captain pulled a splinter from the table and set to picking his teeth. "Aside from having a fair number of unnatural men, why exactly should this railroad require the attention of the Durango Rangers?"

Earl sat down, whipped off his boot, and held a freshly washed foot up on the table to show his missing toes. "It ain't the sort of job a man can leave alive. Mr. Trevisan needs bones for whatever magic he does. Monster bones. He takes bits and pieces from the men, mostly things you wouldn't miss. But every so often, he needs more, and that unfortunate soul never returns to his bunk."

The men leaned close to stare at the wiggling toes, and the Captain shook his head. "Not that I'm doubting the veracity of your claim, boy, but I know for a fact that a monster's bones don't heal. Just ask that coyote-girl. So how come yours did?"

"There's an old man in camp, Grandpa Z. Chine. He has magic or medicine or both. I can't tell you how he did it, but when I went into his tent, I was indisposed, and when I woke up again, I was all healed. Without him, I reckon there's no way the track would get laid. Mr. Trevisan requires a lot of bones, you see."

"Then get your foot off the dinner table and tell me what it is you're asking."

Earl stuck his foot back in his boot. "The Rangers need to stop Mr. Trevisan, sir. Not only because hundreds of men are being maimed and killed and never being paid. But also because whatever it is he wants in Queen-of-Angels is sure to be something no good man wants him to have. Whether it's the same gold everyone else is after or something more sinister, he's not the sort to ship tins of peaches, if you'll be catchin' my meaning."

The Captain leaned back and rubbed his eyes as if trying to excavate fifty years' worth of annoyance and grit. Rhett had to admit he looked decades older than he had the first time Rhett had laid eyes on the head of the Las Moras Company. He looked downright tired, the Captain did. And Earl was just making it worse.

"Son, I got a duty, and that duty is to protect the citizens of Durango from threats of the inhuman sort. Now, I just spent several weeks hunting a damn owl, and now I've got a letter from the head office regarding an overpopulation of sand wyrms down south, terrorizing Durango towns full of Durango citizens. Why the Sam Hill do you believe my Rangers should investigate a private investor's poor work conditions outside of our jurisdiction for a bunch of immigrants who aren't my problem?"

"I suppose that depends on if you got a heart," Earl snapped.

"Oh, I got a heart. But they didn't make me Captain because I chase it around the territory. Now you said the railroad was, last you saw it, around Lamartine?"

Earl nodded grimly.

"Well, then. That's not our district, anyway. You go on out to Lamartine and talk to Captain Eugene Haskell of the Lamartine Outpost. He's closer to the issue, and he's got a bigger company. Problem solved." The Captain sat back and raised his eyebrows.

"But I heard—"

"What you might've heard is far less important to me than my chain of command, son."

Earl's fists slammed down on the table. "Excusing my impertinence, Captain, but the problem is far from solved."

The Rangers shifted, hands on guns and knives, to hear the Captain spoken to as such. Even Rhett's hand was on the butt of his pistol.

"Maybe your problem ain't over, but mine is. Now, we'll give you a horse and supplies and a map back to Lamartine, but this company is committed to head south to Lareda in two days." He looked up at Rhett. "Now, Rhett Hennessy, you look ready to spit nails. You going to leave us again right after your celebrated and long-awaited return?"

The Captain sounded gruff, but underneath it, Rhett sensed he was worried or ready to have his feelings hurt. Maybe both.

Whatever Rhett could do, he couldn't lie to a man like the Captain.

"I can't rightly explain it, Captain. My bones tell me to help this man. Maybe it's my destiny, as it is, or maybe I'm hoping this Grandpa Z can help Winifred get her foot working again. But I..." Rhett rubbed his eye kerchief, feeling a damn fool. "I feel a mighty ache to ride for Lamartine, is all I'm saying, and know that I don't like saying it, not a bit."

"You might have a destiny, son. But me? I got a commission. The Durango Rangers ride south for Lareda in two days. I hope to hell you'll ride with us."

Rhett swallowed, his supper turning into a cold ball of dread in his belly. "And if I don't?"

The Captain's eyes were all sorrowful, but his mouth was grimly set. "Then I reckon I'll write a letter of introduction to Captain Haskell and wish you Godspeed on your next fool quest."

That night, Rhett couldn't sleep. Comforting though it was to be surrounded by the thick air of men snoring and farting, their cornshuck mattresses crinkling as they rolled around, he couldn't find anything close to peace. Destiny was a cruel-hearted bitch, giving him everything he wanted before ripping it out of his hands like a bullying child, again and again.

The porch creaked in the wind, and he was forced to recall the dreams that had lured him outside of this very bunkhouse and out to the butte, to the Injun woman and her wet black mare standing sentinel in the night. Destiny, again, pushing him around. He hadn't wanted to hunt the damn Cannibal Owl, and he sure as hell didn't want to go to Lamartine and fight a rich railroad boss who loved nothing more than cutting off a man's parts, bit by bit. Sand wyrms sounded right homey, by contrast.

Not only was Earl's villain vastly worse than a bunch of big snakes, but following his heart, or the pain in his ruined eye, or whatever it was, meant that it would just be him and the ornery donkey again. No Rangers. No Sam. No Winifred. No Coyote Dan, wherever the hell he was. No nightly belly full of Conchita's delicious tamales. Just a feller named Earl that he respected but didn't like too much, headed toward what was sure to be a mess of trouble that wasn't his business.

Damn Coyote Dan and his wandering off. He was the one who had told Rhett, long ago, or maybe just a few weeks ago, that he wouldn't have much choice in regard to his destiny. That he would feel called to do whatever it was the Shadow needed to do. Damn Dan, damn his eyes, and damn the Shadow. Damn the pain Rhett felt behind his eye kerchief when he considered the simple, uncomplicated pleasures of riding out with the Rangers toward Lareda, sleeping by fires and joshing with the fellers and killing monsters that were nothing but monsters.

Who actually wanted to go to Lamartine anyway? Big dumb town full of big dumb folks.

Better the open air down south, where a man had plenty of room to stretch out.

"Not sleeping, Rhett?"

He turned toward Sam's whisper in the next-over bunk, glad to see those worried blue eyes in the low light of the room.

"Figure I got too accustomed to having the sky overhead," Rhett muttered.

"Is it nice? Flying?"

Rhett considered and settled more firmly down on his bunk. "I reckon so. If I think too much while I'm doing it, I can't do it anymore. So I don't think too much."

"I can't tell you how scared I was, Rhett, watching you jump off that mountain. You got a hell of a pair of balls on you, man."

Rhett rolled onto his back and grinned up at the bunk overhead. "Yeah, well, I figured it would work out all right." Then, more softly, "Say, Sam. What do I look like when I'm . . . that?"

Sam hummed to himself. "Like nothing I ever seen. Like a vulture, but bigger. More colorful. Sort of a peach color in parts, with red-rimmed eyes. You swooped over me, and your shadow was huge."

"I bet Jiddy had some kind thoughts on the matter."

"Yeah, well, Jiddy doesn't like anybody who gets more attention than him. Don't worry about Jiddy. Everything'll be fine once we're on the trail to Lareda. Won't it?"

Rhett sighed and rolled over to his side, facing away from his best friend. "I hope it will, Sam. I sure as hell hope it will."

The next morning, like magic, Coyote Dan was sitting at the breakfast table in stolen clothes, grinning.

"You sure got a way of popping up like a damn prairie dog," Rhett muttered.

"Good to see you, too."

"You find anything while you were off gallivanting?"

"Nothing. Nobody that can help my sister, and you were nowhere to be found. I'll be glad to eat some food that's not raw or strung up on a stick, I can tell you that."

Soon they were all seated and gulping down their eggs and coffee. Earl was more at ease, at least, less like he was waiting for the judge and more like he was waiting in line for the noose and had gotten used to the idea. Conchita slid extra corn cakes onto Rhett's plate, muttering, "Too thin, too thin." Winifred hobbled up and hugged her brother with one arm. Sam just aimed his grin at everybody like a sunbeam that had never seen a lick of rain. The homey scene only served to make Rhett's heart ache all the harder.

The Captain ate quickly, nodded at Rhett, and left, presumably to prepare for tomorrow's leave-taking. Rhett was overcome with the feeling that he was somehow letting the old man down. The Captain was one of the few living folks who knew what Rhett was and didn't hold it against him, and that made the man near godlike in Rhett's eyes. Rhett did not want to disappoint him, but it also went against his grain to agree to a scheme just to please someone else. Whenever Rhett thought of the railroad and Lamartine, his heart felt light. Whenever he thought of sand wyrms and Lareda, it was like walking chest-first into a brick wall of nope.

Which is pretty much the opposite of what his brain told him.

The last thing he wanted to do was go to Lamartine...

Except that's where he knew he had to go.

Damn, but a destiny was a troublesome thing to have.

"What's riled the Captain?" Dan asked, staring at the door.

Sam sipped his coffee and shrugged. "We got a commission to hunt some sand wyrms down south, but Rhett's friend here brought news of a monster causing trouble toward Lamartine."

Dan frowned. "That's Haskell's territory."

Sam nodded. "So the Captain said."

"And Rhett is torn."

It wasn't a question. But Dan always knew everything anyway, didn't he? Or at least he thought he did.

"Yep," was all Rhett said between eggs.

"There's a doctor there," Earl piped up. "In the camp. Fixed me chopped-off toes, and might fix the lass's foot. Lives are being lost every day. Even waiting for the decision is taking too long, if you were asking me."

"And who are you?"

Rhett watched Earl's chest puff out as he prepared to introduce himself and he lost all patience with the world. Picking up his last corn cake, he pushed away from the table and headed outside with Sam on his heels.

"Where you going, Rhett?"

"Where things make sense, Sam."

And that meant the horse corral. Rhett checked on Rag-doll and Puddin' and Blue, scouting out the new horses in the herd and testing their tempers. The Captain was always losing horses in fights and plucking new ones from the wreckage of whatever town he saved or from the werewolves he killed, and Rhett figured breaking a new horse might help him feel less at odds with the world. He selected a short chestnut with a wide blaze who seemed to have a keen eye, lassoed him without too much trouble, and led him to the round pen. Sam went quiet, arms on the fence, and Rhett did what he did best, or maybe second best. Each crow-hop and buck from the gelding felt like a dare that Rhett could answer, and he soon had the horse relatively calm and trotting around. A sweet, familiar ache set up in his rump, which had been too long without a good horse underneath it.

"I admire this about you, Rhett. When you can't make sense of things, you make yourself useful."

But it wasn't Sam who said it.

Rhett swung the chestnut around and glared at Dan. "Admiration is your business, and breaking horses is mine. But if you'd care to try your hand at proving useful, tell me what you think of that boy's story. Is this railroad feller in Lamartine worth my time?"

Dan's grin was smug enough that Rhett wanted to poke holes in it with a fist. "Is it worth the Shadow's time, you mean?"

"Same goddamn thing, ain't it?" He nudged the chestnut into a grudging canter.

"I think you know the answer. You just don't like it," Dan hollered.

"And I think I told you to act useful," Rhett hollered back.

"Lord, but you two grin a lot when you're nasty to one another," Sam said, slapping his hat against his leg.

"A grin's just another way to show your teeth," Dan said.

Rhett groaned, slowed to a walk, and nudged the chestnut toward the fence.

"Are you coming with me or not?" he growled, staring down into Dan's eyes.

Dan wasn't grinning anymore. "I'll follow the Shadow."

"Then I figure we ride at dawn."

"So you're going, then?" Sam asked, looking all hangdog and breaking Rhett's heart again. "To Lamartine with that Earl feller?"

Rhett slid off the horse, handed the rope to Dan, and put his hands on the fence in front of Sam. "I got to. A man can't shake destiny, Sam. I'm sorry. I'll be back as soon as it's settled, if I'm not sand. You can count on that."

Sam's blue-glass eyes were wet, his mouth grimly set. What he said next felt like the opposite of being kicked in the heart. "I won't count on that, you fool. Only way to keep you alive's to go with you, ain't it?"

It was a good thing Rhett was already off the horse, because he was so surprised he might've otherwise fallen right off the gelding's rump.

"You're...going with me? To Lamartine?"

Sam and Dan nodded.

"Winifred, too," Dan added. "On horseback, she's unimpeded. Won't slow us down."

Rhett patted the chestnut's neck and shook his head in disbelief. "I'm going to Lamartine with Samuel Hennessy, two coyotes, and a goddamn donkey," he said. "The world is a damn strange place."

"Wait. A donkey?" Sam asked.

Rhett snorted. "Earl. And just wait until you get to know him. He never shuts up."

"I always wanted to see Lamartine again." Sam grinned and stared toward the east.

"I could do without it, myself." Something caught Rhett's eye, and he found the Captain watching him, thoughtful-like, before jerking his head toward the storage shed and walking in that direction. "The Captain's calling me. If I don't come back, give Lamartine hell for me."

"You'll come back," Coyote Dan said, wearing his coyote grin. "You always do."

Walking toward the Captain was as hard as turning his boots toward the sand wyrms of Lareda, but Rhett did it. That's what a man did—what he had to do. It wasn't always as simple and straightforward as facing down werewolves or sirens. Walking toward a man you respected who was about to tell you he was disappointed in you was bad enough.

At the moment, Rhett would've preferred the werewolves.

CHAPTER
6

Rhett stood in the doorway, giving his eye time to adjust. The storage shed was an old log cabin, the windows boarded up and the logs sloppily chinked. The door wore a mighty heavy padlock on the outside, the general idea being that whatever was inside needed to stay inside. When the Rangers had taken a brief week to train him up, he'd learned that this was where they kept magical and monstery things best left in the dark.

"Over here, son."

Squinting, Rhett could make out the Captain in a dusty corner obscured by shelves of books and old junk, most of which seemed like a waste of space to someone who couldn't read or cipher. The cockatrices and salamanders clucked and hissed as he walked past their cages, glad he'd never drawn the short straw that meant a Ranger had to feed and clean up after the nasty beasts. Rhett well remembered the acid burns on Chicken's hands from the clumsy feller's week of duty in here. That wasn't a problem Chicken would have again, as he was dead, killed by the siren of Reveille. Rhett's heart pinched up, hard and lonely as a nut rattling in a bucket. He'd had so little time with the Rangers and yet seen so much lost.

As for the Captain, he was digging around in a trunk, his back bent to show the bare pate on his hatless head. Rhett waited, patient-like, for as long as he could, which wasn't long.

"I'm here, Captain," Rhett said, just so there'd be a noise that wasn't creepy.

"I know. When I find what I'm looking for, I'll elucidate. Sam showed you your things, I reckon. We brought everything we could find from the mountain. You need any supplies that you didn't already have, now's the time to ask."

Rhett swallowed, his mind reeling and taking stock. "I got bullets and guns. Reckon we could use some road food, if Conchita can spare it. Earl could use a hat so his buttermilk face doesn't burn. Maybe a gun, too, if he can prove he won't shoot his fool foot off." He removed his hat and fidgeted with it, building up the nerve to ask for something he had no right to. "And that stray mule, the feller with one eye. Maybe he could be our pack animal?"

The Captain chuckled and shook his head. "You're just hell-bent on gathering a strange flock, is all I can figure. Only crew uglier than yours I've seen is the one I started out with before I got my commission. You'll take whatever and whoever you can get, at first."

"I'll take whoever's willing to have my back in a fight," Rhett corrected gently. "And they all have, every one of 'em."

"You're stealing Hennessy, too, ain't you?"

"That's his business, Captain."

"I'll take that as a yes. I suspected as much."

"I'm sorry, Captain, if—"

The Captain stood and turned, slow and creaking in his bones. His hand on Rhett's shoulder stopped the words like a cork in a bottle. "Don't be sorry. You're doing what you got to do, and I respect that. I'd send the full outpost to help you out if I could, but I can't, so I'm going to do my best to stack the deck in your favor. Ranger rules allow that younger fellers get sent on quests, from time to time, so you're still on the books and the payroll, and don't take shit off anybody while you're wearing this badge, you hear me?"

Rhett straightened up and said, "Yes, sir, Captain."

"Now, from what Earl tells me, he doesn't know what sort of monster this railroad man is, just that he's got big magic and is mighty secretive. So I'm giving you a copy of this grimoire and all the silver you boys'll need to kill a damn bull elephant."

Leaning over, the Captain picked up a beat-up old black bag similar to the one the horse doc in Burlesville carried around for his doctoring. He opened it up, letting a puff of dust into the still air. Inside, he put a thick leather book, several silver knives, and a pile of glittering silver bullets.

"There's a surgeon's kit in here, too. Laudanum for pain, needles and sutures and whatever the Sam Hill else doctors keep in their little glass bottles."

"But—"

"I know. You and Dan and Winifred and Earl don't need such fripperies. But Sam might. And there could be some humans along the way that need your help, too. Life gets messy around monsters; you know that. I got a feeling whatever you're setting out to do is going to get more messy than usual. Might as well prepare. It's not much for a mule to carry, anyway, even if he's old and skinny."

Rhett let out a breath he hadn't known he was holding. "His name is Blue," he said softly.

"Well, he's almost as ornery as you are, so I reckon you'll be glad of each other's company."

His voice had gone all rough, and the Captain was sort of staring into space over Rhett's shoulder, one hand on the open bag.

"Captain?"

"I feel a tremor in the air, Rhett. Durango…it's changing. Railroads pressing in, wagons tumbling past, full of women and children, and the monsters only seem to be getting bigger and meaner. My time is almost up."

"Don't say, that, Captain! You got twenty good years in you, at least."

That snapped the Captain back. He barked a laugh. "Well, I'm not ready to die yet, I know that much. Might as well go give some sand wyrms the what-for. Ugly bastards, they are. But a long sight better than a monster with a cunning tongue and a bank account." He stepped back and put a hand on Rhett's shoulder. "Winifred told me what you did in that cave. Not all the Rangers. Just me. You did good, son. Best reward I could give you would be a long, quiet life with no more pain, but I reckon you'd look askance at that anyway, considering this destiny of yours and all."

"I never asked for the burden," Rhett said gruffly.

"Nobody does. That's why it's called a burden. Didn't ask for mine, neither. At least I can take that fool woman Regina off your hands, drop her among the townfolk of Lareda, if she lasts that long. Now look here. Hold out your hand. I'm going to teach you the Ranger passcode. Any Captain takes your measure and doubts you, you hold out your hand, look him in the eye, and do this."

What followed felt mighty uncomfortable to Rhett, who wasn't fond of being touched. The intricacies of the handshake were many, and it took several tries before the Captain was satisfied that Rhett could pull it off.

"That'll do, son. Now, one last thing."

Stepping close, the Captain reached for Rhett's Ranger badge. Rhett figured he was going to reposition it, or maybe shine it up a bit, as the Rangers tended to do after a fight. When the Captain undid the pin and removed it, Rhett had his first glimpse of what might make him kill an innocent man, even one he respected as much as the old feller standing slightly too close. But the Captain was soon pinning a new badge to Rhett's collar.

"You're officially a Scout for the Durango Rangers. Jiddy won't like it much, if you come back alive, but we'll cross that bridge when we come to it. Now you make sure you're wearing it shiny and proud when you meet Captain Haskell, you hear? I'd choose to send you into the domain of just about any of my compatriots over him. We never have seen eye to eye. So you remember this: At the end of the day, Captain Haskell ain't your boss. He can't compel you, enlist you, or impede you. So if you don't like what he has to say, you know what you need to do."

"Yes, sir." Rhett nodded and stood up straighter. "Kill what needs to die, with or without his help."

"I'd take one of you over ten of him, so you'd best come back alive."

A knot formed in Rhett's throat, and he could only nod tightly.

"And here's your papers. I know you're not one for lies, but traveling east means folks might have some questions regarding your particular freedoms. Don't let anyone assume the worst."

The papers he tossed in the bag looked old and worn and could not possibly have been legitimate. Rhett burned with fury and relief. So folks might think he was a runaway slave or an army deserter, maybe? And these made-up goddamn papers would convince them otherwise? The only way to fight lies was with more lies, then, in regard to Rhett's history. Just as well. Better to defeat an uppity feller with paper than with a knife in the guts and a rope necklace for Rhett's trouble.

The Captain gave a decisive nod and hobbled out the door. Rhett moved farther into the darkness among the cockatrice cages and allowed himself five minutes of tears. Parting from the Captain was like losing Monty all over again. Except that if he did a good enough job, he could come back, and the Captain might still be around. His job now was simply to stay alive long enough to tell the Captain he'd succeeded.

He was determined to make the Captain proud.

They left at dawn, two companies headed in opposite directions. The Captain led a sturdy crew of hard men armed to the teeth, their horses stomping and breathing clouds against the darkness that still settled around the shoulders of the mountains like a widow's shawl. Regina sat on the wagon seat beside Conchita, both women wearing grim frowns. Rhett raised a hand in good-bye, but she only looked away from him, the fool creature.

Rhett's far smaller posse of compatriots was, by comparison, ridiculous. A crippled woman, a coyote man, a donkey, an uglier-than-usual mule, a herd of decent enough horses, and sweet, optimistic Sam prancing in the middle of 'em like a prize bull. Although Rhett had promised Earl would be fast friends with Puddin', the Irishman had claimed a distaste for sitting astride horseflesh and had chosen instead to trot along in his donkey form. Something about being a hoofed critter apparently made it right peculiar to ride another hoofed critter, which at least saved Rhett the time and trouble of fetching a second mount for himself. As always, a small contingent of injured, old, and raw Rangers stayed behind to guard the homestead and meet any new challenges.

With a tip of his hat to the Captain, Rhett turned Ragdoll toward the shifting dawn and urged the mare into a walk.

Clever thing that she was, she showed some reluctance in leaving the larger, safer herd and heading out in an unfamiliar direction, but Rhett knew his business on horseback and wouldn't take a goddamn mare's mind into consideration. Ponying Puddin' and a heavily laden Blue, he led his crew toward the rising sun.

Behind him came Winifred on the same draft cross the Captain had once lent Regina, a handsome but gentle bay-colored beast named Hercules who had a broad back and steady pace. Sam rode his high-stepping palomino and ponied his blue roan. Dan sat easy on his forgettable chestnut, ponying the forgettable chestnut gelding Rhett had broken just yesterday. And Earl trotted among them, his bag slung over his dirt-brown donkey back and containing all his old clothes, freshly laundered, not to mention a pistol and fresh socks. He seemed especially jaunty, which Rhett had to assume meant he was eager to be headed back toward his brother and friends at the railroad camp.

Rhett wasn't feeling nearly that cheerful. Before he left, Conchita had approached him, her thin lips set in a dour frown. She'd handed him a heavy bag of food supplies and oven-hot tamales and corn dodgers and sketched a cross over him with her thumb. *"Vaya con Dios,"* she'd muttered, and Rhett didn't know what that meant, but it sounded an awful lot like what you'd say to a man marked for dead.

The farther they got from the Las Moras Outpost, the better Rhett felt, which only made him more heartsick. His destiny wanted him to go east, but he wanted to go south and west. How far would the Shadow need to travel to fulfill its duties? Would he be charging down vampires in New Amsterdam or hunting swamp monsters in Shackamaxon? Would the future see him riding in the lower decks of a steamship to Europa? His stomach roiled at the thought. He felt as much a part of

Durango as the dust here, so similar to the color of his own skin. The sparseness of the prairie and the hardness of the desert called to his heart, same to same. Wherever he went, he needed far-off mountains and vastness and a particular wildness, or else he'd start looking for death like a dumb sheep, ready to turn anything into a noose.

It wasn't long at all until the sun shimmered high overhead, marking noon, and they stopped to eat a quick meal of cold tamales and relieve their various needs. Rhett watched as Dan helped his sister down from her horse, the girl's jaw set at the indignity of requiring help. She'd worn pants and a boot for the riding, which was sure to make her task even more challenging. Winifred took up her crutch and hobbled behind some boulders, and Rhett exhaled, grateful that she'd not requested his aid. Try as he might, he couldn't forget the uncomfortable urges he'd felt in the cave with her, naked as a babe, cradled against her chest. He didn't need to be that close to the vexful coyote-girl ever again, even if Rhett was the obvious choice to lean on for her women's troubles.

Men had it so easy, pissing wherever they wished. Most of the time, Rhett had come to feel right comfortable as a man among men, but nothing reminded him of the frailty of his body like the horrors that occurred below his damn belt. Any day now, he'd be bleeding again, and the thought made him grind his teeth and wish for a fairer world. He found a different boulder to piss behind, glad at least that no one was around to witness a clumsiness about his business that few men could claim to understand.

"We still headed in the right direction?" Rhett asked, finding Earl in conversation with Dan over something or other held between them. He assumed it was Earl's blood-crusty map, but when he got closer, he saw that it was the book the Captain had packed in the doctor's bag. Rhett tended to look down on anything beyond his understanding, and the gold-edged book was no different. He spit in the dust and pointed at the tome like it was a fart no one would claim. "Unless there's a map in there, I fail to see how it might be useful."

Dan grinned in that particularly obnoxious way he had. "Said the same person who assured me he didn't need to learn how to make a bow and arrow."

"Didn't need a bow and arrow to kill that siren or the Cannibal Owl. Reckon a gun will keep working, as long as I can pull the trigger."

"But what about when you run out of—"

Rhett stopped him with a hand. "Shut your damn tamale hole and help me reckon the way to Lamartine. I don't care to lose a day to reckless meandering."

Dan chuckled, another noxious habit, and pulled a tan piece of paper out of the bag rigged to Blue's harness, which seemed to hold far more than it had any right to. He unfolded the paper, revealing a creased and stained but serviceable map far superior to Earl's. "Captain gave us this Ranger map, which should get us there. Here's the outpost, and here's Lamartine. First marker on the road's gonna be Bandera, which we'll know because—"

"Because I was there," Sam said, all raw. He'd just moseyed up, but now he had to turn away and stare at the sun, a trick Rhett used himself when he didn't want to see the past play out in his mind.

"Then we'll head up through Waterloo and to Lamartine. Should find some settlements in between that aren't on the map, which we can avoid or seek out as needed." He glanced meaningfully to where Winifred sat on a flat stone, resting, her cut foot stuck out in front of her showing its gruesome circle of live bone. "Now, I know you're not the sort to ache for a fine bed, but any respite we can give my sister would be a gift, provided it didn't carry the taint of pity."

Rhett nodded once and chewed the inside of his cheek. "Understood."

"Let's not forget, lads, that any days spent reclining in bed means that men in the railroad camp are losing fingers and lives both." Earl's voice was clipped and terse, his Irish accent high with emotion.

"It must be a balance," Dan said, using his preacher tone. "If we push too hard, we'll be too tired and worn to fight. If we're in good shape, well fed and well rested, we've a better chance of success."

"Aye, well, and let's recall that we could be discussing such idleness while moving toward our goal."

Sam, who had been watching the argument but remaining safely out of it, smiled widely and clapped both men on the back. "Then let's saddle up—and, uh, donkey up, boys. We still got plenty of daylight left."

Rhett had to turn to his saddlebags to hide the rush of feeling that thrummed through him whenever Sam did something like that. He'd promised Sam they'd just be friends, that they'd have each other's backs. And that meant that he would do everything in his power to hide the fact that he still had feelings for Samuel Hennessy and probably always would, even if he'd want to punch that sweet smile every now and again, just to take out some small amount of his ongoing frustration and pain.

Blue rubbed his long nose against Rhett's shoulder, and he rubbed the old mule's neck, wishing there was some way to discover what-all the beast had been through since Rhett had left Pap's land. At least Pap hadn't beaten the mule, as Blue's ragged gray coat was unmarked by the lash, a kindness Pap hadn't extended to his slave girl, Nettie Lonesome. Which reminded Rhett of a question he'd been meaning to ask but... didn't want to.

Pulling the packet out of the doctor's bag, he held the faded brown papers out to Sam. "I reckon I need to know what's in here, in case somebody asks," Rhett said roughly.

Sam nodded and untied the strings, unfolding the paper and guiding a finger down the chickenscratch writing, his brow wrinkled up in a way that made Rhett's heart crunch.

"Says mostly the truth, or what the truth should be," Sam finally said. "Your name is Mr. Rhett Walker, you're from the town of Reveille in Durango Territory, you're seventeen, and you're an official Scout for the Durango Rangers."

Rhett drew a thumb over his badge and smiled. "Mr. Rhett Walker. I like the sound of that, although I do wonder what made the Captain choose it."

Sam looked at him funny. "You don't know? That's the Captain's name. Captain Abraham Walker." His eyes went soft and his smile lopsided. "He must like you quite a bit, to give you use of his name like that. I reckon he figured it would raise suspicion, two Hennessy boys that look so unalike, traveling together. Rhett Walker's a good name."

"Show me." Rhett edged closer to Sam and allowed himself to appreciate the warmth of the boy's shoulder.

Sam pointed to a particularly clear bit of scribble. "Right here. See, this is an *M*, for *Mister*, and this is Rhett. *R-H-E-T-T*."

"Why's it need two *t*'s?"

Sam scratched his head. "I don't rightly. But Hennessy's got two *s*'s and two *n*'s, so I reckon it's useful for something." He handed the paper to Rhett, and his voice went low and whisper-quiet. "I could try to teach you your letters, Rhett. All this time we got on the prairie, we might as well. A learned man's always respected, you know."

Rhett swallowed hard, overcome with peculiar emotions. He felt the familiar rage that bubbled up every time someone took the trouble to point out one of his deficiencies, but that was mostly smothered out by the lovely dream of being able to read, of being any man's equal. And the thought of cozy evenings by the fire, his hair touching Sam's as they leaned together and puzzled over letters...well, he wouldn't deny himself that pleasure, if nothing else. But he made his voice gruff, just so Sam wouldn't think him weak.

"I reckon that'd be fine, Sam."

Sam turned the full force of his grin on Rhett, whose knees went wobbly. "We'll start tonight. But I reckon we ought to get on the road now, before Earl gets mad enough to spit."

Rhett nodded, checked Ragdoll's girth, and swung up into the saddle. There was a certain sensation, every time he mounted, that would never get old: *his* horse and *his* saddle and *his* guns, won honest. Of all the things he'd ever dared to dream of, these simple things that every other cowpoke took for granted would never lose their shine. He checked his watch as Dan gave Winifred a leg up onto her horse and helped her secure her crutch to her saddle. Earl undressed and transformed into donkey mode, and Sam calmed down his dancing palomino with whispered words of kindness.

This was Rhett's company, and they were back on the road.

Nothing of any interest occurred that day, much to Rhett's satisfaction. He was painfully relieved to dismount by a convenient creek for dinner and thoroughly vexed to discover just how saddle sore he felt. Then again, he'd been a bird for most of his last journey, and that served to make him feel fit and healthy when his feet touched ground again rather than achy and tender.

As if he were truly a captain, Rhett doled out work according to each person's strengths. Sam was set to make the fire, Dan helped Winifred to a rock before going hunting, and Earl helped Rhett with the horses. As if sensing that this man was the same amicable donkey that had plodded by their sides, the horses took to him more than the annoying feller had any right to expect, and Rhett was more than happy to train him in their proper care. As Winifred sat, she sorted through the Captain's black bag by the light of the sunset, exclaiming and humming over what she found and more than glad to have needle and thread. It took so little, Rhett supposed, to make women happy.

By the time the stars came out full force, they all sat around the fire in companionable silence, eating bits of steaming hot jackrabbit and greasy prairie chicken along with cold corn dodgers from Conchita's bag. Rhett was pleased with his first day heading a small crew, grateful that everyone knew their place and no one caused trouble. He would've greatly preferred to ride out with the Rangers, but it was a stark pleasure not to be cheek by jowl with fellers who, whatever their reasons, disliked Rhett. He was soon fat-bellied and licking grease off his fingers, anticipating the sweet comfort of bedding down next to Sam, a pistol under each of the saddles that pillowed their heads.

But first, Rhett gestured them together to discuss tomorrow's plans. Far as they could figure, looking at the Captain's map, it was going to take around two weeks to hit Lamartine, if they didn't run into too much trouble on the way. As Dan held the paper, Rhett studied the various lines and demarcations, wishing he knew what it all meant. Sam was kind enough to point out the sand wyrms that the Captain was hell-bent on curbing, as well as the place where someone among the Rangers had marked off the Cannibal Owl's lair. Some fool had allowed his coffee cup to leave its mark, and Rhett felt sure that Mr. DePaul, who Sam read off as the map's artist, would not have appreciated such carelessness.

"We keep heading northeast, and we'll be there," Rhett said out loud, feeling manly.

Dan's grin was like sand in his eye. "You think it'll be easy, don't you?"

Rhett shrugged. "I reckon I deserve easy, for once. Don't you?"

Taking the map away and carefully refolding it, Dan sighed. "You forget, my friend. The Shadow is called to trouble, and trouble is called to the Shadow. Something strange is coming. I can feel it in the air. Can't you?"

Standing with a sigh, Rhett sniffed the air. "Unless trouble smells like Earl's feet and rabbit fat, I do believe you're mistaken, with that coyote nose of yours."

"Let us hope, for once, that you're right."

But Dan didn't look like he believed it. He never did.

The days slid past, and Rhett felt like thunderclouds dogged his every step. Waiting.

CHAPTER 7

Nettie woke up to a feeling she never wanted to feel again: a man's expectant, probing, curious hand sliding up her knee, the thin cotton night rail not nearly enough armor to protect what she held dear. Her hand snicked for cold metal under the saddle that pillowed her head, but instead of her trusty pistol, she pulled out...an embroidery hoop? The bitty needle wasn't even enough to poke a scorpion. There was nothing else there—no knife, no gun, no palm-sized rock to bash a man's brains in. A shiver of utter helplessness pinged throughout her body, and she sat up, drawing her bare legs together under the shift, her arms protectively hugging her middle and her long braids over her shoulders.

"Please, mister," she said, her voice high and quavering. "Don't hurt me."

The man sitting beside her was a stranger, just a shadow in the night with his black hat pulled down low to hide his face.

"I wouldn't hurt you, honey. I just want to make you feel good."

Nettie bared her teeth. "Bullshit," she hissed. "No man who ever said that was thinking of anything but himself."

The fingers withdrew to stroke a bearded chin. "Is it a girl you want, then?" He gestured with a big hand, and a pretty blond girl in a floaty white shift hurried in from the darkness to kneel on Nettie's other side. The girl's eyes were wide and innocent, her rosebud lips smiling sweetly, her yellow-gold hair half-tumbling in long curls bedecked with flowers. Her soft, moon-pale hand reached for Nettie's shoulder, stroking softly along her arm in a way that made the nightgown slither down, exposing brown skin to the firelight.

Quick as a snake, Nettie slapped the girl's hand away and leaped to her feet, ready to run.

"Sam? Dan? Earl? Where is everybody?"

"Nobody here but us chickens," the man said. His voice was a deep, confident rumble, pleasant-like, if a body didn't feel like it owed him anything. Nettie, for some reason, felt like the man had expectations of her aplenty.

"If you're a chicken, then I'm a monkey's uncle," Nettie said. "What the hell do you want?"

The man made a low hum, like he was considering the question. "To test your mettle. Stripped down, what are you? Even in dreams, you're not what you seem. Peculiar little puzzle of a girl."

"Not a girl," Nettie growled. "And this ain't my dress." Her fingers bunched in the nightgown's flowy fabric as if she longed to rip it off and toss it on the fire but knew that to do so would leave her even more bared than she already was.

She couldn't see the man's eyes, but she could feel them, probing her as if for weakness. The blond girl had disappeared, and even though her two good eyes had adjusted to the darkness and she was leaning forward, all avid, Nettie still couldn't see much of the man. He was a well-built feller, muscular and clad in all black and as hairy as a bear. Nettie could feel that old, familiar wobble about him, meaning that he was some sort of monster. If she'd been a betting creature, she'd have put money that he was something like Jiddy, a bear shifter, or maybe a Lobo who played at acting civilized. The only thing she knew was that everything occurring right now was deeply wrong, down to her bones. This man was not civilized, not at all. And he radiated power as some men radiated stink.

"You got to pay the toll if you want to cross my land," he warned.

"Durango's still free," she shot back.

"Not my part of it."

With a grunt, the man stood and stretched, hairy knuckles seeming to brush the clouds. He turned without a word and walked away, the night gulping him down in one bite.

"What the hell was that?" Nettie asked the emptiness.

"You'll see," the man said from somewhere far off.

A gentle hand grasped Rhett's shoulder, and he swung a fist before he knew what was real.

"Stand down, man! You were crying out in your sleep. Figured you were having a nightmare."

Rhett blinked and found a shadow shaped like Sam Hennessy blocking the starlight, holding Rhett's trembling fist. The fire had worn down, but Rhett knew this man beside him and was glad that, this time, he hadn't bruised the handsome face.

They shared a look so deep Rhett was pretty certain he saw Sam's soul, and Sam released his fist. The moment broke, and both men had to look away.

"Was it the Lobos you were dreaming of? I...I mean, it would be understandable."

Sitting up on one elbow, Rhett took stock. There was Sam, being a good friend. Dan and Winifred slept side by side on their backs, still as corpses. Earl was in donkey form and flopped out in the dust, his wide nostrils flaring with tiny donkey snores. The horses stood loosely in a circle, heads down and tails twitching as they dreamed of whatever horses dreamed.

And Nettie—

No.

Rhett.

He shook his head. That dream had thrown him harder than usual. Its particular tang stank of the same magic that had plagued him as he hunted the Cannibal Owl, the Injun woman showing up after dark to speak words she never had in waking life and alternately beg and threaten.

That was all. It had been a dream. An unpleasant and strange dream, in which Rhett was again trapped in a woman's mind-set and skirts, a thing to be touched and frightened and acted upon. But who was the man at the center of the shadows, hiding his eyes under a dark hat? Could it be this Mr. Trevisan that Earl was running back toward? Or another monster? Come morning, Rhett would have some pointed questions for Dan and Earl about whatever the hell had happened. He wasn't going to mention the dress, though, or the shivers raised by the soft fingertips of the girl stroking down his bared shoulder.

"It wasn't the Lobos," he said, just to reassure Sam.

"What, then?"

Rhett shook his head and settled back down on the hard ground.

"I don't rightly, Sam. But I thank you for waking me."

"Anytime, Rhett. I reckon you'd do the same for me, was I to suffer a nightmare."

Rhett nodded, and they turned their backs to each other to seek sleep. The thought of Sam having a nightmare amused him. How could the sunshine ever experience darkness? Sam probably dreamed of puppies and pies and other pleasant things. But that was too personal a question to ask, and Sam was already snoring softly. Rhett rolled to his other side and matched his breaths to Sam's until he fell asleep. Wherever Rhett's dreams went, the shadowy man and his girl couldn't follow.

After taking a piss the next morning, Rhett walked up to Coyote Dan, all casual-like.

"You have any peculiar dreams last night, Dan?"

Dan looked up from where he was roasting a rattlesnake over the fire and cocked his head. "Describe peculiar. Because I think peculiar means more than usual for you."

Rhett huffed and dug up a rock with the toe of his boot. "Burly feller sitting by the fire, asking personal questions. Wondering what I was."

"Burly?"

"In the way of looks. Lots of black hair everywhere. Like Jiddy. But wearing a hat pulled down to hide his eyes. Dressed like a gambler, maybe. The kind who never loses a hand."

Dan whistled through his teeth and rocked back on his heels. "Did he say who or what he was?"

"Only that you had to pay a toll to cross his land. That I would see. *You'll see*, he said. But it sounded right threatening."

"Was he a cattleman, maybe?"

"How the hell should I know? He wasn't sitting on a damn cow."

"Do you remember anything else about the dream?"

It was Rhett's turn to try whistling, a skill he hadn't yet honed. The sound came out like wind through a reed, worried and fidgety. "Hellfire, Dan. I don't know. He had a girl with him. And he called me a girl. And it was all downright unpleasant, if you catch my drift. I don't want to talk about it."

Turning on his heel, Rhett stormed away, wishing he'd never asked the damn coyote a thing. The feller had said he would see, and Rhett reckoned he would, like it or not, which he didn't like a bit. He could feel everybody's eyes on him, and he didn't like that either. So he did what came natural: got around a boulder, shucked his clothes and boots and hat, and lurched off into the sky, where nobody caused him trouble.

He pushed the human thoughts out of his mind and focused on the ground below him, circling outward to get the lay of the land in the direction they'd be traveling today on the way to Lamartine. Here was a convenient creek, there was an arroyo that would be difficult going for the horses, and just there was a better crossing. Higher and higher he soared, effortlessly riding the thermals, his shadow swirling over the hard ground far below.

There—far off. Farther than he wanted to fly right now. He saw the marking of a town sketched out but not yet grown big. Curls of white smoke, a deliciously rancid trash heap and latrine, enough buildings to harbor the saloon, general store, and bordello every damn town needed to function. Strangely, he also noted rich gardens, an orchard, a sweet river that would soon be polluted. The town was new but on its way to prosperous, and it might have a doc for Winifred. He marked its location, turned, and flew back to the place that called him.

There. A line of horses on the road, his clothes laid out on one of the saddles. Once, a grubby red shirt had been the thing that pulled him back to earth and skin. Now, it was maybe the horses, maybe the clothes, maybe the badge, maybe the people. Hell, maybe all of it. But it drew him like lesser buzzards to blood, and he was soon on two clumsy feet, pulling Ragdoll off to the side and using her body to block anyone's view of his own bareness. Stepping back into his britches, he was glad for something to talk about besides dreams nobody else remembered and he'd rather forget.

The day passed on, as days did. The ground flashed brown and green, the sky going over gray and threatening to rain at any given moment. Thunder waited, just beyond a heavy barrier of thick, dark clouds. Rhett couldn't quite say how far the town was, nor why they might want to aim for it. Being among civilized people wasn't one of his favorite pastimes. And yet it pulled him, tugging at his bones. There was something in that town that needed seeing to, something that made his belly swoop and gurgle, even in bird form. He didn't tell his posse they were headed for it. He didn't say anything, really. His feelings, much like the thunder behind the clouds, were pinned back by a grim frown that no one dared puncture. He simply led, and they followed.

They stopped at the creek he'd found for lunch. Winifred picked some berries, and there was still some snake left over from breakfast. Rhett hadn't eaten then, and he'd filled his belly full of whatever dead things he'd found in flight. He didn't much like the taste on his tongue, after, but it reminded him to drink water along the way, a necessity he often forgot on the trails. His body ached with a familiar, hated feeling, a warm tightness in thighs and belly, and he cursed the unruly innards he'd been given. If only calling himself a man had made his body fall in line. The next time they came across some cover, he yanked his rags from his saddlebag and huffed into the brush to rig them up and prepare for what was certainly bound to happen by nightfall.

Winifred said nothing, but her mouth turned down knowingly. Rhett scowled and looked away. She saw too much, that damn coyote.

"There's a town ahead," Dan said, shading his eyes and squinting.

"You going in?" Winifred asked.

Dan was silent for a blessed moment before shaking his head. "The last town was not kind to me. I'll scout ahead. I'm unfamiliar with this area and would rather get the smell of it first. Rhett, Sam. I can count on you, yes?" His sharp eyes darted to his wounded sister.

"Of course, Dan. You know you can count on us," Sam answered, earnest as hell.

Rhett just nodded. Earl, still in donkey form, did nothing useful.

Dan pulled his chestnut geldings to a halt and handed his lead lines over, one to Sam and one to Winifred. He slipped out of his clothes as easily as a fall tree shucked leaves and stuffed them tidily into his saddlebags, the bulk of his horse hiding his skin. Soon a lean, dust-brown coyote gave a low yip of farewell and loped away toward the hills.

Winifred sighed and clucked her bay into a walk. "He chafes so in a city. I used to think he'd change, but…"

"But they only seem to get worse, and he stays just as stubborn," Rhett finished for her. Remembering his nod to Dan, he kicked Ragdoll ahead so that whatever came at them came at him, first.

Sam nodded, falling in line behind the girl. "Cities getting more citified. It's worse, the farther east you go."

"Then I'd rather stay west," Rhett said gruffly.

Sam cocked his head. "Why are we going to the town at all, then? We don't have to. We can go around."

"Because there might be someone who can help me," Winifred said, her voice sharp. "Or news of the railroad. People have their uses."

Rhett had better reasons, but he didn't say so. He felt just the barest bit of guilt, trotting into a town that gave the Shadow a bad twitch without mentioning it to his friends, but how would scaring them do anybody any good? He was a Ranger Scout. If he found trouble in a town, then he was doing his job, wasn't he? Whatever awaited them, he could handle it. It was just a town.

Did he imagine he felt Sam's eyes on his back? The twinge became a damn pang, and his belly flopped around like a fish.

"Sam, I got that feeling," he said, way low.

"I feel it, too," Winifred added.

The creak of leather told Rhett that Sam was checking his gun.

"Then I reckon we'll be ready," Sam said, sounding like a big damn hero. "But there's something you need to know, Rhett."

He'd never heard Sam's voice get shaky like that, and he turned in the saddle to watch his friend. Sweet, affable Samuel Hennessy looked like he had a mortal pain, his mouth twisted up and his eyes wet and bluer than blue.

"What is it, Sam? You look like you've seen a ghost."

"I wasn't sure of it. Not until just now. You see how the hills come down on either side, up ahead?"

"Well, sure. You'd have to be blind to miss it."

"That's Bandera Pass, Rhett."

Winifred inhaled softly.

Rhett plumbed his memory. "Bandera Pass. There was a Lobo fight. Rangers lost good men. Is that the right of it?"

Sam shivered. "Sure enough my blood is soaked into the ground up ahead. I took an arrow in the leg. There wasn't a town here, back then. It was empty prairie. Lobos were digging farther into Javelina territory and attacking missionaries on their way to San Anton. They surprised us in the pass, and we routed 'em, but... well, if any place is haunted, I figure this one is."

He didn't stop his horse, but Rhett heard him draw his pistol. Rhett followed suit, finding he generally felt better about life when he was holding a weapon. Winifred didn't carry a gun, but she did check the line holding Dan's chestnut to her bay and test her own knife's quickness, silently drawing it from a well-oiled sheath at her waist a few times.

A gasp drew Rhett's attention down, and he found Earl naked and stepping close to his horse. "You feel that?" he asked.

Rhett nodded. "Something in the town up ahead. You going in as a donkey or a man?"

"Donkey all the way," Earl said with a grin. "Nobody shoots a donkey."

Seconds later, he was trotting at Puddin's heels, innocent looking as could be.

The town rose in fits and starts around the scrub, playing hide-and-seek among the hills and little patches of trees. It still had that too-tall, gangly newness about it, like a rangy pup that hadn't settled into its clumsy feet. And yet it didn't seem a clean town. It lacked the tidiness of Burlesville or the infrequent use and barely rubbed boards of Reveille. But, then again, nor did it have the lived-in, sand-scrubbed look of a place like Gloomy Bluebird. Rhett couldn't put his finger on what bothered him about the town, but he knew right away that he didn't much like it and he had to ride into it anyway.

The trail they were on was becoming a road, tents and rough wooden stalls popping up crookedly on either side to sell soap and hatchets and used socks. Rhett pulled his hat down over his good eye and made his spine as straight as possible. Checking his friends, he found that Winifred had wrapped herself in a serape and pulled her hat down and that Sam couldn't stop dashing at his eyes with a red handkerchief.

"Was it here, Sam?" he asked, real low.

"I reckon so. Right about here, they came down upon us, out of the sun."

In that moment, Rhett wished there was something he could do for his friend, thump his back or hold his hand or give him half a roasted goddamn rabbit, anything at all. But he couldn't, so he continued riding, because that was what Sam was doing, and they were both Rangers, and to do otherwise would've been damn shameful.

All the while, riding through the growing town, Rhett scanned the area for the source of his unease. It wasn't a monster town, like Burlesville. He didn't feel lots of monsters all over, just one big, concentrated tummy flop. Everyone he passed in the street was human. And uncomfortably curious. As Ragdoll high-stepped through the muck of the thoroughfare, Rhett began to gather that the trouble was situated where most trouble began: at the saloon. He hoped it was just a harem of harmless vampire whores asleep in a pile, drinking enough from the men at night to stay alive but not enough to cause any real damage or keep their victims from coming back tomorrow night for more of the same.

"Please, let it be vamp whores," Rhett whispered under his breath, mainly because he knew damn well it wasn't going to be anything that simple.

The hitching post in front of the saloon had enough room for his three horses to crowd around, so Rhett waved off the hostler's boy and hopped off Ragdoll to tie her reins on the much-rubbed wood.

"You getting a drink, Rhett?" Sam asked, looking mighty confused.

Rhett shook his head. "I'm scouting. You and Winifred go on and see if they got a sawbones who can help her."

"Ain't you worried about going in alone?"

Glancing back with a rare grin, Rhett answered, "Lord, no, Sam. I got a vengeful donkey watching my back."

Earl bared his teeth and switched his tail but stayed right next to Ragdoll and Puddin' like he actually had some damn sense. Rhett watched as Sam scooted his horses in front of Winifred and hailed a passerby to ask after the sawbones. Once they were on their way, he checked his own gear as if going into a fight for his life. Guns, knives, hat. Licking the pad of his thumb, he scrubbed it over the star of his Ranger badge until it shone as much as a thing could shine under threatening cloud cover. With a pat on Ragdoll's flank, he headed through the open door of the saloon. The sign overhead proclaimed it THE BUCK'S HEAD, a wide spread of antlers nailed above it with faded ribbons dangling limp from the tines.

Inside, the saloon was dozing, as all such places generally were in the afternoon before the dinner bell rang and the men had time to kill. A few disreputable looking fellers and human whores lounged, here and there, looking exhausted and drained and more like meat than people. A slight quiver told Rhett that the vamp whores he'd been expecting were upstairs doing whatever bloodsuckers did during the day, but a more frachetty quaking told him that the monster he truly sought was downstairs and nearby. He turned, boots sliding on scuffed wood, nose up like a dog scenting prey.

"Where are you, you bastard?" he murmured.

"Can I help you, stranger?" said a taciturn feller who'd popped up behind the bar.

Rhett eyed him, taking in the big belly and greasy hair. He was human and stank of rutting, like a goat. No, he damn well couldn't help, as Rhett couldn't flat out ask where a big, troublesome monster was hiding, just waiting to cause trouble.

"Looking for a meal," Rhett said. "Maybe a drink."

The feller snorted, looking Rhett up and down and spitting his lack of being impressed into the spittoon. "We got the latter but not the former. Hotel's across the way and ain't too weevily for supper. Saloon don't get going until after dark, if you catch my meaning."

Rhett nodded. It figured. The feller he wanted was most likely hid away and wouldn't be out until after dark anyway.

"Thank you kindly," he said, tipping his hat and heading back outside, as it didn't pay to be on a barman's bad side.

Just looking at the hotel, Rhett could taste bug parts between his teeth. He'd rather eat snake.

Checking that Earl was still keeping watch with the horses, he headed down the street to find Sam and Winifred. Their horses were parked outside a shabby little shack that gave him no hope on behalf of the girl's foot. She was more likely to die of plague inside that door than she was to find respite, and the fact that she'd gone in anyway told him just how desperate she was.

The door burst open as he glared at it, and Sam stumbled out holding Winifred in his arms, a look of abject surprise on his fine features. A small buffalo barreled out after them holding a piss bucket threateningly.

"Gerrout!" the buffalo shouted, or maybe it was just a small man in a buffalo-skin coat. "Take your damn squaw with you. I don't tend to animals."

Rhett had his gun drawn and against a florid cheek in a heartbeat.

"You don't want to talk to my friend like that," he growled.

Something pressed against his belly. "You don't want to threaten the only person in camp who can sew up what this knife can do to you, half-breed," the buffalo breathed back.

"Rhett, come along," Winifred said. "Not worth it. He doesn't know anything."

Rhett allowed himself a brief fantasy of shooting this feller's head open like a ripe melon before he withdrew his pistol and rammed it home in his holster.

"Rude," he muttered. "Rudest buffalo in the territory, I reckon."

Without looking the doctor in the face, he turned on his heel and walked away, Sam and Winifred in his wake.

"Read the sign!" the feller shouted behind them. "No Injuns!"

"Good. Confine your dangerous negligence to white men," Winifred said under her breath.

"I'd have shot him if I could've got to my gun," Sam growled.

"We've got bigger worries than assholes," Rhett said. "Won't find the monster until after dark. If you got business to do, I reckon you'd best do it now."

"You anticipating trouble?" Sam asked.

Rhett looked around the town, roiling with dangerous types, drunks, and folks giving their small group the side eye. "I always anticipate trouble, Sam. And I'm rarely disappointed." Another twinge pinched his belly, and he grimaced but didn't feel the unfortunate gush he expected. If he had to fight unknown monsters, he'd have preferred to do it as the one who drew blood instead of the one already leaking like a damn girl.

"Where are you going, Rhett?"

He looked at Winifred with a frown. "To find the damn ragman," he said. "Might as well be prepared for what's to come."

It was, in his estimation, the dumbest use of money in Durango.

Little did he know that the night would bring only more blood, and not the kind he was expecting.

CHAPTER
8

Once the lamps were lit, Rhett figured he'd waited long damn enough and headed for the Buck's Head. He wanted to go in alone, but Sam and Winifred wouldn't let him. Even Earl had changed back into human form to join the posse, carefully hiding his red hair under a wide beaver hat the Rangers had given him.

"I feel as jumpy as a cat in a room full of rockers," he muttered. "Don't see why we're here. If your task is to stop Trevisan, then dyin' at some unknown monster's hand in this two-horse town is a waste of your talents."

"Well, I'm sorry I'm not willing to die on your timetable, donkey-boy. But a man's destiny ain't a damn stagecoach schedule. I need to do this before I can do that, so let's go on and get this over with, shall we?"

Earl grinned. "A whiskey would not go amiss."

Rhett's eye cut sideways. "You ain't a drunkard, are you?"

Holding his hand over his heart, Earl attempted solemnity. "Not yet, no. But there's still time."

"Fools, the lot of you," Rhett muttered, mainly as a pretense to stand outside for ten more seconds before heading through the saloon door. His belly wobbled something awful, and not just because of the weevily cornbread they'd eaten at the hotel. "Let's do it, then."

He tromped into the saloon, followed by the clink of Sam's spurs, the hollow clatter of Winifred's crutch, and the Irishman's fond sigh. The man behind the bar shot him a glance of warning but was too busy serving shots to bother saying anything. Earl caught sight of red hair at the bar and bellied up to drink with a man who gabbled in the same singsong tongue as him. Winifred settled at an empty table, and Sam, ever the gentleman, went to fetch her a cup of coffee and get a beer for himself.

Rhett wandered around the perimeter of the room as if looking for the prettiest whore, but really, he was following the different sort of wobbles to their sources. Half the whores were vamps, and half the whores were human, and of the two types of folks, the vamps looked at him with more warmth. It wasn't until he'd done a complete loop that he realized the source of the most powerful wobble was behind a dark red curtain that led to another room. Putting a hand to the thick fabric, he came to the conclusion that in his experience, velvet meant trouble.

"That's for the high rollers."

It was the feller from the bar, appearing with one hand on the curtain and the other on the shotgun over his shoulder.

"How do you know I ain't a high roller?" Rhett countered.

The man snorted. "If you were, you'd already be in there, fool. Now get on. Play a hand or two, if you think you're good enough."

Rhett contemplated just storming on through, but he was decent enough at cards and didn't much like the idea of losing another eye in a bar fight, so he picked a table full of fellers who didn't look too much like murdering curs and fetched some pennies out of his pocket. He'd gathered a bit of coin breaking broncs at the Double TK, and the Captain had paid him for his time as a Ranger, plus three months in advance to cover his scouting mission. Fortunately, no one at the table would believe a half-breed had access to that kind of cash. He made sure to lose a bit before scooping in the biggest kitty yet, once everyone else had taken him for a fool.

One of the nastier fellers pulled a knife, so Rhett tipped his hat, picked a new table, and played the same game there. Being sober, smart, and willing to lose a bit first meant that his gains were big—and unwelcome.

"C'mon, then, high roller," the bar feller said, tugging at Rhett's sleeve as he fleeced the third table of suckers out of their collected ten dollars. "You think you're ready for what's behind the curtain?"

Rhett pulled out a nickel and stuffed it in the barman's breast pocket. "Thank you, my good man," he said, mimicking something he'd heard a dandy say outside the hotel in Gloomy Bluebird once.

The barman just grunted and half escorted, half dragged Rhett toward the curtain. Rhett was deeply amused, not only by the man's behavior, but also by the number of angry, grubby white faces glaring at him with murder in their red-tinted eyes. It was agreeable, pissing off so many folks at once when they'd been expecting to cheat him blind.

Well, blind*er*.

He spun, finding each of his friends in the room and offering them a cunning grin before he was shoved through the curtain.

On the other side, the air tasted decidedly different. The saloon at large was big and airy, the staircase and balcony festooned with loose women and the raw wood walls bristling with antlers. This room, however, was snug and low-ceilinged with forest-green wallpaper, the lamps warm and the curtains thick. Three neat tables sat in the center, a collection of divans and civilized wingback chairs clustered around the edges and draped with shadowy figures. Smoke swirled around the ceiling and wreathed the heads of several gamblers, some of whom sucked on peculiar contraptions displayed on the tables like blooming flowers of glass. The air was hazy and smelled exotic, and the pull of the monster settled around the room like a thick rug. No one paid Rhett the least bit of mind, and despite what the bartender had said about the exclusivity of the room, the high rollers' cards lay untouched on the tables, some showing their faces.

Rhett had no damn idea what was going on, and the smoke had already muddled his head.

"Welcome," said a familiar voice, and Rhett spun with his hand on his gun to find the dark-clothed figure from his dream, just a-dripping with power.

"Who the hell are you?"

The bearlike man grinned with blocky white teeth and tipped his black hat. "Buck Greenwood, sole proprietor of this saloon and Buckhead city founder. And who the hell are you?"

Rhett's back went stiff as his stomach did somersaults. "I reckon you already know," he said through gritted teeth.

"No, I don't believe we've met." Buck settled back in a fancy wingback chair and held a pipe to his lips, the entire thing connected to the machinery in the center of the table. To Rhett, it looked like he was smoking a venomous snake, and the smoke that curled from his lips danced sinuously into the air and burned Rhett's eye.

"I'm Rhett Walker. And I think you're a liar."

The feller—Buck—grinned and held the pipe out to Rhett. "All men are liars, Rhett Walker." His eyes purposefully traveled down and up Rhett's body, a dark eyebrow rising with the sort of punctuating irony that stuck in Rhett's craw. "Care to share my peace pipe?"

"No, sir. I'd like to know what you are and if you mean any harm."

Buck tossed down the pipe and leaned back, laughing. His suit was dark and impeccable, his watch chain glinting in the lamplight. A big man and broad in the shoulders, he seemed utterly at home in his skin, which, to Rhett's thinking, made him right peculiar. His hair was dark and wavy, pulled back but struggling for freedom, and stubble darkened his jaw like a waiting storm. His eyes, now pinned on Rhett and more avid than they'd appeared before, were the light blue of a winter sky lined in eyelashes of funeral black.

"What I am. Well, and wouldn't we all like to know that? All you need to remember is that I run this town, and if you want to leave my land in one piece, you and your friends had best accept my hospitality and pay your dues." He looked past Rhett and motioned with his hand.

The curtain shoved aside, and there they were: Sam, Winifred, Earl. A cold shudder shot up Rhett's spine.

"I asked if you meant any harm."

Buck smiled grandly, leaned over, and crooked a finger to call him closer. "Now, Rhett. Why on earth would I mean anyone harm? I told you. This is my town. My land. I just want to ensure its ongoing prosperity, and I reckon your crew doesn't want trouble. Why, neither do I. Now sit. All of you."

There were four empty chairs around the table, and sit they did, almost as if they had no choice.

"Everything okay, Rhett?" Sam asked, looking all worried.

"I don't rightly," Rhett admitted.

"Oh, everything's fine," Earl said, already drunk as a damn skunk. "I like this lad fine. Reminds me of home. Just the faintest hint of an accent there. D'ye hear it? Where you from, me fine sir?"

Buck cocked his head at Earl and gave him a grin, almost fondly. "Oh, I'm from everywhere, but the green hills of Ireland do hold a special place in my heart."

Winifred was very still, her cheeks sucked in and her eyes dark. "Familiar," was all she said.

"Lay it out for us, Mr. Greenwood," Rhett said. "This smoke's giving me a headache and an itchy trigger finger, both."

"Please, call me Buck. And enjoy your stay. It's rude to reject food and drink, you know." Someone slid a tray onto the table, a dark green bottle with no label and five shot glasses. While Rhett was staring at the sticky residue in the bottom of the cups, another tray shoved in from shadowy hands, this one laden with white wheels of cheese and porcelain bowls of sugar-slick peaches and pears and a plate of dainty little cakes like Rhett had only ever seen in the display window of Gloomy Bluebird's general store at Christmastime. Fancy food. Expensive food. An open jar of golden honey held glistening honeycomb, the whole thing laid out pretty as a picture, surrounded by loose flowers and glossy leaves of a deep green Rhett had never seen before in a Durango vegetable.

Buck poured sloppy shots of deep red liquor and showed his goodwill by closing his eyes, selecting a shot glass at random, and gulping it down.

"Eat. Drink. Take your comfort before we determine the toll. You folks look parched. You don't want to insult my hospitality."

"Hospitality is indeed sacred," Earl quickly agreed, gladly toasting Buck with his drink.

Rhett was disgusted to see the wee Irishman cramming his mouth with a fat slab of cheese slathered in honey, which dripped down his chin. Earl's shot was already gone, and Buck refilled the glass before Earl was done chewing. Glancing at Winifred, Rhett tried to make his eye say that all of this seemed very goddamn foolish. Winifred must've understood at least part of the look, as her mouth turned down at the corners, but she shrugged and drank her shot with a manly surety that Rhett had not expected from her.

"We must," she murmured, licking her lips.

"Well, then. If we must," Sam said, sounding uncertain, but his shot disappeared, too.

"You now, Mr. Walker," Buck urged, his grin too cunning for Rhett's taste.

Rhett felt like a wild horse, cornered and offered grain, knowing that the bucket meant capture but unable to back any farther away without fetching up against the fence.

"If we must," he echoed.

The sweet liquid burned on its way down, floating immediately to his head with a pleasant sort of dreaminess helped along by the smoke. Last time Rhett had gotten drunk, it had been to forget what had nearly happened at the hands of Scorpion and his Lobos. The time before that had been his first introduction to alcohol, and he'd been stuffed with happiness to be counted among the cowpokes of the Double TK, at least until he'd seen the red eyes of the saloon's vamp whores sitting on the laps of his friends.

Now, this time, it was different. The liquor hit his blood harder, thicker, almost demanding in its urgency. He needed more, which was fine, as his glass had already been refilled. A powerful hunger rose up in his wildly flipping stomach, and he caught a slippery peach slice and shoved it into his mouth, licking his fingers clean.

When he looked up, Sam was watching him with a strangely eager look.

"Have some more peaches, Rhett," he said, voice husky. "They suit you."

Rhett suddenly wanted more peaches with an almighty yearning, but he wasn't so drunk that he'd forgotten what few manners he had. Looking to Buck to judge if another peach would be too much, he found the man splayed over his chair, one high-booted leg thrown over the arm, his eyes heavy-lidded and his smug, contented grin on the verge of perversion.

"Go on," he urged. "Eat, if it pleases you." His lips curled. "Eat and drink and honor me."

Rhett's fingers slished in the juice, hunting for a peach, his eye pinned to Sam. The liquor emboldened him enough to ask, "You hungry, Sam?" Leaning forward, he held out the piece of sweet fruit on two fingers.

"I reckon I'm powerful hungry, Rhett," Sam answered.

Taking a deep breath, his blue eyes all soft and dark at once, Sam reached for Rhett's hand, grasping it at the wrist with one hand and cupping the fingers gently with the other. Rhett trembled as Sam drew his hand closer and closer to those warm, slightly open lips, finally letting his tongue caress the sugared palm as he sucked the peach into his own mouth and licked the juice off Rhett's fingers.

Rhett let out a shuddering breath and whispered, "Hot damn, other Hennessy."

Sam leaned forward and licked his lips, and Rhett felt a rush of warmth in his belly, but the good kind. A light laugh drew his attention to his left, where Winifred had let her serape fall to the ground…and her shirt fall off her shoulder. Earl held out a shot glass, which the girl took with a wicked grin, twining her arm around Earl's as they drank their liquor together, their faces flushed and their eyes alight.

"You've a little honey, me girl," Earl said, his accent looser than usual. "Just here." He cupped her face with one hand, running a thumb almost over her lips. Much to Rhett's surprise, the girl leaned into Earl's touch, her tongue darting out to lick the honey away.

"Mine," she said brazenly. "A girl's honey isn't to be taken lightly."

A hand on his knee brought Rhett back to his own situation. Sam's chair was closer, and he held out a slice of peach. "Your turn," he said, all breathy.

Rhett's eye darted to Buck, and for a moment, last night's dream and today's reality merged. Buck had a stag's face, massive antlers branching overhead, tangled with bits of metal and ribbon over his natty black suit. He loomed large, powerful, dangerous, shadowy, his eyes black and as endless as the night, urging Rhett on like a heartbeat. A fire danced between them, and the blond girl in the night shift sat at Buck's feet, her white arms curled around his leg and her upcast eyes adoring. A fawn's skin was draped over her back, a piece of green vine twined around her arm. Buck's hand was on her head, patting her like a fine hunting dog. Rhett shook his head, and the room refocused into wood boards and velvet curtains and sickly sweet smoke. Figures writhed in the corners, but that was just the way of whores and men, wasn't it?

"Rhett?"

The peach brushed his lips, and Rhett gave in to it, swallowing the bit of fruit with a moan and sucking the juice from Sam's fingers. A clatter to the left was followed by a moan and panting. He released Sam's fingers and turned his head to find Winifred sitting in Earl's lap, front to front, their clothes asunder and Winifred's eyes closed, her mouth open and yowling as she rode him like an ungentled bronc. Sam's hand crept up Rhett's thigh, calling him back.

"Do you like peaches?" Sam asked.

"I do now."

"I wonder how'd they'd taste…"

Sam trailed off, caught another peach in the dish, and rubbed it over Rhett's lips, following the sticky fruit with his tongue. Soon they were kissing, and it was like peaches and honey and liquor but better, hot and wet and sweet beyond compare, tongues sliding and teeth nibbling and hands roaming.

"What's happening, Sam?" Rhett asked wonderingly, glad and scared all at once.

His stomach was flopping all over the place, his head swimming, his heart singing, his blood thrumming, his nethers begging.

"I don't rightly know, Rhett, but I like it."

Sam's hands were under his shirt now, counting his ribs and the knobs of his spine and hunting down the back of his britches, and Lord help him, but his hands were under Sam's shirt, and then they fell down, rolling in the grass, and they were on a soft, dark bearskin in front of a fire, and everything was slick and red, and the walls were a deep green forest and the lamps were stars, and Sam touched him in a place where he'd never wanted to be touched before but now couldn't stop moaning for.

"Sam, I don't want… that place…"

"Then where? Tell me."

Sam's hands pulled away, but Rhett pulled them back, placed them carefully on his waist. "I don't know what I want. But I want it. By the gods, I want it."

"I think I know what to do, Rhett." Sam's eyes were soft and starving and dark indigo, wide as the sky, his hands open and cupping and warm. "There's one place where all bodies are the same, and I know what to do with that."

"Then do it, Sam. Goddamn. Do it."

And Sam did. And it was mighty fine for all involved.

CHAPTER
9

Rhett Walker woke up at dawn covered in three things: blood, fur, and the tangled, lanky limbs of Samuel Hennessy. He blinked through stuck-together eyelashes and slid out from under Sam. He was nekkid as a baby and slicked all over with God knew what. Rubbing his eye, he stood to figure out what the hell was going on.

What they lay on was a buffalo coat barely altered from when the beast had worn it. To one side were the remains of a fire, the dirt all around stamped with the prints of bare feet and cloven hooves. On the other side of the embers was a familiar serape. Winifred and Earl, likewise nekkid and messy, sprawled there, senseless. Those two weren't quite as bloody, but that didn't mean they were clean, neither. The funk of rutting and goats rode the air, coupled with the delicious and sickening scent of fresh blood and roasted meat. Slicked-up bones were scattered about, the pork mostly gnawed off.

The whole scene was outside of town in the grove Rhett had noticed from the air. The trees sagged with ripe apples and pears and peaches that glistened like paste jewels in the morning sun. Dewdrops licked the spiderwebs, and a fresh breeze played through glossy leaves. The grass here was strangely soft and bright green, like a carpet. It was goddamn beautiful, all told, and yet Rhett's stomach turned with disgust and wrongness.

For once, that wobbling wasn't about a monster. Whatever he'd been, Buck was gone.

What had happened here last night . . . it hadn't been natural.

"Figured it out yet?"

Rhett's hands jerked over his groin and chest as his head snapped around to glare at Dan, who was wearing all his damn clothes and not in any way impeded by fluids and embarrassment and muck. He had his typically amused grin, and yet his eyes were hard and angry. He was sitting on a rock, a pile of clothes at his feet. Shaking his head in disgust, he tossed Rhett his dirty shirt and muttered, "You'll want to bathe first. You reek, man."

Holding the shirt over his front, Rhett looked around the grove and headed for the burbling creek. With his back to his sleeping friends, he waded into the cold water and quickly dashed it all over himself. It was freezing, but it felt good. Burned, almost. He had to scrub in some places, so thick was the gore that had crusted into hair and flesh. His posterior was tender, and his face flushed with confusion as he probed the area in question and tried to recall what exactly had transpired.

Funny, how it had seemed perfectly reasonable at the time and yet now, he was consumed by shame. Rhett didn't have great faith in shame, nor did he want it attached to his feelings about Samuel Hennessy. Shame seemed like somebody else telling you what to do with your body, and Rhett didn't reckon he'd let other folks decide how he was going to feel. So maybe it wasn't the act that brought the shame so much as the situation and the fact that he didn't remember much about it. As he tossed water over his shorn hair and scrubbed his face clean, he looked to where Sam still lay under the buffalo rug, limp and sprawled out, innocent as a puppy.

Ye gods, please don't let Sam feel shame about it, he thought. *If there's a burden, let it be mine. What I got's already so heavy I probably won't notice the addition at all.*

"He wouldn't want you to feel sorry," Dan offered, and Rhett realized he'd been speaking out loud, and that Dan had snuck up with the rest of his clothes while he stood in the middle of the damn creek, rubbing his face over and over again like a goddamn raccoon.

Dan held out Rhett's chest wrap, and Rhett turned his back and secured his useless anatomy before stepping into his pants. Once his slick-wet shirt was on, he felt slightly more ready to ask, "He who?"

"The horned god."

"I don't see any gods, Dan. Just a bunch of fools and one haughty coyote."

Dan shook his head like Rhett was a willfully stupid child. "Come now, Rhett. You know that what happened last night was by design. The signs are everywhere. Have you never met a god?"

Rhett stepped into his boots and slapped on his hat. "Not that I know of. Do they wear signs? Badges, maybe?" He flicked his own badge, glad to find it was still there.

"If you know what to look for." Dan pointed as he spoke. "A grove under the stars. Cloven hoofprints. Honey. Fruit. Strong drink. A fire. Sexual congress. A sacrifice."

Rhett swallowed hard, tasting blood. "A sacrifice?"

"That buffalo skin was somebody's coat. It's not freshly made, but those bones are."

Closing his eye, Rhett poked around his shattered memory for the truth of what Dan was telling him. Last man he'd seen wearing a big buffalo coat was the doctor who'd refused treatment to Winifred and called Rhett himself by some less than savory slurs. He'd only seen the man once, and yet...

The girl in white had been there, hadn't she? She'd led the doctor out of the dark and toward the fire, her tiny fingers dug into the thick wool of his buffalo coat, dragging him along unwillingly.

"Who's hurt?" the doc had growled uneasily. "I got drinking to do."

"So drink here," Buck had said, sitting cross-legged behind the flames. "I'll want you plenty wet for what's coming."

Then everything went into a blur. Frightened eyes, so wide, fingers tearing into flesh and pulling off strips like barn siding in a windstorm. Incisors on bones, the sweet lap of marrow, hands on thighs and lips on lips and laughing teeth. The buffalo coat, laid down lovingly, Rhett's cheek pressed into the pile as he gritted his teeth and Sam behind him...Sam...

"Oh, hellfire," Rhett spat, opening his eye and shaking his head.

"You remember now?"

"Piss off, Coyote Dan."

Rhett kneeled by the stream and cupped fresh cold water into his mouth, swishing it and spitting it out tinged rusty red. He drank down the next handful, loving the burn down his throat.

"It's not your fault, Rhett. Nor anyone's. The gods have certain demands, and if you don't meet them, you meet your end. He's not the first god to demand his toll, to crave blood, and he won't be the last."

Standing with a splash, Rhett reached for his gun belt. "Then let's kill him. That's what we're here for, isn't it, Dan? To kill what needs to die."

"Gods can't die, Rhett. You've just got to learn to give them a wide berth."

"Is that why you left last night? Is that why you didn't go into town with us?"

Dan shook his head. "No. That was just dumb luck."

"Dumb's right, for sure. So you're saying I can't kill this Buck Greenwood?"

"The only thing that can kill a god is when no one's left to worship him."

"Then why'd my destiny, or the Shadow, or whatever the hell it is, drag me out here?"

Dan's shrug was guileless. "I don't presume to know the way of gods, and I barely understand the Shadow, most of the time."

Rhett snorted to indicate that Dan presumed quite a bit, most of the time.

Walking to a tree, Dan plucked a ruby-red apple and threw it to Rhett. "Here's the thing, Rhett. Everything has a cost. You live in a tribe, you pull your weight. You live in a town, you do your job. You live on a farm, you sweat into the soil. You want something, you suffer for it. Living is not free. Life demands sacrifice. Where gods go, they bring prosperity. Look at this town. Big, safe, no one starving to death, no plague, no horses falling over from bad water. Bite into that apple and tell me it isn't sweet. Folks who live under the protection of gods know they'll be called to do their part, to pay their dues, and they go willingly. For many, it's preferable to politics and government. Let's just say that the tax here is a little different."

"It was different for that doctor in the buffalo coat."

Dan's grin was wry and sad. "If the god claimed him, he did something to deserve it."

"Says who?"

"Says the god."

Rhett's jaw worked in consternation before he gave in and bit into the apple. Sweetness flooded his mouth, juice dripping down his chin. It reminded him of something from last night, but he didn't mind as much now. For a yappy bastard, Coyote

Dan sometimes made sense, and his explanation appealed to Rhett, in part because it excused his mixed reaction to last night. It wasn't natural, but...it *was* natural, wasn't it? It was just that city folks didn't approve of it, done in full light. Well, and what if Rhett would rather pay with his body than with coin? There was nothing wrong with what had passed between Sam and him last night—he knew that much, bone deep. And if it were to happen again without a great horned fool in a black coat watching, it would be all the sweeter.

He just hoped Sam would see it that way, too.

"Will they remember anything?" he asked Dan, tossing his chin at his still-sleeping friends.

"Do you think remembering would be a good thing or a bad thing for them?"

Rhett frowned. "I reckon they'd rather forget."

"Then we could make it easier for them."

Rhett nodded. "Let's do that."

When Sam blinked awake, grinning, the grove was changed and Rhett was wearing a fine buffalo coat. He'd smudged out the cloven hoofprints with a boot and dabbed blood off cheeks and eyelashes with a wet kerchief. Whatever had woken him at dawn, everyone else had remained in a deep sleep as if drugged, unmoving and insensate, and Rhett and Dan had used that time to erase all evidence of the god. Cleaning and dressing Sam's heavy, lovely limbs while the feller slept had possibly been the most strangely intimate thing Rhett had ever done, and that included what had happened last night.

"We outside?" Sam asked, sitting up and rubbing his eyes.

"The Buck's Head didn't have any rooms to let," Rhett answered, slicing off a piece of apple with his knife and holding it out. Sam took it with thanks and popped it in his mouth, sending a shot of memory and desire through Rhett's nethers.

Yes, well, and so that memory was his own. Sam showed evidence of no such recollection and merely chomped agreeably.

"Damn, that's a good apple. We got more?"

Rhett pointed at the grove, heavy with fruit. "As much as you can eat, Sam. I reckon you've earned it."

Sam's eyebrows drew down. "Earned it?"

Rhett looked away, hiding a smile. "Blood watered these trees, and Bandera Pass owes you, Sam."

"Owing or not, I'll take it."

Winifred and Earl woke just after that, their memories likewise blank. Rhett and Sam had moved Earl away from the girl to save them any awkwardness. Everyone seemed, as Rhett did, refreshed and sluggish after their heavy sleep. They stuffed themselves with fresh fruit and drank the cool, clean water. Aside from the blood-soaked debauchery of the night before, Rhett had to admit it was a perfectly pleasant morning. The only dark smudge on the interlude came from one mouthy crow that sat in the limbs of the apple tree and watched them with beady eyes, cawing a rude laugh from time to time.

Finally, Rhett couldn't take it any longer. He picked up an apple core and lobbed it at the oily black bastard. The crow rose from the tree, squawking with affront and flapping off into the morning sun. Rhett felt better once it was gone and had the most peculiar feeling that the bird knew exactly what had happened here last night. Probably waiting for them to leave so it could dig up the fresh bones he and Dan had hidden upon the ridge.

"I should've shot that crow," he muttered.

"Bad luck to shoot it," Winifred said. "Crows are wise. And anyway, it was a raven."

"Bad luck? Bullshit," Earl said, chewing happily. "The Morrigan takes the form of a raven. Brings war and pestilence and death. I'll side with Rhett on this one. Shoot it, next time. The bastards follow the railroad tracks, hungry for blood. Creepy little buggers."

"He's gone, in any case," Sam said, hopping to his feet and dusting off his hands. "And I'm hungry for more than fruit. Let's go find some meat."

Rhett's stomach turned at the thought of killing, at the memory of chewing bloody, undercooked muscle. It would've been a joy, having completely forgotten what it was they'd done last night, the four of them. He wasn't going to want pork for a while, he knew that much. Hunching his new coat around his shoulders, he stood and felt a rush of heat and damp as his body did what he'd been dreading and started his damn courses. He'd tried keeping count once so that he'd know when to expect this unpleasant surprise, but it came and went like a cat, as it pleased and with no regard for Rhett's feelings.

"I hate bodies," he muttered, hurrying to a patch of brush to staunch what he could with his spare kerchief and tie on a new set of rags.

Rhett Walker had had more than enough of blood, then and forever.

Just as a precaution, Dan went into town alone for their horses. Although the others didn't recollect what had happened last night, they knew well enough that if you started drinking in a saloon and woke up outside, you might've gotten tossed out for being unruly, and you might've damn well deserved it. Some small amount of embarrassment was discussed, although no one was willing to hazard a guess regarding what had happened after that first shot of liquor. Dan walked out and shortly returned on his chestnut gelding with his own little herd trailing behind like baby ducks.

"Where'd that extra horse come from?" Rhett asked, tossing his head at a gorgeous little dun paint mare he didn't recognize but quite liked the look of.

"She was tied to the draft," Dan said, one hand on the pretty thing's neck. Her eyes were gentle, her mane and tail long and black. The saddle on her back was new and well-made, the saddlebags over her rump bulging. Rhett moved to Ragdoll and offered her an apple, supposing that even a horse knew when she was outclassed and wanting the mare to know she was loved, anyway, ugly or not.

Winifred hobbled up on her crutch to inspect the mare and gasped. When Rhett moved around to the animal's other side, he saw Winifred's hand fitting perfectly over a bloody handprint planted there. Green vines tangled in the mare's mane, and she turned soft eyes to blink at Winifred, nuzzling the girl gently.

"I reckon that means she's yours," he said roughly.

In the saddlebags, they found cheese and fruit and a jar of honey, and Rhett's memory told him exactly what this meant, exactly who was thanking or reminding them through such a gift. When Winifred pulled out a sharp stone knife with an antler handle and a tiny rim of red along the blade, Rhett had to look away.

"What does this mean?" Winifred asked, her voice low and troubled. "What really happened?"

Dan touched his sister's shoulder, caught her eyes. "You know better than to question the gods, especially when they're still listening. Say your thanks for this gift, and let's put this town far behind us."

"I hate it when you're right," she muttered. But she repacked the saddlebags, checked the mare's girth, and put the reins over her head. Much to everyone's surprise, the horse folded to her knees and looked up to Winifred, blinking her long eyelashes with more intelligence and patience than a beast had any right to possess. Winifred straddled the saddle and sat, and the mare gracefully stood.

"I've never seen anything like that," Sam said, scratching his neck.

"Me, neither." Dan's eyes were narrow as he watched his sister stroke the mare's neck, and Rhett wanted to know what he was thinking but wasn't willing to ask. Whatever Dan thought, staring at his hurt sister on that too-pretty trick horse decorated with Winifred's bloody handprint... well, Dan wasn't sharing it. And that gave Rhett pause.

"Her name is Kachina," Winifred said.

"What the hell's that mean?" Rhett asked.

There was a peculiar look on Winifred's face. "It means *hope*, Rhett," she said softly.

But Rhett wasn't about to ask what she was hoping for. A sensible creature would hope to have their foot healed, hope to stay alive in a world that seemed hell-bent on killing anybody who wasn't cut of stern cloth. Yet Winifred sat her fancy new horse like a queen, one hand shielding her eyes from the sun, staring off at the horizon with a strange smile. Rhett had no idea what the girl might be thinking, and he reckoned he'd never, not a day in his life, understand women.

Before he mounted up on Puddin', he took his saddlebags into the brush and arranged his rags for a long, uncomfortable day in the saddle under the horned god's mocking blue sky.

125

The rest of the day was blessedly normal. Earl stayed a donkey, which meant he was quiet and didn't ask any uncomfortable questions. Sam was his usual cheerful self. Winifred was lost in her own thoughts, and her new horse behaved like a dream. Even Coyote Dan wasn't too vexful. The heavy clouds that had dogged them yesterday had burned off to a fine, clear sky, and the plains remained obliging and free of further troublesome towns ruled over by hungry gods. The entire situation seemed, for lack of a better word, charmed. Grudgingly, Rhett was forced to admit to himself that Buck Greenwood, or the horned god, whatever his true name was…well, he was a fair sort of feller, for a god.

That night over a supper of jackrabbit and cheese, Rhett couldn't stand the polite silence and empty small talk for a second longer.

"Coyote Dan, did you at least learn anything while you were off scouting?"

Dan looked up from the fire. "Nothing useful. Nothing you haven't already seen. Coyotes can't range as far and fast as horses, really, so all I saw was that the road ahead was clear and nothing too dastardly was going on. When I came back and found the grove…" He grinned at Rhett alone and shook his head. "Well, I figured you were in good enough hands and just needed to sleep it off. A little sip now and then can be quite restorative. Although I wouldn't drink too deep of whatever bottles you find in those saddlebags."

"Got any idea what this Trevisan feller is?"

Dan swung his gaze to Earl. "That's where you come in. We need to know everything you can tell us. Where he's from, what kind of accent he has, what he looks like, what he wears, what he does. His habits. His ways."

Earl did his best to swallow an overlarge mouthful of food and managed to choke. With a snort of derision, Rhett got up to fetch the Captain's book from his saddlebags, taking brief respite among the warm, sleepy horses. Horses made so much more sense than people. It had to be right nice for Earl, to be something close enough to horses that he could move among them without spooking them. If Rhett became the bird this close to the docile beasts, he reckoned the poor creatures would stampede, screaming, into the night. At least Sam wasn't scared of him in that form, whatever it was.

"We should look through this book," he said as everyone turned from watching Earl splutter to stare at him. "Captain said it might help, whatever it is."

Dan took it with reverence and cracked the spine. "It's a grimoire."

"I know that."

"But you can't read it."

"Hellfire, Dan. I know that, too."

Rhett sat down, wishing he'd just thrown the damn thing in the fire, for all that it made Coyote Dan even more bothersome than usual. Back at the Ranger outpost, Rhett had spent several stolen moments flipping through the book as if perhaps his recently gained powers might magically include reading. Much to his consternation, the little black squiggles still made no damn sense, although the book was riddled with fabulous drawings of beasts and almost-men that drew his eye like the candy display in a general store. He'd found pictures of something like the siren he'd killed in Reveille as well as harpies, werewolves, and shapeshifters. The biggest bird among them was a vulture, though, and everybody who had seen him change said he wasn't one of those. He'd slammed the book shut, then, assuming whatever secrets it held were for another man to decode.

"I didn't get much of a chance to look at it before, but it's useful," Dan murmured.

Rhett spat into the darkness. "Further information of which we are already aware."

Dan ignored that. "Earl? Are you recovered enough to tell us what we're facing?"

Earl's ruddy face was redder than usual. "Don't know how useful I can be, but I'll try. A shot of something to loosen me tongue would not go amiss."

Sam fetched a dark green bottle from Winifred's saddlebag and handed it over. Earl pulled the cork out with his teeth and took a deep swig. As he wiped the bottle's lip and set it down, he grinned and said, "Not to reinforce the common slurs against my people, which are many. But delving back into that dark place requires a bit of liquid courage, lads." He burped softly and stared into the fire as if seeking further fortitude.

"I came from Galway. I told you that much, did I not?" Seeing Rhett scoff, Earl wagged a finger in admonishment. "None of that, now. We're a people of storytellers, the Irish, and I've been sorely lonely, so you'll listen and listen well. The famine back home was hell, and the boat that brought us over was hell, and then landing in New Amsterdam was hell. Me and Shaunie and some lads from back home figured we'd make enough money to send on, maybe even enough to bring our families over, if the Federal Republic of America was the land of milk and honey we'd been promised. Jobs aplenty, they told us. Gold running down the middle of the street and fruited plains abounding." He spit into the fire and laughed darkly. "What a load of shite. The labor gangs were waiting for us, but we were too smart for that, see. The railroad was where the money was, plus travel out of the crowded cities back east. Rooms stacked like crates, people sleeping twelve to a room. No green, anywhere."

"What-all cities did you see?" Sam asked.

Rhett stifled a grin. Wasn't that just like Sam, to focus on the wonder?

"Just the two biggest ones. New Amsterdam and Checagou, where we signed on with the Checagou and Galena Railroad. Rough work but honest. At least we were out of doors, Shaunie and me. Then one day, a feller came through in a fine black suit, no coal under his fingernails, claiming he was hiring for a new railroad headed west to Calafia. Pay rate he offered was triple what we were drawing, so when they chose us both, I expected it was on account of my being sober and ready and keepin' Shaunie on the straight and narrow like I'd promised our mam. We said good-bye to our mates from back home and headed on for greener pastures, which was really more a field of bones."

Shaking his head, he took another swig from the bottle.

Rhett opened his mouth to tell him to get the hell on with it, but Dan held out a hand. "In his own time," he said. "Storytelling is sacred. Every detail will help."

When Earl had drunk his fill, he looked up, eyes hard and determined. "The camp divides itself by origin, as men tend to work best and argue less among their own kind. The Chine are the largest group, in part due to numbers and in part due to the power of their magic. They handle the blasting and tunnels, far ahead of the train, mostly, where we rarely saw 'em. We Irish—well, we're mostly shapeshifters and a few hedge witches, see? Only good for running rails and smoothing things out. Not specialty work."

He spit a glob of his disgust in the fire. "I heard there was a big crew from Afrika, all from different regions but banded together by brown skin and anger at being brought here in chains. They're mostly stuck with grading. There's a team of Injuns and mixed-blood lads like you. Some quiet folk from the old Crusade lands, maybe, clad in robes and wearing towels on their heads and streaks of black under their eyes. Dunno what their magic is, but it must've been useful, as they were the most likely to disappear with Mr. Trevisan. Most all the bosses, scouts, guards, and gangers are white and wear bits of faded Confederate uniforms. If any of the groups could speak together and band against Trevisan, they might yet overthrow him and destroy the railroad, but as it is, they're distrustful of one another and fractured in their power. Can't even talk to conspire."

"Does Trevisan push this fracture?" Winifred asked.

Earl nodded thoughtfully. "Oh, to be sure. Shows favor to whichever group is doing the best work, punishes groups for the individual's failings. Pulls out one lad as his valet or offers promotions to likely bodies. Thus are quotas kept: through fear and the censure of comrades."

"Who are his lieutenants?" Dan asked. "His friends?"

Earl barked a laugh. "Friends? Trevisan? No one, I reckon. He's got a second, the feller who scouted me. Big lad, name's Adolphus. He can sniff out the magic—and trouble, too. Handy with a whip. Knows just where to cut you to cause pain and keep you working. Other than that, it's rotating toadies. Grandpa Z is the Chine doc that keeps the laborers healthy enough to labor, but I don't believe he has any love for Trevisan—just looking to keep his people safe and in favor."

"And what does Trevisan look like?"

"Handsome son of a bitch," Earl spat. "Pale and blond and shiny and clean. Sharp as fresh-cut ice. A dandy. Can't reckon his place of origin, though. Somewhere in Europa, maybe. The snow lands or Italia. Born with a silver spoon in his mouth and a blade in his hand, accustomed to being in charge and listened to. Fine clothes, all perfectly matched with his gloves and carefully tied cravats. You'd think he was a weak thing, easily broken as a flower stem." He paused to take another drink. "But you'd be wrong. When his fingers wrap around your bones, you feel the bruise. Like touching cold, hard ground."

"What of his magic?"

Earl threw a handful of dirt in the fire, making it spark. His words slurred with rage as he spoke. "Hellfire with your questions! If I knew his magic, I'd know how to fight it, wouldn't I? Wouldn't be dragging me sorry self across the damn desert on half a hoof, begging strangers for help. Save me own brother and kill me own monster, wouldn't I? I've never seen Trevisan brought to pain. He didn't sweat in the sun nor shiver in the rain. Never showed a cut from shaving or a bruise from dropping his teakettle. Any man who stood up to him was cut down by Adolphus, slish slash. Whatever magic he has, he does it in that personal train car of his. No windows, no door that I've seen. He's untouchable. Hence the problem."

"But you were in there..." Rhett trailed off.

Earl's frantic eyes looked like they wanted to pop out of his head. "Would you remember every detail of a place where you was strapped down and tortured? I was in a tent, and then I was in the room, and then I was in a tent again. I know what the chair feels like, what the charred air smells like in that damned box of a room, and I know that I lived to see the sun again, but that's the only memory I have of it."

The only sound, for a moment, was the crackling of the fire and the soft stamping of horses. Earl picked up the bottle and drank, long, deep, and defiant. Dan nodded thoughtfully and picked up the book, flipping through it with his lips pursed.

Winifred pulled her blankets down and lay on her side, her dark, wide eyes reflecting the fire.

"Well, what do you think of that, Rhett?" Sam asked.

Rhett leaned back on his elbow and ran the ball of his thumb over his gun's wood grip. "I reckon I haven't gone into a fight yet knowing what I was up against, and I managed to live through it."

"You've been lucky, so far." Dan's voice was dry and obnoxiously matter-of-fact. "A monster that commands other monsters with magic will be harder to fight than a child-stealer, hiding alone in the mountains. This Trevisan could be anything. A rogue Lobo, a shifter, a powerful witch. He's smart. And he'll be on the lookout for trouble. And he has a scout. Adolphus."

"We got a scout, too. Me." Rhett pointed at his badge.

Dan's eyes did that thing where they kinda pitied Rhett while also being amused with him—that thing that made Rhett want to scuffle with the feller even more than usual. "One of the only things we know about Trevisan," Dan said slowly, "is that he only takes on monsters to work in his camp. Even though you're a shifter, because you're the Shadow, you're undetectable. Therefore, Trevisan isn't likely to take you on."

"What's this Shadow thing you all blabber about?" Earl asked, sloshing his wine. "Is our birdie friend special, then?"

Rhett rolled his eyes, knowing Dan would answer for him. Not even worth trying to get a word in first.

"Rhett is the Shadow," Dan said in his preacher voice. "He has great powers. He is a shifter, but even the sharpest scout won't recognize that he has magic. His eyes don't shine, he has no scent, he doesn't set stomachs wobbling. I once told him myself that he was…how did I say it? *As human as human can get*. Normally, this helps him hunt his prey. But this time, he has no way into Trevisan's graces."

"Oh, well then. That explains why he doesn't make me as ill as he should."

Rhett tipped his hat. "Many thanks for the compliment."

"What we need," Sam said, getting back to the topic at hand, "is a plan."

"I got a plan," Rhett muttered.

"Let me guess." Dan leaned back on his elbows. "Rhett, you want to ride up, guns blazing, and start shooting anybody who's white and not in chains."

Rhett nodded. "That sounds about right."

"If you want to get us all killed, sure. But we don't know how the other groups feel, who's loyal, if he has hidden sympathizers. We don't know who is acting under duress and who is part of the problem. And, most of all, we don't know if their sawbones can help Winifred."

"What's your point, coyote-boy?"

"It's got to be me. I'm the only one here who's an obvious monster, who's unknown to the camp, and who's sound of body. I'll go in as a scout, find out what I can, and escape."

"Fool! You can't just be escapin' whenever you wish, you grand ninny," Earl slurred, the bottle clutched in his hands like a life rope. "'S'not that bloody easy."

Dan grinned. "It will be for me."

"You're not going in without me," Rhett growled. "This is my goddamn destiny, and I'll goddamn live up to it."

"Did you ever think that sometimes your destiny is to wait two damn days and then save everybody with a little bit of well-timed help?"

Rhett looked up at the moon, remembering how it had hounded him on the road to the Cannibal Owl. "I reckon my destiny's as restless as I am."

"Then you'll both have to trust me and learn patience."

Rhett rolled over, his back to the fire. "I reckon we just need a better plan than yours."

CHAPTER
10

Every nerve in his body sparking, Rhett waited until the familiar snores of his friends joined the low crackle of the fire. He sat up slowly, feigning sleepiness and scratching the fuzz of his shorn hair. Checking that they truly were asleep, he buckled on his holster, shook out his boots, stuck his feet into the worn leather, and wandered away to piss and change his rags. When he came back, certain that no one was close to wakefulness, he picked up his blanket, saddle, and bags and walked to the horses. Ragdoll sleepily snapped at his hand as he tightened her cinch, but no mere grouchy horse was going to stop him. He had business to do, and Coyote Dan didn't get to jump in line and get himself hurt.

A long nose bumped into his back, and he cussed under his breath. If he didn't take Blue, the damn mule would bray his fool head off as he left. He unhobbled the rangy critter and ponied him off Ragdoll as he rode away from the fire and into the darkness.

He didn't need the sun and moon to know which direction was the right one; the flop and wobble in his belly told him. The moon, at least, was cooperative, giving enough scant white-blue light to keep the horse shuffling along. Rhett couldn't help thinking about the many dark creatures that might be hiding out here—Lobos, sirens, and worse. Maybe even some of the Captain's dreaded sand wyrms. It was right funny, to think that he'd once considered rattlers and scorpions the most danger the world had to offer, outside of Pap's whip. When an armadillo popped up in terror and trundled away, Rhett didn't even blink. If the critter had meant any harm, Rhett knew he would've felt it in advance.

It wasn't long before time lost all meaning. Everything was heavy with blackness, and if Rhett looked for too long at the glittering stars overhead, he started to feel like maybe he was upside down, the world shifting and sliding sideways. Ragdoll knew her job, surly as she might've been about it. She stopped, once, to rub her face on her leg, but Rhett knew that trick and kicked her on before she could drop to the ground and roll him off. A man's destiny didn't offer leeway for laziness, and Rhett didn't have time for anything that would allow Coyote Dan to get the drop on him.

That Trevisan feller belonged to Rhett. To the Shadow.

Letting someone else kill him was bound to feel like never quite scratching an itch.

And letting Trevisan kill Dan and leave Winifred alone in the world and neck-deep in sorrow? He couldn't let that happen, either.

As the night wore on, Rhett had to correct Ragdoll's path using the wobble in his belly like a compass. Trevisan was building a railroad, after all. Who knew which-a-way he was taking it? Without Rhett to guide them, the others didn't have much of a chance of finding one little camp in all of Durango, even with Earl's shoddy map. So long as those coyotes didn't catch his scent before the sun was up, they'd be hard-pressed to catch him in the days before he'd found his quarry. Blue, at least, was no trouble. The stupid animal was happy just to be along for the ride. If things went real bad, Rhett could always trade him. Or eat him. At least that's what he told himself.

The edge of the horizon was just starting to consider lightening up when Rhett saw some right peculiar shapes drawn in stark black against the moonlight. He expected buttes and rock piles, hills and valleys and arroyos and tablelands, all the general natural furniture that made Durango right hard to traverse. But these shapes were unnatural, disconnected and peculiar. It wasn't a town, and it sure as hell wasn't a railroad, but it was something man-made for sure. He squinted, trying to puzzle it out from over a mile away, but his one good eye couldn't make heads nor tails of it.

Wait. Except…there were some heads and tails, weren't there?

Cows, maybe. Some horses. A unicorn?

"Goddammit," he muttered, angry at not knowing what the Sam Hill was going on.

He knew well enough he had to stop before Blue gave an earsplitting welcome to whatever creatures were sleeping up ahead. Rhett slipped off Ragdoll, undressed, tucked his clothes in her saddlebag, and tied her to a raggedy tree. As annoyed by this turn of events as the mare was by everything that happened when Rhett went off alone, she nudged him with her nose and turned her bottlebrush tail on him.

"Right back at you," Rhett muttered, shivering in the night's cold as he gave her rump a conciliatory scratch.

He walked off a few paces, took a deep breath, and…changed.

Blue was already asleep, but Ragdoll looked over and snorted as Rhett hopped away and into the air. Worry and anger fell off him as he swooped upward, his brain making easy sense of what he saw but not quite able to grasp the why of things. It was so much easier, being a bird. What was, was. It didn't need a why, so the bird didn't need a why.

But he did need breakfast of the unrotten sort, and so did someone else. With leisurely flicks of his feathers, he returned to the now-impatient horse and mule and landed as gracefully as he could.

As soon as he'd transformed, he was muttering, "I know. I know! I'll get your damn grain."

His human brain had to pick apart what his bird brain had seen. There were animals aplenty, mostly cows and horses and, sure enough, a unicorn. The blocky things that looked like buildings were wagons, some with bars on them instead of wooden sides. His nose, or beak, or whatever the hell he had that helped him find dead things to eat—it had smelled live things, and lots of 'em. To the bird, all that breathing flesh smelled better than Conchita's breakfast, far as he could figure. But the damnedest thing about the whole scene was that there wasn't just one monster. There were dozens. Maybe hundreds. The animals were all monsters. And it wasn't the railroad camp, so what the Sam Hill was it?

Only thing Rhett could reckon was that if he just acted like a traveler, he might find out. Being the Shadow was an encumbrance most of the time, but at least it meant that he could pretend to be a dumb human, easy enough. He dressed right quick, burrowed into his new buffalo coat, saddled up, and did his best to look like a born fool.

The camp was a mile off or so, but Blue acted like it was across the country and required a good bit of hollering. The mule's bray was enough to chase the sun up, and by the time the sky was purple fringed in red, all sorts of creatures were answering his call.

The first thing they came across was a herd of cows, but these cows were like nothing Rhett had seen before in Gloomy

Bluebird. They were black and heavy-built, but their faces were just horned skulls of long white bone. They could moo well enough, but they had no eyes in their stark black sockets, and as Ragdoll rode into the herd to the tune of Blue's braying, the cows' heads clicked curiously. They didn't seem mean, at least, and the ones with horns didn't try to use 'em. But cows, in Rhett's opinion, definitely required faces.

Up close now, Rhett could hear horses whinnying, dogs barking, birds cawing, and one very annoyed human. From somewhere among the wagons, an old woman's voice called, "Be gone. The show aims for Zodiac. See us there."

Rhett swallowed hard and pitched his voice low. "It's a show?"

A tall, hunched-over figure appeared from behind a wagon painted bright violet. She scurried nimbly up the steps to sit on the driver's seat, her slitted eyes peering out from a shawl that had seen better days, possibly as a saddle blanket onto which a cow had given birth. The woman reached out and tugged a rope, and a piece of canvas unfurled, showing swoopy letters that didn't make a lick of sense.

"I ain't got my letters," Rhett grumbled.

"'Course you don't." The old woman chuckled in a mean sort of way. "What it says is, *Prospera's Menagerie: Magical Beasts Revealed!*"

"Well, that ain't catchy. It don't even rhyme."

"Folks don't come here for the wordplay, boy. They come for the monsters."

Rhett laughed, startling Ragdoll to a sidestep. "Monsters? Lady, did you fall and hit your head? They're just cows."

The old woman, Prospera, supposedly, hopped down from the wagon, unexpectedly quick and spry in her heavy boots and ragged skirts. "Didn't look close, did you? Nobody ever does, not till I tell 'em to. Folks don't like to see the truth. Come on, then. You give me a quarter, and I'll give you a special show."

"You want me to pay you two bits to look at your cows?"

The lines of the old woman's face showed her long familiarity with this particular brand of rage. "If you aren't surprised, and if you still think they're cows at the end, you can have your two bits back, plus another two. What you'll see here is real. Realer than anything else." Her hand crept out, palm up to show wrinkles and calluses and burn scars.

Amused for a variety of reasons, Rhett fished a quarter out of his pocket. "Figure I'll do it for the wager if not the show, ma'am."

The quarter disappeared, and Prospera unfolded and drew herself up tall, like some fancy statue. Her face went over solemn, and Rhett could see that she might've been beautiful and queenlike, once. With his belly wobbling all over the place, he looked her up and down for any signs of what sort of monster she might be, but all he knew was that she wasn't a vampire, as her eyes were gray instead of red and she was standing proudly in the morning sun.

"Step close, my friend," Prospera said in a cultured, practiced voice that echoed back off the buttes. "For you will see, today, the monsters of antiquity that draw fear into a man's heart." She walked, all swoopy-like with arms outstretched, toward the nearest wagon and whipped back a canvas curtain in dramatic fashion, flinging dust into the morning sunlight and making Rhett sneeze. Behind the bars were several weird-looking rabbits. Rhett saw the usual fanged kind, which he found quite tasty, plus some with antlers, and even some particularly large ones with antlers and wings, both. Considering Prospera was looking at him expectantly, he gave a gasp of surprise.

"What the Sam Hill are those things?" he asked.

"Jackrabbits, jackalopes, and the more esoteric Wolpertinger, brought all the way from Germania." Reaching into her pocket, she pulled out a scrap of dried meat and tossed it behind the metal bars. The rabbit-things fell upon it in a ball of fur and flying teeth. "Unseen by most innocent souls, these beasts surround us every day, waiting for the opportune moment to feed on the unwary."

"So how come I ain't never seen 'em before?"

Prospera smiled coyly. "Only my great magic can reveal their horror to human eyes."

"I reckon they're still just rabbits, ma'am."

Prospera's smile twisted into a cruel sneer. "Then let me show you something that isn't a rabbit at all. My newest addition. The Elmendorf Beast."

The next wagon was considerably smaller, and the curtain opened to reveal a snarling dog-thing that made Rhett's hand itch for his gun.

"What is that—some hairless coyote?"

He knew it wasn't, though. He could feel the wobble in his stomach, the strangeness calling for release. The beast's skin was the color and texture of stone, wiry hairs standing up here and there. It had a ferocious overbite and glowing red eyes, and it lunged at the bars, teeth scraping on metal. A thick leather collar and heavy chain held it at bay, the monster's throat red and raw where it rubbed.

"The Elmendorf Beast killed hundreds of cattle in Bexar County, ripping the helpless calves to ribbons and littering the ground with bones and blood. Most women pass out, looking upon its hideous face. But you, fine sir, I can tell are made of sterner stuff." She threw a piece of meat to the beast, and it snarled and sneered at the tidbit. "Likes its food alive and screaming, that one," Prospera added, whipping the curtain back down.

Rhett stuck his thumbs through his holster and said, "So you got some messed-up animals. That ain't worth a quarter."

Prospera snorted. "A disbeliever. Yes. How original. What do you think about...this?"

When she whipped the canvas off the next wagon, Rhett didn't have to feign amazement. He stumbled back and drew his pistol, his heart yammering in his chest. He knew this creature well. Bright blue eyes in a buzzard's face, dark gray wings with blades for feathers, dangling dugs with long, brown nipples, talons coated with gore gone black.

It was a goddamn harpy.

"What the hell?" he snapped.

"Finally. Something impresses you. Behold: the harpy!"

"Gonna kill you, bitch," the buzzard-woman spat, lunging to peck at the bars with her razor-sharp beak.

Prospera ignored that. "This creature of antiquity was seen in the works of Homer and Hesiod, captured by the great storytellers in their mythology, as I have captured her here."

"Bitch. Cur. Gonna eat your liver. Gonna rip the old woman apart like a rag doll."

Whether Prospera was troubled by the harpy's words, Rhett couldn't tell. The lady's smile remained smug and arrogant.

"Please lower your gun, sir. She's entirely harmless so long as she's caged. Just squawks and pecks. You're as safe as safe can be."

"I don't think she likes you very much," Rhett muttered, ramming his gun back in its holster as he noted the fresh silver claw marks on the otherwise dull and tarnished bars.

Prospera waved her hand at the cage. "I don't think she likes anyone."

Rhett backed away from the harpy, remembering all too well what one of the creatures could do when let loose on the world. Could this very one have helped carry him to the Cannibal Owl's lair or hunted him through the desert? They all looked alike, really. And they all died alike. Rhett was mighty tempted to shoot this one and be done with it. But he needed to act dumb so he could learn more about Prospera's magic. If whatever she did revealed monsters, maybe it could lift the Shadow's disguise, show that he was a monster, and get him into Trevisan's labor camp, neatly trouncing Dan and his attempt to take the reins and get his fool self hurt.

One more step back, and Rhett fetched against something huge and hairy. He spun, gun out again, ready to fight.

"Excuse me, good sir," the creature said, its voice cultured and soft around huge teeth.

"William, you're supposed to be cleaning cages," Prospera said, the sweetness of the words caught between angrily gritted teeth. "Not getting in the way of paying customers."

Rhett stepped away and reholstered his gun, because whatever this thing was, he wasn't supposed to be seeing it, apparently. Prospera would've charged a hell of a lot more than two bits to see something like this. William was at least eight feet tall, maybe more, roughly human shaped and completely covered in long chestnut-brown hair. He wore a beat-to-hell top hat and carried a broom, and his eyes were big and deep brown and very, very sad.

"Yes, Miss Prospera. Of course."

"Do a better job than yesterday, or there will be no dinner for you."

"Of course, Miss Prospera. Do excuse me, good sir."

His long, hairy legs clanked as he shuffled away, and Rhett noted a slender chain buckled around one of his boat-sized bare feet and trailing back to Prospera's purple wagon.

"Do pardon our mess," Prospera said. "Good help is so hard to find. William is a laggard, practically inexcusable, even for an indentured servant. All the way from the frigid wilds of Kanata, if you can believe it." She laughed like a church lady, secure in her place above everybody else, and Rhett tried to laugh along like he hadn't just met a Sasquatch sweeping up rabbit shit in the middle of Durango.

Prospera showed him several more wagons that were really just cages with roofs. There was a Wampus cat, a hellhound, a ghost deer, several cockatrices in chicken cages, and salamanders sticking to the sides of big glass jugs still wearing the rim of old brown liquor. It was possibly the saddest thing Rhett had ever seen, and that was saying a lot. He began to realize, as they moved from wagon to wagon and he pushed himself to feign wonder, that part of Prospera's presentation involved whipping back the canvas curtain on each wagon, making his nose itch and showering dust on the creatures within. Considering he could already see the monsters as they were, his best guess was that the powder changed something for normal folks. For once, being the Shadow didn't give him an edge; it only made it harder to see the truth.

What finally got to his swallowed-down heart was the unicorn. Now, he'd gentled unicorns before and felt no sadness for their shorn horns and nuts, as everybody knew stallions just caused trouble on the trails. He could accept a working animal kept well while earning its keep. But this unicorn was a mare, dainty and blue-white, glimmering like a broke-off sliver of moon in the new morning. Her horn wasn't the death spike of the males; it was delicate and almost see-through, like a fine piece of twisted quartz, and her tail hung low between her hocks like she was expecting a beating. Rhett—once Nettie— knew that feeling well.

"What about this one?" he said, jutting a thumb at the hobbled creature.

Prospera gave a cloying smile. "That old nag? Just a lame cart horse. Nothing more."

Rhett held out a fist for the mare to sniff, but the unicorn only flinched and shied away.

"What'll you take for her?" he asked, knowing that he wasn't supposed to see what was really there, this time.

With a wave of her hand, Prospera led him in a different direction. "She's worth nothing but to the knacker, and she'd die on her feet before you found one. But here is a creature to amaze you." She threw back the curtain on some sad-looking beaver-duck thing, but Rhett wasn't listening to her bullheaded prattle. He wanted that unicorn set free, his heart tugging toward it as surely as his belly did. Was that what his destiny wanted, shoving him toward Prospera's show when he had real business at Trevisan's labor camp? Was the Shadow just here to set a damn unicorn free?

He shook his head. Whatever the Shadow wanted, Rhett wanted to drop all goddamn pretense and take care of business.

"What about you?" he asked suddenly.

Prospera spun around to stare at him, half-amused and half-wary. He pulled his hat down over his eye.

"What about me, good sir?"

"What are you?"

Her laugh reminded Rhett all too much of the whores at the Leaping Lizard back home. Practiced, light, and entirely lacking truth.

"My dear boy, I am but a humble caretaker for this fine collection of specimens, bringing joy and wonder to the world, one town at a time."

"No, really. You're something. Shifter?"

She wrapped her shawl more tightly around her shoulders and turned away. "I'm sure I don't know what you mean."

Rhett grabbed her shoulder and spun her around, holding her in place. "I'm sure you damn well do."

The old woman lurched back, drawing a tiny pearl-handled revolver from somewhere in her layered garments. "Don't you dare," she hissed. "Don't touch me. I cannot be bought. I am not part of the show."

"But you're something."

"Nothing that's your business."

"Well—"

Before Rhett could explain that monsters were damn well his business, Prospera shot him in the shoulder. They were pretty close, which meant he got to experience the exquisite pain of a bullet going in one side and popping out the other. For one second, he felt wind whistle through the tunnel, and then his skin started knitting up, a warm and itchy sensation.

He huffed a sigh and poked a finger through the new hole in his buffalo skin. "Hellfire, woman. I just got this damn coat, too."

A look of complete horror grew on Prospera's face, and the longer Rhett went on standing up straight, glaring at her without doubling over in pain, the more her grimace made her look like a shriveled-up potato that had caught wind of its inherent doom.

"What are you?" she asked, voice low as she pointed her gun at his good eye.

"I reckon I'm the feller sent here to kill you," he answered, drawing his gun. The first round, he knew, was regular, but the second was silver.

Without another word, he unloaded them both into where he figured her heart might be.

CHAPTER
11

Prospera did the dumbest thing possible: She squawked and flopped over dramatically on the ground, wailing and spluttering. Rhett kicked her over onto her back and whipped out his knife, wondering where the Sam Hill the whatever-she-was kept her heart. The siren at Reveille had been like this—disinterested in dying easy, with a heart protected by a cage of whatever such things had for bones. But the siren had also laughed and fought back, while Prospera seemed totally taken up with hysterical death throes.

"You keep your heart somewhere else?" he asked, squatting down on his heels.

Her mouth moved, but nothing came out. Except blood, dark as syrup.

"Mistress?"

It was William, galumphing out from the wagons with his hat in his gigantic hands. He stopped at a polite distance and cocked his shaggy head.

"Good sir, what has happened?"

"Well, I shot her. But she didn't explode into sand, so I'm trying to figure out why. She got a particular sort of anatomy?"

"To my limited knowledge, she is the same as any human."

Rhett's blood went cold, and he probed around under Prospera's shawl, popping the buttons of her shirt to reveal more layers, all soaked in blood. The last layer exposed an all-too-human chest, blood oozing from two bullet holes.

"Are you saying…she ain't a monster?"

The Sasquatch kneeled at Rhett's side, and even though William was big and burly enough to rip him in half, the feller didn't feel like a threat under the current circumstances.

"She was a monster in heart if not in body. And now, she is nothing." Huge fingertips alit like moth wings to brush down her eyelids. In all Rhett's worry about her heart, he hadn't looked at the old woman's face as she died. But she was gone now, sure enough.

Rhett stood, took off his hat, and held it in his hands.

"I reckon it's a lot easier to kill things that turn to sand," he said. "I…I never killed a human before. Much as I've wanted to, now and again."

"Do not feel too bad," William said, putting his top hat back on and standing straighter, cracking his back. "I assure you she deserved it, and worse."

Rhett turned around, taking in the little camp. The cows and horses went on doing their creature business of not giving a shit. The things in the wagons kept on being in their wagons. The unicorn simply stared at Rhett with great black eyes.

"So what the hell now?"

William cocked his head. "Well, you're the one with the gun."

They regarded each other for a moment, the wiry cowpoke in the buffalo coat and the Sasquatch two feet taller and three hundred pounds heavier. There wasn't any threat in it, as far as Rhett could reckon, but there was a question. And Rhett, somehow, was the only person who could answer it.

"Well, what do you want to do, William?"

The Sasquatch took a moment to consider it. "I want to be free of this chain."

"And then what?"

"That's as far as I can think, good sir."

Rhett pulled his Bowie knife and squatted by the giant hairy feet. The chain in question was slender and tarnished but definitely silver. Where it encircled William's ankle, the hair had rubbed off, leaving raw pink skin. Rhett looked up, squinting his one eye. "You ain't gonna kill me, are you?"

William looked down with gentle dignity. "I am a pacifist."

"Don't know what that is, but it doesn't sound like revenge." With one quick slice, the chain dropped off William's ankle and slithered to the ground, and the great Sasquatch sighed in happiness and shook out his foot.

"I don't know what you are, but I am in your debt," he said.

Rhett stood and looked around the camp. "Just tell me what to do with all these damn critters. Except the unicorn. Her, I'm setting free."

William nodded, and when Rhett stalked toward the unicorn, the Sasquatch followed. As they approached, the mare danced around as much as her silver hobbles would allow, snorting in fear like any horse who lacked trust in mankind.

"Whoa, there, filly," Rhett murmured, doing his best to calm her and knowing she wouldn't be calm until she'd galloped out of his reach. "Hold her halter, would you?" When William had the mare in hand, Rhett leaned down to slice off the silver chains, careful to cut them away from her hooves and leave no trace of the metal against her flesh. As soon as the last bit of silver had fallen away, William pulled off the halter, and the unicorn bounded over the makeshift fence and away, head high and dainty hooves kicking up dust.

Rhett picked up the chain, expecting it to hurt his hands somehow. It didn't.

"Why silver?" he asked William, holding it out. "Doesn't it only hurt on the inside? Knives and bullets?"

The Sasquatch flinched away from it. "Prospera had magic. Whatever she did to the silver made it painful to...us. To our skin. Not to humans."

"I ain't human."

"Then you must have magic, too."

Chewing his lip, Rhett rolled the chain up around a twig, then started rolling up the chain William had left behind. The Sasquatch followed along behind at a respectful distance until Rhett found the hook bolting it to Prospera's wagon, where he had originally met her. He sliced the end of the chain and tucked it all into a pocket. The Captain would've called it spoils of war.

"This wagon is where she kept her things?"

William nodded.

"You reckon there's anything in there that could hurt me?"

"I don't know," William said. "I've never been in there. I wouldn't fit."

And he wouldn't. The wagon was a solid wood rectangle with an arching canvas roof, and the door in the back was small enough that Rhett had to duck to get through. The inside would've been dark if not for the sunlight filtering through the fabric. There was room only for a platform bed mounded with pillows and furs, a small table covered with cooking-type instruments, and a heavy old trunk on which sat an interesting sort of book. It was bound in leather and very thick, the pages scrawled in dark brown ink instead of the usual printing-press stuff. Even harder to read, if Rhett had been able to do so.

"You lettered?" Rhett called.

"Minimally."

"Then I'm taking this book. You don't mind, do you?"

"Good sir, you freed me from servitude. Take the entire camp and I'll not complain."

"Don't want the damn camp," Rhett muttered. "Just want the magic."

Dumping a pillow from its case, he stuffed the heavy leather book inside, adding to it something he recognized as a mortar and pestle from the table. Inside the trunk, he found some fire stones, sharp knives, and another length of chain. Most importantly, there was a cunningly crafted wooden box full of all sorts of powders, each labeled in the same spider-writing as he'd found in the book. He was about to rifle the bed when Blue's bray split the morning's calm.

"What the Sam Hill now?"

William cleared his throat. "Good sir, several riders approach from afar."

Rhett sighed. "Let me guess. A flashy palomino, two fat paints, a bay draft, some forgettable chestnuts, and a goddamn donkey."

"Accurate to the one."

"Take this, will you?" Rhett stuffed the bag and box into William's huge hands and crawled on out of the wagon. "Before they get here and start meddling, you and me should make a plan. What do you reckon should happen to this camp? Are these monsters dangerous?"

William looked around, tapping a finger on his chin. "Who can say? Many consider me dangerous, and I know for a fact that you are dangerous. But neither of us belongs behind bars, nor would we choose such a life."

"That ain't exactly what I'm asking. Which of these monsters would kill people, given the chance?"

"I would assume all of them."

"Well, ain't you a goddamn philosopher?"

Rhett dusted off his hands and pulled out his knife, considering his options. He was the Shadow, and his destiny had led him here. The tug on his belly had lessened as soon as Prospera was dead, and as he looked to the opposite horizon, on the other side of the camp, he was now compelled to hit the trail in that direction. Whether or not the Captain would consider it the right thing to do, Rhett's job had been to kill the old white woman, the human, holding all these supposed monsters in thrall. And now, before Dan's preaching and Sam's sunny disposition and Winifred's kind heart arrived to muck up his thoughts, he had to finish the job on his own terms.

"The cattle and horses. They eat folks?"

"The horses are merely beasts of burden, to pull the wagons. The black mare bit me once but didn't draw blood. As for the cows, Prospera called them Death's Head cattle. I don't know what they eat, but they seem complacent enough."

Rhett nodded and ran to the makeshift corrals, kicking down the posts and slicing the wire away with his Bowie knife. The horses erupted in a dust cloud as they galloped away, tails held high, but the cattle only moved a little away and stared at him with empty night-black eye holes. Hurrying back to the wagons, Rhett took a deep breath and considered that if there were gods, this might be what they felt like. He'd have known better what to do if he'd rolled the damn dice. Kill the wrong thing, and there was unjust blood on his head. Let the wrong thing live, and who knew what critter might rampage through a, killing folks. Either way, the wrong choice made him all the more monstrous, and he felt monstrous enough as it was.

"To hell with it," he shouted. And then he decided.

The Elmendorf Beast, which looked like a coyote's shadow—it growled at him, and he shot it in the heart, leaving black sand on the floor of its wagon. Same with the Wampus cat, which took a swipe at him with long claws and looked like it might eat babies just for fun. The harpy was opening her foul mouth to cuss him like a dog when he shot her in the heart, immediately feeling himself relax as her sand hit the floor. Rhett couldn't imagine a day he'd let a harpy live.

He let the wagon of rabbit-things go and enjoyed watching them bound and flutter into the brush. He had his gun cocked at the hellhounds until one whimpered and reached out a long tongue to lick his hand. With a muttered "Aw, hell," he unlatched the wagon and let them run off into the hills, silent and swift. The ghost deer, as it turned out, were held in by a single loop of silver chain wound around the bushes, and the moment he pulled it down, they leaped away, white tails flashing like starlight. All that was left by the time his posse rode up were the cockatrices and salamanders, creatures that seemed mostly below notice.

Dan stopped his chestnut a few feet away and grinned down at Rhett, who was panting from exertion as he wound up another coil of silver. "Do I even want to ask what happened?"

"The Shadow happened." Movement reminded him of his manners, and he nodded to the Sasquatch, who held his top hat in his hands. "And this is William."

"I prefer Bill, actually."

"Well, hellfire, then. Bill."

"We saw a unicorn," Winifred said, making it more of a question.

Rhett shrugged, feeling the fool. "I let her go. Big damn eyes. I let just about everything go that didn't growl at me. And I don't want to hear a goddamn thing about it. Just figure out how the old lady was using magic to make normal folks see monsters, and I'll be obliged."

Taking the pillowcase of loot from Bill, Rhett shoved it at Dan.

"There's a book and a bunch of powders in there. She kept them in with silver chains and shackles that burned from the outside. Might could figure that out, too."

"Why'd you leave us behind, Rhett?" Sam said, impatience failing to mask his hurt. "Don't you know you can trust us? We came to help you."

"I know, Sam. I know." He sighed but refused to hang his head. "I don't know why I do what I do, but it sure as hell feels like I don't have a choice."

"Now that you've sown your oats, are you ready to ride, then? To Trevisan?" Earl was back in human form, dusted with dirt and red-faced with annoyance.

Rhett shook his head. "I reckon we'll camp here today," he said.

Earl looked like he might explode. "And why's that, lad?"

Rhett tossed a look over his shoulder, to the body in the dust. "Because I've got to dig my first grave."

Prospera's caravan didn't have a shovel, but it did offer a pickax with a rusty-red tip. Rhett didn't want to know what the hag had used it for; he just wanted to get her in the ground so he didn't have to look at her anymore. Dan and Sam and Winifred had checked out the camp, hobbled their horses, and tried various ways to get Rhett to talk, but he wasn't damn ready and couldn't be forced. His annoyance only made the hole easier to dig in the hard, sandy ground.

It wasn't a very good hole. It was all cattywampus and not flat at all, and the edges kept crumbling in. He'd never dug one before. Pap hadn't exactly trusted Nettie Lonesome with sharp objects, especially ones that could be used from farther away than he could grab her by a braid and yank her to the ground. All Rhett could do was slam the pick down, again and again, and shovel out the scree with a pan Bill was kind enough to bring. But when it seemed like it might be deep enough to hold what was left of Prospera, Rhett stood back and nodded at the ground like they had an understanding.

The posse had given Rhett a wide berth, which was good, because he would've snapped at anybody who showed up to stare at the tears merging with his sweat and rolling down his face and into his eye. When he stopped and threw down the pickax, though, Sam sidled up, not quite staring at him but just being there, much as Rhett himself would approach a skittish colt.

"You want help carrying the body?" Sam asked, voice pitched low and private as he held out a fresh kerchief.

"Much obliged," Rhett answered, taking the rag to mop off his face. "You reckon the hole's big enough?"

Sam shrugged. "She's pretty fresh. She'll fold up."

Rhett flinched away, and Sam put a hand on his shoulder.

"You did what you had to do, Rhett. That's all you can ever do."

"Then why don't it feel right?"

Sam stared down into the hole as if it held the answers to all of life's questions.

"Because when killing starts to feel right, you're doing something wrong."

Without a word, Rhett quick-walked back to where Prospera had fallen. Someone—not him—had pulled a chunk of canvas off one of the wagons and draped it over the still form. In the afternoon light, Rhett couldn't help noticing the glittery dust coating the heavy fabric. Reaching down, he dragged a finger through it and looked right close. It was like ashes and cobwebs and felt smooth, not at all like sand. He'd noticed it earlier, dancing in the morning sunbeams as Prospera whisked the curtains away from each wagon. It had softly fallen on the monsters within. Was he right—could it be the secret to regular folks seeing monsters was in the dust?

He touched the tip of his finger to his tongue, tasting only dust, maybe something mineral behind it, like a pebble in his grits.

"What are you doing, Rhett?" Sam asked. Rhett turned to tell him he didn't know what the hell he was doing, but Sam gasped and stumbled back a step.

"What is it, man?"

"Your eye, Rhett. It...it ain't natural."

Rhett scrabbled around his good eye with his fingers, finding nothing strange about it. No pain, no lumpy bits. Just to be sure, he reached for his gone eye, too, but the damn thing still hadn't had the sense to grow back. "I don't feel anything peculiar. Has the sun tetched you?"

Grabbing his shoulders, Sam spun him around and gazed with his face uncomfortably but welcomely close. "It used to be dark brown, like a swole-up river, a-churnin'. But now it's... moon-yellow, with red around the outside."

"Like a vampire?"

"No, nothing like a vampire. Just different. I ain't saying it's horrible, it's just...well, like Dan's coyote eyes. How he looks like what he is. You look like what you are. I swear it wasn't like that, just a minute ago. Were you about to...change?"

Rhett shook his head and blushed a little. "Not in front of you. I'd have to get...nekkid first, and the whole thing's just horrible and awkward. I wouldn't make you watch that."

Sam let go of his shoulders and looked away, blushing himself. "Well, now, it might not be the worst thing. I mean, it would be interesting. I never seen that sort of thing before. Not saying that I want to. But you ain't horrible at all, and I'm not worried about…aw, hell. It's still you either way, ain't it?"

Rhett grunted. "It is." And he started walking for Prospera's body.

Six people stood around the makeshift grave, piled high with sand and stones. The men held their hats and Winifred clasped her hands as best she could while leaning on her crutch. Nobody looked at anybody else. It had been silent for far too long, and Rhett was sick of it.

"Bill, you knew her best. Care to say a few words?"

The Sasquatch looked up, placid and solemn. "Prospera bought me in Okla Humma and kept me in chains. She charged people money to laugh at me. When I spoke too much or out of turn, she beat me. The only words I have to say are that I hope there is a hell and she's in it."

The silence after that was even more uncomfortable. Finally, Rhett slapped his hat back on and walked toward the circle of stones where Dan had started a fire.

"To hell with her, then, and welcome," he said. "Dust to goddamn dust."

The others followed, each taking their place around the fire. Rhett regretted letting the jackrabbits go, considering the critters he'd saved were all of the inedible sort unless he wanted an entire, possibly undead heifer. There was no game to be found, whether because Prospera's magic had driven them away or the monsters themselves had scared away the local wildlife. The company ate what was left in Buck's saddlebags, passing chunks of cheese and bottles of wine around wordlessly. As much as Rhett figured his friends generally talked too damn much, he hated the eerie silence of the prairie punctuated only by the creaking of the wagons settling, the rattling of the cows, the caws of far-off carrion birds, and the canvas curtains flapping in a breeze that somehow never reached his face.

"Coyote Dan, I reckon you've got something to say. Some bit of teachin' or preachin' or wisdom."

Dan drank some wine and leaned back on his elbows. "I'll talk when you don't look apt to bite my head off. Care to discuss what troubles you?"

Rhett took a gulp of wine and slumped over. "What troubles me? Hellfire, Dan. What don't trouble me now? We're after this Trevisan monster, and I was going to do it myself to save you, and you followed me anyway! And then I got here and everything was muddled, and I thought I was shooting a monster, but it was just somebody's grandma. But she was mean as a damn snake. But she was a person, and this Ranger badge says I'm supposed to protect people like her from people like you. From people like me." He flicked his badge with a fingernail. "So did I do the right thing or didn't I? Because I don't know anymore."

In the silence, Dan stared up at him, and Rhett saw something quite rare: surprise.

"Rhett, your eye."

Rhett didn't look away. "Yeah, Sam told me."

"I can tell what you are."

"No shit, Dan."

"Something changed."

Rhett stomped to the nearest wagon and dragged a finger over the canvas curtain, holding up a gray-stained fingertip. "It's this dust, close as I can reckon. I think it's the magic that lets regular folk, folks who haven't killed, see monsters. So whether it's because I touched it or licked it, it means the Shadow isn't invisible." He touched the dust to his tongue and smiled. "And it means I'm the one going in to kill Trevisan."

CHAPTER

12

To hell with the silence. Now everybody was talking at once, mostly arguing against Rhett's cunning plan.

"It's not safe. We don't know how this magic works," Dan said.

"And if Trevisan knows magic, he might recognize you using it," Winifred added.

"I just don't like the idea of you going in alone," Sam muttered.

"I swear to God, I don't care who goes if they'll JUST GO SOON!"

This last bit of hollering from Earl, of course.

Bill simply sipped tea from a cracked porcelain cup. No one knew where he'd gotten the tea or the cup, but nobody wanted to ask, far as Rhett could tell. At least the Sasquatch wasn't bickering.

"I think it's fairly obvious to everyone who ain't thick-headed that we'll get moving in the morning when we can see our damn hands in front of our damn faces, Earl," Rhett said, at the end of his patience. "And if you want to go in with me, Dan, I reckon that would be fine, so long as you let me be the one to make stupid mistakes. And if you lettered fools would crack open the witch's book, I suspect you could find out everything you want to know about the goddamn powder. Does that about solve all your goddamn problems?"

Everyone nodded.

"Good. Then let's go to sleep and stop acting like goddamn idiots."

He flopped on the ground, arranging his buffalo coat, saddle blankets, and saddle into the most comfortable lump possible. Dan carried Winifred to Prospera's wagon and helped her through the door, since sleeping inside would be more comfortable and keep the sand from collecting on her stump. Earl turned back into a donkey, claiming that he only had nightmares in human form and the ground seemed softer when he had fur. William simply sprawled where he was like an island of silky mops, his snores deep and long and strangely musical.

Rhett rolled over and watched Sam Hennessy saunter back from his customary pre-sleep piss. Sam's bedroll was right by Rhett's, and Rhett took a moment to let that fact sink in with a smile as the blond-haired cowpoke settled in for the night. Did Sam remember anything about their night at the Buck's Head? If he did, would it make things strange or serve as a reminder that Rhett could function as a man in all the ways that mattered? Rhett didn't know which alternative was preferable, but if they for some reason had to stop in that town on the way home, he'd play dumb as a log and hope it maybe happened again. He didn't know if that made him a bad person or not, but he couldn't stop thinking about it.

Sam grinned like he didn't have a care in the world and settled down on his back with a contented sigh. Rhett did the same. No matter how bad the day was, no matter how bad tomorrow was bound to be, there was still something fine about listening to your best friend breathing, even and sure, as you fell asleep.

This. This was what Rhett understood. Sleeping under the stars, beholden to no man, back aching and hands calloused from a hard day's work, even if that work was the kind he'd just as soon forget. The horses stamped and swished, the coyotes yodeled in the hills, and the fire quietly died down to a comfortable crackle. Rhett didn't even realize he was holding his breath until Sam rolled over and spoke.

"Hey, Rhett?"

"Yeah, Sam?"

"I got something to say."

Rhett rolled over on his side and propped his head up on an arm. "Then let's hear it."

"What you said earlier today. About digging your first grave?"

"What about it?"

"Well, I just thought...I mean...you never killed a person before?"

Rhett shook his head.

"I been thinking about it. You just seemed really upset, and I wanted you to know that you're not alone. I killed people before, and on the Captain's orders. You weren't with the Rangers for long, so I guess you never had to do it. But there are people who aren't monsters who still need to die. That lady today...sounds like she was a witch. I've seen them before. And brujahs, which are like the Aztecan version of a witch, I guess. And there's ghouls and warlocks and whatever the hell else happens when folks who got no business with magic overplay their hand."

His bright blue eyes were wet and pleading, and Rhett wished he knew if his own eye was back to being mudwater-brown or was still red-and-yellow, which didn't sound like the kind of eye anybody would want to look at for long.

"So was it hard?" he asked.

Sam nodded, his neck-apple bobbing like it did when he was trying not to cry. "It's the sand. If you kill something and it turns into sand, you don't got to deal with it. No digging a grave, no touching the body when it's rubbery as all get-out. No standing over a mound of rocks and hoping the vultures don't claw it open. No offense," he added hurriedly.

Rhett shrugged. "None taken. Pretty sure I never robbed any graves."

"I'm just saying…it's easier when you can tell yourself it's a monster, that it's not like you. That it's bad. It's easier when there's no mess to clean up. But that doesn't mean the killing is wrong. You heard Bill. That lady was no damn good. You did the right thing, Rhett."

Rhett could only nod, fighting tears himself.

"And Rhett?"

"Yeah?"

Just then, Sam did the unthinkable: He reached out and squeezed Rhett's hand. "You might be a monster, but you're a good person."

Despite all the crap feelings that had been weighing him down all day, Rhett suddenly felt as free as a damn bird in the bright blue sky. He smiled, and Sam smiled back, and that was the purest magic in all of Durango.

Rhett fell asleep happy, and that was saying a goddamn lot.

The next morning, nothing and everything had changed. Rhett had killed a person and dug a grave, but he still had to piss and build up the fire and see to his horses, which meant he had to get up and moving. He was vexed to find his flux hadn't abated and had, in fact, made a mess in the night. Of all the things he had to deal with, he could leave most annoyances behind by killing them or walking away, but this one thing he was stuck with, a painful and messy reminder that no matter what he did and told himself, he was still something he didn't want to be.

A woman.

It felt all wrong, and he could ignore it most of the time. But not now.

Cussing to himself, he fetched the wad of rags and scraps he kept in his saddlebags and rigged everything into place feeling like a chunk of beat-up meat before heading to the nearby creek to wash out his britches. At least everyone else was still asleep so there were no witnesses to a situation that shamed him something awful.

When he returned to the fire, Winifred was sitting on a cushion from the wagon, her forehead wrinkled as she watched Dan hook Hercules into the harness.

"He wants me to ride in the wagon," she said, throwing bits of grass in the fire. "Like an old woman. Like an invalid."

"Well, you are missing a pretty important part—" Rhett began.

Winifred shushed him with an angry slash of her hand. "So are you. You want to ride up there with me? I'll let you sit on the box and point out ways we're broken."

"Hell, no. I can still ride."

"So can I."

"But if you fall off in a fight, you're as good as dead."

"Say something like that again and I'll shoot you myself."

Sam rubbed his eyes and sat up. "What're you shooting Rhett for today?"

Winifred huffed like she wanted to get up and flounce away but couldn't. "Being mule-headed, same as usual."

Dan finished settling Hercules in and returned to the fire looking pleased with himself. "Looks like he knows what he's doing. We'll tie Kachina to the back, and you'll be all set."

"I don't need to be set. I don't need to be looked after. I don't need cushions and a roof. This isn't who I am."

Dan inclined his head toward her foot. "It is for now."

Winifred grunted something in another language and struggled to stand on her one good foot. They argued in heated tones that didn't need translation before Winifred hopped toward the horses.

"If he comes after me, Rhett, I give you permission to hurt him," she called.

Dan didn't budge, but he radiated anger, his arms crossed over his chest. "She can't accept what is," he said. "That's always been her problem. Thinks things will stay the same if she wishes it hard enough. Thinks things will change around her, because of her. Thinks she gets to choose." He shook his head. "Experience is a bad teacher. She thinks she's hurt now, but it could be a lot worse."

As they watched, she unhobbled Kachina, whispered in the mare's ear, and put the reins over the mare's neck, carefully balancing all the while. Kachina gently lay down, and when Winifred was settled on her bare back, the pretty little horse climbed back to her feet. With neither bridle nor saddle, the girl guided the horse away at a stately walk, the morning breeze blowing back Winifred's black hair and her horse's black mane and tail like they were one creature.

"Looks like she don't give a shit about learning anything but what's over that hill," Rhett said.

He didn't let Dan see him smile. He'd do what Winifred was doing, too, if Dan tried to stop him. Hell, he'd done so just a few nights ago. The moment he'd left Pap's house was the moment he'd decided that nobody else got to tell him who to be or what his limitations were. Winifred might've been a woman, but she was brave and stubborn, and Rhett could respect that.

"Guess we better catch up, huh?" he asked.

Dan sighed. "Looks like I'm the one driving the wagon."

A short while later, Bill smothered the fire with his huge foot, and Rhett struggled with what to say to him.

"I reckon all this is yours now," he said. "For whatever use you might put to it."

Bill stuck out his chin. "I have no need to possess what was my prison."

"Then take what you can use and be gone with you. It's your choice."

"Yes," the Sasquatch said solemnly. "Yes, it is."

"So what will you do?"

"As you say: leave."

"To go where?"

Annoyance flashed in Bill's dark eyes, and he bared long canines that had been hidden until just then. "Home. Up north. Kanata. Away from this dire place."

"What's it like?"

Bill thought a moment, his face going slightly dreamy. "Vast. Cold. Green. Your Durango is empty and hot and dry, but Kanata is an endless labyrinth of trees and snow and stone. Here, people gape at me. There, no one will ever find me again."

Rhett nodded slowly. "Feller, that don't sound half-bad."

"Good luck with your journey," Bill said, clapping a huge hand on Rhett's shoulder that drove his boots an inch into the sand. "May you kill this thing that requires it."

"Same to you."

The giant shaggy man turned and strode purposefully northward without looking back. Just as he was almost out of sight, he plucked off his top hat, stomped on it, and threw it as Rhett had thrown flat cow patties as a child, just to watch them soar.

"He's a weird feller," Rhett said as Sam came to stand beside him.

"Ain't we all," Sam added. "Ain't we all."

Things were pretty normal for a while. Normal, that is, for two coyotes, a donkey, a Ranger, and some sort of big ol' bird-thing that refused to act like a girl. As it happened, Earl ended up happy to drive the wagon, claiming he didn't like riding astride a horse but would direct one from the wagon-box just fine while giving his hooves a rest. They caught up with Winifred by noon and rode along together through the hottest part of the day. Rhett was goddamn miserable, considering the heat and the lack of meat and the ongoing fact of his bleeding, which was at least drawing to a close.

By nightfall, everyone was glad to settle down, especially considering Dan had managed to snag a scrawny little mule deer with his bow at sunset. The world looked brighter with a full belly. For a day or two, everything was like that. Everything was fine. Everybody behaved. Rhett's body behaved and quit its bleeding. Hell, even the weather and terrain behaved.

But then something regrettable happened.

They came across a road.

It wasn't much of a road, as roads went. Rhett hadn't seen many roads in his lifetime, and most of them just ran down the middle of one shitshow town and then petered out to nothing on the other side. But what he didn't like about this road in particular was that there were bound to be other travelers on it. He kept expecting Dan or Sam to say something to that effect, like pointing out the obvious: This had to be the road from Waterloo to Lamartine. But no one said a damn thing, which only confirmed his fears.

Among his friends, among the Rangers, or at the Double TK, he knew who and what he was. Among strangers, the type of strangers who felt the need to parade across the territory for no good reason, he felt downright peculiar, and he suddenly understood completely why Bill the Sasquatch had lit out for his beloved Kanata. Rhett was now exposed and guaranteed to run into curious people who were bound to be rude. And if there was one thing Rhett hated, it was rude people who didn't quite deserve to die.

It was easy enough to travel, at least. The road was just a strip of dirt tromped down by hooves and boots, the hay-dry grass on either side trying unsuccessfully to overrun it again. Signs of life popped up here and there: a tin can, a thrown horseshoe, a chunk of broken harness or rope. Rhett hated it. A pile of manure was natural and useful, but just tossing out broken things to impede the way of others? Rude. Just plain rude.

Rhett was hollering at people in his head when he first noticed a cloud of dust heading toward them from the horizon. He was riding Puddin', out in front of his posse like the Ranger Scout he officially was. At first, he thought about transforming into a bird and flying over to see what was headed their way, but then he remembered that…roads were for people. Not outlaws. Not Lobos. Not monsters hell-bent on eating babies. Just regular folks too scared and foolish to make it alive across the prairie on their own. Being scared of folks on the road was about the same as being scared of cattle. They were big and dumb, but you had to remember who was the dangerous one.

"Let's make camp," Dan said, trotting up on his chestnut.

Rhett nodded. "Might as well. Getting crowded out here, all of a sudden."

"That it is."

They pulled off in a place where folks had been pulling off for a while. Dirt ruts from past wagons led to a pretty clearing by a stream surrounded by weeping willows. A fire pit was burned black, ringed by logs and rocks about the right size for sitting. Rhett couldn't deny that it was mighty pleasant to have half the work already done. Of course, his relief disappeared as soon as he realized how far he'd have to go to scavenge firewood without chopping down a waist-thick willow with his Bowie knife. Still, it was a pretty walk, following the creek through copses and plucking up whatever twigs and dead branches he could find. At least he knew that by the time he got back, someone else would've hacked into the mule deer and gotten it ready to roast.

When he returned to dump a load of kindling in the pit, he was taken aback to hear unfamiliar voices raised in laughter, a fire already crackling. A fierce jealousy rose up in his throat. Those were his people, and who were these new folks, just joining the camp as if they had a right?

Up close, he saw a big wagon parked across the clearing from Prospera's wagon—or Winifred's wagon, now, whether the girl wanted it or not. Two matched brown draft horses cropped grass amicably with Hercules, while another mule traded joyful scratches with Blue. When Rhett approached the fire pit, chin held high and mouth set in a grim line, he found Winifred in conversation with a white woman and two little girls with long blond braids trailing down their backs over faded sprigged calico. Winifred's stump was carefully covered.

"This is Mr. Rhett Walker. Rhett, these are the Muellers," Winifred said carefully in her most white-sugar voice. "They're on their way to Waterloo to start a farm. This is Betsy, and her girls are Minnie and Molly."

"Howdy do, Mr. Walker," the woman said softly.

"Howdy do, sir," the girls echoed at her nod.

When Rhett didn't immediately say anything, Winifred's eyebrows went down sharply, her eyes demanding he cobble together some sort of politeness.

He pitched his voice deep. "Uh, howdy do, ma'am. Ladies." He tipped his hat, settled it lower over his eye, and hurried past. One of the little girls had gasped, probably at his single eye, and he didn't want to be gawked at any longer.

Over by the wagons, Dan had the mule deer strung up and was slicing off bits of it as a man in faded farmer's garb smoked a pipe and yapped in a growly voice.

"Name your price, I said. Don't you like money, boy?"

"He's not for sale," Dan said, carefully focusing on his work.

"Everything's for sale. Farm needs a good donkey. What do you need it for, anyway? It's not even being used to pack out. Wasted, that is."

Rhett took an instant dislike to the stranger for several reasons and was sorely aggrieved to recognize that he wasn't any sort of monster that needed immediate killing.

"He's not an it, and he's not for sale," Rhett interrupted, his hand on his gun.

The man turned, looked Rhett up and down with an ugly sneer, and snorted foul smoke out his nose. "Where'd that Ranger go? Maybe he has some sense in his head."

Shaking his head in disgust, he stomped away toward where Sam was carrying in water from the stream. Earl did a little

169

kick and brayed, and Dan savagely cut off a chunk of meat as if he wished he were cutting on Mr. Mueller.

"Tomorrow, we get off this fool road," Rhett muttered. "I'd rather take supper with a harpy."

"It's not so bad," Dan said. Then he caught himself and laughed, sharp and dark. "Well, it is. I guess I'm used to it. Point is, Mrs. Mueller has a pot and can cook up the grub with some flavoring and greens, and maybe we can do some trading. We're stuck with them tonight, in any case. And Winifred's smiling, so there's that."

Rhett followed his line of sight to find Winifred in good spirits as she played a game with the little girls and their two ragged dollies. The girls laughed, and it was indeed a sweet sound. Mrs. Mueller kept watch over a cauldron set in the fire, her face drawn down and her mouth a thin line. Well, and who would look happy, when they were married to Mr. Mueller?

"He can't have Earl, and he can't have any of the horses. Look at his animals. The mule's skinny, and the horses' hooves are all grown out. He doesn't even brush their manes." Rhett spit in the dirt, hands on his skinny hips. "I got no respect for a man who doesn't care for his beasts." Earl stamped a foot, and Rhett added, "You'd best turn back into someone who can talk back or he'll try to steal you in the night." Earl nipped at his hand, but not with an eye to bite off a finger.

Dinner was a tasty but stiff affair, as Sam was the only person Mr. Mueller saw fit to talk to in between sips from a dirty glass flask. Prospera's wagon had included a variety of mismatched and dented-up tin plates and cups, so the meal was uncomfortably civilized after weeks of eating nearly raw meat off sticks. Betsy was mostly silent, answering questions in a quiet voice when asked and instructing the girls on proper behavior. Winifred did her best to carry on a conversation, but any time Betsy spoke too much or too loudly, Mr. Mueller gave her a hard-eyed look, and she pursed her lips and focused on her food.

"Your boy told me you was headed to Lamartine," Mr. Mueller said to Sam, who looked more annoyed and aggrieved than Rhett had ever seen him.

"If you mean my friend Dan, then you heard correctly." Sam's voice was sharp, and he was sitting as stiff as a preacher, his sweet eyes gone cold.

"We just came from there."

"I figured."

A few moments passed in silence. Mr. Mueller finished his plate of food and shoved it at Betsy with a grunt. She hurriedly refilled it and handed it back.

Looking down at it, he shoved it back at her, harder, slopping sauce onto her shawl. "Well, fill it good. Stingy slattern."

The air around the fire practically crackled with anger. Dan, Sam, Winifred, and Rhett were all tense and silent, their food forgotten.

"You need a wife?" Mr. Mueller made to elbow Sam in the ribs.

Sam leaned away, his face a grim mask as he changed topics. "The food is mighty fine, Mrs. Mueller. We're all much obliged. We've been so used to trail food that it's right nice to eat something fully cooked with some salt to it."

Mr. Mueller grunted. "Too much salt. Always too much salt. I joke that she's trying to kill me with salt."

"Didn't know seasoning was a weapon," Rhett muttered, and Mr. Mueller's head jerked up.

"Don't you mutter at me, boy. You mind your betters."

All slow-like, Rhett set down his plate and dabbed at his mouth with a kerchief. "Mind my betters?" he said. "Well, if I should see one, I'll remember that advice."

Quicker than Rhett expected, Mueller had a fist tangled in his shirt and was dragging him to standing. "What the hell did you just say to me?"

Rhett jerked away and straightened his shirt. "Pretty sure I didn't mutter that time."

Mueller looked down to Sam. "You better tell your boys to show me some respect or I'll teach them to behave."

Sam stood, towering over the stockier man. "You seem to think they work for me, but I assure you they are free men. Heavily armed ones, too. And Rangers to boot."

"Like hell," Mueller spat.

Rhett rubbed a thumb over his badge. "Shiny, ain't it?"

Dan had pulled his own badge from wherever he kept it and pinned it on his collar slowly, his eyes locked on Mueller. "Captain Walker wouldn't take to you threatening Durango Rangers, *sir*."

Mueller's grin went twisted and cruel. "Well, this here ain't Captain Walker's territory. This is Captain Haskell's land. And he ain't going to like you boys too much, from what I hear. Them Haskell's Rascals ain't known for their tolerance."

"I reckon even an intolerant man won't abide you insulting the Rangers," Dan said. Rhett was coming to realize that so long as Dan was smirking, things were fine. As soon as Dan got like this, his face impassive and his voice even, things were headed south.

Betsy put a gentle hand on her husband's arm. "Gregory, please. The children are tired."

Without looking at her, he jerked his arm away and shoved her to the ground. The most telling detail Rhett noticed as time seemed to slow down was that the little girls didn't even act surprised. They clutched at each other and backed away into the shadows with wide, wary eyes. Once they were under their wagon, Rhett turned back to face Mueller, his hands in fists.

Rhett was the first to roll up his sleeves, then Sam and Dan. Betsy's mouth quivered as she pulled herself back to sitting and tried to settle her shawl and hair.

"Please," she begged. "The road makes us weary. Let's all just go to bed."

Her husband ignored her and stood, his face lit like a demon from the fire below. "They'd like that, I bet," he said, voice low and almost cloying. "Think you boys can talk back to me? Where I come from, there are consequences for insolence." He glared at each of the men in turn, his eyes settling on Rhett as he rolled up his own sleeves.

With a snort of amused murderousness, Rhett flexed his hands. "I don't know what insolence is, but I bet it's not half as offensive as your rudeness. If you like hitting women, I reckon I'd like to kick your ass."

And then the fight began.

CHAPTER
13

Mueller's lip curled, and he threw a haymaker that Rhett had no trouble ducking. Before Rhett could hit Mueller back, Sam and Dan had him by the arms to haul him away.

"Rhett, stop and think," Dan muttered. "What do you hope to gain?"

"Beat the shit out of an ass who deserves it?" Rhett struggled against them, realizing for perhaps the first time that he wasn't as strong as he thought he was.

"You want his girls to see that?" Sam asked. With one hand, he turned Rhett's chin, pointing his eye at the wagon from under which four bright, wet eyes were watching as Mueller breathed through his nose like a bull.

"Well, I—"

Mueller landed a punch in Rhett's belly, and all the air whooshed out. The pain was nothing compared to the rage, and soon Sam and Dan were struggling to hold him back for real.

"Let me do this, Sam," Rhett shouted. "You know he deserves it!"

Sam pulled Rhett close to speak directly into his ear. "I know that if we let you go, either he kills you or you kill him. I can't live with the first, and his family can't live with the second, so

I'll keep holding you back even if it means I have to sit on you all goddamn night."

Much to his surprise, the fight drained on out of Rhett at that, his body relaxing. Sam and Dan still held on tight, most likely believing it was an act, as that was exactly the sort of dirty fighting Rhett would've preferred to indulge in.

Mueller stepped forward to go for another coward's shot, and Winifred muttered, "Don't," from her place by the campfire. She was still sitting, but she had her leather sling and stone whirling in the air, her beautiful eyes narrowed with hate and threat.

In the shadows, a pistol cocked. "Yeah, you don't want to be doin' that," Earl said.

Holding his hands up in defeat, Mueller backed away until he was out of striking range.

"You okay?" Sam asked.

Rhett nodded, and they let him go. He readjusted his shirt and resettled his hat as if such civilized motions could clear the air.

"Oh, I'm fine. So long as I'm not expected to share my fire with that feller again."

"Oh, you won't," Mueller said. "Uppity mongrels." He kicked over the cauldron, spilling the rest of the food into the fire. "Now you can't eat my scraps." With that, he spat on Rhett's boot and strolled to his wagon with his head held back, tippling from his flask.

Betsy was crying silently, and Rhett understood now that the purple smudges under her eyes weren't from lack of sleep.

"I'm sorry," she said before scurrying behind her husband, back toward the wagon.

The posse pretended not to watch as Betsy laid out pallets for the girls on the ground and climbed into the wagon with her husband. Once the wagon started rocking rhythmically to the tune of animalistic grunts and soft sobs, Rhett stood and walked hurriedly away to the horses. Normally, he'd bring over his saddle and blanket and curl up by the fire. This time, he set up his bedroll by the stream, on the other side of the horses. Cold and the familiar reek of manure were better than the red-hot fury he'd feel if he tried to sleep near that bastard Mueller. At least he had his buffalo robe to curl up in, not to mention the heat of his anger.

He twitched when he heard footsteps, but it was only Sam, saddle and blanket in hand.

"Dan's staying by the fire so he can keep an eye on Winifred in the wagon. He doesn't trust that Mueller feller, and neither do I."

"Me, neither."

Sam set out his things and settled down in his usual place. The only difference was that there was no fire and no one else, just them and the horses and the cool night wind ruffling the burbling water. The stars were bright, twinkling through the weeping willow as whip-poor-wills gave their mournful calls.

"What good are Rangers if we can't stop folks from doing wrong?" Rhett finally asked, although whether he was asking the moon or Samuel Hennessy, he didn't rightly know.

"We can stop plenty of wrongs," Sam answered, all gentle. "We're on our way to do just that. But some things...well, they got no good answer. You just got to measure the balance and do the best you can. If we had let you kill that feller, who rightly deserved it, either his family would be alone on the prairie with no man to keep them safe or we'd have to take them on, and then we couldn't hunt Trevisan. So we've got to let it go, even if every one of us'll be chewing over it all night like a piece of gristle."

"That poor woman," Rhett fumed. "Those poor little girls."

Hours or possibly years went by before Sam spoke again, just as quiet as the doves cooing somewhere along the stream. "Was it like that for you, before? Were you somebody's...? Did some man...?"

The question hung between them, and Rhett's emotions had a knock-down-drag-out in his heart. He was grateful as hell that Sam hadn't finished either question, but he always wanted to be honest with Sam, if he could.

"You've seen my back, Sam. You've got some idea of where I come from."

Sam's continued silence was a question, too.

"Nobody did that other thing, though. Lobos tried." He knew well his grin was a feral thing. "And boy howdy, they failed."

"Sometimes I try to see you in that life, wherever you were before, and I just can't. You ain't that. It about gives me a headache, trying to puzzle it out."

"It doesn't matter," Rhett said, tired all of a sudden. He rolled onto his back and suffered the weight of the sky pressing down on his tightly wrapped chest. "This is me. This is my life."

"I reckon I feel the same. Regarding if it matters. What you are. Or me. Or what I...I used to think...oh, hellfire."

Rhett chanced a sideways glance at Sam, who was on his back now, arm over his eyes, cheeks flushed red. It was a tightrope of a moment, and Rhett felt as if he held a handful of corn and a little bird was just about to hop into his palm. So he did the kindest thing he could.

"It doesn't matter, Sam. You're you. This is the way you are. There ain't a thing wrong with it, and I'll shoot anybody who disagrees in whatever tender place you request. It's nobody's

business, what either of us are. It feels like enough to me, sometimes, just knowing you know. And that you don't mind."

"I...I used to mind, Rhett. But then I figured a man's born
to be whatever he is, and there can't be nothing wrong with
that."

"Oh, just kiss already!" Earl shouted from the darkness.
"Nobody gives a shit!"

Rhett and Sam hurriedly rolled over, back to back. Rhett's
face was as red as Sam's now, he was sure.

"Night, Rhett," Sam said.

"Night, Sam." He paused, staring off into the darkness.
"And you can go to hell, donkey-boy."

Sam was soon sleeping, because that was just one of his gifts.
Rhett, however, was all riled up and couldn't calm his mind.
The uncomfortable talk with Sam, overheard by a jackass; the
altercation at the fire; the unfriendliness of the road and the
unfairness of life. It ate at him, ragged as chupacabra spit working on a cowhide.

He got up and walked away, figuring that if Earl was drunk
and awake they could maybe get in a friendly sort of fight in
which nobody would get hurt but everybody could work out
their antsiness. He found the feller in donkey form, hidden by an
especially weepy willow and snoring on his side. Pulling back his
boot to give the meddling bastard a nudge in the ribs, he found
he couldn't. The fuzzy donkey was just too goddamn charming,
and as much as Rhett didn't mind beating up a man, he wasn't
the sort to hurt an animal, even if it was a man underneath.

Walking back toward the camp, he spotted Dan asleep by
the fire, on his back and solemn as a corpse, as usual. The little
Mueller girls were curled together, face to face, holding hands

under their wagon. As if that could stop the world from prey-ing on them. Tender little things, one all arms and legs and the other pudgy as a pot of honey. When Rhett thought about Mueller striking one of them, the rage came back, hot as ever.

Walking past the fire, Rhett stood beside the wagon and lifted the dirty canvas at the edge to peek inside. The hot, wet reek of rutting struck him first, a smell that brought only con-fusion and, in this case, disgust and anger. No way had Betsy wanted what had been given to her, right there for all to hear. Mueller was a beast displaying power; that was all.

As his eyes adjusted, Rhett could see them sleeping. She lay curled into the wood wall, her bare shoulder wearing finger-shaped bruises and her breathing light and fast, like maybe she was outrunning him in her dream, but only just. He was on his back, spread out and openmouthed, his chest wet with sweat and one wide, dangerous hand sprawled through springy blond curls. Quietly, so quietly, Rhett pulled his Bowie knife from its sheath and slipped it inside the wagon's tent, holding it just above Mueller's neck.

Right there.

That's where I'd cut, he thought.

It would be so satisfying.

Well, until Betsy woke up with blood soaking her night shift, her husband gargling and sputtering and clawing at her as his life pumped out. Until the little daughters woke up to their father's corpse and learned they would be batted about by the whims of the world like tumbleweeds in a tornado. Until Betsy tried to harness the draft horses herself and started crying because no one had ever taught her how to make untenable beasts behave.

No, the satisfaction would be short-lived, and Sam was right. There was no good answer, no justice here. Leaving the Mueller women without a man was crueler than letting them keep trudging along under his thumb. In the kindest world, which it certainly wasn't, the posse would cart them off to the nearest town and leave them there in the care of someone like the Widow Helen in Burlesville. Rhett couldn't even imagine what the ride from here to there would be like. As much as he'd regretted the burden of carting Regina around twice, it would be all the more unpleasant with a suspicious widow and two children, all looking at him like maybe he was the bad guy. He silently slipped his knife back out of the wagon and drove it home in its sheath on his belt.

"It would be sweet, wouldn't it?"

Rhett's head whipped around, but no one was there. Because Winifred was in her wagon, wasn't she? Her voice had seemed to come from everywhere, almost as if the moon had spoken. But the quiet, patient rage floating on the night breeze belonged only to the coyote-girl.

Winifred's wagon was across the clearing from the Muellers' wagon, almost as if Dan had anticipated trouble when he'd brought them here. No lantern was lit, and the canvas was tied down more tightly than the Muellers'. For no reason he could name, Rhett wandered over that way, his hand on the butt of his knife.

"I'm not gonna do it," he murmured, right up by the canvas.

"I know," Winifred answered, sounding amused. "You're growing up."

Rhett huffed a sigh. "We're about the same damn age. Not my fault if you and that brother of yours think yourselves uppity preachers."

Winifred laughed, and Rhett heard her moving around in the wagon. When the door around back creaked open, Rhett swore under his breath and walked around to see what the Sam Hill she wanted, other than to needle him.

"I'm sorry. You're right. I shouldn't tease. I wanted to kill him as badly as you did tonight."

"Ain't no way that's possible, coyote-girl."

The laughter drained out of her face so markedly that Rhett could see it by moonlight, cut as it was by shadows and the rippling canvas. "And why's that, Rhett? Because he thinks so much of me, as compared to you? You he saw as someone's servant, but me...he didn't even see. Not a word, all night. So which is worse? Being seen as lesser, or not being seen at all?"

He shook his head. "I got experience with both sides of that coin, don't forget."

"But you took something more for yourself. Shed your old skin like a butterfly's cocoon. You decided which side the coin would land on. And I'm stuck here, a woman and an Injun and a cripple. At least your eye healed up. You think you have it so bad, but you don't."

Rhett put a hand on the wagon and leaned close, his rage a colder thing and collecting like snow. So soft and deadly, he asked, "Why are you trying to pick a fight with me when you know damn well I've a mind for violence tonight?"

"Because I have anger, too, and I get tired of feigning politeness." Winifred leaned farther out the door, her hands gripping the jambs. "I tire of being overlooked completely. Of not being seen when I wish to be seen."

Rhett realized in that moment that he hadn't really looked at her since that day in the Cannibal Owl's cave, when she'd held him close to her warm, bare skin, rocked him like a child and taught him the key to becoming what he was. He did her the favor, now, of looking at her. Really looking at her. Seeing her, as she was. Her hair was down, loose and rippling, brushed out from the braid she wore to travel. Her face was all planes and lines and plushness, her eyelashes dark frames around darker eyes. Coyote

181

eyes, now that he noticed it, as Sam had said. No matter how many white petticoats this woman wore, her eyes would still be wild. She wore the man's shirt she rode in every day and washed in every stream they crossed, but its puddled looseness suggested she wore nothing else. The wagon was all full of her smell, earthy and green and kissed with rose soap, feminine in ways that Rhett recognized he would never be, had never wanted to be.

And yet something about it squirmed into him, tugged on him.

He liked it.

"I see you, Winifred Coyote," he said, still soft and deadly, but in an altogether different way.

"Sometimes, I think you do." Her lips quirked up, her canine teeth lending her smile a feral edge. "But I do wonder what you see."

He grasped the curving wood bow overhead, his face not so far from hers. "If you're looking for sweet words, you should recall that I don't know any."

Her chuckle was a purr. "Said I wanted to be seen, not flattered, didn't I?"

"I never know what you want."

She leaned all the way out, holding her face up to his, her eyes big wet pools of something. "So ask. Or better yet, don't."

Winifred's lips landed on Rhett's, soft and plump as springtime. Fire flared up in the pit of him, as if a tiny spark had caught a world of paper and set the sky ablaze. He let loose the wagon with one hand and curled fingers around her jaw and chin, holding her there, where he wanted her. He didn't know what this was, and he had no goddamn idea what he was doing, but he knew he wasn't ready for it to end.

Winifred, at least, knew what she was about. She murmured something lovely into his mouth and tangled her fingers in the front of his shirt, pulling him toward the door as she deepened the kiss. Rhett didn't much like being ordered around generally, but he chose to make an exception this time, considering that every particle of his being urged him to get closer to the coyote-girl's soft heat.

As Winifred edged backward into the darkness of the wagon, towing him along, he climbed up with her, keeping the kiss going as much as possible and being careful of her body, especially that one leg. Winifred herself didn't seem to much care, her pain all but forgotten. Rough and fierce, she reclined on her back, pulling Rhett with her onto the platform bed and the pile of pillows until he lay over her, lined up in all the right sorts of places, taking his weight on his knees and elbows so he wouldn't hurt her. They weren't much different in size, and yet he felt protective of her, as if she were as light-boned as a bird.

"Why'd you stop?" she asked, all breathy.

"Don't want to hurt you," Rhett mumbled.

"I'm tougher than you think." She grabbed his head and pulled his face to hers again, her mouth open and hungry. When her tongue slipped out, it surprised the hell out of Rhett—not to mention sped up his breath and sent whirls of heat pooling all over him. But he'd seen the saloon girls kiss like this, hadn't he? And at the Buck's Head, hadn't he and Sam—? So maybe that was the way of things. Not that it mattered when it felt this nice.

"Come closer."

Winifred's hands slid down his shoulders and waist, pulling him down with a knee between hers, lining up their middles in a way that struck Rhett as mighty personal. Did the coyote-girl know what she was doing? What her hand did next assured Rhett that she did. He grunted in surprise, then the grunt slid into a moan. That place—he didn't even touch himself there—he didn't think he ever wanted to be touched there—and yet it sent undeniable shivers and thrills to every inch of flesh on his body.

"Are you sure we—"

She caught the question in a punishing kiss. "Shut up, Rhett. You talk too much."

So he quit talking.

Silence had never been so goddamn golden.

Hours later, still a bit before daybreak, he crawled out of the wagon a changed man. Sam didn't stir as Rhett settled down on his blanket, his head limp against his saddle. Exhausted as he was, and wrung out as his body felt, sleep didn't immediately come. His thoughts spun out as he stared at the stars, trying to puzzle out what was what. The coyote-girl had—and it had been—good Lord—but what—? After figuring out how tongues worked, he hadn't given a single consideration to what had passed between him and Sam in Buck's grove. The two experiences were as different as night and day. And he couldn't forget, of course, that whatever spirit had held him and Sam had also, as far as he figured, come over Winifred and Earl.

Had she liked it, he wondered? More than she'd liked—? But what had passed in the grove hadn't been a choice, had it? They'd all been in the grip of a god, drunk on his wine and lost to his will. He couldn't blame Winifred for that any more than he could blame himself.

They'd all experienced it, but he was the only one who remembered it.

And where had Winifred learned to—do what she did? She'd taught him, clumsy and shy as he'd been, moving his fingers and urging him on with soft moans as he found the way of bodies. Was that a normal thing that happened, that folks were doing all the damn time behind closed doors? It had never been like that between Pap and Mam, and it didn't seem like that with the Muellers, but Rhett and Winifred couldn't do what those folks did, and from what Rhett remembered of the act, he didn't want to. Too much yowling and grunting involved. Him and Winifred—well, they were all nicely soft and squishy and quiet in the dark. And yet he and Sam could do what Mam and Pap did, what a stallion and a mare did, but that didn't feel right, and neither of them wanted it. What they had done in the grove had felt right in the moment, if a bit peculiar, but Rhett figured Sam wouldn't be interested in a repeat performance when he was sober, which made Rhett oddly sad.

But did Winifred want to do this again? Would she expect Rhett to visit her wagon at night, and would they speak of it come morning? Was it a regular type thing, or an accident of fate, pulling them together in united hatred and incidental pleasure against a man who didn't see them as people? Worst of all, was Winifred expecting...to be courted?

Rhett shuddered. Lord, but the confusing situation of his body had gotten even more goddamn complicated.

A brief thought surfaced and dove back deep like a fish. If Winifred and Earl had coupled, did that mean it was possible that she was...?

Rhett shook his head against his saddle. Surely not. The coyote-girl had more sense than that.

Didn't she?

CHAPTER
14

They hit the trail at dawn to avoid dealing with Mueller again. Blue had to bray his good-byes, but the wagon canvas didn't stir. For just a second, Rhett wondered if maybe Winifred had managed to hobble over there and slit the man's throat herself. But no. She wouldn't do that to the little girls, who were already stretching and standing sleepily to attend to the camp's chores.

"Roads are more trouble than they're worth," Rhett grumbled.

"But far less likely to end with a horse being shot for snakebite or a broken leg," Dan said cheerfully, only vexing him all the more.

Rhett had watched Dan and Winifred, quiet-like, all morning. Watching Winifred for some sort of sentimental attachment or troublesome expectation, and watching Dan to see if the feller knew what had happened in the wagon last night and might want to break his nose for the transgression. They'd acted completely normal, and he'd therefore done likewise. Now they were on the road like nothing had happened at all, with Sam leading out front on his palomino, Dan and Rhett in the middle, Winifred behind them on Kachina, and Earl in back driving the wagon.

"You been to Lamartine before, ain't you, Sam?" Rhett asked.

Sam nodded, his hips swaying with the saddle. "A while back. It's one of those places that's getting too big for its britches. Townfolk wanted to build a bridge across the Rio de los Brazos de Dios, if you can believe it."

"How far off are we?"

"Hard to tell. A few days, I reckon."

"We might know more if you'd use your bloody gifts to give us a bird's-eye view," Earl shouted from the wagon-box. "Anytime now, you great oaf! Do something useful, aside from nearly getting us all killed, why don't you?"

Rhett tamped down his anger and didn't turn around. "I reckon we should've sold you to Mueller. You two would've gotten along right fine. Cantankerous and demanding."

"Don't needle him," Dan said, quiet-like, riding up beside Rhett. "Can't you tell he's scared?"

"I figured him for angry and annoying."

"We don't always show our true feelings."

Rhett glanced at him, eye slitted against the sun, but Dan didn't seem to be talking about anything else, like Winifred. The feller seemed downright balmy, like always.

"But he's right, Rhett. We'd learn more if you'd transform and check the route ahead, maybe see how close the railroad camp is. We'll continue on the road. And if you're back before dusk, we can return to your lessons with the bow."

With a snort, Rhett shook his head. "I didn't take to it with two eyes, and I reckon I'll be worse with only one. Unless you think they'll let me mosey into a railroad camp carrying a quiver of arrows, I figure I'll save myself the trouble."

"That's the whole point, Rhett. You can mosey in empty-handed and make a bow when you need one. You don't strike me as the kind of person who would turn down a weapon."

Rhett huffed and hopped off his horse, tossing his reins to Dan and stalking off behind the wagon, where nobody could see him. He hated Dan's bow lessons as much as he hated Sam's alphabet lessons, both of which made him feel like a stupid child. He'd ached for that quiet, shared time with Sam, and they'd tried it for two nights before the Muellers showed up, but the letters made no damn sense. Rhett hadn't even managed to write his name in the sand. Sam's kind, patient encouragement made him feel like a bitty baby learning to do something everybody else could already do without a thought. And he didn't want Sam thinking about him like that.

Shucking off his boots, clothes, hat, guns, and eye kerch, he stuffed everything into the door of Winifred's empty wagon, took off at a run, and changed. Soon, he was soaring into the sky, grateful that in this form, nobody tried to talk him into any damn thing. It was good to finally have some silence.

The giant bird landed on clumsy feet, hopping toward the fire with its great curved beak open and screaming. The people sitting there watched it, curious.

"Nobody understands you, you great git," Earl said, waving a hand as if to shoo it away. "Change back."

"What is he?" Sam asked from over by the horses, his hand on his gun as if that would actually do anything useful if the bird proved a threat.

"Not a vulture, apparently," Dan said. "I thought he was a vulture. I haven't seen him this close before, but I've never seen anything like it."

Winifred cocked her head and tossed the bird a strip of deer meat. "Neither have I. He must've come from far away. His people must've."

The bird gobbled up the meat, ducked its head, and hobble-hopped behind the wagon. A short while later, Rhett emerged, fully dressed and feeling more self-conscious than usual.

"You-all got any idea what I am?" he asked, voice rough.

"No, but it's impressive," Winifred answered with a smile that was a little too fond for his taste.

"The camp," Earl urged. "What did you see of it?"

Rhett had to think back, hard. Although he'd gotten better at it, remembering what he saw as a bird was as hard for him now as remembering the point of being human when he was a bird.

"Road goes on into the city, crosses the bridge Sam mentioned, and heads north like it's got business up there. I reckon I saw the railroad near there, but it didn't make sense to me, then. Tracks, sky filled with black smoke, tents, bodies. Horrible smell, and that's coming from a creature that likes its food a week gone. Just a big ol' mess of trouble."

"Well, how long until we get there?"

Rhett scowled at Earl's constant pugnacious, pushy, demanding attitude. "Well, shit, donkey-boy. I didn't check my fine pocket watch while I was a-flying overhead."

Earl jumped up with his hands in fists, and Rhett put a hand on his gun, and Coyote Dan stepped between them.

"Rhett, I made you a bow. Let's go practice." When Earl opened his mouth again, Dan raised a hand. "A couple of days, give or take. Isn't that right, Rhett?"

Rhett shrugged. "Give or take."

"Then come on."

Dan led him away from the road to a clearing with several prickly pears standing sentinel on the prairie. Three arrows sat on a scrap of chewed-up leather that Rhett remembered from all the way back when he'd first met Coyote Dan. The feller always carried it in his mouth when he was in critter form and kept it nearby when he was a human. The arrowheads were knapped stone, just like Rhett had seen Dan shear off before he'd fought the Cannibal Owl. Dan had made a whole pile of sharp rock shards, and Rhett had kept one and slashed the owl's eye wide open with it, just like Delgado had slashed his with a silver bullet. Funny, how those little details came back to a person, much later.

"Do you remember what I said about materials for your bow?"

Rhett scrolled through his memories. "Something orange, something ash. Hellfire, Dan. That was a long time ago."

Dan gave him a lopsided smile. "Rhett, that was barely two months ago."

"Well, it feels like forever."

"Osage orange, cedar, ash, willow, juniper. Hard and flexible, I said." Dan grinned. "Much like you."

"So what's this one?" Rhett inclined his head toward the bow in Dan's hand.

"Juniper. Plentiful around here. Do you remember how to hold it?"

Rhett took the bow and stared at it like it was a live snake. "I remember how to hold a gun."

Dan muttered something under his breath in another language, grabbed an arrow, and moved to stand behind Rhett, arranging his hands in a way that could only ever be awkward between the two of them. Rhett let him, his whole body stiff. No wonder he could never find the way of it, with Dan standing so close to him. With a gun, you didn't need to touch anybody else. Not to learn to shoot, and not to kill.

"There. Do you feel it?"

"Hell no, Dan. It doesn't make a lick of sense to me."

"Now hold out your elbow here, and draw back the string to your cheek, and then release it with one finger."

Rhett tried, and the arrow flew and skittered in the dust.

"Were you even aiming?"

"What the Sam Hill was I supposed to aim for?"

"Anything! Pick a cactus! It doesn't matter what you hit, so long as you decide to hit it and then you do."

Rhett tossed the bow on the ground. "Well, and how am I supposed to aim with only one eye?"

"Idjit," Dan muttered, picking the bow back up and holding it out. "Most folks shoot with an eye closed anyway. Stop letting your self-pity hold the goddamn reins."

Rhett took the bow, but he wasn't happy about it. He was even less happy when he noticed that Dan closed an eye to aim, meaning he was telling the truth about that bit. Rhett's powerful lack of skill had nothing to do with his gone eye.

Dan tried, again and again, to teach him the proper way to hold a bow, to aim, to release, but it was as wrong to Rhett as a dog walking on its hind legs. It didn't come natural, and Rhett had no interest in accommodating things that didn't come natural, and Dan grew increasingly frustrated. And took to hollering at the sky in his own language. The more annoyed Dan got, the more amused Rhett was, and so the whole thing was pretty much a big goddamn waste of time for everybody.

"How am I supposed to teach you to survive if you won't learn?" Dan finally shouted, throwing the bow on the ground.

"How am I supposed to learn if you're teaching me something I don't need to know? You want to help me, you teach me how to read the damn grimoire. Help me figure out what this Trevisan feller is I'm up against. I'm going in blind, and I guaran-damn-tee you that a handmade bow won't be the thing that saves my skin this time." He picked up an arrow and tested the tip on the pad of his thumb. "Or at least teach me how to bang rocks. One of these blades did me good, once."

Dan got himself under control and stared at Rhett like he was an animal nobody'd ever seen before. "For an idjit, you sometimes make sense," he said. "But there's not enough time to teach you how to read. If you think shooting an arrow is hard, wait until you try to spell *receive*." He kicked the ground, but thoughtfully. "And I don't have a supply of the right kind of stone nearby. Thing is, I think you'd be great at shooting, if only you wanted to. If you'd give it a chance. Once you shut your fool self off, nothing can get into your skull. Stubborn as a mule."

Rhett twanged around with the bow but still found the whole damn thing as mystifying and cumbersome as Coyote Dan himself. "Shutting myself off makes sure only the right things get in."

Dan nodded thoughtfully, his expression going dark. "That's a good point, Rhett. Let's try it one more time. I'll help you."

Taking a step away, Rhett said, "Well, I reckon that's all right, Dan. One more bad shot won't teach me nothing."

The coyote-boy's smile was dangerous. "Oh, it might." He held out the bow. "C'mere."

To Rhett's reckoning, he had to take the bow or admit he was, for the moment, more than a bit fearful of his friend. Most of the time, Coyote Dan was an even-tempered man who talked too haughty and too much, but just now, Rhett saw the Dan that lurked underneath that calm shell. This Dan was watchful and carried threat in every line of his body, especially in his coyote-brown eyes. But Rhett would rather die than let Dan know he was worried, so he gave a firm nod and took the bow.

Dan moved around him in his usual way, one arm holding the bow on one side of Rhett and the other holding the arrow. The cage of his body was taut as the bow's string, and Rhett held his breath and tried not to move.

"Pull to here," Dan said, voice low. "Then hold it. See how strong your arm is. Sight along the arrow." His hands left the bow and the juncture of arrow and string, and Rhett held it against his cheek, hoping to stay on whatever good side Dan had.

Something hot pricked through his shirt to his skin, just under his ribs, and Rhett struggled not to show the fear shooting up his spine.

"Now, about my sister," Dan said, cool and low and deadly.

Rhett took a deep breath. So that's what this was about.

"Well, what about your sister, Dan?"

"Be careful in your dealings with her."

Rhett snorted, the blade breaking his skin as he exhaled, not that he showed it. "You worried I'll break her heart?"

"No, idjit. I'm worried she'll break yours. Or that she'll make you forget your mission. If you're mooning about like a calf and sniffing after skirts, then you're not focused on the goal. The Shadow doesn't have time for love, Rhett."

"And who said I loved her?"

The knife bit in and twisted. "You don't. I know you don't. That's the problem. You're both like cats, always holding back and toying with others until you get bored. You'll join and squabble and hiss and join again while the rest of us burn."

Quick as a flash, Rhett spun, dropped the bow, and knocked Dan in the jaw with his elbow, knowing full well the knife would leave yet another damn scar. He looked down to inspect the red-dabbed hole in his shirt as Dan ran his sleeve across a split lip.

"You don't seem to think much of me. Or her."

Dan laughed bitterly and spit a wad of blood into the dirt. "Do you think you're the first one she's called to her side in the night? She'll take her pleasure where she will, on her own terms, with no fuss from me. It's the aftermath with you that I'm worried about. Just trust me on this, Rhett: Move on."

It was a peculiar feeling, knowing that Dan's disapproval just made Rhett want something more. Being told not to do something in such highfalutin, clear terms was mighty compelling.

"I reckon you're not the boss of me," Rhett said. He grinned. "Or her."

"I know that. You think I don't? If there's one thing I know, it's that neither of you does what they're told, much less what I'd personally prefer. But trust me on this: Keep tangling with Winifred, and one way or another, you'll regret it."

Dan's lip had healed by now, and he reached for the bow. As he stood, he slapped Rhett across the cheek with it with a solid *thwap*, drawing a hot line of blood.

"And if you're so keen for blades but won't learn to shoot, just yank off the arrowheads and keep them in your pocket. My gift."

He turned to walk back to camp, shoulders heaving with rage. Rhett leaned down to pick up the arrows. Using his knife, he popped one of the arrowheads off and held it up to the light. "Little small, ain't it?" he called.

Without turning around, Dan shouted, "A man like you can't speak to size."

Rhett colored with rage and nocked an arrow, the movements at least coming smoother without Dan so close and critical. He pushed out his elbow, pulled back the string to his cheek, aimed for the middle of Dan's back, and released. It fell far, far short, damn his single eye.

"I don't need size to stab you in the night," he muttered.

As far as their arguments went, he considered it a draw.

When Rhett got himself under control and returned to camp, everything was as normal as could be expected for three monsters and a man eating charred snake around a smoky fire.

"You all right?" Sam asked with an innocent smile.

"I reckon I'll do," Rhett said. He almost brushed his fingertips over the thin, raised scar where Dan had struck him with the bow. "You got any more of that snake?"

Winifred reached toward the fire and held out a pointed stick with sizzling meat threaded on it. "I saved you the last piece. It's not much, but it's still good," she said.

Rhett gave her a smile he hoped was charming. "Well thank you, darlin'. I'm not a large man by any means, but I suspect this here tidbit is tasty enough to satisfy me."

Coyote Dan growled out a sigh and looked like he wanted to leap across the fire and strangle Rhett with his bare hands, which Rhett found enormously satisfying.

"Did you boys have fun romping about the prairie?" Earl asked, his voice going clipped with impatience. "Was it a pleasant afternoon, then?"

"Not this again," Sam muttered.

Rhett ripped into the meat, letting the juice run down his chin. "Damn, donkey-boy. You were annoying when it was just us, but now you're downright hateful."

Earl hopped up and marched over to where he sat. "Oh, well, and considering that every hour we add to our trip means me brother and friends are losing fingers or possibly their lives, I do get a bit riled up when we stop just after lunch for a party, thank you very much."

"Now, boys. Let's not fight," Dan said, and when Rhett cast him a doubtful and questioning glance, he shook his head and held up his hands. "No, really. We all know the score, and none of us need more scars. We're close. We'll hit the camp in a couple of days. We need to make sure Rhett and I are ready to go in. That means we talk about our plans and discuss weaponry. Now, I'm sorry if you don't like it, but that's how the Rangers do it. An extra hour of sleep or planning can be the difference between a victory and a massacre. Isn't that right, Sam?"

Sam nodded agreeably. "It is, Dan. You boys do what you need to do."

"Now, have you and Winifred been going through the grimoire, trying to figure out what we're up against?"

Earl deflated and sat back down. "Oh, sure, and it's no help. Whatever he is, it ain't in there. But the witch we met recently wasn't in there, neither. Some things . . . well, far as I can figure, lads, some things wish to remain secret."

They went quiet for a moment, chewing that information along with their meat. Rhett swigged from his canteen, grateful for the cool, clear water they'd collected from the stream that morning. Who knew? Next time he refilled it might be with the water of the Brazos in Lamartine, one of the biggest cities in Durango. It made him right itchy, thinking about that many people. Probably thousands, maybe more, and most of 'em wouldn't think much of him on sight. Like Mueller, they'd probably take him for Sam's servant. And he'd do anything for Sam, but he'd never be anybody's servant.

It bothered him, how Dan had brought up love earlier, thrown it in his face. As if Rhett couldn't love. Because sure enough, he loved Sam. Didn't he? Maybe it wasn't what most folks would consider commonplace, but that didn't make it any less true. And if he loved Sam, why had he done what he did with Winifred, and why was he hungry to do it again? Sam had admitted from the start that he could never love Rhett that way, and the only time they'd shared in an intimate fashion had been drunk and drugged and being used as rag dolls of the gods, flopped around in someone else's hands.

He looked at Sam, then at Winifred. A smile arrived, unexpected and unbidden, on his face. Just like everything else in Rhett's life, perhaps this didn't have to be an either/or choice.

"We did find one interesting thing, though," Winifred said, interrupting Rhett's thoughts.

"And what's that?" Rhett asked playfully. He looked up at her with a cocky grin, but his attention was caught by a single black feather, twirling into the fire.

And that's when hell erupted from the sky.

CHAPTER
15

It was hell, and hell was a million birds.

The moment they descended, their caws rent the night in a cloud of black feathers and earsplitting cries. Rhett pulled his hat down to protect his eye, drew his gun, and headed for a collection of boulders he'd pissed behind earlier.

Rough claws plucked at his hat and shirt as he ran. Birds landed on his head and shoulders and back, much heavier than he expected birds to be. One hand on top of his hat and one on his pistol, he fired over his shoulder, the gun aimed up, knocking off the bird that was currently using its beak to tear at his ear. The bird screamed and its weight disappeared, but Rhett didn't feel any blood or splatter. Still, the momentary confusion of his gunshot bought him the time he needed to get behind two boulders and wedge himself in, his ears ringing all the while.

He couldn't see the campfire from his hiding spot, but he hadn't been able to see it from anywhere, not once the birds had attacked. He'd never seen anything like this before—the flock must've been silent in the air, their ink-black feathers merging with the night sky. There'd been no reason to look up.

Rhett's blood told him to charge out, shooting pistols with both hands. But the Ranger in him said that was a great way to shoot all his friends full of holes. And Sam Hennessy, so human and soft and tender, might not be able to survive a single bullet. All Rhett could do was wait until the damn birds returned to their senses and their rightful place in the sky.

Wait.

No.

There was something else he could do.

Something *only* he could do.

Shedding his clothes, he shoved the bundle between the rocks and changed. A few hops outside and he was flying into a flock of angry black birds. Birds much smaller than he was. They cawed, but he squawked, tearing a hole through the swirling flock. Reaching with his huge talons, he grasped, crushed, and dropped fat, feathered bodies. His beak snapped them out of the air. His great wings beat them down, knocking them silly. When he opened his mouth to give what passed as a laugh of triumph, a bird flew right in, and he landed on the ground, tipped back his head, and swallowed it whole.

The flock seemed to thin, but he couldn't see the people who should've been there. Fine. More food for him. Hopping around, he ate as many birds as he could hold, silencing their dying coughs. As he hunted around for something else to kill, the rest of the flock rose as one and swirled off into the clouds like a tornado, silent again but for the susurration of their wings.

Soon the only birds left were on the ground and broken. The giant bird was delighted—at least until a big, flappy human ran out, shouting at him in garbled words. He dropped the last prize and hopped away behind some boulders. A few moments later, Rhett Walker moseyed out with a painfully full and grumbling belly, reloading his pistol and counting heads.

Sam. Winifred. Dan. Earl.

The order in which he looked for his friends did not surprise him.

They were all there and not close to dying, although Dan held a blood-soaked kerchief to the side of his head. Someone had stoked the fire back up, throwing wild shadows on their scratched-up faces.

"You get pecked on, Dan?" Rhett asked, swallowing down a rancid belch.

"Not exactly." Dan pulled the handkerchief away to show that the entire lobe of his right ear was missing.

"Well hellfire. Guess you can finally join the Club of Folks with Missing Parts." Rhett tipped his hat, winked his remaining eye, and bowed sarcastically. As he leaned forward, the roiling in his belly surged violently up his gullet, and he fell to his knees as he vomited a torrent of filth onto the prairie dirt. It hurt more than a vomit usually did, and once he was able to open his eyes, he realized why.

In front of him and splattered over his knees were…things.

Not food.

Not the chewed-up, partially digested bodies of twenty black ravens.

Things.

Rhett wiped his mouth on his sleeve and picked one up as his friends edged closer.

"You okay?" Sam asked.

"He's fine. What are those?" Dan said.

The thing in Rhett's hand was a small ball of black wax stuck through with a feather and coated in slime. As he turned it over, he found a flake of gold, a chip of bone, and an elaborate seal pressed into the slick black goop.

Earl pointed. "BT. Bernard Trevisan. Them fancy letters. That's his seal."

"So he sent the birds," Dan murmured. "But they weren't actually birds."

"Ravens," Winifred added.

Rhett's throat was all scraped up, and the slime around the object was burning his palm, so he dropped it and wiped his hand off on his ruined pants.

"That ain't what I et," he rasped.

Dan had picked up one of the wax balls and now carried it over to the wagon, crawling through the door and digging around within. He returned with the Captain's grimoire and flipped through it by the light of the fire. He'd completely forgotten about his ear, seemed like, and the flesh was already scabbed over and nearly healed. That earlobe wasn't growing back, and it gave serious ol' Coyote Dan a lopsided look that made him slightly more likable.

"You look good with half an ear," Rhett said, hunting around for something to eat to calm his still-angry belly. Winifred flipped open a saddlebag and handed him a sad-looking apple.

"Not a good sign," Dan murmured, running his fingertips over the pages. "It had to be intentional. Marking me. We took no other injuries. They weren't trying to hurt or kill us."

"So?" Rhett asked, biting into his apple.

Dan looked up, annoyed. "So for whatever reason, Trevisan will know me. What the ravens did, they did on his command. He must be a dark shaman. Warlock. I've heard of those who command the dead, but never this kind of magic. Turning an object into a..."

"Messenger?" Winifred asked.

"Minion," Earl muttered.

"But why birds?" Rhett chewed the apple, considering. "Why not folks with guns?"

Dan sighed heavily. "Birds travel fast and silently through the air. No one expects a flock to bring danger. Their large numbers confused us. They must be scouts for him."

"Then why'd they go after you in particular?"

Meeting Rhett's glare, Dan carefully set the book down. "Because while everyone else dove for cover, I sheltered my sister with my body. She couldn't run, so I stayed in the open and didn't move, even when I felt the creature biting through my ear. Perhaps if you'd been more heroic, you'd be missing more parts, too." He gave an ingratiating smile. "Except not you, of course, Rhett. Because no one can sense that you're a monster unless you wear the witch's powder. You haven't taken it lately, so it's worn off. The ravens didn't even trouble you, did they?"

"There was a bird tugging on my ear, but I shot it off." Rhett scratched the back of his head and looked away. "Once I turned into a bird and started eating 'em, they didn't really have a chance."

"One went for my ear, but I turned into a donkey and ran." Earl sniffed. "Never said I was a hero."

"I was under the wagon. Hellfire, Winifred, I'm sorry I wasn't looking out for you." Sam sounded so sorrowful and hangdog that it just about broke Rhett's heart.

Winifred gave him a kind smile. "Kill some fresh meat tomorrow, and we'll call it even. I don't need three men jumping on top of me. One was bad enough."

That lightened the tension, and Earl put on his shirt and started setting the camp to rights. Sam, ever glad to be useful, made a torch out of a stick and a rag and pulled out his knife as he set out in the dark. That boy would come back with something to eat or die trying, Rhett figured. That left only the coyotes and himself sitting around the campfire, which made him itch inside his skin, even if Winifred had thus far never acted, in word or deed, as if she remembered their time in the wagon.

"There's a page in here on warlocks and witches, but it doesn't describe what happened tonight," Dan said. He held out the book to Rhett, pointing to an old-fashioned-looking feller in a long black dress holding a dead cat by the tail. "This Trevisan is something different. But at least we know now that magic is involved. Might make him easier to kill."

"Might make him harder to kill, too," Rhett added.

"The point is, tonight changes things."

"It sure as hell does. I'll never look at a raven kindly again."

Dan shook his head. "No, fool." He pointed at his ear. "I can't go into camp with you now. Earl said Trevisan wanted monsters, and the birds must be sent out to find them. They tried for Winifred's and Earl's ears, but they got mine. Anyone who works for Trevisan and sees a notched ear doesn't even have to ask. They just drag you away to the camp."

Rhett nodded slowly. "They marked you. They already know Earl. They wouldn't want Sam. You protected Winifred from them. So you're right. It's just me."

"Then why are you grinning like a fool?"

Rhett was, he realized, doing just that. "Because that's how I always wanted it to be," he said. "Just me in the railroad camp. Just me and Trevisan. Just the Shadow doing what the Shadow does best. Nobody else getting tortured or cut on or hurt."

"I've got a bad feeling about this," Dan groaned.

"You always do, but it always ends up fine."

Dan flicked his mangled ear with one hand and pointed at Rhett's eye with the other.

"Does it, though?"

Rhett just grinned wider.

Sam brought back a fat rattlesnake, and they ate it with singed fingers before it was cooked all the way. Rhett's belly felt like it had been scrubbed out with rocks, and he almost transformed into the great bird to take advantage of its iron stomach. He didn't, though. The sinking feeling whenever he thought about what had happened tonight—that was shame. He hadn't thought to protect anyone else; he'd simply gotten the hell away and taken his revenge as a brainless animal. It didn't help that Earl had made the same choice. Rhett didn't much respect the donkey-boy, outside of his enduring stubbornness. No, he'd rather be like Sam, owning up to and repenting for his damn sins. Now he wished he'd brought Winifred a dead thing, too.

Dan ate his share and stood. Staring down at the pile of wax balls and feathers, his lips twitched. Finally, he picked one up, carried it away from the fire, picked up a big rock, and dropped it on the thing, turning his face away like it might explode.

Nothing exciting happened. He picked up the rock, and Rhett moseyed over to stare at the pile of dust, bone, gold, and ruined wax.

"We should destroy them all," Dan said. "In case he can track them or reawaken them." Scooping up the trash, he threw it in the fire, where it burned as readily as anything else.

With a nod, Rhett delivered the wax balls to Dan, who crushed them one by one with his rock until they were useless trash. As the pile of dross built, Rhett scooped up what he could and dropped it in the fire. The scent of burnt feathers rose, the fire turning a peculiar green and sparking mightily.

"Goddamn magic," Rhett muttered.

"Goddamn magic indeed," Dan said.

Soon all evidence of the ravens was gone, the wax and feathers burned up and Rhett's belly almost back to normal. Even the gold went in the fire.

"Now that that's done, you're agreeing we're close now, yes? Hence the birds?" Earl said, standing over the fire with his hands on his hips. He'd already taken off his boots and pants, which meant he was ready to sleep. It was something, how accustomed Rhett had gotten to the wee man's peculiarities. But of course he couldn't let everyone go to rest until he'd unleashed his cantankerousness on them.

"We're close," Dan agreed. "And even closer to the Lamartine Outpost of the Durango Rangers, which will be our first stop."

Earl looked like his eyeballs might explode, and Dan held up a hand.

"You asked the Rangers for help, and we're Rangers, and Captain Haskell's got even more Rangers. In the best possible world, Haskell would shut down Trevisan right then, no questions asked." He paused and met everyone's eyes, one by one. "But this is not the best possible world, and we all know Haskell's not going to help."

"But the Captain told us to stop there, so we're duty bound to do that," Sam added.

"Right." Dan gave Sam a nod of thanks. "And then we'll head for the railroad. Once we can see the smoke, it's probably best if we pick a hidden camp and send Rhett on alone so Trevisan and his men won't be suspicious. I'd stick with the road, if I were Rhett, to make myself seem stupid and innocent."

Rhett snorted. "If you were Rhett, then horses would walk on their hind legs and wear high collars and go to church on Sundays."

"He's right, Rhett. If you sneak up sideways, they'll never trust you," Sam said. "I, uh, worked in a railroad camp. In charge of a work crew. Not for long. It was awful. But they watch you careful, if they think you're not dumb as a post."

"Act dumb," Rhett said. "I don't know how that's rightly possible, but I can try."

"Not dumb, you great fool. Ignorant. I'm not dumb," Earl said, turning as red as his shirt.

Rhett held in his laugh. "Says the man who isn't wearing britches."

Dan stepped between them. "Both of you are being foolish. Save your anger and energy for Trevisan."

The moment boiled for a time before Rhett shrugged. "Well, considering I won't punch a donkey, I might as well concede."

"Well, and I don't punch women," Earl snapped.

Then Rhett dove for him, and they tussled on the ground like goddamn puppies, elbows and fists flying everywhere. Dan and Sam pulled them apart, and Rhett allowed himself one moment to savor the feeling of Sam's chest tight against his back, the man's breath against his cheek.

"It ain't worth it, Rhett," Sam said.

"That ain't the point."

Rhett relaxed, and Sam let him go. Dan likewise set Earl back down on the ground. Rhett drew himself up tall and straightened his shirt and eye kerchief. Earl spat in the fire and stormed off, muttering to himself in another language.

"Exciting night, ain't it?" Rhett said. "Reckon I could take a piss." He wandered away to do just that while he waited for his hands to stop shaking.

The fight hadn't meant anything—Rhett didn't really want to hurt Earl, and he knew Earl didn't really want to hurt him, either. Not much, at least. They were just letting off steam, as fellers often did. And yet his body and feelings didn't seem to agree on that topic. For a long while, he sat on a boulder, counting the heartbeats in the hollowed-out place where his eye used to be until his blood had slowed the hell down.

When he returned, putting unusual effort into his mosey, Sam had laid out his bedroll as usual and brought Rhett's things as well, laying them out side by side. Rhett sat down and tipped his hat in thanks.

"Glad that damn Mueller feller is gone," Sam said with a grin.

"Being attacked by ghost birds is nicer than talking to an asshole," Rhett agreed.

When Sam lay back on his saddle with his hat over his eyes, Winifred dusted off her leg stump and made an inquiring-type noise at her brother. Dan helped her into her wagon and laid out his blanket on the other side of the fire. Earl, thankfully, had already turned into a donkey and was snoring peacefully. Rhett copied Sam, lying on his back and staring at the cloudy sky, considering.

"You asleep, Sam?" he whispered, all hopeful for a comforting-type conversation.

The only answer was gentle snores. Rhett was thinking about nudging Sam when another voice called to him from the darkness.

"I'm awake."

His eye twitched toward the violet-blue wagon waiting in the scant moonlight like something out of a fairy story. A hand appeared through a hole in the canvas and beckoned.

"Are you now, coyote-girl?" he whispered.

Tomorrow, he'd head out on the road alone to face a warlock. Tonight, he'd take comfort where he could.

He got up, walked to the open wagon door, and crawled inside.

CHAPTER
16

It was a regular morning, if regular meant that everything was goddamn peculiar. Rhett woke up before everybody else, so disgusted with the funk of his body that he launched into bird form and flew lazy circles until he found a creek worth bathing in. He told himself it was because he would hopefully be meeting Trevisan's railroad soon and didn't want to smell like a whoremonger, but the look Winifred gave him when he returned with water droplets caught in his shorn hair was bemused and accusatory.

"Feel better, Rhett?" she asked.

"I felt fine to start out with," he growled.

"Well, you smell just as fresh and clean as a daisy."

He tossed a jackrabbit into her lap, where it landed with a sick and boneless thump. "Don't say I never did nothin' for you." Before she could say anything else cunning, he left to see to the horses.

Sam was there, of course, his first smile as bright as the morning.

"Sleep well, Rhett?"

Guilty flashes of Winifred's bare skin in dappled lantern light assaulted Rhett's memory, but he just gave Sam the best smile he could muster. "I reckon I did. Wasn't attacked by birds or feisty redheaded men, so it was an improvement."

Just then, Rhett realized that Sam had been brushing Ragdoll to a shine, as much as an ugly appaloosa with a bottlebrush tail could shine. Ragdoll looked pretty pleased about it, at least, one leg cocked and ears perked up.

Rhett inclined his head to the currycomb in Sam's hand. "You get bored? Or has she been nuzzling up to you, makin' eyes?"

Sam blushed. "Oh, well, you know how it is. You're going off on your own soon. Wanted you to present well. Can't have you riding off on a dusty mare, can we?"

But Rhett noticed that Sam had groomed Puddin' and Blue, too. The mule was asleep, his long lips hanging loose and his ears all cattywampus.

"That's mighty thoughtful of you, Sam."

"Wish I could go with you. You need somebody to have your back. Don't know what you'll be up against in that railroad camp. At least we'll all be together when we ride up to the Ranger outpost today."

Oh, shit. Rhett had entirely forgotten that part.

He was just fine with riding into servitude in a hard labor camp run by a mysterious warlock, but he was so against the concept of talking to Captain Eugene Haskell of the Lamartine Outpost of Durango Rangers that he'd mostly managed to forget that was part of their quest. Again. Perhaps Dan was right about how he had a habit of shutting down when he didn't like what he was hearing.

"Maybe I could skip that part and just head on up to the railroad," Rhett said. "We don't really need the Rangers."

Sam's eyes went big and panicked. "We do, though, Rhett. You ride into another Ranger's territory without setting up your bona fides, you're likely to get court-martialed. Or shot. It's part of the code. It's how we keep from stepping on one another's toes out in the wild."

"Haskell's not going to help us, Sam. It's useless."

Sam took to nervously currying Kachina's flank. "I don't reckon anybody ever thought Haskell would help you. Help us. But we've got to give him our report. Tell him we're on the Captain's business. Or else the Captain gets in trouble, see? And the Rangers need our Captain. He's one of the good ones."

Rhett gulped behind his kerchief. "Well, how close are we then?"

"Real close, as far as I can reckon," Sam said. "Outpost is on this road, near Lamartine. We're passing by it whether we want to or not."

"Not," Rhett muttered. "Definitely not."

Sure enough, they found the Rangers just after noon. The outpost was hard to miss, as there was a weathered wooden sign out front, right where a dirt-rut trail ran off the main road.

"Durango Rangers, Lamartine Outpost," Sam read, mightily slowly. "Haskell's Rascals. Major Eugene Haskell presiding. Half doller per Injun scalp."

"I like him already," Winifred said.

Dan's jaw worked with rage. "You and Earl are staying here."

Winifred snorted a laugh. "What, so he won't scalp me?"

"So I won't have to kill him when he insults you."

Rhett expected Winifred to have something to say about that, but she just nodded and walked Kachina around behind the wagon, and that's how he knew things were serious.

"So we're going in with one and a half Injuns, then?" Rhett said. "Why, that's seventy-five cents."

"We're going in with three proven, badge-wearing Durango Rangers," Sam said. "Even Haskell can't bring us harm." He spit on his thumb and rubbed it over his badge, and Rhett and Dan did the same.

"You got your papers, Rhett?" Dan asked.

Rhett poked around in his saddlebag and pulled out the packet from the Captain. He'd hoped to make some progress learning his letters on this trip, but after those two frustrating sessions, he'd been too busy fighting, flying, and...spending time in Winifred's wagon. Still, he could point to his name, at least.

Rhett Walker.

And it was time for Rhett Walker, Ranger Scout, to speak man-to-man with his nearest superior.

"Let's go," he said, pitching his voice low.

Sam led on his palomino with Rhett on Puddin' next and Dan on one of his too-dull-to-tell-apart chestnut geldings. A cabin with a long porch and a row of shiny glass windows perched on the trail like a monster waiting to gobble them all up. It was so similar to the Las Moras Outpost, and yet to Rhett's eye, it radiated menace.

"Don't get scalped," Winifred called behind them, but not too loud.

At that, an unholy racket started up, and all three horses spooked as a hell of a big black dog burst out from around the side of the cabin. Rhett had his gun out and ready, but the thing hit the end of its rope and stopped. The barking and growling didn't let up, and the horses didn't stop dancing and gnawing their bits, but since it was tethered out of biting reach, Rhett didn't have to shoot it, at least.

Well, and no wonder it was so damn loud. It had three heads, all of them built like a shovel and packed with teeth.

"You'll have to forgive Ol' Debil. He don't take kindly to strangers."

The voice came from behind them, and Rhett felt like he'd fallen for the oldest trick in the book. He spun his horse around and found a mean-looking man in a beat-to-hell gray uniform standing there with a shotgun over his shoulder and his finger on the trigger.

Before Rhett could say something that got them all shot, Dan said, "We're on business from the Las Moras Outpost, here to see Captain Haskell."

"I don't speak Injun," the man said, spitting a glob of tobacco on the chestnut gelding's hoof and making the horse dance back. "You're in Rascal country now."

"If you spoke Ranger, you might've understood me," Dan said. He sounded calm and wry, but Rhett knew him well enough to note the tension in his jaw and the hand on his knife.

The man ignored him and turned to Sam. "You don't keep a tidy company," he observed with a shit-eating grin.

Sam looked down on the man with a sneer. "Well, I ain't the Captain, and I ain't in charge. We're of equal footing, as all Rangers under a Captain are. Now, would you be so kind as to take us to Captain Haskell?"

The man snorted and walked around them toward the cabin. "Major Haskell. Figure I have to take you around, seeing as how we're all Rangers together. Of equal footing." He shook his head. "You boys from out west got low standards, is all I'm saying."

They followed him on horseback, and Rhett didn't take his hand off his gun. The dog had stopped barking to lick its biscuits, at least, and no other rude sons-of-bitches showed up to give any lip. The man led them to a water trough, within which lounged a feller in a fine hat, only his head above the water, smoking a cigar.

"And who the hell is disturbing my cogitationals?" the man barked. Under the hat, he had a wide, gnarled face like a knot of old wood and a mustache as thick as a horse brush. Rhett immediately disliked him, but that was more about the look of disdain and disgust than the man's lack of appealing features.

"We're on business from the Las Moras Outpost," Sam started, but the man held up a hand.

"Don't much care for your Captain, then," he said. "Tell me your business and get the hell out of my territory."

Rhett reached into his saddlebags for his papers and heard guns drawn behind him.

"Easy, boy," Haskell said. "Wouldn't want you to get accidentally shot full of holes."

"This one's a monster, Major."

Rhett looked down to find a beanpole of a white boy close enough to kick in the teeth. But the scout wasn't looking at Rhett; he was focusing on Coyote Dan. And at his words, the guns cocked.

"You can see my badge plain enough," Dan said, failing entirely to hold up his hands or show any weakness. "All our badges."

"Badges can be stolened or sold. Road agents, outlaws. I'll need real proof."

"Considering my guns are on my hips, it should be clear I'm reaching back in my bag for my papers," Rhett said. "Unless anyone objects to paper?"

"Get on with it," Haskell muttered, the cigar clenched between his teeth.

Rhett slowly fetched out the packet of papers and nudged his horse forward, close enough to lean over and hand the Captain—no, the Major?—his papers. Haskell took them in a wet hand and scanned whatever he saw there. Rhett winced as he noted water from the man's hand carelessly bleeding the ink in places.

"Fine. So you're apparently who you say you are. What is it you're hoping to gain by coming here? Because I make it well known I don't take on Injuns or..." He stared Rhett up and down and held out his papers. "Whatever the hell you are."

"We're here scouting—" Sam started, but Rhett stopped him with a cough.

He'd just noticed something right peculiar as he took back the papers. There was a heavy gold ring on the Major's fat ring finger with a design that would've meant nothing to him just a few short days ago. But Rhett didn't need his letters to recognize the seal of Bernard Trevisan, exactly the same initials as the image pressed into the black wax balls, albeit now backward.

Sam looked to him, and Rhett said, "We're here trailing a Sasquatch, but it looks like he cut north. We just wanted to stop in and pay our dues before we left. Wanted to make sure you didn't feel we'd trespassed if you heard tell of us later."

Everyone stared at him.

"So we'll be going now. Headed north for a bit and then back home. Thanks kindly for your time. Fellers?"

With a tip of his hat, Rhett turned Puddin' and rode back around the cabin, his spine straight and his hand off his gun but damn anxious to return to it. After a few moments of awkward silence, Dan and Sam caught up at a trot. Rhett waited for one of the fools to open his goddamn mouth, but they apparently knew him well enough now to trust that he wouldn't do something that cowardly and stupid unless he had a good reason.

"You turn on around and go home. And tell that milksop Walker to keep his boys out of my territory," Haskell shouted in their wake. "And tell that woman of yours out front that if she can't walk, she's welcome to work for us lying down."

He and his men burst into rude laughter, and not turning around and murdering everybody was possibly the hardest thing Rhett had ever done. He'd had trouble getting over killing his first human, but he reckoned there'd be no guilt attached to ridding the world of this vile bunch.

"You holding up, Dan?" Rhett asked.

"Long as I don't turn around and see their faces, I hope so."

"Just for the record," Sam added, "I got your backs if you should decide in that direction."

Rhett kicked his horse into a trot, then a lope back to the road. Ol' Debil barked like crazy and strained at his rope, and the guards and sentries who'd been watching them stepped briefly out of the brush to nod their smug satisfaction at the hurried leave-taking. Earl and Winifred were parked a bit away and began turning around as soon as Dan twirled a finger in the air. As much as Rhett hated the road, he was damn glad to see it and even more glad to be headed back south on it. For a moment, he let himself pretend they were truly headed back to Las Moras and the Captain and the simple everyday pleasure of getting on Jiddy's nerves. The burly scout was a snoot, but he would be a welcome sight after Haskell's Rascals and their bastard of a leader.

"How'd it go?" Winifred asked, riding up on Kachina. "And why—"

"We'll tell you later," Dan snapped. "For now, let's see how fast that new pony of yours can go." He kicked his chestnut into a canter, and Winifred whooped and urged her paint to join him.

"And what about all these ponies?" Earl asked, gesturing to the string of horses and mules tied up to his wagon. "I can't keep up with that sort of a gallop, never mind that they're going the wrong—"

"They're going damn fast," Rhett finished for him. "You just keep on going yourself, fast as you think's safe. Me and Sam'll stay with you. We got to get back home to Las Moras and report to the Captain." He gave Earl a significant look and hoped for once the feller would prove smarter than a pile of bricks. "And we got to hurry."

Earl's eyes narrowed, and he clicked his tongue at the horses and shook their traces. "Oh, to be sure. Let's hurry home."

They rode for half an hour before they caught up with Dan and Winifred, who sat companionably as their lathered horses drank from a pretty little pond.

"We safe here?" Rhett asked.

Dan nodded. "I reckon so. Unless you were followed?"

Rhett spit. "Hell, no. They think we're idiots headed home. Why would they bother to follow us? No need to send those fine, upstanding fellers after us when we've been put in our place and swept out the door. Not when there's bathing to do in the horse trough."

Dan snorted, then started shaking, then started full-on laughing. Rhett had never seen him do so before, and it was downright contagious. Soon they were all laughing like fools, even if they didn't know why. It fell off to chuckles, and Rhett rubbed a hand over his laugh-sore belly.

"You gonna tell us what happened back there now?" Sam asked. "Because that wasn't what was supposed to happen. It wasn't going well, but..."

"But the Shadow sensed something," Dan finished for him, back to owl-like solemnity.

"Hellfire, Dan. The Shadow didn't sense shit. I saw Haskell's ring when I gave him my papers. It's gold, and it's got the same letters on it as those wax balls I yarked up. Bernard Trevisan's letters. So I reckon him and Haskell..."

"Are in league together," Sam said. "Damn, Rhett. It's lucky you saw that and got us out of there before we mentioned it."

Dan nodded thoughtfully. "There's sense in it. Dastardly sense, but sense. Only thing Haskell hates more than monsters is Injuns, and he probably isn't a big fan of any color other than white. Trevisan comes through and puts the monsters all in chains, works 'em to death. That's a lot less work for Haskell, but he looks like he's cleaned up his territory. Like he's keeping his cities safe."

"I reckon that's why they kept calling him Major," Sam said. "He must've gotten promoted."

"Well I'm just glad such an upright feller's in charge," Rhett said. "Makes me downright pleased to be in Lamartine." He looked around. "Or just outside it, since there's no thoroughfare full of wagons hereabouts."

"Time is wasting," Earl snapped. "Let's get on with it. On to the railroad. Stop skulking around in the road."

Dan shook his head. "We're off the road now. We can't pass the outpost again or go through Lamartine. We'll have to travel north and head the railroad off."

Rhett's eye was drawn to the sky, which was currently blue and wide as all get-out. With no buttes or mountains, there was nothing to hold it all in. It made him feel breathless and strange, that the sky could be so big and he was just a tiny thing under it, trying to do his tiny work. Far off, across the pond and near the edge of the world, he saw a black line. Smoke, coiling into the air.

"I reckon we found the railroad," he said, pointing.

"Now we just need to get there in one piece," Earl snapped.

CHAPTER 17

It felt good, to be off that goddamn road. No more Muellers. No more chance of something worse than Muellers. No three-headed dogs. No hateful Rangers, hopefully. Just a tolerable handful of familiar folks and horses, striking out across the prairie.

They made it across the stream, wagon and all, and the grassland spread out before them, less prickly and lumpy than what Rhett was used to, first in Gloomy Bluebird and then up throughout the Captain's range. Blue sky everywhere, green underfoot. His blood was zipping through his veins, his spirits high.

"Hey, Sam," he said.

"Yeah, Rhett?"

"I'll race you to that tree!"

With a whoop and a holler, Rhett yanked off his hat, kicked Puddin', and streaked across the prairie. Sam followed suit on his leggy palomino, and soon they were neck and neck, the horses putting their heads down once they realized it was a race. Fat little Puddin' wasn't as fat as he'd been, his gut made lean by the road. Rhett had never ridden him like this before, and the black-and-white mustang had a hell of a dead run, sure-footed and flat and smooth. Sam's horse almost seemed to dance, his long legs stretching like swans' necks. Rhett again felt that peace, that joy that only came at full tilt on horseback when he rode for the feeling of flying. Once, he'd raced like this back home and wondered what it would be like to be a bird.

Now he knew.

He liked this better.

Not only because bird thoughts were tiresome and mostly involved eating rotten carcasses, but also and mostly because he could share this moment with Samuel Hennessy.

They passed by the tree at the exact same time with another whoop and let the horses slow of their own accord.

"That's some mighty fine riding, other Hennessy," Rhett said, a little out of breath himself.

"That fat pony of yours has some heart," Sam responded. His cheeks were red and their time in the sun had browned his skin and lightened his hair, making his blue eyes all the brighter. Rhett's heart could've burst with his feelings for this good-hearted cowpoke, but they were getting along so well as it was, and it wasn't worth risking such a beautiful moment to say something dumb and have everything go all cattywampus again.

"And your palomino's legs haven't snapped like toothpicks, so I reckon he can hold his own."

Hoofbeats pounded toward them, breaking the calm as Winifred rode up on Kachina, the girl's hair streaming behind her and the horse's elegant neck stretched long.

"Third in the race. That's what I get for starting late," she said, wearing a radiant smile. At times like these, Rhett completely forgot that she was missing a foot and had to be in near-constant pain. She trotted her mare in a circle and slowed.

Looking from one to the other, her eyebrow went up. "Am I interrupting something?"

"Hell, no, coyote-girl. Just enjoying the day."

Winifred laughed lightly. "I bet you are. The day is so much more cheerful than the night."

Rhett's smile went flat. Winifred was bad about giving him sly looks around Sam, and he always carried the worry that she would say something, whether about Rhett's continued feelings for Sam or, more recently, their time spent in the dark wagon together, figuring things out with fumbling fingers. Was it... could it possibly be that the girl was jealous?

No. That was just plain ridiculous.

But Dan had warned Rhett about her, and Rhett didn't want Dan to be right.

Rhett let Puddin's head go so the paint could graze a little. This area was pretty and green, and as he looked beyond, out toward the column of black smoke, it only got greener.

"I reckon there's a stream down there," he said, pointing at a lush ribbon of trees. "Maybe an offshoot of the Brazos. Might be a good place for you-all to make camp."

Sam looked, too, and nodded. "Close enough to ride there within a day but far enough away where they wouldn't find us. Normal enough for folks to camp out next to a stream. Durango's still a free country, ain't it?"

"Depends on who you ask," Rhett muttered. "But the plan seems sound. Winifred, why don't you ride back and direct the wagon to follow us? Me and Sam'll scout ahead. Make sure there's no ambushes lying in wait."

Winifred's eyes danced with mischief and amusement. "Yeah, you'd better check all those bushes real good, Rhett. Keep us all safe from something in the bush."

Wheeling her pretty mare with a laugh, she loped back the way they'd come.

"Women make no goddamn sense," Sam muttered.

Rhett waited for him to say something like, "Present company excluded," but he didn't, which made Rhett so happy he could jig. Whatever Sam had thought about him when he first found out what Rhett was, he'd apparently come to terms with what Rhett had decided to be.

"Let's go on, then," Rhett said. "Find a nice place for a camp. Maybe hunt up something edible that ain't a snake."

"I like the way you think, other Hennessy." Sam beamed and nudged his horse forward.

For once, Rhett didn't mind following someone else's lead.

It was a good day. Sam got a white-tailed deer, and Rhett took down a strange, fat bird that was horribly ugly but promisingly meaty. They found a sunny little clearing by the stream and set about cleaning their game, collecting firewood, and generally being manly and useful. They didn't talk much. They didn't need to. Working side by side on a beautiful day was pleasant enough, even if a feller was up to his elbows in deer guts.

By the time the wagon bumped in with a herd of bugling horses and mules strung out behind it, Rhett was about as close as he got to relaxed. Meat was strung up and cooking over the fire, and Sam had headed off for a quick bath. Rhett had wanted to accompany him for various reasons but knew well enough that such was not a task to which men invited themselves. For his part, Rhett had used that time to transform, take to the air, and quickly scan the land around their camp, just to be sure there was nothing dangerous nearby and to gauge how close they were to Trevisan's railroad. It was closer than he would've guessed, but headed in a direction that wouldn't bring anyone within hailing or viewing distance of the camp, and out here, travelers were a regular-enough thing.

The railroad itself was a daunting beast of a venture. Even in bird form, Rhett knew not to fly so close as to attract undue attention. They still hadn't figured out what sort of bird he was, but he was unusual enough as to arouse suspicion.

A long way out in front were wagons and tiny figures with sticks. Then came fellers with shovels and axes, making the way even. There were carts and mules and machines laboring up and down the path. At one point, he flew high over a group of figures that scattered quickly, right before a little hill exploded. The bird squawked and climbed higher, wheeling on. Then came the tracks for miles and miles, scurrying with sweaty laborers. And at long last he found the train itself, a metal snake belching black smoke and carrying its own wood and metal and coal, the whole thing surrounded by a city of tents and a clutter of clapboard buildings. The last car of the train stood out as peculiar, clean and shiny while everything else was coated in powder and muck. It made no sense to the bird, but when Rhett returned to camp, landed, and changed, it made perfect sense to him. That was Trevisan's car, the one where fingers and toes disappeared. Fellers, too.

He relayed all this information to his posse as they ate around the fire, well after dark. Rhett had been gone much longer than he'd planned. Earl was twitchy as hell, his eyes darting in the direction that made them all uneasy.

"So we need to discuss the plan," Dan started, licking the meat juice off his fingers.

"I thought we already had a plan," Rhett answered. "I go in and kill Trevisan."

Earl snorted, and Dan gave his lopsided smile that meant he figured Rhett for an idjit.

"It's not that simple. It never is. You need to talk to the people already in the camp and find out more about how Trevisan's magic works. Find out if he has any weaknesses. You need to talk to the sawbones who might know how to heal Winifred's foot. And you need to do all that while making Trevisan and his men think you're a fool and never letting them see you as a bird. When you have a firm grasp of Trevisan's true nature, you let us know your plan. And then we strike."

"I don't want you-all involved," Rhett muttered, his eyes shooting to Sam.

Sweet, easily killed Sam. As easily killed as Monty.

"You do," Dan started, but Winifred interrupted.

"Rhett, did you ever try to pull the queen out of an ant nest?"

"What the Sam Hill do ants have to do with this?"

She grinned darkly. "Ants are peaceable creatures, mostly. But if you go for their young or their queen, they all join together to attack you blindly. Warlocks can be like that, too. Their magic is what powers their lair. We already know Trevisan can command ravens. What if he has traps or other powers? What if he can command bigger creatures, too?"

"Then I'll kill them."

"What if they're monsters who don't want to die?" Dan said.

"Then I'll just keep killing. It's what I do."

Winifred shook her head mockingly. "It's what you do until someone else turns you to sand. You lost your eye last time, but there's plenty still to take."

At the mention of his missing eye, the damn thing began to itch horribly. He wouldn't let himself reach under the kerch to worry at it.

"Fine. If you're all agreed that I need to shake hands like a damn mayor before I get on with the killing, then I reckon that's what I'll do. Any more hellfire rules?"

"You need to change clothes," Dan said.

Rhett sat up straight, affronted and furious that they might suggest he go into the camp in Prospera's old skirts. "Why the hell would I need to do that?"

"Because if he can see by using the birds, then he might not recognize your face, but he might recognize your hat and shirt." Dan held up a hand. "Just switch with me. If you're worried I'll taint you, we can go wash everything out in the creek first."

And it made sense, to be sure, but Rhett mightily hated the thought of wearing another feller's clothes when he had his own. He was comfortable as he was, and he'd spent most of his life previous in various forms of discomfort, so he wasn't much ready to change his ways.

"I'll switch hats with you, Rhett," Sam said, holding out his oiled leather hat. "I ain't got nits, if you're worried."

Shyly, Rhett pulled off his own hat and handed it to Sam. "I ain't got nits, either, other Hennessy, and thank you kindly." Sam's hat felt strange on his head, not at all molded to his shape by sun and sweat, as his own was. But it smelled deeply of Sam, as personal as tasting a feller's breath, and he took undue interest in watching Sam put on his own beat-up hat and wiggle it around until it sat right.

"Now, if you don't mind a bit of sweat, let's go change clothes," Dan said, standing up and dusting off his britches. Rhett stood, too, glad at least that his courses were over and he'd since washed his pants. That was one shame he'd prefer to keep completely secret. Just because Dan knew it happened didn't mean he needed a reminder.

They set off for a couple of trees, and Dan inclined his head for Rhett to head behind the biggest one. Rhett shot him the sort of glare the lead mare gives an uppity stallion before putting two hoof-shaped indentations in his belly, but he went behind the indicated tree and hurriedly tossed Dan his faded red shirt and britches. Before he was done, Dan had tossed back his own pile of clothes, and Rhett dove into that old blue shirt like nobody's business. At least he still had his chest wrapped tightly—no reason for him to give that up.

Rhett expected Dan's shirt to feel peculiar—crispy, maybe, or stretched out across the shoulders, as Dan was a stockier man than he was. But it fit about like any shirt did, and the pants were maybe even softer, and Rhett slipped his arms through Dan's suspenders and buckled on his own gun belt and stepped into his boots and reasoned that maybe tomorrow wouldn't be so horrible.

Well, except for the part where he walked into a railroad camp run by a bone-stealing warlock.

Dan was sitting at the fire and eating more meat as Rhett moseyed back out, his buffalo coat over his arm. Sam and Winifred both stopped whatever they'd been doing to take his measure.

Sam smiled like the Fourth of July. "You look right fine, man."

"Blue suits you." Winifred's smile was altogether too knowing for Rhett's taste.

"So what else do I need to know?" Rhett asked, ducking his head to cover his blush.

Earl leaned back and stroked his bristly orange chin. "Well, for one, whatever group you're put in, you'd best get in good with the leader. Me brother Shaun's with the Irish, so if you get lumped in with my people, he'll have your back. The Afri-kan fellers won't like you much, but the Injuns might. Feller in charge of them is by all accounts fairer than most. Wherever you go, do your best to fit in. You need protection from your own or you'll get abused, see?"

Rhett considered it. "Find some big feller and make nice. Got it."

Earl's sigh was meant to sound patient but failed utterly. "You can't just rush at Trevisan with a rock the moment you're in his camp, lad. Much as I hate to say it, you've got to get the lay of the land."

"What would happen if I did rush at him with a rock, though?"

"Well, I once saw a lad run at Trevisan with a railroad spike in his hand as a weapon. Trevisan pays his bosses well and gives favors to workers who prove useful. The lad with the spike was shortly a pile of sand, and the crew that killed him had whisky and double helpings at dinner. But also remember you're supposed to be excited at a new job opportunity. You're not supposed to be scared, at first. Most of the lads who arrive will be acting like Trevisan might be their savior, hat in hands and all. Like the sun shines out of his fancy-britch ass. The pay is rumored to be good. So do your best to act inferior and hopeful."

"Unlikely, but I'll try."

Earl cleared his throat and twitched his fingers into and out of fists like he still aimed for a fight but was trying to hold back. His voice had a deadly, sweet calm about it. "Listen, then. You'll catch on to the rhythms of the camp fast enough. You won't be in irons, but there are sharp-eyed, well-trained scouts on top of the cars and stationed at intervals along the outside of the camp. Men with long-shot rifles and men with repeater pistols. They won't aim for your heart, though. They'll go for your legs and try to take you back alive. That's when the chains come in, see?"

"So how'd you escape, if it's so goddamn impossible?"

For once, Earl's face went hard and tough. "Didn't say it was easy, did I? All the Irish were in on it. Saw two of me mates get turned to sand. I took a bullet in the ass, another in me back leg. Only thing that saved me is how awkward it is to shoot a

226

donkey. And that I kept running even when they screamed for me to stop." Standing in a huff, Earl stomped over to the horses and rummaged about until he found the last bottle of Buck's wine. He pulled the cork out with his teeth and drank deeply, the red liquid running down his chin like blood.

"I'll have my guns," Rhett started, but Earl waved a hand.

"Like hell you will. You think you can walk into a labor camp and keep your bloody weapons? No, fool. They take them away. For your own good, they say. To keep everyone safe. But nobody ever gets to leave, so nobody ever gets 'em back." He drank again and shook his head. "If you value something, best not take it in at all."

Rhett's hand went for the leather pouch that hung at his belt. The objects within might seem useless to another person, but he'd been collecting them since before he was really aware he was doing it. Since killing that first stranger with a piece of Pap's twig fence, he'd added weight to the small bag: vampire teeth, his first earned coin, the silver bullet that had taken his eye, a little curly feather from his own bird body. The thought of handing it over to some other feller and possibly never seeing it again pained him mightily. He untied the strings and handed it to Winifred, who'd taken care to bring it down from the Cannibal Owl's lair. She accepted it with a solemn nod, not even a smirk.

His gun belt was just as hard to take off. He stood, unbuckled it, and handed it over to Sam, who'd kept it safe during the Lobo attack. Sam, too, nodded. Rhett's Bowie knife and pocket watch went to Dan, just so the feller wouldn't feel left out. Standing there, wearing nothing but his clothes and boots, Rhett felt nekkid and light as an eggshell.

"Well, I reckon that's it, then." Rhett rocked back on his heels.

"I've been thinking," Dan started. "We have the surgeon's kit. What if you go in saying you've worked with a sawbones? Then you'd maybe get close to the feller who does the doctoring."

"Grandpa Z," Earl said. "And he already has an assistant. His granddaughter, Cora."

Rhett scoffed. "But I don't know shit about doctoring. And what the Sam Hill kinda Chine name is Cora?"

Earl just about choked on his meat, spit out a wad of fat, and pointed at Rhett from across the fire. "It's always something else with you, isn't it? What, you think I had time to stop and ask her while they put me under to fix up me damn toe stumps? You think we had acres of time to take tea and discuss why our mams named us stupid things? I know no more of the Chine than you do of the Irish, so you can stop it with the rude little comments."

"Rude?" Rhett's hand went to where his gun should've been. "You calling me rude, donkey-boy?"

"Come on, now, Rhett," Sam said, standing and putting a hand on his arm. "Tensions are high, but there's no use to fighting."

"No. No, Sam. I want to know why. Why Earl thinks he can talk to me like I'm a child or an idjit and not the only person in the goddamn territory who can go into this godforsaken devil camp and save his brother? Isn't that the whole reason why you're here, Earl O'Bannon?"

Earl launched to his feet, his hands in fists. "Oh, it is, lad, to be sure, but I don't think you're the right man for the job. I've no faith in you! How could I? I expected the celebrated Durango Rangers, world-renowned fighters of monsters! Strong, determined men with a good moral compass. I imagined them hearing my plea and riding off into the sunset, a hundred brave lads with guns a-blazing, dead set on doing what's right! I never dreamed in all my life that I'd end up here in the bloody desert, camped close enough to almost hear me old friends and me brother singing their sadness. But now here I am, supposed to have faith that some mixed-up, hot-blooded vulture-girl can go in and save them all. What kind of fool do you take me for?"

"A pretty damn big one!" Rhett launched himself at Earl, but Dan tripped him, and Sam still had his arm in a strong grip. All he managed to do was stumble in the dust and feel the rage burn up the back of his neck, along with embarrassment.

"Earl," Dan said, soft and deadly. "In your haste to lash out, I think you struck some unnecessary targets. Rhett is the Shadow. He's a legend. He's the right man for the job. And if you don't believe that, if you're not willing to have some faith in that, then walk away from this campfire and don't come into my sight again or I'll shoot you myself, because you're insulting all of us who stand with him."

Sam let go of Rhett's biceps, crossed his arms, and nodded. "That's right."

"If anyone can defeat the warlock, it's Rhett," Winifred added.

Rhett lifted his chin, feeling like a million damn dollars. "Like it or not, I'm all we've got."

"I don't like it, but I'll shut me trap. Worst thing that happens is you die and leave me in peace, eh?" He tipped the bottle at Rhett like a toast and drank again.

Rhett sat back down and cocked his head, watching Earl. "We got along fine for a while there, didn't we? What's got you so riled against me? What'd I ever do to you?"

Earl sat back down, too, seeming half his size again now that his anger had drained. "You're hard to get along with, harder still with more folks around. You know that, right?" Rhett

CHAPTER
18

Rhett had done some dumb things in the past, but this might've been the dumbest one. To avoid the simple truth that pretty much everyone already knew, and to save himself the pain of meeting Sam Hennessy's eyes, he'd walked off into the darkness, alone and unarmed. He didn't even have a horse under him. All he had was a goddamn sawbones kit, which at least meant that if he had to cut something out of his own stupid skin, he probably could. Not that he'd need to sew himself up, considering his skin could just squish back together. When he recalled what it had been like, not so long ago, sewing Mam's ripped nightgown or darning Pap's threadbare sock, knowing he'd be beaten whether he did a good job or not, he still would've chosen to be here, now, walking toward his doom in the cloudy night.

It didn't pay to show up somewhere new after dark. Folks were right jumpy, their trigger fingers sleepy or well lubricated. A man hunting a job would arrive in the morning. Better to find some quiet place to curl up and sleep as best he could until the sun was up. Never had he missed his saddle and blanket more. Hell, even Winifred's wagon and knowing smile would've been welcome. More than welcome, truth be told. He licked his lips, feeling oddly thirsty for something that wasn't water. Why'd Earl have to go and open his fool mouth, anyway? Everything was easier when Sam just kept on not knowing the truth of things, walking like a fool off a cliff, blind to the tomfoolery happening around him.

For just one moment there, Rhett had considered telling Earl what he remembered of their night in Buck's orchard. Of the red-haired man servicing Winifred Coyote from the back like a horse, wine dripping down his throat and onto her honey-gold skin. Earl had been rough, crazed, drunk. He wouldn't know how to please that girl, how to move softly in the darkness and urge her to quieted screams behind his hand. Rhett himself hadn't known, just a few days ago. But now he did. And he wouldn't have minded throwing it in Earl's face. But he didn't want to hurt Winifred, and he didn't want Sam to know it had happened, and that if he had any say, it would happen again. But he wasn't sorry for it, neither.

Dan had warned Rhett away from Winifred for Rhett's sake, but if Rhett left off, it would be for Sam and Sam alone. Complicated as his feelings had been back in the Cannibal Owl's cave, cradled against Winifred's nekkid chest, it was pretty easy to figure out his feelings once he was sliding around in the wagon with her. And that was: good. It felt damn good. Even if it didn't mean anything.

Especially because it didn't mean anything.

And yet part of why he was doing this, walking off alone without proper farewells, was to save her the trouble of losing her brother, who would still try to join Rhett if he could. If Rhett ran off alone, nobody else had to get hurt. Nobody else had to lose anything. And what did Rhett have to lose, himself? Not a damn thing. It was better, this way.

Looking up at the clouds, he figured he might as well stop here as anywhere else. Worst thing he could do, really, would be to stumble into the railroad camp and take a lucky shot to the chest from a drunk feller. This part of Durango was unfamiliar and strange to him, with altogether too much green and not nearly enough mountains and crags and tablelands. Rhett was accustomed to orange. Orange dust, orange rocks, orange sunsets. But here, the trees were taller than him, and some of the damn things had actual leaves. He'd wandered away from the stream, angrily walking in the direction where he knew the railroad camp lay, following the tug behind his belly button, but he had no way of knowing where he was compared to where it was, distance-wise.

And, yes, he'd half hoped Sam would come barreling after him and drag him back to the campfire. But...Sam had done no such thing. Probably because he was too disgusted by what his friend had been doing with his other friend while he slept innocently a few paces away.

"Hellfire," Rhett muttered.

He felt lost in every way.

With mountains, a man knew where he stood. There was something to put your back against, with a mountain. Out here, it was just piddly trees, and they all looked alike. Rhett tried sitting with his back against one and then another, but they were both equally uncomfortable. And the ground was almost...wet.

"I hate trees," he told them.

The trees did not respond, so Rhett kept walking. Finally, he just found a pillow-sized rock and flopped down on his back.

"This place is too horrible for rattlers," he told the clouds. "No nice, comfortable caves. No flat, sun-warmed boulders.

Just…" He dug his hand into the ground and pulled it up. "Dirt. Sandy dirt. To hell with Lamartine and to hell with Major Eugene Haskell and to hell with Earl Donkey Boy O'Bannon."

But even cussing all the malcontents on his list didn't make him feel better. Finally, sick of himself and his current situation, he stripped, turned into a bird, fluffed his feathers, and went to sleep on a pile of his own clothes, blessedly free of such sticky things as thoughts and feelings and especially guilt.

The bird startled awake and leaped to its taloned feet, beak already open in readiness. Just out of striking range sat a thing. The bird's brain said DANGEROUS and then it said NOT EDIBLE and then it said GODDAMN COYOTE DAN.

The thing dropped the leather bundle in its mouth, became a man, and purposefully turned his back to the bird. In response, the bird turned back into Rhett Walker and stood. Rhett yanked his shirt—well, Dan's blue shirt—over his head, glad it covered him down to his knees.

"Come to wish me well, Dan?" he said.

"When you stormed off, you forgot the witch's powder. Without it, Trevisan's camp won't see you for a monster and hire you." Dan held out a small pouch quite similar to the one in which Rhett had previously carried his treasures.

Rhett took it, hefting the weight and feeling the contents squish within.

"The book said nothing of it, so I don't know what it is or the best way to use it, but it seemed to work, whatever you did last time. Winifred made the pouch in our tribe's traditional way, so if you say it carries your mother's ashes, anyone familiar with our people will neither question you nor take it away."

"And if they ain't familiar with your ways?"

"Then you do your best to act upset and sad and like taking it away would break your heart and make you a bad worker with a bigger grudge than usual."

Rhett pulled open the drawstring on the bag. The powder inside did look like fine ashes. He pressed the tip of his pinky in it and looked up at Dan. "Anything?"

Dan cocked his head. "No."

With a shrug, Rhett touched the tip of his pinky to his tongue and swallowed the grit of the fine powder, which tasted nothing like ashes. When he looked up again, Dan smiled and nodded.

"That eye is something else."

"Guess having one only makes me half as ugly, huh?"

Dan sighed that sigh that said he was right consternated. "Rhett, you are the Shadow. You're meant to be deadly, not beautiful."

"Don't mince words, friend." Rhett slipped the bag's leather tie around his neck, turning away so Dan wouldn't see how much that smarted. "Thanks for the ugly powder, I guess."

"I didn't take you for the vain type."

"Well, maybe I am. Maybe you don't know what type I am."

"I've been watching you for a long time. I have a good sense of what type you are. And my sister must like the look of you enough."

Rhett snorted at that. "I reckon one person feels about the same as another when you're lonely in the dark."

"Then you haven't touched many people."

Turning his back, Rhett stepped into his britches, pulled on his socks and boots. For now, the shirt hid his chest, and he wouldn't let Dan witness the personal process of wrapping it down with the long sheet of muslin balled in his fist.

"Why do you always got to be throwing such things in my face? No, Dan, I haven't much felt a kind touch in my young years."

"Winifred knows who you are. What you are. She welcomes the feel of you."

"She might be thinking about somebody else."

Even Rhett could feel the twinge of hurt in those words, a sentiment he'd taken pains to keep to himself.

Dan gave a small chuckle. "Whose name does she call when you touch her?"

"I don't know, Dan. I don't speak your language."

The morning air trembled, and Rhett didn't look up.

"The word she says is *Shadow*, Rhett. She knows well enough who she's touching."

Rhett could only nod at the gently spoken words, his throat working as he tried to swallow down that knowledge. He'd wondered—hell, he'd worried. But now relief flooded him. He didn't love Winifred, and he didn't want Winifred to love him, not like that. He knew that much. But he still cared for her and he still wanted to be wanted for himself, to know that he wasn't being used randomly, just a pile of skin and clever, calloused fingers.

"Well, I reckon I knew that," he said.

When he looked up, Dan was grinning. "Oh, I figured you did."

"So I got my powder..." Rhett turned to stare at the black smoke already riding the morning breeze. "Reckon I should go."

"We need to discuss communication," Dan started.

"I prefer it when you don't talk at all."

At that, Dan laughed for real. "I know. But if you get into a tight spot, you might wish to call for reinforcements."

"Haskell's not going to help. You know that."

"I do. But you've got three friends who are decent shots, two of whom are hard to kill."

"And the donkey could probably kick somebody in a tender place."

"Possibly."

"You hate him, too?"

Dan smiled. "He's rude, Rhett. Why must everyone be so rude?"

Rhett gave a rare chuckle. "Let's hear your plan, then, while we're agreeing on things. But keep it quick. I got to piss."

"I'll follow you today—in coyote form," he added before Rhett could protest. "We'll find a lonely spot between scouts, maybe near the privy. If you have a problem, you find three big stones and build a little house, like this." Dan scrabbled around until he'd found three flattish stones and stacked them, two on the bottom and one on top. "That's the signal. You hit the latrine the next day, and I'll try to get close enough to talk. If it's really bad, so bad you need us to come riding in with our guns out, you stack two rocks on top." He added another rock. "And if, for some reason, you can't get far enough away to do that, just find a way to make this symbol. Use a stick to scratch it in the dirt, or carve it onto a tree. That work for you?"

"I reckon it will," Rhett said, swearing he'd never make that symbol for any reason.

Dan held out his hand. "Then good luck, my friend."

"You keep 'em all safe while I'm gone, Dan."

Rhett shook his hand, enjoying the manly punishment of their mutually squeezing grip. Then he nodded, picked up the doctor's bag, kicked over the pile of stones, and headed out.

He'd never let Dan know it, but hearing the coyote trot along behind him was almost like walking with a good friend. He liked Dan just fine when the feller couldn't talk.

237

The smell and the noise came all at once, and Rhett understood well enough when Dan made a sad, whining noise.

"Shit and smoke," Rhett murmured. "It's gonna be a pleasure of a time."

They were in what was left of a forest that had been logged within an inch of its life. Nothing bigger around than Rhett's wrist was left, the stumps of the bigger trees squatting sadly among their plucky lessers. The smaller trees clacked together in the early autumn wind, their still-green leaves rustling and dropping every so often to the ground like they were in a fight to see who could die first. The birds were mostly gone, and Rhett longed for the heavy tug of his gun belt around his hips.

A louder yip caught Rhett's attention, and he turned to find Dan sitting by an especially large stump, his tail tucked and his ears back. He nudged the stump with his nose and stared hard at Rhett with those uncanny eyes. Rhett noticed that a big chunk of the coyote's ear was missing.

"Sure. This forest. That stump. Or any stump nearby. A pile of little rocks. I got it."

Dan glared for a moment more.

"I said I got it!" Rhett flapped his hand, but Dan didn't budge. The coyote tilted his head sideways and slowly and deliberately closed his left eye.

Rhett almost laughed, it looked so comical. Then he realized what Dan was trying to tell him. "Oh, more powder. Good point. You win that one, Dan." The coyote nodded and let his tongue flap out, and Rhett reached into the bag around his neck and touched a dab to his tongue. "You think more, maybe? Just to be sure?" The coyote nodded. "Fine. Fine. Now git!" And Dan shook his coyote head, his clipped ear flapping, and ran off.

For the first time since he'd leaped off a mountain and become a senseless bird, back before Earl, Rhett was wholly alone, and it was both a relief and a curse. He'd learned, since leaving Mam and Pap, that being alone could be a hell of a pleasant thing, with no responsibilities and no getting beaten for not upholding them. But he'd also grown accustomed to the pleasant feel of living among a group of men—and Winifred, damn her. The joshing, the insults, the jostling and thumps on the back, the burps and farts and spitting and roughhousing to let off steam. Most keenly, though, he missed the feeling of knowing he was surrounded by fighting men, men bristling with guns and knives, ready to back a feller up, even when they didn't know or like him that well.

Rhett reckoned that where he was going, he'd have a hard time finding a group that would accept him as readily as Monty and the Double TK Ranch or the Captain and his Rangers. Still, he was going to walk in like he wanted to be there, so he wrapped his chest tightly in muslin armor, picked up the doctor's bag, lowered his shoulders, stuck out his chin and headed for the ruckus like he couldn't wait to get to work.

As he emerged from what was left of the woods, he tried to puzzle out what he was seeing. Even though he'd flown over this very spot, he'd somehow been expecting a railroad and an orderly line of men hammering at it. He'd thought a train was a couple of big boxes with wheels rolling around. What he wasn't expecting was an entire goddamn town, one bustling with activity and enough people to make him downright twitchy. There were tents everywhere, the canvas stained with mud and muck. Pigs and horses and chickens were corralled or roaming around or tied up, and men of all colors and types did work that Rhett found mystifying. The scents of manure and burning coal and unhappy flesh all crowded together like bad stew under brewing storm clouds.

"You lost?" a man asked.

Rhett looked up, unsure whether to smile or frown. He'd been told that his smiles could look more like he was about to bite somebody, the first time he met them. The feller in question was mostly white under a face full of dirt and soot, his clothes likewise stained the color of wet ashes. The disgust on his face suggested he was hoping Rhett was, in fact, lost, and the man could beat him to a pulp and steal whatever goods he had on him.

"Just looking for work," he said, making his eye hard and his voice rough.

The man stuck a thumb toward a row of tents.

"See Griswold. Tent says *Foreman*." The man made like he would spit but didn't. "Don't got no letters, do you? Can you count, at least? Third tent from the left." Shaking his head, he walked off. Rhett couldn't help noticing the man wore no weapons, which struck him as downright pitiful. If a white man couldn't carry his guns, what was the point of being white?

Rhett's boots squelched in mud as he walked toward the tent the man had indicated. There was something a little like a road, although it was beat to hell and half made of manure. The tent openings facing it were mostly closed, but the third one was tied open with lettering above it. Inside, a surly-looking old dwarf sat at a small desk, and Rhett walked toward him, preparing his speech.

"Hey, lad! There's a line!"

Well, hellfire. Rhett hadn't noticed the group of slightly cleaner men lined up along the thoroughfare.

"Sorry," he muttered, going to stand in back.

The men ahead of him grumbled, all white and mostly Irish, from the sound of it. Like a whole crew of Earls, which was just too much for Rhett.

"Any of you fellers know a Shaunie O'Bannon?" he asked.

"Piss right off," one said.

He was quieter after that.

As Rhett waited, he tried to put his finger on what was so peculiar about the camp, and then it hit him: It was all one big belly wobble. He hadn't really noticed it as he approached because it was so all-encompassing—like walking in fog. Every man here was a monster of some sort. It didn't pay to look strange men in the eyes, but he suspected that doing so would reveal rectangular pupils like Earl's and all sorts of other strange eyeballs that were anything but human. And when they looked at him, thanks to Prospera's powder, they'd see one red-and-yellow bird eye, sharp and canny. They might not like him, but in a way, he was one of them. A monster. The feeling was both comforting and scary.

If they really didn't like him, they knew exactly how to kill him.

And he likewise knew where to aim if he wanted them dead, but he had neither guns nor knives, and stout twigs were hard to come by when the forest had been stripped bare. For all of his strength as the Shadow, Rhett felt downright vulnerable. And he didn't like it.

The noise of the camp was something, too. Sounded like they had a whole herd of blacksmiths, and about a million pickaxes. Horses whinnied and water sloshed and men hollered and somewhere, up ahead, a group of men sang a bawdy song together about some lady who was going to feed them dinner, the words breathless and chanted in time with their work. The line seemed to go on for hours, the hot sun beating down and the stink rising up off the mud. Rhett took a step forward, from time to time, but it all blurred together.

Too damn much, it was, rubbing up against his elbows.

"Son!"

Rhett looked up. The old dwarf at the little table was staring at him, one hand out.

"What's it take, an invitation from the queen?"

"Sorry," Rhett said as he hurried into the tent and sat on the low stool, feeling it sink into the muck under his weight.

"Sorry, *sir*," the feller said. "You here for work, boy?"

"Yes, sir." The word tasted like poison, but Rhett said it, and he didn't even sneer.

"What's your name?"

Rhett had to swallow before he answered. They hadn't discussed this part. But since Haskell knew the last name he'd traveled under, and since his first alias was probably wanted for murder back west...

"Ned Hennessy."

The dwarf raised a bushy eyebrow. "You don't look like a Ned."

"If I ever find my daddy's grave, I'll dig him up and tell him that."

Barking a laugh, the dwarf scribbled in a book. "You worked in a camp before, Ned?"

The dwarf wore Confederate gray and had an accent much like Sam's. Same as the people of Burlesville, he was short and stocky and bald as an egg, his long beard tucked into his jacket to keep it out of the muck. His pince-nez had slid down his sweaty nose, and his eyes were hard and gray.

"No, sir. Worked under a sawbones." Rhett held up the bag. "Brought his kit."

"And what happened to your sawbones?"

"Lobos got him. He was human. I couldn't save him."

"How'd you escape?"

It was Rhett's turn to raise an eyebrow. "By being harder to kill."

"What are your skills?"

Rhett sighed. "Breaking broncs. Good with horses. Can help a sawbones. Got a strong stomach for that sort of thing."

"Let me rephrase that, son. Can you swing a pickax?"

"I don't mind hard work. But my true talents are—"

"Mr. Trevisan don't run a talent show. He's building a railroad. And you're not white. So the best you can hope for is to be the sort of strong, silent type who can follow directions and keep working."

Rhett nodded. "I reckon I can do that."

The dwarf wrote something on a slip of paper and handed it to Rhett. "Your walking boss is Mr. Shelton. You can start on the cut line after lunch. First, you'll report to the physical evaluation tent. You take a right and head all the way down the thoroughfare, and you'll see it."

"What the hell's a physical evaluation tent?" Rhett asked.

The dwarf put a finger to the side of his nose and winked. "You'll see, Ned. You'll see."

CHAPTER
— 19 —

Outside the tent, Rhett couldn't help but feel like he'd been swindled somehow. The only other job interviews he'd experienced had involved breaking a bronc and surviving Delgado's beans, but he would've preferred either activity to visiting whatever the hell a physical evaluation tent was.

The clouds were pressing down, the air wet with men's sweat and the ground even worse. Rhett slogged down the knee-deep mud and filth of the thoroughfare, marveling at how different it was from the dusty thoroughfare of Gloomy Bluebird, which was too dry for even a tumbleweed, most days. As he watched, a feller flopped out his pizzle and added to a puddle under a rogue cow, and Rhett kept his face a mask as he walked on. For all the different folks he'd met thus far, with their different customs, he didn't find much to recommend a railroad camp.

The same group of Irish lads from the foreman's line had made an identical line outside a large tent planted directly against the last car of the train. Rhett instantly recognized it from Earl's descriptions and his own scouting: This was Trevisan's lair. The damn thing was pitch-black and slick as a wet horse with that godforsakenly fancy BT business painted on it in gold and bone white. It made Rhett's skin crawl, really. The car, from what he could see, had no windows at all, and the tent before it loomed large like a flapping maw. For no reason he could reckon, Rhett did not want to go in that tent. But he would, anyway, so he got in line to wait, using his time to make a mental map of the filthy little city.

All the while, men went into the tent, and they didn't come back out. That would've worried Rhett, except that...well, it's not like they were killing fellers in there. The railroad needed workers—they'd said that even in Gloomy Bluebird. Then, they'd spoken of the Yerba Buena railroad stretching from the west coast out to the Messourita River. But it was the same for any railroad, even if other companies treated their men like men instead of animals. Tracks didn't lay themselves. And he wasn't hearing screams. And that meant that there had to be another door to the tent besides the front one, which made damn sense, because a tent wasn't even made of wood, was it?

Man after man went in. These fellers couldn't have known what they were truly facing, as they were relaxed and joshing, if annoyed by the wait. Rhett couldn't pick up much of what they said to each other, between their accents and some foreign words the likes of which he'd heard Earl muttering or singing to himself from time to time. No man stood behind him in line, and nobody talked to him, either. Which was just as well, as Rhett was right jumpy and unpleasant of temperament when he wasn't sure what he was walking into.

"Next," someone called.

Ducking under the flap, Rhett stepped into the tent, squinting his eye against the brighter lights within. The room had several lamps, all centered around a nasty-looking chair with straps on the arms and footrests.

"Welcome to Trevisan Railroad Holdings. Your paper?" The voice was fancified and bored.

There were three fellers waiting, staring at Rhett. One was tall and broader than Bill the Sasquatch and a hell of a lot meaner looking—he had his arms crossed over his all-black suit and wore a hungry smile, and there's no way those fancified words could've come out of those bullet-like teeth. This had to be Trevisan's second in command, Adolphus.

The feller to his side was smaller and scrappy-looking with off-putting eyes, a bright yellowish green with black knives for pupils. He had his hands up like he was getting ready for a gunfight, even though he wore no guns, and Rhett had never seen a feller who looked like him, with gold skin and straight ink-black hair. The third feller was the scariest one, though. For one thing, he was the fanciest dresser Rhett had ever seen, even fancier than Boss Kimble at the Double TK, and far less likely to have eaten half a chicken with his bare hands while riding a horse.

The man was of middling height and weight, but he was pale as a milk-white stone, with ice-blue eyes and white-gold hair slicked back and curling up over his high collar. His outfit only made him look paler, considering it was all in shades of black and pink. Rhett didn't know much about fashion, especially not about what folks chose to parade about in back east or in Europa, but he figured this feller knew and deeply cared. Even his black boots were polished like mirrors.

It had to be Trevisan.

"Paper," he said again, but not in an angry way. Like he was so patient that snow wouldn't melt on his tongue.

Rhett nodded and handed over the slip that Griswold the dwarf had given him. The man took it in pink-gloved hands, stretching it and tilting his head to read it.

"Ned Hennessy. Tell me, Ned. Which do you favor—your hands or your feet?"

"I'm right fond of them all, actually."

"But which do you use more?"

"Well, a man's gotta walk, I reckon. Am I hired?"

"Have a seat," the man said.

Rhett didn't want to have a damn seat, but they didn't give him a chance to protest. They moved like a machine, the big one grabbing Rhett around the chest and the smaller one capturing his ankles as they forced him into the chair and strapped down his arms and legs. Rhett fought as hard as he could, but there wasn't a goddamn thing he could do. His doctor's bag had fallen to the ground, where everyone ignored it.

"Are you healthy, Ned?"

"I was until you strapped me into this chair. Now I'm feeling a bit shifty."

"Do you have the cough? Are you costive? Have you ever had fainting spells?"

"No to all."

Well, and so what if he'd fainted a little when Delgado had shot him full of lead and silver and the harpies had carried him to the Cannibal Owl's lair? That didn't count. A man with that much metal in him was bound to get sleepy.

The man in the gloves—Trevisan—knocked off Rhett's hat and pulled back his eye kerch and gently tugged his skin this way and that, looking in his nose and ears and even forcing Rhett's mouth open by pinching his cheeks. Rhett had never felt so violated and furious, which was saying a lot, and it had been a long time since he'd felt so helpless. Tied down, with the other men grinning on, there was nothing he could do but thrash and growl at the unwelcome investigation.

"What are you, Ned?"

Goddamn the man for his calm, silvery voice and his strange accent.

"I'm angry is what I am. Did I pass my physical evaluation or not?"

The gloved hand slapped his cheek in warning—not so hard as to make a bruise, though.

"No, Ned. What's your magic? I know you have it, and you know I have need of it in my camp, or else you wouldn't be here."

"I was just told you needed bodies and paid a good wage."

"Then you're a terribly unlucky fellow, aren't you? What do you become?"

"Well, when people slap me around, I turn into a—"

He was going to say *asshole*, but the hand was poised to slap him again, and the tension in that goddamn pink glove told Rhett it would hurt a lot more this time.

"I turn into an animal. Not the sort that can build a railroad, so I don't see how that's important, but there you have it."

"What kind of animal?" That voice, cold as the snow Rhett had never felt.

Rhett swallowed hard and looked away. "Big bird. Don't know what kind."

The man nodded and smiled, serene as a churchman. "That explains the eye. Vulture?"

"No."

"How interesting. We'll have to test it and find out."

Rhett's heart jumped into his throat. "Oh, well, now, that's a private thing, ain't it? You don't need to watch that. I can just...go behind a screen, or..."

The man looked down at Rhett's bound hands and feet as if to remind him. The big feller snickered. The smaller feller put his hands on Rhett's boots as if to remove them.

Before they could start stripping him, Rhett did a stupid thing, a thing he'd never done before. Reaching deep inside, he

pulled that golden cord and turned himself inside out, into...
whatever he was. The bird surfaced furious, tangled in a pile of
fabric and screeching. Its eye met that of the man with the pink
gloves, and then he was Rhett again, his clothes a mess but still
mostly on. His chest wrap was a wreck, but the shirt was roomy,
so he just wriggled down deeper into his pants and pulled his
eye kerch and hat into place, wishing his boots hadn't fallen to
the floor and glad to be out of the restraints.

Of course, the next thing that happened was that they
strapped him right back down.

Trevisan leaned closer, his face alight with happiness. He put
the cold palm of his glove against Rhett's cheek, and it was
everything Rhett could do not to turn away in disgust.

"You are a lammergeier," the man said softly. "The lambhawk. My first one. A fierce bird from Afrika and the Caucasus. In Persia, they call you Homa, and to be touched by
your shadow is good luck. Eating your meat is forbidden. A
fortunate creature. One of your parents was from Afrika, yes?"
Whatever went over Rhett's face as he learned this news told
the man what he needed to know. "Poor creature. Both the
orphan lamb and the lambhawk, aren't you? We'll give you
work. Idle hands are the devil's playthings, are they not?"

"Work would be good," Rhett said, hating the shakiness of
his voice. "I was told I'd be on the cut line after lunch?"

The man pulled a glittering silver pocket watch from his
pink waistcoat, popped it open, and snapped it closed.

"Ah, well, that will depend on Grandpa Z, won't it? And
how good of a patient you are."

Rhett nodded. "Real good. Good enough to unbuckle me,
I reckon."

The man smiled, and it was like being caught in a tornado
of ice. "You will call me sir, but to you I will be a god. I'm

Bernard Trevisan, and this is my railroad. And you said feet, didn't you?"

"Feet?"

"Feet, *sir*," said the big man as his hands clamped down on Rhett's shoulders.

Panic shot through Rhett like a rabbit writhing in a snare as the smaller man caught his knees in an iron grip. Mr. Trevisan—Mr. Trevisan, by God—knelt at Rhett's feet like he was worshipping at a pew. He yanked Rhett's right sock off with the tips of his gloved fingers and reached for something that made a sloshing noise. Too late, Rhett recognized that part of the warm heat of the tent and the sweat on his brow was a cauldron of water boiling over a brazier.

As Rhett opened his mouth to holler his fool head off, the big man slid a leather-wrapped stick between his teeth.

"Best bite hard, friend," he said, but not like he meant the friend part.

Hot liquid gushed over Rhett's foot, and he growled wordless screams around the leather, his toes clutching painfully together. Something cool sloshed over them next, a welcome respite, and the scent of red wine filled the room, reminding him so much of Buck's drink that his head swam a little.

"This little piggy went to the market," Trevisan said, wiggling Rhett's big toe. "Did they teach you that rhyme, where you grew up?"

Rhett's head thrashed back and forth.

"And this little piggy stayed at home." Trevisan wiggled Rhett's second toe. "This little piggy had bread and butter." He wiggled the third toe, and Rhett's skin crawled as he realized what was about to happen, what Earl had told him would happen. But Earl, that goddamn bastard donkey, had not said *when* it would happen, because then Rhett might not've walked into camp like a goddamn fool. Earl had described it like a punishment, not an initiation.

Trevisan wiggled Rhett's fourth toe. "This little piggy had none. I suppose you have had none, too, have you not, Ned? Very skinny. Don't you think, Adolphus?"

"Pretty skinny, sir," the big man agreed.

"And this little piggy," Trevisan said, his fingers delicately grasping Rhett's little toe, pinky up as if he held the handle of a dainty teacup, "went *wee wee wee*, all the way home. Good-bye, little piggy!" With terrifying gentleness, the man cupped Rhett's wine-wet foot, slid a midnight-black stone knife against his little toe, and sliced it clean off into his waiting hand.

Rhett made himself a liar by passing the hell out.

The next thing he knew, he was in someone's arms and swaying. He squinched his eye shut and tried to ignore the raging pain in his toe and act asleep, or maybe dead—at least until he understood what was going on. The light was different, and cold rain splattered and sluiced down his skin, soaking his clothes. So he was outside the tent, back in the thoroughfare. Slumped against Adolphus's chest, the hard thing was not yarking all over the feller, who smelled like he'd sewed himself into his drawers a year ago and wouldn't emerge for a bath until next year. The man said nothing, and Rhett forced himself to remain limp. His toe stump throbbed in a peculiar-type way, and he realized that was his heartbeat.

Thump-thump. Thump-thump.

How the hell did Winifred live with it?

Well, by reaching out to feel something of her own choice, maybe.

Canvas scraped his face as the light went dark.

"Last one today, Z," Adolphus said. "Here's his belongings. If there's something you can use in the doctor's bag, big boss says it's yours."

The only response was a grunt, but the grunt managed to say quite a bit about how put upon it was and how it was damn sick of doing whatever it did and that stolen leftovers in a black bag wasn't about to make up for it.

With more care than Rhett would've expected, Adolphus transferred him to a rough, narrow cot with a scant pillow for his head. The sound of canvas flapping shut told him Adolphus was gone. A few seconds later, he opened his eye just the tiniest fraction.

This tent smelled much better than the last one, although it was likewise moist with boiling things. Herbs hung from the ceiling, giving off a fresh, hay-like scent. A squat old woman with a long gray braid, a funny hat, and a floor-length green dress edged in yellow stood with her back to Rhett across the tent, working at a table—probably the source of the grunt. In a low, rushed voice, it spoke, but not in a woman's voice and not in any language Rhett could reckon. Someone spoke back in a younger, softer voice, and soon a boy dressed in gray was popping open the Captain's doctor's bag, his back to Rhett and his black hair in a stubby ponytail. Rhett mightily wanted to shout at him or punch him in the snoot for rudeness, but he reckoned he'd learn more if he pretended to be asleep.

The boy pulled out the needles, the thread, and the leather roll of instruments, gabbling at the older man in triumph. The old man grunted again and nodded, and the boy disappeared, probably to squirrel away his find.

When the old man spoke again, it was more of a bark, and there was some urgency to it. Soon they stood, the old man behind Rhett and holding down his shoulders as Adolphus had, and the young man kneeling at Rhett's feet. When Rhett dared another glance through his lashes, he realized it wasn't a boy at all—it was a girl in boy's clothing. She had golden skin and black hair like the smaller feller who worked for Trevisan. Her eyes were strange and hypnotizing, like blue-green skies sparked with lightning and an angry black sun in the center, the pupils deep as hatchet marks. But the twist of her fine lips—well, that was something altogether different. She was looking at him the same way he looked at a particularly fine horse that needed breaking, as if she were the only one who could do the job right.

Tenderly, she wiped Rhett's toe with something cold and soothing that had a sharp smell, and his foot twitched without him meaning it to. The old man barked again, and the girl did something he couldn't quite see with his toe and muttered in a clear, sweet voice, "Yap yap. Like a dog. I know, Grandfather. I know. He'll be awake soon. I'm hurrying."

When she looked up again, her eyes met Rhett's only eye. She knew he was awake. The tiniest smile almost gave her a dimple. Almost.

Rhett's eye slammed shut. Almost.

But he had to watch what she was doing, because he understood now that this had to be Grandpa Z, and this was his granddaughter Cora, and they were about to seal his lopped-off toe. This was the magic he needed as much as he needed Trevisan to die. This was the way to help Winifred live a normal life without pain. So he watched through his eyelashes, ignoring his own agony and buzzing with more excitement than he cared to contemplate to discover their secret. Earl had been asleep every time he'd lost a limb, but Rhett was awake and watching avidly.

The girl shoved her hair out of her eyes, briefly holding a finger over her lips. Then she looked down and took a deep breath. When she breathed out again, hot air billowed over Rhett's foot, and he smelled…smoke? Cora's delicate fingers were cold, though, and as he watched, they grew bright orange scales, like a snake, tipped with curved talons. He'd never seen anything like it, the way her scaled hands flowed into her human wrists—unless you counted how a Lobo could howl with a wolf's head on a man's body.

With dainty, exacting care, Cora pinched the skin around where his pinky toe used to be, holding the edges of flesh together like she was going to sew a seam on a shirt—which Rhett knew wouldn't help the skin heal at all. But she didn't sew it. She put her lips so, so close, and blew on it, a gentle sigh. What came out wasn't air this time, but a smoky sort of fire.

And goddammit goddammit goddammit, but it burned, as if his whole damn foot was melting off and dripping onto the floor. Despite himself, despite his dedication to feigning sleep, Rhett bucked against the old man's grip, his teeth snapped together, and his body bowed up off the cot.

"Shhh," the girl breathed, and it was a deep, unnatural sound.

The already-warm tent filled with the scent of cooked meat, and the girl pulled away and dashed a pot of cold water over Rhett's foot, instantly cooling it. When he looked again, she was just a girl, round faced and smiling sweetly, blinking eyes that still burned with the dragon's fire. The scales and the smoke and the deep, godlike voice of the dragon had fled. Rhett had heard of this, once—that the Chine could turn into beasts far more powerful than anything in the Federal Republic. But if they could be dragons, why the Sam Hill did they stick around here? Why not set the whole damn camp on fire and fly away?

The old man grunted, and the girl nodded. "Yes, Grandfather. He is awake now. How do you feel?" This last question was directed at Rhett.

"Like a chunk of meat," he said, voice raspy. "Half-cooked."

The girl brought him a dipper of water, and he sat up on one elbow and drank it with a grateful-type look in his eye.

"Welcome to camp."

Rhett cleared his throat. "The welcome wagon here needs some work."

The girl laughed into her hand, her bright eyes dancing. "You should see the leave-taking committee."

The old man grunted and walked around to Rhett's line of sight. His face was a saggier, more ravaged, more troubled version of the girl's, and he had a long gray mustache and goat beard to match his braid around back. He gabbled angrily, made the motion of a finger slicing a throat, and pointed at the door.

"I am Cora, and this is my grandfather, the honorable Dr. Zhang. Everyone calls him Grandpa Z. I am sorry to say you will see us again. But now, you must go." She gracefully raised her hand and bowed her head as if welcoming him out of the tent and into the pouring rain.

"What do I do now?" he asked, sitting up and feeling the world spin dizzily.

"I would start by putting on your boots. The crews will be in the bunk cars and tents while the rain is hard, repairing canvas or doing other useful work. Have you been assigned?"

"Shelton."

Her mouth pursed. "Rough crew. Cutting lines and cleanup. Don't show weakness."

Rhett nodded his thanks and hunted around for his missing sock, which he found draped over his doctor's bag. It was closed, as if it had never been rifled through while he was supposedly asleep. That rudeness, he supposed, could be overlooked, considering the kindness Cora had just performed. Before pulling on the sock, he took a long look at the place where his little toe used to be. It was just smooth, pink scar tissue now.

"That's a right handy trick," he said. "How'd you do it?"

The girl smiled in a fake but practiced way that didn't seem like her at all, a way that reminded Rhett of the whores at the Leaping Lizard saloon. At least they were going to play like she didn't know he'd been awake.

"Ancient family secret."

"Well, I thank you for it." He pulled on his boots and stood, wobbling for a moment as he learned how to balance while missing a toe. It didn't hurt as much to stand as he'd thought it would. "Bunk cars, you said?"

Cora nodded. "If you walk up the train, you will find them. The number eighteen is on the side of the car."

Rhett's brow wrinkled. "Oh, eighteen. Well, sure."

The girl reached into the fire like it was nothing and pulled out a cherry-red piece of coal, crushing it between her fingers as if it were a clot of dirt. Taking Rhett's arm in one fire-hot hand, she turned his palm over and wrote *18* on it in warm black ash.

"Many thanks," he said, feeling weirdly choked up. "To you, too, Grandpa Z."

The old man, whose back had been turned during their discussion, only grunted. Rhett tipped his hat to Cora, picked up his far lighter bag, and did them the favor of not mentioning their thieving. His toe felt remarkably not horrible, considering it had been cut off and the skin sealed over with dragon fire. It was a decent bargain, as far as he was concerned.

He had come to this camp with two objectives, and he'd already got one under his belt. Now he just had to survive long enough to kill Trevisan.

CHAPTER
— 20 —

It was a different world outside their quiet, warm, tidy tent. The camp was filthy, and the pounding rain didn't help. It sluiced off his hat and shivered down Rhett's back and into his boots. In seconds, he was drenched, his feet squelching as he walked past Trevisan's caboose and up the line of train cars. Earl had told him a little, but not much, which meant he had to pay attention and figure it out for himself. There were numbers on each car, and he'd just have to walk until he found the right one.

Off to one side of the train were pens for cattle, pigs, and horses, the creatures mired in knee-high mud and caterwauling. Between cars, he could see that on the other side was the city—but it was not a real one. Even from here, he could tell the buildings had false fronts and weren't nearly as big as they looked. A feller didn't need his letters to know that their signs boasted liquor, women, and cards. Rhett was glad he'd chosen to walk along the side with the animals.

He would've liked to have seen the train up close in the sunlight. As it was, the dark shape seemed to go on for-ever under black clouds, and he couldn't even see the engine up front, obscured as it was by sheets of rain. He smelled a butcher, somewhere, and iron and coal, and blood mixing with mud. The cars he passed began to have open doors, and sullen men watched him as he passed. There were all sorts of fellers, many of whose general types he'd seen before, like the broad, freckled Irish or the dark-skinned fellers from Afrika, many of whom he knew had been recently freed from slavery back east—although he'd heard tell around Gloomy Bluebird that not much had changed for such folk. They glared fiercely at him while he passed, their cat-eyes gleaming green and yellow. Rhett would not have admitted it to anyone for all the world, but he wouldn't want to tussle with them, much less ask about shared relatives.

He'd kept his hand in a fist to keep the rain from washing out Cora's scribbling, and he opened his fingers briefly to be sure the number on the train car matched the one on his palm. He reckoned it did, so he stopped in front of the slid-open door. The car was dirty, the dull gray of bare wood, full of holes, and half-full of a motley crew of part-Injun fellers and other in-betweeners.

A dark-skinned man with raised bumps on his face in peculiar shapes bared his stark white teeth in what might've been a grin.

"What're you staring at, podner?" His voice had a honey-slow twang that didn't go at all with his ferocious looks, not that Rhett planned to comment on the discrepancy.

The man held himself like he knew his own importance, so Rhett nodded to show his respect. "I was told to report to Shelton in bunk car eighteen for work."

The grin turned up at the corners in welcome, and the man held out a hand—missing the tip of his pinky. "Well, come on in and welcome to hell. You already met the big boss man and know you made the mistake of your life, right?"

Rhett looked down at his foot before taking the man's hand and stepping up into the car. "That I did."

"Then I'll show you around. I'm Digby Freeman. You like that name?"

Having never been asked such a question, it took Rhett a beat to answer, "Well, sure."

Digby nodded. "Chose it myself. You know what they called me after I got kidnapped off a sugar cane plantation and grew up among the Sioux? Cat Who Falls Twice. So I figured I'd pick something better. What's your name?"

"Ned Hennessy."

Digby cocked his head like that tickled his ear. "Hm. That does not roll off the tongue. You don't look like a Ned." He shrugged. "Doesn't matter. You'll get a nickname, soon enough. Everybody does. So let's see."

They were standing with their backs to the open door now, and Rhett got the layout of the bunk car. It held only hard cots, and fellers, although there were no blankets nor any other sign of comfort. Rain showed through holes where boards were missing, and a full piss-pot was swarming with flies. All the men wore shades of gray and black, their faces sweaty and grimed with dirt and their eyes wary.

"Mr. Shelton's in the shebang with the other walking bosses and foremen—you know what that means?"

"Reckon it means they're in charge and I'd best watch my mouth."

Digby nodded. "You catch on quick, which tells me you been in a position to get whipped if you didn't. When Mr. Shelton ain't around, I'm in charge, and neither one of us is so bad, comparatively. You like that word? *Comparatively?*" Rhett nodded because he didn't appear to have a choice. "I do. Nice, meaty word. Means it could be a lot worse. Now this here's Jackrabbit, and that's Pegleg Lemmy, and that's Notch, and that's Beans and Pup Dog and Buzzard and Wild Ed and Little Jim and Preacher. He ain't a real preacher, mind—he just talks like one."

"I know a feller like that," Rhett murmured.

The men were all sewing at canvas and looked up briefly with a nod when their names were mentioned. Cora had called them a rough crew, but they mostly looked like beat dogs who just didn't get up anymore after they got kicked.

"What kind of monster are you?" Digby asked.

"The dangerous kind."

Digby snorted. "Lot of that goin' around, for sure. But we like to know a man's capabilities before we sleep locked up in this stinkin' piss-box with him." He leaned close, his eyes gone flat and hard, waiting. "So what are you?"

"Lammergeier," Rhett said, his tongue tripping over the unfamiliar word. "Big-ass Afrikan vulture."

Digby nodded. "That explains that big ol' red eye. Now, what tribe are you?"

Rhett shrugged. "Don't know. Didn't know either of my folks."

"But you're a black Injun?"

"Ask me as much as you want, but I still won't know."

Still staring at Rhett, Digby said something in a tongue like Dan and Winifred's, and a couple of the fellers nodded along. One laughed cruelly and responded in kind. Rhett's hackles went up.

"A feller stands in front of me and talks in another language, I figure he's trying to keep me in the dark," he said, his hand going to where his knife should've been.

Digby's grin came back, full force. "Just checking to see if you were lying. I reckon you ain't. Now, can you sew?"

Rhett nodded.

"Then you can take that extra bunk in the back, Red-Eye. There's a hole in the floor under it, I'm afraid, which lets in the wind and cold right fierce, when they're a problem. And Beans farts something awful. I'll get you some tenting and a needle and thread. Until the rain's done, that's all we got to do—patch up the tents while the big men enjoy themselves. Once it clears up, they'll put us on a handcar, twelve deep, and send us out to smooth the way."

"Different day, same story," said the feller Digby had called Notch. Just like Dan, this feller was a long-haired Injun missing a chunk out of his ear. But Notch seemed easygoing, which meant Rhett didn't want to punch him yet.

"Thanks kindly for the welcome," Rhett said, tipping his sodden hat and heading for the bunk in back.

"If your britches are soaked through, might want to take 'em off before you sit down," Beans said. "It's always damp as hell in here, and your bunk'll be wet for days." He pointed down at his wiry brown legs poking out of a leather breechclout like Dan's.

Rhett considered what he had on under his britches and shook his head. "I don't know you boys that well, and you might poke fun of my skinny limbs," he said. The other fellers chuckled, and Rhett hoped that was the start of fitting in.

It rained all afternoon, and Rhett sewed on the rough canvas with the same violent rage he'd felt while fixing Mam's and Pap's shirts back in Gloomy Bluebird. It irked him something awful to have escaped slavery and then walked right back into it on his own. He wanted to ask a dozen questions, but he didn't know if Trevisan might have spies sprinkled among the men or pay the kind souls who brought him word of mutiny. So he just did his work and listened in and tried to get a feel for Digby, who seemed like a top feller and well-liked by all.

At dinnertime, Digby solemnly checked his beat-up time-piece and had the men get dressed and line up at the door right before the bell rang. They followed him out to the feed tent, their hats pulled down and their shoulders hunched up against the driving rain. It was a longer walk than Rhett had antici-pated, and by the time they got there, he was again soaked to the bone. No one bothered to complain.

Once inside the tent flaps, everyone relaxed. It was warm and smelled good, and they slid onto long wooden benches along with dozens of other men. In front of Rhett was a bowl, but when he went to pick it up, he found it nailed down. Soon a big ladle appeared over his shoulder, slopping down overcooked beans with bits of bacon and beef mixed in. A hard biscuit was tossed down beside it, plus a tin cup of water.

"Eat fast," Notch said, his elbow digging into Rhett, so closely were they crammed in. "Or they'll send you out with food still in your bowl."

Rhett didn't have a spoon, but plenty of the fellers didn't. He had to make do with his fingers and biscuit. The water tasted of tin, and he'd just finished everything when the bell rang and the flap opened and a new batch of hungry workers showed up to take their places. A one-legged Aztecan feller went all down the table, swabbing what was left out of the nailed-down bowls with a mop and leaving dirty water pooled on the benches.

"Like horses at a damn trough," Rhett muttered.

"Yeah, well, and you might've et horse, too. That beef was tough as leather," Digby said with a laugh, appearing behind Rhett. His big hand landed on Rhett's shoulder, and he leaned close before they ducked out of the tent. "Just a word of warn-ing. If you try running, they'll make sure you never run again. You saw that one-legged feller, right?" Rhett nodded. "Don't be like him. First strike, you get whipped with silver. Second strike, you lose a leg so they can still get some work out of you. Third strike, you're sand."

"I thought this was a job."

"Then you ain't looking close." Digby turned Rhett toward the far side of the tent, where the cookwagon poked halfway in. A few wooden shelves were lined with big, greasy-looking glass jars. Each jar was full of sand and had writing on it. "Those boys tried to run."

"What do the jars say?" Rhett asked, a chill creeping up his spine.

"Runs with Bears. Juan Rodriguez. Shaun O'Bannon. Samuel Sykes."

Rhett swallowed hard to keep the food in his belly. "You got your letters?"

Digby spat a laugh. "Hell, no. I remember the day each one of those bastards got executed. Trevisan made us all crowd around to watch. Told us their names. Told us to remember. Now we got to stare at what's left of 'em, every time we eat."

Rhett wanted to ask him if he knew which jar belonged to Shaun O'Bannon. Maybe, somehow, he could steal that jar and take it back to Earl, or at least tell the bastard what color his brother's remains were. Earl would take it hard, knowing his brother had died while he escaped. But Digby's hand on his shoulder, shoving him back out of the tent and into the rain, suggested that further questions about the dead folks weren't the best idea, now or ever.

They trudged back to the bunk car to sleep, and Rhett did his best to get comfortable on the swaybacked cot. He wished to hell he'd found a moment of privacy during the day to rewrap his chest after transforming for Trevisan's amusement, but there was no privacy in the train camp, and that meant the damp muslin was pooled around his waist. He tossed and turned and couldn't relax. Digby hadn't lied—Beans clearly had belly issues, and their corner of the train smelled like a dead cow left in the sun. Settling himself on his side, facing the hole in the wall, Rhett let his gaze soften and stared out into the night.

A wobble went up in his belly, and his skin went over cold. Through the sluicing rain, he saw a shape approach and hurry by with stern, bold steps. Wrapped in a black cloak, it was dark, so dark, and held a black bumbershoot, on which perched a familiar-looking black bird. A raven. Rhett squinted and could just catch the shape of a pale white face by the light of the shebang.

It was Trevisan.

And he was alone.

Rhett bolted up to sitting as the figure disappeared down the road of filth and muck. Sticking his freezing feet back in his still-sodden boots, he moved toward the train car's door, his eyes searching around for some sort of weapon that could pierce a warlock through the heart and end him. But as he wrapped shaking fingers around the handle, something warm grabbed his boot around the ankle.

"Where you think you're going?" Digby asked. His voice, usually so jovial, sounded right threatening, as if he knew exactly what Ned Hennessy thought he was doing.

"Going to take a piss," Rhett muttered.

"Use the pot."

"Might have to do more. Dinner's gone sour."

"Yeah, I bet it has. Now you do whatever you got to do in the piss-pot, and no man'll blame you for it."

Rhett's teeth ground together as he considered how much of a lead Trevisan now had on him in the dark in an unfamiliar place full of hiding spots just as pitch-black as the man's cloak. "I ain't afraid of a little rain, Mr. Freeman, and what I need to do is bound to be messy."

"I reckoned that was so, but I like you, Ned, so I'm gonna tell you a secret. Night like tonight, a man might get some ideas. The kind of ideas the big boss man and his scouts would consider malevolent. Pretty word, ain't it? *Malevolent*? Means hateful. Means a man might put his hands to dark deeds. So even if you wanted to go out and do something messy, you can't. We're locked in."

Rhett swallowed hard. "Locked in?"

"You go on and pull that handle a little and see if it ain't so."

With a silent growl, Rhett did just that, and the door wouldn't budge.

"That clank you hear is the pin put through our lock by a man on the outside."

"What if there was a fire? What if—?"

Digby sighed like he carried the weight of the world on his shoulders. "Son, you think they give a shit about us?"

Rhett's head hung. Digby was right. And the moment was lost.

"Yes, sir, Mr. Freeman," he said softly and returned to his bunk. He didn't bother with the piss-pot, and Digby didn't mention it.

When he put his eye back to the hole, all he saw was a miserable night.

Trevisan was, of course, long gone. No man lingered in the rain, especially not one who thought himself so fine. The railroad boss was a peculiar feller, even before you got to the part where he sliced off fingers and toes. He had dangerous men close to him, not to mention unseen guards planted around the camp. Grandpa Z was not the friendly feller he sounded like, but at least Rhett didn't have to try to squeeze him to find out how to help Winifred. He already knew the how; he just had to figure out how to get one of the two healers out of the camp and back to Winifred. Of the two, he'd naturally choose Cora, who was right pleasant and had already shown several traits that Rhett could appreciate. She dressed like a boy, she didn't rat him out for feigning sleep, and she was easy on the eyes. Tomorrow he would learn how to build a railroad, and hopefully how to get close to Trevisan. Tonight, all he could do was go to sleep.

His little toe itched and twitched, but Rhett didn't indulge in a scratch. He'd pretended for too long that his eye would grow back, somehow. His toe, he knew, was gone forever. But what was Trevisan doing with the damn thing, anyway?

The next morning dawned fair, the last of the rain dripping away from every eave and sagging tent. The first thing Rhett did, even before he opened his eye, was to rummage around under his shirt and dig a fingertip into the pouch of ashes and touch his tongue, just in case the effect had worn off. Surrounded by nothing but monsters, his only hope of staying hidden was to pretend to be normal. Normal for a monster. Or not the Shadow, anyway, considering he was in with a whole crew of Injuns and half-Injuns, and who knew if they were familiar with the legend?

If Rhett had considered his life with Mam and Pap to be horrible before, it was only because he'd never worked at a railroad camp. Digby rounded up the fellers of Car 18 and marched them in a line to a supply car, where they were each handed a numbered pickax, their tips purposely filed down to bluntness. Rhett's new number was eleven, which was easy enough for him to remember. 11. Just two little lines, like a man's legs. It was carved into his pickax, and Rhett considered it damn lucky nobody carved it into him. The *18* Cora had drawn onto his palm had long since been rubbed away, but if he thought about it, hard, he could still feel the warmth of her fingertip pressing gently against his skin.

Pickaxes over their shoulders, Digby led his men to the front of the train, which Rhett had never seen before. The engine was a big, dangerous-looking thing, like a damn buffalo—which is what the little grille on the front was for. If some dumb cow or a buffalo got on the track, Digby told him, well, the train just plowed on through, and some fellers were sent out on handcars afterward to collect the meat.

The track ended way ahead of the engine, and it was Crew 18's job to grade the area, meaning it had to be level enough for the rails. They crowded onto a little car, banging one another with boots and pickaxes, and then Digby and the next biggest feller pumped the machinery that moved the car on down the freshly laid rails. It was a long, bumpy while before they reached the end of the train tracks and the handcar stopped to let them off, right before a whole other set of cars containing wood and metal and spikes beyond counting.

Other crews crawled over the site like ants, some setting out with scraggly mules or much-abused handcars, carting dirt and supplies and dynamite to wherever the hell such things were needed. Rhett caught sight of a group of worried-looking Chine men carefully carrying big crates as if they contained precious, raw eggs and concluded he was glad that blowing shit up wasn't his job.

Once Rhett had hopped down in the puddle-filled trench and started banging his pickax into the quickly drying mud, he couldn't watch what anybody else was doing. All of his focus went toward not breaking a foot or hitting his workmates. He learned immediately that Digby was a different man outside the bunk car, a sharp-voiced, angry-eyed bastard spitting orders and keeping everybody in line. Rhett took to his pickax quickly, although the work was awful and hard and stupid. He tried to stop one time to wipe sweat off his brow, and Digby stuck the end of a whip in his face.

"I don't wanna quirt you, son, but I will. If Mr. Shelton or a foreman is watching and you stop working, I'll whip you. And if the big boss comes by while you shirk, I'll beat you near to death."

Rhett almost said something smart, but he could well see the desperation begging behind Digby's eyes and reckoned the man had a good reason for saying such things. "Yes, sir, Mr. Freeman," he said softly, and he went back to his work. Digby at least gave him a nod of apology.

Lunch was a dipper of water and a piece of hard tack that was mostly weevil. Rhett chewed in disgust as he watched the blisters on his hands reseal.

"They'll be back soon," Preacher said, stretching out his own pink palms, a mass of callus. "Such is our Sisyphean task."

"This ain't a task for sissies at all, far as I can reckon," Rhett said.

And then Digby was back with his quirt, and Rhett took up his pickax, the handle moving loose over wet palms and a new layer of blisters.

By dinnertime, Rhett couldn't lift the pickax another time. His arms were limp as old reins, and his head felt like it was stuffed full of moldy straw. His legs and back ached, and so much sweat had run into his eye that he reckoned he'd processed a cloud's worth of moisture. His kerch was wet and crusted with salt. He turned in his pickax and felt as light as a damn feather, like he might just float off into the sunset. It was more than a bit like sleepwalking, slogging along to the food tent. He ended up next to Notch, their elbows bumping as they shoveled in their food. Rhett barely tasted it—it was just fodder.

"Meat's tough tonight," Beans observed.

"Better than going without," Preacher intoned.

"Mr. Trevisan eats rare lamb," Notch said, his voice gentle. "Or veal, sometimes. Gives his valet the scraps. Hard to go back to this shoe leather, after that."

A piece of weevily bread bounced off his head, and he ducked. "Shut up with that chatter, fool," somebody muttered. "You ain't special no more."

Rhett's head slowly swiveled to stare at the quiet feller by his side. Notch was a good-looking man, young and lithe and quick and not too unlike Rhett, although his skin was a world lighter and his eyes a bright, keen gold. His hair was sun-kissed brown, long and straight. Must've been half-white, the lucky bastard.

"How do you know what the big boss eats?" Rhett asked quietly between gulps. "And what the hell's a valet?"

"Big boss keeps a servant. Calls him a valet." The feller's voice was soft and cultured. "Tried to train me up, and it wasn't hard work. But I got too proud. Thought I was smart. Thought I could run. He caught me. The marks on my back and the notch in my ear are my first warning." Notch touched his ear, quick as a worried rabbit. "Next he'll be taking my left leg to go with the bit of finger he already kept, or so he told me."

Rhett's food was all but forgotten as he realized that this feller might just contain all the information he needed to accomplish his task without another day at the pickax. "Did you live in his caboose, then?"

Notch chewed and swallowed before shaking his head. "Naw, I slept on the floor of the walking boss car and just visited to help him dress. Mr. Trevisan wouldn't trust anyone to sleep in there. Except Meimei, but it's not like she can do anything."

"Who's Meimei?"

Notch looked over, all crafty. "You mean you don't know?"

"I just got here. I don't know nothin'."

Preacher put a hand on Rhett's arm. "Less you know about that, the better."

And then they were being hustled away to make room for the hobbling mop boy and the next crew.

That night, as Rhett collapsed into his bunk, he felt a breeze on his face and put his eye to the hole in the wood. Not so far away, lanterns hung outside the ersatz city, and all the white fellers—or at least the ones that had a job instead of an enslavement, as far as Rhett could tell—were headed for the saloons. Woman-shaped shadows flounced around, and Rhett couldn't help being curious if these were more vampires or human women, and if there were vampire work crews who slept in bunk cars all day and worked all night. Shelton—the foreman Rhett had never met, thus far, but whom Digby had pointed out as a very kind drunk—walked by with some other fellers, laughing and sharing a bottle. It was funny, as far as Rhett considered, how two such very different lives were unfolding, so near and yet so far away.

Rhett was too tired to move, but most of Car 18 was in the corner, shaking dice and gabbling in their languages while Digby kept watch at the door and Preacher prayed by his cot, loudly, for their eternal souls. The voices and clattering made a pleasant-enough noise, although Rhett vastly preferred a crackling fire, softly stamping horses, and the nighttime conversation of one Samuel Hennessy.

A body landed in the cot beside him, and Rhett prepared himself for a world of stink. But instead of farting, Beans started talking.

"She's Grandpa Z's other granddaughter," Beans whispered.

Rhett rolled over. "Who is?"

"Meimei. So if you wonder if the Chine will ever turn on the big boss or be friendly-like, now you know who they're loyal to. She's just a baby thing, and Trevisan treats her like a little pet, but if Grandpa Z ever showed his claws…" In the shadows, Rhett could barely see the shape of a finger drawn across a neck.

"Why're you telling me that?" Rhett asked.

"I saw your medicine bag this morning. Didn't mean to pry, but there you are. My ma was Comanche, too." He held out something similar from his own neck. "Reckon you're the closest thing I got to family in here, even if your habits are a little peculiar. And I hate Notch parading hisself around like he's special. So now he ain't."

Rhett grinned. "I reckon I owe you one, then, cousin."

Beans made a personal noise that Rhett was glad to ignore. "I can accept that," he said.

The next morning, Rhett woke up early for the chance to piss alone in the sad excuse for a privy. He made sure to go before dawn so nobody would be around to see what he didn't have or witness him rewrapping the sweaty muslin on his chest. But when Digby slid open the door to let him out, the world was a fresh new hell. Every damn inch of space outside was covered in black birds. The cars, the sagging lines of the tents, the wagons. Even some of the mules and cows. And not just normal birds, but the exact same kind that had assaulted them around the campfire and nipped off a chunk of Dan's ear.

"Ravens," he muttered.

"An omen of evil," Preacher said from his cot.

Rhett turned around and found several pairs of eyes watching him warily.

"Now you know good and well they're not biblical things," Digby said, patting him on the back. "They're Trevisan's creatures. Nothin' god or devil about 'em. They ain't even real."

"They're real enough," Notch said, one hand fiddling with his ear. He was all shrunk back in his bunk, and Rhett didn't blame him.

"Why ravens?" he asked.

Digby snorted. "Why are you what you are? Why am I this? What is, is, son. The big boss tells a flock of birds what to do, and I reckon he tells a flock of men what to do. If I can't defy him, why should they?"

"Okay, but what's he use 'em for?"

"Sorcery," Preacher started, but Digby waved it away.

"This and that. They're good for seeing the lay of the land, finding out what's over the ridge. We always know what the weather's gonna be, and when there's a herd of buffalo, well, we know that, too, and we eat well that night."

"I've heard they find the gold in graves," said Beans. "Pick through the pockets of the dead."

"And eat what else they find in there, besides," added Jackrabbit, who only seemed to speak up when there was something gruesome to be said.

"Nature's cleanup crew," Digby said with his big, wide grin. "The Lord loves a useful animal."

"He keeps one in his car."

Rhett turned to look at Notch, but the man had gone quiet—and two shades paler, curled up like a child after a nightmare.

"In his car?" Rhett urged.

Notch nodded. "In a cage, like Meimei. Two identical cages, lined with red Chine silk and pillows. He pokes their food in between the bars."

"What's the bird eat?" Rhett asked.

Notch didn't answer. He just shook his head, stood, and hopped out of the car.

"Be smart," Digby said to Rhett, a hand on his shoulder and a meaningful look in his eye. "Learn when to shut up. Like Notch."

"If Notch is so goddamn smart, why's he back in here with a chunk cut off his ear?"

Digby's smile was sad and pitying. "He wasn't smart before. He's learning now. Best get to the privy while you can. The birds'll head off, soon."

And they did. Sometime in the morning, the whole flock took off in a great black cloud, swirling like a tornado and flying off purposefully into the blue. Rhett stopped digging, his pickax stuck into ground that had been mud a few days ago and was now dry, unforgiving, hard earth riddled with hateful rocks.

"Keep on keeping on with that ax," Digby said. "Don't be buyin' trouble on my time."

This time, he barely had to waggle his quirt before Rhett got back to work.

CHAPTER
21

The Shadow soon discovered the taste of humble pie. What had he told his friends—that he'd swagger into camp, kill Trevisan, and swagger right back out? Hellfire. At least they weren't here to see him suffering for his pride.

The problem was that Rhett had figured he'd have plenty of access to Bernard Trevisan, but he hadn't seen hide nor hair of the man since that night in the rain. Not overseeing the camp, not riding about on a snow-white horse. Rhett hadn't even seen the man's underlings, nor had he manufactured a chance to visit Cora and Grandpa Z again. Rhett had begun, to all effects, to be as helpless as Earl himself had been. And the one time he'd tried to talk to an Irish crew, the feller had spit on him and told him to go to hell.

And so he stood in his ditch and did whatever Digby Freeman told him to do. Some days, it was the pickax. Other days, they transported fill dirt onto a handcar and shoveled it into holes. Some days, they sat in the tent to avoid rainstorms or sandstorms, doing women's work and being miserable in a different way. After a week, Rhett was no closer to accomplishing a damn useful thing. He'd expected some sort of lucky break, but none had come. He was always on the lookout for Trevisan, whether walking through the camp or spying through the hole in the car. Other than that night in the rain, however, he hadn't seen his quarry again. And although the flock of ravens had flown over his head, back and forth, again and again, cawing to hell about their dark deeds, he had no idea what news they brought. He just hoped Dan and the rest of his posse had the good sense to stay hid and allow him the time he needed to accomplish his goal.

Every few days, as the track was laid and spiked and smoothed up ahead, the engine would fire up, pumping its rancid black smoke into the air and puffing along the tracks with a powerful grunting like thunder having a big belch. Even then, Trevisan wasn't seen, but of course, that would've been like looking for one particularly shy ant in a hill gone mad. Rhett had never seen such carefully orchestrated insanity as the tent city and shebang all packed up into wagons and train cars, the men hanging off the sides as the engine pulled them a few miles to the next site. The ants swarmed again, and within hours a new city stood with a new thoroughfare already beginning to collect its puddles of piss and tobacco spit and piles of horseshit that would melt at the first fat drops of rain. The places they left behind were filthy and flatter than buffalo wallows, nothing but train tracks and ruin in their wake.

What Rhett couldn't quite figure out was how Earl had ever managed to run off at all. Maybe the Irishmen were trusted more than Rhett's crew, but it was all he could do to keep his fellers from finding out he was distinctly lacking in the pizzle department. That spot he and Coyote Dan had agreed on was about as far away as the damn moon, after the train had moved twice. About the only freedom he had involved turning from one uncomfortable side to the other in his damn crappy little cot.

One morning, he woke up and stretched, the gunshot cracks of his aching back loud enough to wake the dead, although not quite enough to wake a train car full of exhausted graders. He kept his eye closed until he'd tasted the witch's powder, of which there was increasingly less. When he looked up and blinked, he was surprised to find dawn's rosy fingers prying open the door of the bunk car. It wasn't open all the way, but it was open enough to let slip a slim sort of feller who didn't eat enough.

His eye darted left and right as he shoved on his boots and silently tiptoed to the door. Normally, one Digby Freeman would be guarding the door from the inside. But when Rhett looked out, he saw Digby getting what looked like a nasty sort of dressing-down from Shelton. The foreman had his hands on his hips and was jawing off, taking out his hangover on the much-larger man, who looked like he was trying to cower right into himself, softly muttering, "Yes, sir," and "No, sir," anytime there was a break in Shelton's hollering.

Neither man was looking at Rhett, though, and that was the important thing.

Because what Rhett needed wasn't to actually run away, as Earl had. He just needed to get caught running away. Because he was sick of waiting for a lucky break, and Earl had said Mr. Trevisan had given him those scars on his back, hadn't he? And Digby had called that kind of punishment a man's first warning. Rhett was willing to risk what was left of the meat over his own spine if it meant he was in Trevisan's presence again. And who knew what might happen, when a canny and tenacious feller like the Shadow was left alone in a locked car with a pompous magician who thought he was the damn King of Durango?

Anything was better than waiting for luck that never arrived.

The Shadow would make his own luck, for good or ill.

Pulling his hat down, Rhett hopped lightly to the ground, which hadn't gone entirely mucky yet, which meant his boots didn't make a squelchy sound and give him away. He didn't want Digby to be the one who caught him, though, so he slipped around the corner of the car and considered his options. Was it better to get caught actually running, or was it preferable to look like he was getting up to no good? If he ran, he might take a gunshot to the heart, but if he sauntered along, surely someone would stop him with less permanent measures. But would such a minor infraction as getting lost on his way to take a piss get him into Trevisan's clutches? Hellfire, Rhett had spent most of his life trying not to get beat, and now he was aiming for the biggest beating of his life—on purpose.

So he wouldn't run and risk getting shot. But he wouldn't fumble around the privy, neither, and just get slapped for waywardness. Stealing wasn't a good option. What he needed, he realized with a sly grin, was to get in a fight.

He glanced back at the train car, but the fellers inside were a sorry damn bunch. Stringy to a man, like Rhett appeared on the outside. He'd feel right bad for popping any one of 'em in the face, and aside from Preacher's vexful jawing, he had no real quarrel with anybody.

Just then, he saw exactly the sort of target he needed: a big, dumb Irishman. He was roughly the size of a haystack and about as dim looking, with a bright green shirt that even the rough work of the railroad hadn't yet dulled. The feller was walking, alone, toward the privy trenches, looking a lot like a bigger, meaner version of Earl. And Rhett took off at a steady jog and darted right in front of the redheaded bull moose.

It was about the same as walking into a brick wall.

"'Scuse you," Rhett muttered, stepping back and looking up with a sneer.

"What the damn hell, man?" the feller said, his eyes squinched down in honest confusion.

"You ran into me, that's what."

"Are you lookin' for a fight, wee manny? Because there's no one around here who can talk to me like that."

Rhett glanced left and right. "Well, that's sure enough. I don't see any damn girls about."

He was ready for the punch and turned slightly sideways so it glanced off. Still hurt like hell, but it was like the knock that opens a locked door, the locked door being Rhett's temper. Rhett's lips curled off his teeth in a feral grin as he clocked the feller in the chin. The Irishman staggered back, looking ornery and dizzy as a drunk ox. But Rhett was overcome with a mad sort of rage, and he didn't pause to think about it, just tossed himself right back at a man twice his weight, socking him in the gut and landing a hook in his kidney.

"You—"

Rhett shut him up with a fist in the teeth and let go a sigh he'd been holding for weeks. Hellfire, but it was good to punch things when he felt hopeless.

Before he could land another punch, strong arms yanked him back by the shoulders and cold steel knocked his hat aside and kissed his temple.

"Just what the hell's going on here?"

"Little bastard attacked me!" the Irishman blustered through bloody lips.

"When a bull ox runs into me, I run right back into him," Rhett said calmly.

"Freeman, this one of your men?"

Whoever was holding him yanked him around to face Shelton and Digby. Rhett tried hard not to grin and failed.

"Yes, sir, that's Red-Eye Ned."

"You not keeping a good watch?"

"Well, sir, I—"

"It's on me, sir. Mr. Freeman was talking to Boss Shelton, and I snuck out to hit the trenches for my morning movement, but then this feller ran smack into me and nearly busted open my bowels, so I politely asked him to give way, and he started pounding me about the face."

"That's not true!" the Irishman shouted, sounding truly offended.

Rhett shrugged. "That's how I saw it. I am sorry, Mr. Freeman, if I'm out of bounds."

Digby's eyes were near to falling out of his head, and Mr. Shelton looked like he kept a church bell in his skull and it wouldn't stop ringing, and whoever was holding Rhett shoved him roughly away.

"No fighting," the feller said. Rhett didn't recognize him, but most white folks looked about the same, anyway.

"Yes, sir. I will keep that in mind."

The man sighed and rubbed his stubbled cheeks. "Ten lashes each should be a fine reminder. Can't have workers busting each other up. Come along."

Rhett nodded and struggled not to grin in triumph.

"Red-Eye, you best do whatever Mr. Lowery says, you hear?" Digby said nervously, to which Rhett nodded his assent.

The Irishman leaned over and muttered, "I'll kill you for this, lad."

"Good luck trying, son," Rhett whispered back. "I don't take shit off donkeys."

Mr. Lowery moved behind the two of them and cocked his pistol. "Just go where I say and don't try anything stupid. I got no problem blowing both of you malcontents to sand."

He directed them around the maze of tents, nudging them

with his gun to save spit. As they moved, Rhett realized the camp matched perfectly the layout he'd first encountered, minus the knee-deep mud. But they didn't go to a tent, and they stopped way short of the false fronts of the shebang still being raised; they headed for an open space between all the construction. Hammers and saws filled the air with rough music as the buildings came together piece by piece. Rhett quickly saw that Lowery was directing them toward a corner-type beam sunk deep in the ground, a pile of dirt and rocks holding it upright.

Almost like the sort of thing you'd hang a man from.

Rhett's step faltered, but the gun barrel against his back kept him on track.

"Bring the cat!" Lowery shouted, and some far-off feller nodded and ran into the nearest storefront.

Rhett was about to mouth off about liking cats, but the snarling faces of the men gathering in a loose circle suggested that more than one man would be glad to make him bleed. His fight rage had drained off, and now he became aware of a thousand tiny sensations. The way his sweat-scratchy shirt clung to his back, the fact that his eye kerch had slipped in the fight, the rude rattle of dirt in his boot. The day wasn't horribly hot—yet. Rhett had seen much hotter. And yet sweat began to trickle down his spine.

He'd expected to be escorted directly to Trevisan's car to explain himself or just to face the whip. He had not considered that punishment might happen in a far more public way without Trevisan present at all.

Rhett licked dry lips. "What about the big boss?" he asked.

Lowery walked to the wooden post, putting a palm against it and leaning in to determine its strength. The damn thing was well planted and didn't budge.

"Wouldn't bother the big boss for a piddly thing like fighting," he said. "Now, if you'd tried to run, that'd be a different story. But you won't want to run for a while, not after I'm through with you." He laughed, and the knot of gawking onlookers tightened, and Rhett looked up at the big Irishman, suddenly feeling like a right bastard for what he'd done.

"If it's worth much, I'm sorry for this," he muttered.

"It's not worth shit, and I'll be payin' you back one day," was the reply.

The crowd split to admit the feller who'd been sent for the cat, which most certainly was not a cat. It was a whip like that three-headed Debil dog at Haskell's outpost, but nine separate heads sprouted from the handle, each tipped with a silver spike.

"Don't think I like cats anymore," Rhett grumbled.

A hungry sort of laugh went up among the men. One produced a rope, frayed and filthy with what looked and smelled like crusted cow shit, and Lowery tossed it over the top of the gallows and tested its strength by dangling from it.

"Who goes first?" he asked.

Rhett looked at Lowery, and then he looked at the Irishman, and he reckoned that whoever went first would get the harder lashes, while maybe the second feller would take a lighter load, accounting for Lowery's arm getting tired from beating the first one half to death.

"I'll go first," he said, hating the upward squeak in his voice. He cleared his throat and added, "I never did get to take my piss, and I'm getting antsy."

The Irishman glared at him with slitted eyes, not sure about the gambit. Rhett figured the feller would try to kick his ass either way and settled for giving him a manly nod.

Lowery nodded. "Well, come on, then. Folks got business to get to."

Rhett stepped up, and Lowery yanked on his wrists, knotting the rope around them and tugging until Rhett was up on his toes.

"Aw, shit. Forgot your shirt," Lowery muttered, loosening the rope, and that's when Rhett nearly lost it. If they took off his shirt to whip him, they'd realize he was...well, he had the parts of, at least...a girl.

"I don't mind being punished, but I'm awfully shy about my scrawny chest," Rhett squeaked. "You got any alternatives to the whipping?"

A rumble of laughter went through the crowd.

"Not in general, but considering the way that big Irish bastard's looking at you, I reckon we could come up with one on the fly, seeing as how it's unofficial."

He yanked Rhett's wrists back up and pulled the rope hard before handing it off to a mean-looking feller who kept on yanking. It was all Rhett could do to stay on his toes and not have his hands jerked right off his arms. He spun a little as he found his balance and turned to face the Irishman.

"See if you can beat 'im to death," Lowery said, clapping the Irish feller on the back.

Rhett smiled.

The Irishman smiled, too, and he did his goddamn best to comply.

After the first punch to his gut, Rhett didn't smile anymore.

At some point, he must've passed out. That's all Rhett could figure, as the last thing he remembered was a bone-juddering series of punches to the ribs and the crowd crowing like a pack of Lobos. He woke up lying on his back, eye swollen closed, trying to decide which part of him hurt more.

"You are a fool," said a soft voice, not without some amusement.

"That you, Cora?" Rhett struggled to say through a mouth that felt like it was stuffed with broken glass and rocks.

A soft, warm, wet cloth brushed over his eye, and he did his best not to wince and whimper like a damn baby.

"Of course. You've been out for quite a while. If you were human, I suspect you would have a crushed skull and brain damage. You made Big Red very angry."

Rhett barked a laugh that made his ribs burn. "Big Red beat Red-Eye black and blue. Why, our names go along like cows and shi—" He cleared his throat. "Like sunshine and blue-birds, begging your pardon, ma'am."

"Quiet, now." He couldn't see her, but he heard her draw in a deep breath, and then something very hot covered his eye with an unwelcome pressure. But she'd told him to stay quiet, so he did, pursing his split lips to hold in the scream. A wet cloth followed, and when it was removed, she said, "You should be able to see now."

Rhett gingerly opened his eye, finding it far less swollen if still gritty and tender. He just barely spied Cora hiding her orange-scaled hand, busying herself with the cloth and water bucket floating with green herbs that filled the air with a sharp, clean scent.

"You're very strong," Cora observed as she went about cleaning his many cuts with the cloth. "Lowery said he'd never seen someone so small last so long under such a vicious assault."

"He said that?"

A chuckle. "No. What he said was something like, *That cocky little bastard just flat out won't die, even after a solid hour of beating, so fix him up and get him back on the cut line.*" She'd done an admirable job of mimicking Lowery's twangy accent. "But I heard the men talk as they brought you in. For someone who seems to find trouble, at least you are capable of with-standing it."

The cloth touched Rhett's split lip, and he hissed. "We're all hard to kill. That's why we're here, I reckon."

A secretive smile. "Something like that."

She dabbed at him, here and there. He allowed it. When she unbuttoned the top button of his shirt, though, he gently caught her wrist in bruised fingers. "Keep it above the neck, sugar. Nothing to be done for me, down below."

Cora smirked. "As you say."

Rhett couldn't puzzle out what she meant by that, but he liked lying down and holding still and being dabbed at as he healed, so he did his best to relax and oblige her.

"You do this a lot?" he asked.

"What, patch up men who get in fights? Not all that much. Few return for a second whipping. Most know that you only get three chances here. And then . . ." She flicked her fingers at him. "Poof! Sand."

"Wait. What happened to Big Red?"

Cora shrugged. "They gave him five lashes. It was enough. I spread them with salve. He did not thank me—they never do—and was sent back out to work. Only one more chance for him. He tried to run, once, you know. A whole group of Irish tried. Many died. If he wasn't so big and strong, they might've just killed him on the spot. But he does the work of three men and doesn't shirk or drink, so there is a chance they will con-tinue to be lenient. So long as he will work."

Rhett's split lip twisted. He hadn't thought about the conse-quences of picking a fight with the feller and had only seen Big Red as his golden ticket to Trevisan. Now, because of Rhett, and for no other reason, the feller had only one more chance to behave. And Rhett himself was no closer to killing the big boss.

"Did that hurt?" Cora asked, dabbing her cloth at the blood crusting his busted knuckles.

"Probably not as much as I deserve," he muttered, feeling like maybe he was the one who was a complete and useless ass.

It was after lunch but before dinner. Every part of him that needed tending had been tended, and the bruises elsewhere were already fading. No real harm had been done, except another tally added to his failures. Grandpa Z looked him over and grunted to indicate that Rhett was ready to go back to work. Cora opened the tent flap and bowed him out.

"Thank you kindly, ma'am," he said, tipping his hat.

Her smile was radiant, her cheeks rosy. She always looked like they were in together on some secret joke that never failed to amuse her. "You are welcome, Red-Eye."

He squinted against the afternoon sun, considering. If he ran now, he'd have his second strike and maybe that meeting with Trevisan he so coveted. But he was beat to hell, aching in every bone, still sticky with dried blood, and hungry as all get-out, not to mention awful fond of his legs. Now was not the time to try anything clever. Failing once per day was more than enough. And there was a scout with a rifle on top of one of the train cars, watching him especially closely now.

Rhett tipped his hat at that feller, too, and headed off for the pickax man. With his tool slung over his shoulder, he walked slower than usual to the front of the train, where somebody would eventually show up with a handcar to deliver Rhett out to the dig. Every step, he knew he was being watched. He'd have to sit tight and toe the line. For now.

CHAPTER
— 22 —

From then on, Rhett focused on something he thought he'd left behind: behaving.

He swung his pickax, ate his slop, slept hard, and held his piss at inopportune moments. His bowels became as regular as sunup, and he no longer thought about how far the engine had pulled him away from Dan's meeting place. He tried to lure Notch into talking about Trevisan, but the feller had gone sullen and silent, or sullener and silenter, for whatever reason. He usually ended up arguing with Beans about which kind of horse was best just so he'd have something to do.

For the first few days after the fight, Digby Freeman kept an especially close eye on him. Feller even pulled his cot in front of the door every night, and Rhett had to reckon that the freshly nailed board over his little hole in the wall wasn't a kindness on the boss's part to keep out the cold.

They didn't want him to get more ideas about going outside on his own.

"Thanks for blocking up that rain hole, sir," Rhett said, tipping his hat to Digby. "It's right nice, how it keeps out the cold and noise."

Digby nodded back and said nothing else about it. So long

as Rhett did his work, nobody seemed to notice him. The men were kept quiet during the day and too tired at night to talk much. They hit a hard and sunny patch, no rain for a week, and Boss Shelton sobered up for five minutes and hollered that they were by God and the devil going to hit ten more miles by the first frost or die trying. So they tried. They tried hard.

Rhett knew he had to bide his time and wait for the right moment or risk losing his chance at Trevisan. He'd only hurt Big Red this go, but now he understood that his actions would ripple down to Digby, the men of Car 18—hell, the whole camp. He just had to push himself so hard that he didn't have time to chew on his frustration like a worn-out plug of chaw. He was dropping weight and constantly thirsty, and it wasn't much of a surprise when his monthly flux was barely a brown trickle.

One day, he was singing along, minding his pickax, when his belly gave a big wobble. He jerked upright, pickax still in the bank, and looked around for the trouble. It wasn't Trevisan or a Lobo; it was a sound he knew well: a wagon. But it was coming way too fast, and nobody else seemed to notice. Two mules were running full tilt, straight for their cut, dragging an unmanned wagon full of spikes right at Rhett's crew. And Digby Freeman, his back to the wagon and his hands clasped, was singing his song and completely unaware.

It seemed to Rhett like everybody was in slow motion except for him as he leaped out of the cut, shoved Digby into it with a shoulder, and waved his arms at the mules, flapping his hat and hollering.

For one mad, glittering moment, Rhett was pretty sure he was going to get run over by two tons of horseflesh and a mess of metal, but the mules turned in time and took off across the prairie, the wagon on two wheels, leaving nothing but spikes and shit in their wake.

"What the devil?" Digby asked, looking up from the hole, one hand to his forehead like he thought he might have a fever.

"Runaway mule team," Rhett grunted, readjusting his eye kerch and pulling his hat back down.

"I know that, fool. They woulda run me down, turned me into a pile of gravy."

"Possibly."

Rhett held his hand down to Digby and pulled him back out of the hole, then jumped in himself before he got hollered at. He already had his pickax going before Digby caught his attention.

"Stop, Red-Eye. What I'm asking is: How the hell'd you move that fast? I didn't even see those damn mules, and you were up here and waving them off before I could open my mouth."

Rhett shrugged in between swings. "Reckon I can do what needs doing, sir."

"I reckon you can," Digby said, scratching his head and shoving his hat back down. "I reckon you can."

The next morning, Rhett woke up to a hand on his shoulder and prepared himself for a fight, but all he found was Digby Freeman standing over him. He kept his arm thrown over his eye as if he were ashamed of his empty socket instead of trying to hide what he looked like before the witch's powder had taken effect.

"Mmph. Sir?"

"You're pretty fast, ain't you, Red-Eye?"

Rhett grinned. "Faster than a jackrabbit with a lit match up his hole, sir. But you know that."

Digby stood up and nodded. "Reckon I do. And I reckon

you proved yourself here. They need a new rail runner. You got to be fast, but you got to be strong, too. You got to be a veritable Hercules. You know what that means? Kinda like a god. Think you can do that?"

"I can do that, boss," Rhett said, completely unsure of whether he could do it and having no idea what it was anyway.

"Reason I'm choosing you," Digby said, all slow and meaningful, "is because you're bad with a pickax but never shirk. You did me a good turn yesterday, and I done vouched for you, so you better not try anything stupid. I know damn well you could've hopped on one of them mules and been gone from here, fast as you are, but it didn't even occur to you, did it?"

Damn if that didn't make him feel half-proud and half-stupid as hell. "It did not, no."

"Then go on. You do me proud, you hear?"

"I will. Thank you, sir."

Rhett sat up, turning away to arrange his eye kerch and hat and sneak a precious few grains of powder.

"Go on down to the front of the engine. Big Irish boss in a brown hat's waiting for you." He gave a lopsided grin. "It ain't Big Red, I promise."

Rhett walked to the door, and his throat tightened up a bit as he nodded at the fellers in the car. They were all watching him from their sad swayback cots, looking jealous and hopeless and older than their years. But they looked that way every day, didn't they? Only difference was that he was leaving now. It wasn't so much that he'd miss them personally, but they'd been good enough to dwell among.

Digby clapped Rhett on the back briefly and hollered, "The rest of you-all shirkers better wake up and get ready for work! I ain't one for malingering, which is a damn pretty word means that no man'll dodge a task in my car. We're a man down, but we're not gonna show it."

Rhett didn't say good-bye or anything of the sort. He was going to take this one fine chance Digby had given him to get the hell out of that hole in the ground. If they wanted something fast, and if being fast would get him a step closer to freedom and Trevisan, so be it. He started running toward the front of the train, and it felt damn good to move his legs and pump his arms. Leaping over tools and dirt and dodging around mule whackers and tent poles, he soon stood, a little out of breath, in front of a big Irish bastard who, to be honest, looked an awful lot like Big Red.

"You're the new rail man, is that so?" he asked.

Rhett nodded.

"Me name's Bruiser, and you can guess why."

Rhett eyed the feller's bulging arms and mean eyes and nodded. "Reckon I can, sir."

"So you won't want to be starting any trouble with me."

"Reckon I will not, sir."

"What's your name?"

"They call me Red-Eye."

"Well, walk along with me, then, Red-Eye, and let's see if you keep up longer than the last lad from Digby's crew."

"How long did he last?"

Bruiser's grin was a twisted, cruel thing missing quite a few teeth. "Which parts of him?"

Rhett didn't ask any more questions.

❧

Truth be told, running rails was a pleasure compared to digging the grade. The runners were all quiet, medium-sized fellers like Rhett, the kind of men who looked like they were made of wire twisted around mesquite thorns and stuck together with hornet blood. They were a mixed bag outside of that, with several whites, a few dark-skinned fellers, and some medium-brown folks like Rhett himself. Apparently, the big, strong men weren't quick enough, and the wee, quick men weren't strong enough, so the men in between landed here, if they lasted long enough and proved they could get along in camp. Taking a beating in public had given Rhett quite the reputation for toughness, which the other runners shared and respected.

He caught on quickly to the work, which happened in short bursts. Rhett and another man grabbed a rail off the car, one on either side, and then four more men grabbed it in the middle bits and they all ran it to the marked place, where they dropped it carefully in position and got the hell out of the way for the next set of six runners with a rail. Once the rail cart was empty, they tipped it over and off the track to make way for the new cart, all while a man on a fast horse delivered the empty carts back to the train at a furious gallop that Rhett mightily envied. It was a peculiar sort of dance, runners weaving in and out of line, all pulling their weight equally, and it was easier to lose himself in the work, as compared to beating on the ground all day without much to show for it but more dirt. You had to be careful to run rails, but being careful took up most of the time a man would otherwise spend worrying.

As the afternoon drew long, one of the runners must've done something wrong. Rhett didn't directly see what happened, only that the rail was lying out of place, five men were standing in a circle, hands on hips, and Bruiser was hollering and cussing fit to be tied. With the sharp authority Rhett had come to admire, Bruiser ordered the biggest man in the crew to carry his fallen comrade back to Grandpa Z. As they hurried past, Rhett smelled blood and saw a flash of bone poking out of the injured man's ripped trouser leg.

"What can Grandpa Z do for somebody like us?" Rhett asked.

"Set the bone," said Arrows, the dark-skinned feller he'd been paired with all day. The man's accent was somehow both sharp and mellow, his *t*'s sharp and his *o*'s long.

"That happen often?"

Arrows shrugged. "All bad things do. At least a broken bone grows back stronger."

That made a hell of a lot of sense to Rhett in a lot of ways.

"Back to work, you bastards," Bruiser shouted, and everybody hopped to, setting the dropped rail back to rights and reentering their intricate dance.

But Rhett had a plan.

That night, he bunked in a different car with the rail running crew, which he took to mean he'd done a decent-enough job that he wasn't getting sent back to Digby and the cut line. The rail crew car was slightly nicer, with whitewashed boards and a cleaner floor and cots that didn't smell quite so much like mold and sweat and piss. Rhett realized that he'd left his doctor's bag behind in the old car, but what good was it anyway? Cora and Grandpa Z had already taken what little wealth it possessed, with no thanks to the bearer. All Rhett owned now were Dan's clothes on his back, Sam's hat, and the leather pouch Winifred had crafted to hold the magic powder that made sure everybody knew why his name was Red-Eye. He slept hard that night, as he had every night in the railroad camp, exhausted to his very bones.

The next morning, the rail crew passed the pickax crew on the way into the breakfast tent, and Notch and Beans and all the fellers acted like they'd never met Rhett, nor worked and slept alongside him. Digby gave him a slight head nod of respect, but that was it. Apparently moving up in the world was frowned upon. Not that it mattered, because Rhett was about to undo all the good he'd done, getting promoted to a slightly more comfortable life.

The first couple of rails he delivered quick and sure, but the fourth one he fumbled in a spectacular fashion. He'd been mentally preparing himself for it, knowing that if he didn't commit one hundred percent, if he didn't at least punch a bone through his own flesh, then they'd just brush him off and set him back on his damn feet. But no. He did it. He dropped that rail right on his leg and fell over it. He was rewarded with a pain like all the fires of hell, and he saw his goddamn arm bone jutting out of his skin in a gush of hot blood that made him feel just as mortal as a little old church lady tiptoeing through town.

The pain was so bad that Rhett maybe fainted, but not in a womanly fashion. Arrows had him cradled up in his arms like a baby and was breathing hard as he ran Rhett to the handcar and pumped him back to the train and its little town that moved magically along with the engine. Rhett's vision faded in and out, the prairie rolling by, and he couldn't help noticing the black shadows of sentinels on horseback. Had he and Arrows turned and run for the hills, there'd have been no escape from those fast horses and faster rifles. No matter how fast men might be, they couldn't outrun horses, nor could a bird outfly gunpowder. Rhett didn't doubt Trevisan kept sharpshooters ready to punch men like him out of the sky with bullets. All the while, his arm screamed, the pain almost as bad as being peppered through with silver and lead. He was careful not to look down at the wound lest he make a further mess of himself.

Things went dark. Next thing he knew, his head was sticking through the tent flap.

Cora looked up from Grandpa Z's table. "Another? Go on back. We have him."

Arrows dumped him on the cot and left without a word, at a run.

"Tripped on a rail, did you? Still foolish, I see."

With a sigh, Cora left her work at the desk and kneeled at the side of the cot looking more annoyed than kindly.

"Hell of a nurse you are," Rhett muttered. "Not even a whimper of sympathy."

"I am not a nurse. I am a doctor. And this is going to hurt." She took Rhett's arm in her small hands and said, "Deep breath now."

"Wait," he said, although it was a bit of a splutter.

"For what? The bone to set incorrectly due to negligence? Fool."

"I need to tell you something."

She leaned down only slightly, looking distrustful. "I will listen. But know that I have a knife, and I know how to use it."

"Good. That makes me like you better. Now, you want Meimei, right?"

Cora changed entirely, going from a vexed woman to a dragon bitch in the space of a heartbeat. Her eyes flared with white-hot fire as she leaned closer, a curl of smoke escaping as she hissed in an altogether different voice, "What of Meimei?"

"Well, I reckon the only reason you and your grandpappy don't turn into giant dragons and burn the whole damn railroad down is because Trevisan has your sister in a cage in his caboose. But if you could save her, you could just kill everybody and leave, right?"

She cocked her head like a lizard. "Perhaps. Why do you say this?"

"Because I want to help you do it. I want Trevisan dead."

"Many people want that, but more people still want him alive. What do you propose?"

Rhett grinned, or tried to. He was in a powerful lot of pain, slipping in and out of sanity, and he could feel his lips quivering. "I propose we break her out."

Cora's eyes half closed, and she stroked her chin with a dragon's claw. "I believe I begin to see your plan. You just want to die quickly. Now hold your tongue."

Before Rhett could say anything else, she grasped his arm in two places and did something that involved the worst, most grinding pain in the damn world and a loud snap. Rhett swooned before relaxing into the cot as boneless as a snake, the pain fled. He knew without looking that his arm was back in its right place, the bones already knitting together.

"Thank you kindly," he said weakly.

"You won't thank me, should you try to rescue my sister."

"I'll thank you for trying to help."

He closed his eyes, just for a moment of rest. Cora placed a cool, wet cloth that smelled of herbs on his forehead, and he sighed. Next to going to sleep across from Sam or fumbling in the dark with Winifred, this was about as close to heaven as he'd been—this sudden removal of abject pain.

The next thing he felt was the cold prick of a knife over his heart.

He'd been still—but he went stiller.

"So tell me first—why should I trust you, Red-Eye?"

Rhett opened his eye, but not quickly, like he was afeared. Slowly, as if to match her deadly, measured, reptile-like way of doing things.

"You don't have to trust me. You just have to listen to my plan and do what I say."

"Trevisan might kill you outright."

Rhett shook his head, his eye never leaving hers. "I don't think he will, though. He likes torturing things. I'm something different and rare. You might even say he considers me down-right interesting."

"Then why has he put you to dangerous work?"

Rhett shrugged a little, like it was nothing. "All the work here's dangerous. He's curious to test my mettle, maybe. Botched that up right fine, didn't I?"

Cora withdrew her knife from its precarious place and drew it over the glittering scales on her palm with a screech, a small smile tugging at her mouth.

"To be honest, I am also curious. Why do you pretend to be a man?"

At that, Rhett went still, his eye narrowing and his fingers clenching painfully into fists. "Now, why would you say that?"

"Don't be angry. I am a woman who dresses as a man so that the hard men of the railroad won't think to look at me, but I live my inside life as a woman. You are a woman who dresses as a man, but I sense that you truly wish to be one. I have met people like this before, back home in Yerba Buena. I make no judgment. I am merely curious."

"You're not from Chine?"

She snapped her claws at him and chuckled. "Tit for tat. I understand you, and I will play your game. My honorable parents came to Calafia when I was small, and I have lived only here, in the Federal Republic. My grandfather joined us more recently. My ways are new ways, different from those of my ancestors. I am a new thing, and I am unashamed. Perhaps your ways are new ways, too?"

The wings of her eyebrows rose to spur him on. Was she saying what he thought she was saying? That she wasn't all mares-and-stallions, too?

"Tit for tat," he grumbled. Before he went on, though, he scanned the tent for the green cloak and long gray braid of Grandpa Z, who didn't seem to be nearby. What Rhett was going to say wasn't something he wanted shared around. "So maybe I was born wrong, but being a girl brought me nothing but trouble and discomfort. I live how I want to live. And that's in pants, among hard men, on horseback, with a gun in my hand. I'm glad to shoot anybody who has a problem with that."

"Your name is not really Ned, is it?"

Rhett looked at her like she was dumb as a possum. "Names don't mean shit, and you know it. I could change my name to Lord Percival Montgomery Assface tomorrow, and it wouldn't change who I am."

At that, Cora's dragon face finally cracked, and she laughed behind a hand. "This is true, and something I had not considered."

Rhett gave as much of a shrug as he could, lying down, then realized he could sit up and not look like a damn baby. His arm was sore and achy but mended, and it felt better to be upright, on the level and staring Cora in her peculiar, beautiful, hypnotizing eyes. "I reckon I'm on my fifth name by now, and I'd bet good coin it won't be the last one I travel under. Doesn't really matter what you call me. I'm still me, and that's never going to change. And I tell you now that I'll do my best to save your sister if I can just get myself into Trevisan's caboose."

"Few who enter his car leave alive." She cocked her head, amused, and her eyes somehow smoldered like a banked flame and went back to a cool blue-green. Rhett suddenly realized he had a powerful yearning to kiss the hell out of that smart mouth of hers.

"What makes you think you'll succeed where others have failed, Red-Eye Ned?"

He gave her his cockiest grin. "I got something they don't."

Her eyebrows rose, her fingers—now soft girl fingers, not dragon claws—grasping Rhett's chin. "And what's that?"

"Pluck," he said softly, leaning in to kiss her quick, before he lost his nerve.

He half expected Cora to give him a new scar with her talons, but instead, her fingertips moved to his jaw, holding him lightly in place and bringing him back into the kiss. His eye flickered to the tent flap, expecting Grandpa Z to bustle in and ruin everything, but the world, for once, didn't interfere. Kissing Cora was entirely different from kissing Winifred, which Rhett had not expected. The girl had a soft precision to her that Rhett liked, a little cat tongue that darted about curiously and gentle but persistent hands that didn't hesitate to put Rhett where she wanted him.

When Cora pulled away, she was smiling, and so was Rhett.

"I did not expect that," she said.

"Pluck has its rewards," was his response.

They considered each other in the silence, which wasn't really silent, thanks to the constant pings and bangs and shouts of the camp.

"So will you do it?" Rhett finally asked.

"I don't want to bring you to harm." Her voice was gentle, apologetic, but firm. "Selfishly, I wish to keep you around. We could explore many things together in stolen moments like this one. But I spend every moment of my life knowing Meimei is in a cage, and any enjoyment I take is at the expense of her pain. So I will do this. I will help you kill Trevisan. But I ask for one thing."

"What's that?"

Rhett was expecting the worst. That she wanted to get married, or to be escorted to Calafia with her cantankerous grandfather, or that he kill Trevisan a certain way that wouldn't be nearly as fun. What Cora said, however, surprised him.

"Time. With you. Alone." If Rhett had been the type to swoon, he would've. "Now. Before Trevisan kills you."

Cora's wicked smile almost took the sting out of her words.

"Why? Why me?"

"Because you are like a specific spice I have never tasted and might never find again."

"How much time do you need?" Rhett said, his voice all husky.

"Not much."

She kissed him, and he decided she was an unusually reasonable woman.

Cora sent a runner boy in the thoroughfare to tell Bruiser that Rhett required some watching, which wasn't unusual. Some bones knit more easily or correctly than others, apparently, and some men stayed unconscious all day. She turned back from the slice of daylight wearing that dangerous smile and silently tied the tent's flaps shut—top, middle, and bottom. The tent went dark and quiet, shadows dancing through the canvas.

"What about your grandfather?" Rhett asked.

Cora flicked her fingers. "He is a peculiar man. He goes for long walks to find plants."

"And Trevisan lets him?"

"Trevisan sends a guard with him. Grandfather very much enjoys making his guard uncomfortable, in walking very, very slowly."

"And Trevisan doesn't guard you?"

With each question, Cora stepped closer to the cot—not that she had far to go, considering it was a small tent. Her arms were behind her back, as if she were pretending to be an innocent, harmless little thing. Rhett didn't buy that for a minute, and he liked that about her. He imagined those dainty hands behind Cora's shapely back edging into claws, sharp and glittering.

"Trevisan knows I do not require a guard. He holds Mei-mei's life in his hands, and that means he holds my life, too. I will be good so that he will be good to her. That is my curse." She smoothly kneeled between Rhett's knees, curling her dragon claws over his thighs. "But it is also my salvation. I am not watched."

Emboldened by her brazenness, Rhett caressed her hair and pulled the leather thong that held it back, letting the inky curtain brush Cora's cheeks. "You take your salvation often?"

She shook her head, letting her hair play. "Not since I came here. These men are crude, hairy beasts. I am accustomed to... softer flesh."

Rhett wondered, for just a moment, if Cora was calling him a woman. But when she started touching him, he didn't care anymore.

Hours later, after they'd talked and kissed and done a hell of a lot more than that, someone hollered and tugged at the tent flap, and Cora leaped up from the cot, tying her jacket closed and pulling back her hair.

"One moment!" she called, flapping her hands at Rhett.

He indulged in one good, luxurious stretch before setting himself to rights and yanking his hat down to hide any love bites or bruises that were hopefully already fading. The girl had shown him her claws in more ways than one.

"You must be careful with your arm," Cora scolded, her voice shrill and rude. "Come back tomorrow so that I can check the dressing. Keep it clean!"

"Yes, ma'am. Thanks mightily for the doctoring," he answered, likewise overloud, a lazy smile on his lips.

Cora chuckled and leaned close. "You can count on me," she said. "But you had better be as good as your word, Red-Eye Ned, or whatever your name is." She leaned in close enough to bite his ear with her sharp teeth. "I am not done with you. Kill Trevisan and free Meimei, and you will see."

Rhett stood.

He very, very much wanted to see.

CHAPTER
23

At breakfast the next morning, he realized he'd been betrayed. Rhett was sitting with the rail runners, shoveling down his food as fast as he could, when the dining tent suddenly went silent. He looked up to find Adolphus towering over him like a hungry mountain.

"Can I help you?" Rhett asked, wiping his mouth off on his sleeve. He swallowed his food, and it tumbled like a cold ball of lead down to his belly.

"Big boss wants to see you," Adolphus said, his grin as friendly as a cave-in.

"What'd he do?" Bruiser asked, doing some towering of his own.

"I reckon I got promoted again," Rhett said, standing and sticking out his chin.

"Like hell," Adolphus said. "Cora told us about your little plan."

He punched Rhett right in the gone eye, and everything went black.

Well, black*er*.

"Come now, my little conspirator. Time to wake up."

The voice was cultured, with a peculiar accent that bounced

like a hard trot. And it sounded as delighted as a rich kid at Christmas.

Rhett blinked sand out of his eye. His head was pounding and his mouth tasted of copper. His palms and wrists burned, and when he looked down, he realized his arms were bound. He was in another damn chair, although this model was much, well, prettier than the one from the tent. Shiny chrome gleamed like a mirror in the lantern light, and instead of leather restraints, there were chains. And spikes through his hands, pinning them down, far too similar to the one the Cannibal Owl had favored.

Silver. Hence the burn.

Of course.

So he couldn't heal, and he couldn't change.

Bernard Trevisan was a right bastard, but he knew his business.

The man himself stood just a bit in front of Rhett, looking down at him like Rhett figured a doctor looked at a dead body. Like it was only kind of interesting, and only if there was something unusual and freakish about it. Lucky for Trevisan that Rhett had quite a bit unusual about him. Rhett spit a glob of blood at the man's shiny black shoes and raised his head warily.

"They ought to hire you out as the timekeeper," he said. "Even if you're a few hours late for the wake-up bell. I'm sure you'll catch the hang of it by supper."

Trevisan's snow-pale face lit with delight. Last time, he'd worn black and pink, and today he was in all lavender with pink trimmings, right down to his gloves and a floppy cravat that would've been just the right size for strangling the man with. Rhett's innards recoiled at the sight of such a fancified, lady-like dandy.

"Oh, this is going to be fun. Isn't it, Ned?"

"I believe we do have different ideas of fun. *Sir.*"

"One moment, please, while I prepare myself." Trevisan bowed his head slightly and turned his back to mess with whatever he planned to use to torture Rhett.

Rhett let his head slide forward like he was swooning, but really he was scouting around the room. Last time he'd faced Trevisan, the two thugs had been there, too. Now they were alone, and they weren't in the tent. They were in a train car. If Rhett was lucky, he'd finally made it into Trevisan's personal car, the seat of his magic.

Only problem was, the damn car had no door. No windows, either.

Excluding such regular things as doors and windows, though, there was a lot crammed in the smallish space. On one side was a pigeonhole desk stuffed full of papers and velvet bags and evil-looking glass bottles. A leather knife roll much like the one from the Captain's doctor's bag lay there, but the instruments were far more complicated, clean, and shiny. This set looked like they could whittle Rhett up into a thousand twisty pieces that would never fit back together.

On the other wall were two shrouded shapes that Rhett figured for birdcages, each under a twilight-purple velvet cloth. Rhett would've bet Sam's hat that Meimei was in one of the two cages, and he would've bet his own hat that Trevisan's pet bird was under the other. But why were they covered? Either so Rhett wouldn't know about them, or perhaps so their occupants wouldn't see whatever dark deeds Trevisan had planned for him.

The wall directly ahead of Rhett was taken up by a long workbench covered in what he could only figure for witch business. Peculiar drawings of not-quite-letters were scrawled on the wall overhead in black as if burned there, elegant and sinister as the devil's own curling mustache. The bench itself was the messiest thing in the room, sprawling with bowls, cups, cauldrons, crucibles, oddly shaped glass gewgaws, tripods, books, and stains ranging from fresh blood to old blood to burned blood. Tall, drippy black candles were stuck everywhere like charred rib bones. The air crackled with magic and ashes, making Rhett's nose twitch.

Worst of all, Rhett could tell that there was at least half a train car's worth of space behind him, looming empty the same way a storm cloud does. The rustling of wings and rasping of sharpening beaks told him that Trevisan's birds roosted there, black eyes bright. Maybe sometimes they were black wax balls stuck with feathers, but just this moment, they were a dark-winged jury that didn't know the word *innocent*. Rhett didn't need his one good eye to know they'd gladly carve him up before Trevisan found his way to the beating heart underneath all that meaty flesh.

Rhett was right where he'd wanted to be. Right where he'd asked Cora to put him by turning him in to Trevisan's men. She hadn't liked the plan, but in the end, she was as good as her word. He hoped she would receive some sort of reward for her part in their carefully planned betrayal. That was the good news—he was finally here.

The bad news was that he had no damn idea what to do now.

Being the Shadow might've given him an edge, but it didn't give him much sense.

Oh, if Coyote Dan could've seen him now. He'd have laughed his fool head off. Of course, he'd have to find a way into the car to do it, first. And in order to do that, he would've had to have seen the crudely drawn pile of stones Rhett had scrawled on a south-facing tent with a chunk of burned wood last night on his way back from the privy. The camp had moved several times since they'd parted ways, and there was no way for Rhett to get back to that particular stump in the forest, even if he could've found it. So a clumsy drawing was the best he could do, and he'd done it more so Dan couldn't scold him later than in the hopes that his ragtag posse could somehow ride into Trevisan's camp and do anything useful. Truth be told, he didn't want them to show up at all. He'd fare better here believing they were safe, far from the fate that he now faced. Their safety was the sole reason he'd come here alone and gotten himself into this fine mess.

"Ah! Here we are now. Hello again, Ned. Or would you prefer I call you Red-Eye? I know the men do enjoy their little monikers."

Rhett's head jerked up to find Trevisan standing over him, holding...something. It looked like a tool he'd seen blacksmiths use to shoe a horse, like a long metal pincer. Rhett didn't like the look of that thing one bit, and Trevisan's avid smile cinched it.

Nope. Rhett was against witches with pincers.

"It don't matter what you call me, so long as you don't call me—"

Trevisan's salt-white eyebrows rose, and he squeezed the pincers knowingly, *click-click*.

Rhett flinched. "Ned'll do."

"Fine, then. Ned. Please explain your plans to...what did Cora say? End me?"

Rhett took a deep breath, and Trevisan snuck his pincers into Rhett's mouth and grabbed his tongue. Silver again. Rhett had no way to pull away, with his body strapped into the chair, and turning his head to the side only made it hurt more. His heart started yammering and he nearly pissed himself.

"Did I mention that I don't like lying?" Trevisan said casually. "And that I could yank your tongue out right now?"

"Ih yuh dih—" Rhett started.

The pincers released his tongue, and he swallowed desperately before repeating himself. "If you did that, I couldn't tell you my plan, though."

Trevisan smiled like Pap had when Nettie—*Rhett*—was little and struggling to learn something difficult, like starting a fire. It was a smile that said you had maybe one more minute of patience before the whip came out.

"Tell me your plan now, then, while you still have your tongue."

Rhett cleared his throat but didn't open his mouth wide this time. "Revenge. Simple as that. You killed a friend of mine, and I was hoping to find help in taking you down. Figured the Chine girl had probably met everybody in camp and had some idea of who-all might want to throw in with me."

"Tsk." Trevisan actually looked...slightly sad. "That's not the truth. Men who burn with revenge don't talk about it like it is yesterday's biscuit. Revenge is anything but simple. And a man seeking revenge would begin among his crew, whispering with his equals. He would not seek out and seduce the only woman in the camp."

A blush crept up Rhett's neck, and his eye slid sideways. "I don't know what you mean by—"

"Come now. I have spies everywhere. For example, I know Cora is not the only woman in camp. And I know that you never spoke to anyone on your crew—on either of your crews—about fomenting rebellion. So what is it, then? Is it the money or the magic? Because let us be honest. It is always the money or the magic. I have killed far greater men than you."

He winked solemnly with one ice-blue eye. "And women. They die much the same in this chair."

"And how's that?"

"Piece by piece until there is nothing left. Why do you think there's so little sand in some of those jars in the feed tent? Just a handful of grains. Just a heart left, at the end, still beating."

"Why?" Rhett asked.

Because it had worked with the Cannibal Owl, hadn't it? Asking all his fool questions to prolong the inevitable? And because he truly wanted to know.

"Oh, poor Ned. You don't understand how interrogation works, do you? The thing is…"

The lavender glove reached out to pinch Rhett's nose closed. He struggled to tear his face away from the iron grip, but Trevisan was fiercely strong and as patient as stone. Finally, Rhett had no choice but to open his mouth if he wanted to stay conscious. When he did, the pincers yet again snagged his tongue.

"Gahammit!"

Seconds later, Trevisan had snaked another instrument into his mouth, and Rhett shuddered as something tightened around one of his teeth. Not a heavy molar in back, not a pointy one in front—one of the middle ones. As Rhett realized what was happening, his struggle hit a frantic note, his fingers digging into the arms of the chair and his body bowing up off it as he howled wordlessly.

The sound and the feeling were equally goddamn horrible as Trevisan wrestled the tooth out of Rhett's jaw with a crunch, the roots pulling out with a long, painful snap. Rhett was breathing hard, panting around the pincers as Trevisan held up a pair of pliers latched onto a blood-tipped tooth, staring at it with a love that some men only showed to bibles or whores.

"Do you know what this is, Ned?"

"Ugh oo!"

"Ah. The tongue. Sorry."

The pincers withdrew, and Rhett probed the blood-filled socket in his jaw tenderly with that sore muscle. His whole skull rang with the hurt and wrongness of it, his chin trembling with shock.

"It's my goddamn tooth, you son of a bitch!" Rhett hollered.

Trevisan nodded kindly. "Oh, but it's so much more than that. It's life to me, Ned." His eyes took on a crazy light, as if he really needed Rhett to understand. *"Life."* The floor didn't even creak under his shiny shoes as he moved to the workbench and dropped the tooth into a glass jar full of what Rhett now realized were more teeth. Teeth, and little bones. Pinkies and little toes, most like, all white and shiny and streaked, here or there, with rusty red, probably twenty in all.

Rhett's mouth was sore as hell as he said, "You're one sick bastard. Anybody ever told you that?"

"Only for the last three hundred years or so. It doesn't really hurt my feelings anymore. What's your real plan? Lie again, and you'll lose more than a tooth."

Rhett snorted and shook his head. "What is it with you bad guys? Always pinning a body down and acting like you're owed the hellfire truth. I never signed on for that. I don't owe you shit. I'm here to kill you. It's that goddamn simple. You're a bad man, and I'm a Durango Ranger. I kill what needs to die."

Trevisan looked up from lovingly patting his instruments. "A Ranger? No. That can't be. Haskell hates monsters like you. And more than that, Haskell and I have an arrangement."

"You think I don't know that? Why the hell you think I'm here alone instead of riding in with fifty friends? Hell, man. I thought you were smart. After you're dead, I just might go after Haskell as dessert."

"Eugene would kill you."

"Eugene ain't the only Ranger captain."

Trevisan put down the knife he'd been caressing and slunk to Rhett's side like a hungry cat. "Tell me, then. Which is your outpost? Not Garland or Houston. Must be Las Moras or El Paso. Lubbock's nearly in my pocket. This is important now."

"What'll you give me if I tell you?"

A small laugh.

"I might let you live a little longer."

"Oh, well, praise the lord. I'm enjoying life so much right now. In fact, it's been a right treat for the past seventeen years. Please, let's keep on. Just like this."

"I see." Trevisan's face went dark and distant, and he turned away.

The throbbing in Rhett's jaw warred with the ongoing burn in both palms. Realizing that the harder he clenched his fingers around the arms of the chair, the more the silver spikes tore through his hands, he took a deep breath and tried to relax, which proved impossible.

But did it mean he truly couldn't change? That was obviously what Trevisan was guarding against—letting Rhett go from a well-secured, fleshy human to a half-wild animal that had slipped its bonds. Sure, most folks wouldn't be able to change in this situation, considering thick hooves or wide paws. But what was the point of being the Shadow if the same rules applied? Rhett reached for the golden cord—

And found Trevisan perched over him with a silver spike and a hammer, the spike's tip hovering over his heart.

"I can kill you quicker, then, if you think that would be wise."

"Didn't say it was wise. Just didn't think vinegar was the best way to catch a fly."

"Oh, you want sugar, then, Mr. Red-Eye? Perhaps some sweet red wine? That's what we used to catch flies in my time, when things were civilized. Before we crossed the ocean and found this land of milk and honey, of gold and blackflies. Do you know that Italia has no naturally occurring monsters? We had to learn to make our own magic there. We had to struggle for our greatness. Now, will you talk, or shall I end it here?"

Rhett sneered. "Reckon I'll talk eventually. If I'm to die, I'd rather do it under the sky."

Trevisan smiled again. *"Molto bene."* He carefully placed the spike and hammer back on the tray. "I have no honey. My wine stores are low. Do you wish for more vinegar, or will you tell me, once and for all, why you're here?"

"I already told you—"

Trevisan's smile went brittle, then feral.

"Allora."

He nodded once and turned to his instruments, his fingers dancing over them like he was playing a piano. With only seconds left before the man turned back with another one of his goddamn devices, Rhett reached inside, pulled his golden string, and turned himself inside out. It always hurt, at least a little, although the transformation had gotten better when Earl had taught him to accept himself, whatever the hell that meant.

But this time, the change burned and tore, and the bird flapped out of a blue work shirt screaming, its wings ripped and trailing blood and feathers. It hopped across the room, away from the man, shaking loose of everything that had held it down. The man spun and shouted nonsense, and soon the air was full of beaks and feathers and talons, the flock of ravens swarming around the great bird, the lambhawk, the lammergeier, even as it fluttered around the floor, wings broken and unable to fly.

The ravens attacked him like a giant fist, beaks punching and claws ripping for his remaining eye, for his flight feathers, for his breast. But the big bird knew what to do, even if he couldn't take to the air. His beak and talons were bigger and sharper and stronger, and he thrashed out with his own weapons, ripping their smaller bodies apart and swallowing chunks of what was left.

It was the man he wanted to kill—he knew that much. But the cloud of birds stood between them, and on the other side, the man had weapons of his own. Somewhere, on the edge of his awareness, a child's voice was crying, the bars of a cage rattling in fear or rage, but that barely registered. The bloodlust had him in its grip, even if the birds he felled contained no blood to soothe him. Soon the floor was littered with balls of wax and bits of string and fluttering, broken feathers. The mad ravens were too few and too fractured to pose a real threat.

The bird almost changed back into a man, but Rhett was there, too, and Rhett had a plan.

With a great heave, the bird hopped across the floor and stabbed at the shiny black shoes, causing the man in lavender, the enemy, to dance back, a great gleaming knife in his hand. The man stabbed at the bird, but the bird stabbed back. A hot metal punch landed in the bird's back, but it didn't find home in his heart, and the bird managed to slash the man's leg, drawing blood and tearing the hated lavender pants.

Deep within the bird, Rhett grinned, missing one tooth.

The man shouted and danced back, and that's when the bird hopped aggressively forward and became Rhett again, a naked, skinny creature dripping blood from a dozen places.

Standing unsteadily but filled with red-hot rage, Rhett snatched two knives from the roll on the desk and took a step toward Trevisan. Naked, torn, trailing red-dipped black feathers underfoot, Rhett stalked Trevisan around the room, still half animal in his thoughts.

Whatever Trevisan was muttering wasn't in any language Rhett knew, and it sure as hell didn't sound like the man was begging for his life. His trembling hand sketched signs in the air as he brandished his knife, and Rhett reckoned that this was how magic happened, with baneful words and stupid signs and a whole bunch of frilly bullshit that didn't do a goddamn thing. So he slashed for Trevisan's hand with one knife, and when Trevisan clutched his bleeding hand closer, Rhett punched the man in his teeth with the handle of the other knife, hoping to make it as hard for him to talk as it was for Rhett just then. His busted knuckles burned as they always did, but Trevisan's pain was worth it.

"Stop, Ned. Just...listen. I know the secret. To living forever. I'll teach you. I'll teach you whatever you want. Just stop. No more blood."

Rhett sucked on his knuckles and laughed with red-splashed teeth. "No more of *your* blood, you mean. You'd be pleased as goddamn punch for more of mine spilt."

Trevisan was backing away from him now, looking altogether smaller as fear bit deep. Rhett had somehow wondered if the man would bleed black or maybe be full of feathers like a fancy white pillow, but the witch, or whatever he was, bled as readily as anyone else. And the cuts on his hand and leg weren't healing like Rhett's were.

With another violent slash, Rhett split open the man's lavender sleeve. The blade was so sharp that it was almost a pleasure, slick as...well...other things Rhett had discovered recently.

"You'll never survive without me," Trevisan said, as if casting about for just the right words as he clutched at his bleeding arm. "You and Meimei won't get out of this car. You'll never find the door. Cora would kill you for that alone, but you'll starve to death until your heart gives out and turns you to sand."

Trevisan was backing behind the chair now, past a swinging chandelier where Rhett figured the ravens had been roosting before. Rhett caught his reflection in a tall mirror, just a flash of a half-familiar, half-hated body, all brown and bones and unwanted curves and a gaunt, haunted face that would never need shaving. He lashed out, bashing the mirror with his fist to make it crack into a thousand glittering shards.

"Money? Gold? You can have it all, Ned. I'll tell you the combination to the safe. Riches beyond your wildest dreams. You'll live forever, and you'll do it in whatever fashion you like."

Rhett's next slash was meant for Trevisan's throat, but the man lurched back and took it across the jaw instead. Trevisan dropped his knife and put a surprised hand to the deep cut, touching the bone beneath in abject horror. He licked his lips, panting, one hand out to Rhett in desperate supplication.

"You said you were going to kill me because I was a bad man, but what does this make you?" he said, holding the flaps of his face together with shaking hands. "You began a monster, but you'll end a monster of a different sort. This is torture. Playing with me, like a cat with a mouse. You can still stop. You don't have to do this. But if you keep going, you will be as bad as you think I am."

"Wrong."

Trevisan had backed himself into a corner now, and Rhett stood tall, naked and unafraid before the cowering man in his fine silk suit.

"I'll never be what you are, Mr. Trevisan. Because I'm going to kill you, open all the doors, and walk the fuck away."

"Don't be stupid—"

"Can't help that," he said. "It's in my blood."

Whatever his name was, he slashed Bernard Trevisan across the throat.

CHAPTER 24

Trevisan fell.

Not in a dramatic way, but like a weak man who knows he's done for and can't do a damn thing about it. Rhett didn't let go of either knife. He knew well enough by now that monsters usually got up for a second round of pontificating and fighting, even those whose skin wasn't knitting itself back together in preparation for another round.

But Trevisan just lay on the floor in a puddle of red, shivering and growing paler, the lavender and pink of his suit soaking up his own blood. Rhett's wounds had already closed, the holes in his palms no longer burning and the kiss of the silver chains burned away to slightly raised scars at his wrists.

"You done?" He nudged Trevisan with a long, bare foot that made memories of Winifred rise, sharp as the morning, in his mind.

Trevisan's body was done moving, but his fool mouth wasn't. He was curling in like a bug, getting older and wrinklier and more frail by the minute. He started up in that language of his, and a bobbing, dancing, evil thing it was, full of syllables that sounded like spit and punches. Shaking his head, Rhett walked over to where his boots sat at the base of the chair, stepped into them barefoot, walked back over, and landed a kick square in Trevisan's mouth. Feeling teeth break was one of the more peculiar things Rhett had experienced, and he watched, fascinated, as Trevisan spit out white and red shards and kept mumbling around whatever stubs were left.

For a split second, Rhett considered fetching those damn pincers and ripping the man's tongue out, but that seemed cruel now, and Rhett had no admiration for cruel men.

Thing was, though... Trevisan's neck was split near in two, his blood all pumped out. So why was he still able to move his lips at all? If he truly was human, he should've died as quickly as Prospera had. Even his eyes had gone that odd, glassy dark that dead eyes did. But still the lips moved, spitting and punching and lisping inelegantly.

"Why don't you have the good sense to die when you're dead?" Rhett said, hunkered down on his haunches with a knife in each hand.

The dead eyes rolled up to look at him, the lips still fluttering. Trevisan said one last thing, breathy and wheezing, something that sounded like *Amen*, and smiled with his broken mouth. And then he finally stopped moving and seemed really, truly dead.

As Rhett stood, a sound began somewhere he couldn't pinpoint, and the room filled with a wild gust of wind. Black feathers and bits of string whipped across his face as what felt like a cyclone swirled in faster and faster circles, carrying a loud roar that sounded a little like a human scream of terror and triumph. Rhett fell to his knees, dropped the knives, squeezed his good eye shut, and slammed his hands over his ears. The sound tore at him like wind trying to find the chinks between boards and rip a prairie lean-to apart. Rhett held his breath, tensing his entire body and every damn sphincter he had against the ripping, pulling, hungry onslaught of sound and air. It felt like it sought to tear the very skin from his bones, like it wanted to crawl right down into his throat, and he shook his head and pinned his lips and denied it that pleasure.

The wind carried pleading and screaming and the caws of a million ravens.

The wind carried madness.

The wind begged and demanded and commanded and cajoled, and still Rhett hunkered down further in his skin and mind and refused it any damn toehold. And then someone else screamed, a high, mad child's scream, and Rhett didn't know if it was him or the wind, and then the damn wind let up and he realized it was coming from one of the covered cages.

The train car was bizarrely quiet as Rhett stood and brushed snapped black feathers off his ravaged skin. Everything was thoroughly wrecked, the surfaces littered with wax and shattered glass and spilled bones and seeping liquids. With a peculiar sort of clarity, Rhett plucked a whole tooth off the floor and stubbornly jabbed it back in his jaw where it belonged. The roots tickled as they re-formed, and he moved his mouth around and probed his gums with his tongue, pleased to find that whether it had originally been his own tooth or not, it was now.

Glass and bone and sand cracked under his boots as he trod, naked, to the still-covered cages and whipped the indigo velvet fabric away. On the right, a dead raven lay, feet curled up, on the bottom of the cage. Unlike the creatures of wax and magic, this one had been real, apparently. On the left, a little Chine girl with silver-white dragon eyes regarded Rhett in fear, tear tracks tracing long lines down her chubby cheeks.

"You're Meimei, I reckon?" Rhett said.

She couldn't have been more than six, maybe, and her baby

fingers wrapped around the bars of the cage briefly before shuddering apart as if burned. More silver. She sat cross-legged in a red silk robe, her hair in tufty little tails.

"Cora," she said with a sniffle. "Want Cora."

Rhett nodded and swallowed a sniffle of his own. If there was one thing he knew, it was what it felt like to be a small thing living without love, kept caged to be used by a cruel man with no warmth in his heart. He kicked shit around the room until he found a shiny silver pair of nippers. Snip by snip, he cut a hole in the cage and pried the pieces apart so that Meimei could uncross her legs and slide off her silk cushion. The little girl fell as soon as her feet hit the floor.

"Legs asleep, huh?" Rhett said, not unkindly. He held out a hand to help her, but she shook her head and stood on her own, a stubborn set to her round little chin.

Seeing the tiny girl so helpless and determined reminded Rhett that he was standing nekkid in his boots, and he hurriedly shuffled into Dan's shirt and pants and found Sam's hat, battered and beaten in a corner. His wrap had landed in Trevisan's blood, and hell if he wanted that bound tight to his chest. For now, he'd do without.

"You want to go find Cora?" he said, turning back and holding out a hand.

Meimei nodded but didn't reach for him. Her hands were clasped tightly to her chest. Well, and why would a little girl who'd been kept in a cage trust anybody, especially a scary-looking stranger?

He nodded his understanding and said, "Where's the door?"

Meimei walked with an odd, weightless delicacy to the wall behind the chandelier and pressed her small hand against a panel, which smoothly moved aside to reveal a sharp spear of sunlight and the noise of a construction camp hard at work.

Rhett shielded his eye with his hand and gazed out, expecting to find Trevisan's lackeys waiting with guns arrayed against him. But not a soul looked to the car, and work went on as usual. Adolphus and his skinny friend were nowhere to be found. Still, Rhett held up a finger to Meimei, hurried back into the wreck of the car, and palmed one of the smaller knives, just in case.

Rhett hopped down the stairs first, and Meimei followed with the carriage of a princess. The little girl stopped, just outside, and pressed a panel that closed the door again.

"Smart," Rhett said. "We don't want anybody to know he's dead, do we?"

She solemnly shook her head no.

"Cora," she repeated, eyes wide and earnest.

When Rhett led her toward Grandpa Z's tent, Meimei walked at his side, not close enough to touch, but close enough to show she was scared of the camp. The child shared her older sister's peculiar calm and steadfastness, never wincing as her satin slippers landed in mud or filth. It was a short stretch to their destination, and Rhett's every sense was on alert, his fingers clutching the knife so hard they went numb. But nothing came at them or after them, and he couldn't help his grin as he pulled back the flap on Grandpa Z's tent and put a hand on the child's back.

"Go on, sugar," he said softly.

The soft cry from inside the tent filled him with warmth, and he stepped within and tied the flap, his back to the sisters to give their reunion the sort of privacy such sentiment required. They babbled at each other in their language, laughing and hugging and crying. Meimei spoke very little, and Cora treated her like a newborn kitten, as if she were breakable and easily startled, which the poor little critter had every right to be. As

Rhett watched, Cora attempted to examine the little girl, but Meimei pouted and crossed her arms and shied away from her sister's hands. The tears in Cora's eyes and the firm set of her mouth told Rhett that she was hurt by her little sister's coldness but that she understood the sad truth behind it. Maybe Meimei had reasons she didn't want hands touching her body against her will right now.

Good for her, Rhett thought. *Still got spunk.*

"Ned," Cora breathed, and then she was hugging him, filling up his vision and heart and making a sweetly painful lump rise in his throat. "You did it."

"Reckon I did," he said, voice husky with feeling.

"I owe you a debt of gratitude. We owe you."

He patted her awkwardly and tipped his hat a little. "I'm a Durango Ranger, darlin'. This is what I do. You're free now. Trevisan is dead."

She pulled away and looked at him like he'd hung the damn moon, her bright eyes afire and wet at the same time. "Are you sure? How?"

He allowed himself a little grin. "Gave him a nice smile," he said, drawing a finger across his throat from ear to ear. "For all his power, he fell as easily as any man. Any human, I reckon. I watched the last of his blood pump out. He's well and truly gone."

She shoved hard against his chest as if trying to burrow in for winter. "You have brought me my dearest wish, and I will say prayers for you all my days."

Letting himself fully enjoy her warmth, he wrapped his arms more firmly around her, lining them up all along the front in a pleasant way and rubbing her back. "There's better ways to repay me, ma'am," he said, voice pitched low so the child wouldn't hear.

She pulled away with a mischievous look in her eyes. "As you would say, I reckon there are. And plenty of time, now, for repayment."

Much to Rhett's surprise, things went well after that. Grandpa Z spoke to his Chine boys, and Rhett sought out Digby and Bruiser, and even if nobody believed him at first, the whole damn camp soon had Adolphus and the skinny feller cornered, mud-smeared pickaxes pressed to where their hearts should've been. Once those two evil bastards were sand, the scouts riding in to stop the trouble turned their mounts promptly around and galloped for the hills. A crew of terrifying but beautiful dragons crawled up on top of the train cars and took out the snipers, bullets pinging off their scales like the notes on a badly tuned piano. Rhett was pretty sure most of the sentries got et, and that seemed pretty reasonable, as far as punishment and repayment went.

After Trevisan's men were gone, Rhett didn't know what to expect from the rough crew of a railroad camp, whether they'd go for weapons and whisky or food and gold, but they'd been so beaten down and fearful for so long that they didn't immediately get to carousing. The bosses met in the feed tent and decided to divvy up what wealth they could, considering the workers had never been paid for a day of their labors. Griswold's desk became the place a man could go to tally his time and reckon what he considered fair recompense for fingers and toes and years. Luckily, Trevisan had enough gold around the camp to satisfy men who were happy to simply taste freedom again. A good number of fellers went to visit the shebang, which at least kept them out of worse trouble.

The glass jars of sand on the feed tent shelves disappeared

quietly, one by one, as men came to claim their friends. When Rhett arrived, the Irish were sitting at the bench around one such jar, handing around a bottle of whisky and toasting Shaunie O'Bannon and whatever had become of his stubborn bastard of a brother.

"I know him," Rhett said quietly. "That Earl O'Bannon."

The burly fellers turned to stare at him with wet red eyes and distrust.

"Like hell you do, Injun," one started.

"Little feller. Has an unhealthy attachment to his burgundy shirt. Missing two toes. Turns into a donkey. Snores something awful. Loved his brother. Won't stop pestering a body until they go back to the railroad camp and kill the big boss. Sound about right?"

They looked him up and down like he was a lame mule.

"You?" the same feller asked. "You're the one who did Trevisan in, then?"

Rhett nodded and held up his palms to show the starburst-shaped scars from the silver spikes. "I am."

"How?"

Rhett grinned, knowing they wouldn't believe the truth. "Inde magic," he said solemnly.

The Irishmen glanced at one another in unspoken conversation, and the biggest one, even bigger than Bruiser, pushed the jar of sand toward Rhett. "Maybe you'll be takin' this to wee donkey-boy, then? Tell him his brother died brave."

With a manly nod, Rhett took the jar. "I'll get it to him." Then he allowed them a small grin. "I been callin' him donkey-boy, too."

The big Irishman grinned back. "Hates it, don't he?"

"That he does, lad. That he does," Rhett said, and the big feller toasted him with the bottle, and they laughed, every one.

The camp was clearing out. The train and tents had been sacked of anything of value that could be easily carried, and Rhett had no doubt that his doctor's bag and anything else he'd once considered his was long gone. Men collected into groups, hitching up wagons or doubling up on mules or perched on donkeys or getting bucked off half-wild mustangs or turning into wild beasts with glowing eyes, not caring that they looked like fools if it meant they would make it back to civilization without losing any more body parts or falling prey to other monsters. Rhett left them to it; he had two good horses and a mule waiting for him with his friends. But as he watched the last of the mules being fought over by Beans and Notch, he did wonder how Cora and Grandpa Z planned to get their supplies and Meimei back to Calafia. Could you even drive a wagon in dragon form?

With a grunt of self-satisfaction, he walked purposefully to the mule lot, hoping to find a creature left with four good hooves and not too many teeth. He hadn't dared think it, much less speak it out loud, but he reckoned he'd like life in general a good bit more if Cora was nearby. She was like no one he'd ever met and didn't get on his nerves much at all. She was a hard worker, had a sense of humor, was never rude. He liked her body and what she did with it, and she'd fit in right well with his friends. Maybe the Captain would take her on for doctoring and such, considering the man didn't mind if folks were odd. But she wouldn't want that, would she? She'd want to go home to Yerba Buena and do whatever it was she'd done in the big city by the sea, long before she'd met a mixed-up cowpoke with a habit of getting shot at and losing pieces of himself in the bargain.

The only thing he could find was a donkey too small for the other men to ride. It wasn't the most pleasant of creatures, but he figured it could hold Meimei, and that's what Cora would care about. She could come with him and ride in Prospera's old wagon—hellfire, after fixing Winifred's foot! And then they could all go back to Las Moras or Gloomy Bluebird or any ol' town near the Las Moras Outpost. Even if Cora was a day or two's ride away, he'd still be glad to see her a few times a month.

Fashioning a rough halter from a bit of broken harness, he towed the donkey behind him, missing the reasonable good sense of a horse—any horse. He'd tossed an old feed sack over the creature's angrily hunched back, and the donkey had already bucked it off several times. He put the jar of sand on the ground where the creature couldn't kick it and tied the harness to the wagon waiting outside Grandpa Z's tent.

But when he poked his head inside, he found nothing but trouble.

It was mostly empty, the cots and rugs and worktable long gone. Only Cora was left, sitting cross-legged in the mud beside a sodden blanket and sobbing like her heart had fallen out. Despite himself, Rhett ran to her and fell to his knees with a splatter.

"What's wrong? Is she hurt? Did they take her?"

Cora shook her head and muttered in her own language before dashing her tears away. She looked at him, dragon eyes fierce with rage and sadness, and flipped back the top corner of the blanket to show a pile of silvery sand.

"Meimei?" Rhett asked, feeling his own tears rise up.

Cora shook her head. "Grandpa Z. My Meimei is nowhere to be found."

CHAPTER

— 25 —

Not knowing what to do with a heartbroken woman, Rhett settled for wrapping his arms around her and patting her and murmuring the sort of soft things he would say to a frightened horse. It worked for a moment, but then Cora exhaled angrily, pushed him away, and stood. Her hair was askew, her face puffy and her clothes spackled in mud. He'd never seen her in pieces before, but it didn't bother him.

Rhett stood, too. "You want me to go find her?"

His mind worked the calculations. All he had to do was go outside, shove a feller off a horse, and follow the Shadow's instincts. But Cora just shook her head.

"Ned, there was no one else. I left them here together while I readied the wagon, Grandpa Z and Meimei. They were playing games and laughing, sitting on this blanket. I have not seen him so happy in many years. When I came back, there was only sand, and this." She held up a shiny silver spike, small and sharp. Rhett recognized it immediately.

"That was in Trevisan's car. He threatened to kill me with it." Turning it over in his head, he made the connections. "She must've brought it with her. I...I didn't see it after..."

In the wet mud, small slipper prints were clearly visible,

a slick spot where a small, wee body had wriggled out from under the tent.

"Why?" Rhett said, his voice suddenly small. "Why would she do that?"

Cora's head dropped. "I don't know. Who could know? What poison did Trevisan whisper to her? He kept her with him for two years. I asked her what he did, if he touched her, made her drink anything. She would only smile and shake her head and call me Beloved Sister. Like he had broken something inside of her. Like there was nothing left but a doll."

"I can find her," he said. "She can't have gotten far. I can change—"

"Then change. Go. Bring her back. I don't care if she's broken. I will fix her."

The girl's eyes flared white, fathomless and hot. A thin curl of smoke rose from her lips.

Rhett stood and kept his eye locked with hers as he tossed off his eye kerch, Winifred's pouch, Sam's hat, Dan's clothes. He stepped out of his boots, his bare feet sinking into the soggy ground. He didn't mind her seeing him nekkid, not like this or anything else. Not that he was proud or wanted to impress her or seduce her, and not that he was altogether comfortable in his skin. Just that he knew it didn't matter, compared to real love like she had for Meimei.

Tugging the golden string inside, Rhett became the bird. Lammergeier was the word Trevisan had used, and that word didn't mean anything to Rhett. But Trevisan had also called him the lambhawk, and Rhett reckoned maybe that meant he could find the lost little lamb. For Cora. As the bird thoughts took over, he bobbed his ugly head, flapped out of the tent, and fumbled into the sky, leaving taloned prints in the muck.

The bird thrashed into the blue. His wings ached slightly

from where the silver spikes had torn them, right near the biggest flight feathers, but he didn't waver. He was missing a claw, too, but he didn't care. His one good eye could see, and his body still knew how to fly. They could keep on carving bits off of him, and he would keep on riding the wind just to spit in their eyes. All of them. Humans scurried below doing senseless human things, but he soared out in a focused circle, looking for one thing.

A little girl in a red silk jacket.

But he knew he had to look for other things, too. A little girl in a disguise. A horse or donkey with an extra lump. A small creature on foot, lost and confused. A man hurrying too fast, alone, carrying a sack. A wagon where no wagon should be. Maybe she'd left on her own, as Cora supposed. Or maybe someone else had taken her again. Little creatures were so easily stolen, as Rhett knew well enough.

The bird wobbled in flight and dropped a bit as Rhett realized that he was having man thoughts and bird thoughts, all at once. Together, both creatures sought the same thing with the same intensity they'd once given Earl O'Bannon's red shirt.

Find the child.

Wider and wider he circled. The man's mind ticked off and catalogued what he saw. There, Digby and some of his crew, traveling on foot behind a mule pulling an open wagon full of food and a couple of pickaxes, their only weapons. There, a great dragon, big as a train car, leading the Chine men on foot. There, the Irishmen, a tidy line of donkeys, sheep, and goats with bags strung around their necks or over their flanks, hot-stepping toward Lamartine. Most folks were headed that way, and few had anything to hide. Humans only saw what they wanted to, didn't they?

Circling away from the city, Rhett saw figures he recognized, Notch and Arrows and Beans, each alone. He heard Preacher preaching before he saw him, not surprised to note the uppity man had collected some of the sadder fellers in a wagon, including the one-legged Aztecan from the feed tent. But he didn't see anything that could've been Meimei, and his Shadow-self didn't wobble in any particular direction except back toward the camp. So when he'd exhausted his possibilities, he raced the sun back to earth and landed by one of the last remaining tents, where a beautiful girl waited by a hunchbacked donkey, her eyes streaming as she watched the oddest-looking bird in Durango Territory turn into the oddest-looking man in Durango Territory.

"No sign?" Cora asked, knowing the truth already.

He shook his head grimly and took the shirt she held out to him. "I'm sorry," he said, although it didn't seem like nearly enough. "I felt for sure I'd find her. I always know how to do what needs to be done. But this time...I just don't."

"Maybe she's gone." Cora raised her hands as if taking in all the sunset-tinged prairie. "Just more sand amid so much sand."

"She ain't sand." Rhett knew the hard truth of that, too, as the words left his mouth. "I know that much. She ain't sand."

Cora fell to her knees in the mud, startling the donkey. "Then, what? What else? What now?"

Rhett yanked down the tent's canvas until it covered the mud in an unwieldy heap. He caught Cora around the waist and dragged her back against him until they lay together, him curled around her spine and her curled around whatever hope she had left.

"Then we sleep, a little more free than we were yesterday. And tomorrow, I'll take you away from here." His voice was soft, sweet, a whispery voice he hadn't known he contained.

"If I go away, I will never find her again."

He brushed her smooth hair back over her cheek. "Staying won't bring her back."

"Stay. Go. It is all the same. She was my only compass, and now she is gone."

"Sometimes things come back. Sometimes there's a better path. But you have to leave, first, to find it."

Cora sighed as the stars began to peep out, one by one. Her body relaxed against him, just a little. "Perhaps you are right, Ned."

"My name is Rhett," he said, so quietly that the stars couldn't hear. "Before that, it was Nat. And before that, it was Nettie. And before that, it was something Injun."

Cora turned her face to put her cheek against his, smooth and cool. "Which name do you like best?"

"Rhett Hennessy Walker."

"Thank you, Rhett Hennessy Walker."

He gulped, well aware that he'd failed her. "For what?"

"Freedom," she said after a thoughtful pause. "And maybe, hope."

The morning dawned pink and cool with just the faintest hint of the winter to come. Rhett saw one good puff of breath before the heat started to find itself. He didn't move, though. He would prefer to stay curled around Cora for the rest of time, or at least until one of them had to attend to bodily needs. So far as he understood it, things were about to change again. Things had changed a lot, after he'd left Gloomy Bluebird. Most of the time he didn't mind, but this time, he was mighty uneasy.

He hadn't yet asked Cora which direction she favored. And he hadn't yet allowed himself to consider what he would choose if she wanted to head east or west instead of south toward his friends.

Beside him, Cora exhaled and stretched, arms up and legs down, her body going rigid and then boneless as she rolled to her back.

"She watches us," Cora said, and Rhett was about to ask who, but he looked where she was looking and saw the moon's coy smile.

If Rhett had had any sense, he would've kept track of the damn thing, at least to time his courses. But he resisted, as if resisting could change anything. There was something sly about that silvery crescent that plagued him lately. Ever since the Cannibal Owl, he'd figured he was better off not giving the moon that kind of power over him.

"It's like she's grinning at her own joke," he said, considering. "I don't know if I trust her."

"That's what is so funny," Cora said lightly. "She does not care, either way. She will go on, waxing and waning, ebbing and flowing, long after we are sand."

Rhett licked his lips and considered his next words carefully. "I don't know which way you want to go, but you said you owed me, and I reckon I should call in that debt before you get too far with your planning."

Cora rolled toward him, her small, fine hands dragging down his chest in a way that made him tense with hope. "And so here is the asking," she said, half-playful and half-suspicious.

"I got this friend," Rhett said.

"Do you?"

Cora's hands traced the more sensitive places of his anatomy, and he almost shut his damn mouth and gave in. Instead, he said, "And her foot got cut off."

The hands pulled away, and so did Cora. The air between

them went cold, and her voice dropped. *"Her."* A pause. "You wish me to heal her?"

Hating himself and shaking his head in loss, Rhett said, "I reckon that if I got one favor to call in, that'll be it."

Cora sat up with a sigh, maybe of disappointment, or maybe of resignation. Rhett didn't understand women well enough to know.

"Where is she, this friend?"

"About twenty miles south from here, I reckon. Maybe closer. I got a whole posse, armed to the teeth and waiting on me. We got horses and a wagon. And I hate to admit it, but we got a better tracker than me, and he could have an idea of where Meimei might be."

He propped himself up on one elbow and looked around at the empty camp and the long, dark train standing sentinel, the only shape rising from the flat prairie for miles. It might never move again. But if Rhett knew railroads, or at least the sort of men who built them, it would keep on chugging across Durango, with or without Trevisan. Damn thing would probably build itself just out of sheer stubbornness.

"I don't get it, though. My belly usually leads me toward whatever I'm supposed to chase, and my belly says I'm right where I'm supposed to be."

Cora rubbed his belly with a glint in her eye. "Just like a man. Following your appetites."

"Not like that. I just get a feeling. That's all." He almost told her what he was—the Shadow. But something stayed his tongue.

"Maybe you're supposed to stay with me," Cora said.

In her eyes, Rhett saw mischief war with longing, and he ached to roll her over onto her back and give the moon something real to see. But he didn't.

He looked toward the west, trying to imagine how far the land might stretch until it met some magical goddamn thing called an ocean.

"Maybe," he said, but he gave her a grin that said it wouldn't be such a horrible fate, staying with her a while longer.

Rhett stood and held out a hand to pull Cora up beside him. He felt big and capable next to her, although hellfire knew she was capable enough in her own right. And a damn dragon to boot. He hoped to see her change, someday, but was too shy to ask about it. It seemed a mighty personal thing to do, if someone's life wasn't currently on the line.

The donkey was still tied to the post, although it looked even grouchier than it had yesterday and had left several nasty piles of wet slop in the area. Rhett was glad he'd left the jar of Shaunie O'Bannon's sand far away from the frachetty creature. The wagon still waited, its contents covered with a rug, the horse twitching its tail. Rhett felt a quick twang of guilt for having left the creature in such a state overnight, tethered to future work.

"You got everything you need?" Rhett said.

Cora kneeled and dug around the tent's rumpled canvas until she found the blanket containing her grandfather's sand. A gust of wind whistled through the camp just then, and she clutched the blanket close as her hair whipped across her face. In that moment, Rhett thought she was the saddest and most beautiful thing he'd ever seen, and his heart wrenched in his chest something fierce. He wanted to protect her, but how could he? The world had already taken the two things she wanted most.

"Do you want to . . . bury him?"

Cora shook her head sadly. "That's not our way. This is merely sand, and it must return to the earth so new plants can take root. I wish I could lay him to rest on a hillside in Yerba Buena. Or in his home village, far away. Grandfather loved the sea. But he will return. Even without burning the paper and reciting the holy books, he will return. I wonder what form he will take." A smile played at her mouth. "In forty-nine days, he will be reborn. I only hope his karma was good enough for a better life than this one."

"Reborn?" Rhett said. "Like, from that sand?"

With a light laugh, Cora pressed the corner of the blanket to Rhett's chest. His fingers closed reflexively around it as she stood on her tiptoes to kiss him. When she pulled away, the blanket fell open, and the sand caught on the wind in a soft cloud. Rhett closed his eye almost all the way, watching through his eyelashes as the sand dispersed in a soft cloud, glittering in the morning sun.

"No," Cora said. "His spirit will take a new form. Everyone has been born before, and everyone will be born again. Such is life." She took the blanket back from him and folded it neatly as if it were just another piece of cloth. To her, now, maybe it was.

"He seemed like a good man," Rhett said softly.

Cora nodded. "He was. He considered it his duty to help others. I inherit this duty from him. He grew angry here. Angry at Trevisan, at himself, at me. He said we would never get Meimei back, that a fisherman never expects to take back his minnow whole and still wriggling. Perhaps he was right. But then again, he stayed anyway. And I never thought of my sister as a minnow." Walking to the wagon, she tossed the blanket on top of the rug and cocked her head at the seat. "Do I ride up there or walk?"

Rhett shook his head like he was trying to clear out the cobwebs. "That's it? You're ready to go? Just like that?"

Looking around the camp with her hands on her hips, Cora shrugged. "Here isn't here anymore. We will go, and I will help your friend."

"And then?"

"And then, we shall see."

Rhett had figured Cora would tear at her hair and cry and wail and maybe yank a bonnet down over her head. He didn't have much knowledge of women with grief, aside from Regina and Mam, both of whom he considered soft in the head and foolish. It was right peculiar to him, sitting up on a wagon-box by Cora as she quietly commented on the prairie they passed and asked him questions about the various sights. They purposely strayed from the train's path, set a hundred miles ahead by surveyors and graders, a red-dirt mound pushing endlessly west. Instead, they headed south, back the way Rhett had come. His only real worry was running into Haskell or his Rascals. That, or finding Meimei's bloody jacket fetched up against a prickly pear. So long as they headed south, Rhett reckoned they'd find his friends again, eventually.

As they moved, his senses told him they were headed in the right direction. He considered turning into the bird and scouting farther ahead, but the thought of leaving Cora alone in the wagon caused fear to burn up his throat like stomach acid. Sure, she was a dragon, but she was still a dainty little thing, and they didn't even have a gun between them. There could be Lobos out here, or even a ragtag group of railroad workers with their minds set to mischief. If there was one thing Rhett had realized since leaving Gloomy Bluebird, it was that no matter how many peculiar and dangerous creatures he met on the road, there were still more waiting to be discovered, in the form of both monsters and men.

His thighs ached for the saddle and his hips felt light without a holster, and sitting in the wagon made him feel slow and useless and plodding. No wonder Winifred had refused driving. It didn't help that the donkey ponied alongside would occasionally take up braying for no good reason, further cementing his dislike of donkeys. He'd only really brought it along in case of catastrophe, and maybe to mess with Earl, when they found him again. When life got rough, you could always eat the donkey.

"Shut up, you ass!" he hollered after at least an hour of screeching.

He snapped the reins to hurry the wagon horse along, and Cora wrapped her hands around his arm, pillowing her head on his shoulder. "Is it strange that I think you were more at home working in that camp than you are in fleeing it?"

Rhett shook his head as if to dislodge a fly but made no attempt to dislodge the girl. "I'd rather have work to do. I don't do well with empty hands. I need something to aim at, or I get all ornery. That whole time in the camp, I was just waiting for my shot at Trevisan."

"Not every moment."

He chuckled. "No, not exactly."

The donkey took up a new tone of angry braying, and Rhett was just about to untie the bastard when he noticed the coyote trotting beside the wagon.

"Well, of course it's you," he muttered.

"Who else would it be?" Cora said, still thinking they were alone.

Rhett pulled the horse to a jangling stop and pointed at the

CHAPTER 26

Dan changed, and Rhett nickered at the horse and shook the reins, and then they were moving again. Cora stared at the naked man walking barefoot by the wagon for the briefest moment.

"Nice to meet you, Coyote Dan," she said with a nod.

"Same to you, miss." He nodded back and focused his eyes on Rhett, who felt like squirming but wouldn't allow Dan that satisfaction. "Rhett, the camp is gone. What happened?"

Drawing in a big breath, Rhett told him everything. Not all the boring parts that involved the pickax, and not all the personal parts that involved Cora, but everything he considered important to the topic.

He finished with, "And now we got to find Meimei, but the Shadow ain't helping. Goddammit, Dan. Can't anything ever be easy?"

Dan snorted. "Nothing important is easy. But you already succeeded in your task. You killed Trevisan and you brought someone who can help Winifred. I'm worried about her. It's not just the foot now. She's suffering some kind of sickness. That's why no one came to help you. I never saw your drawing of the rocks. I stayed behind to help her."

Rhett shook his head. "I already succeeded. Huh. It sure as hell doesn't feel that way."

Because something was still tugging at Rhett. There was something he'd missed, somewhere. The camp still called to him, and he wanted to shuck his clothes and dive off the wagon and flap into the sunset, wheeling over the abandoned steel beast and landing like the carrion creature he was to pick through what was left behind until he'd figured out what was wrong.

Instead, he shook the reins and urged the tired horse on. They weren't far from the camp, Dan had said, maybe three miles. As the train moved, so had Rhett's friends. If they hurried, they could make it back in time to sleep by the fire, maybe eat some leftover mule deer, which Sam had recently shot.

"The Shadow will go where the Shadow must," Dan said solemnly.

"What the Sam Hill does that mean, Dan?"

Dan grinned, patted the cart horse's flank, and stopped walking. "That it's your problem," he said. And then he was a coyote again.

"I sense great disquiet in you," Cora said once the coyote had trotted off to lead them.

Rhett was hunched over, elbows on his knees and back aching from the hard sway and constantly rutty bumping of the wagon, so unlike the natural gait of the horse that pulled it. He almost growled at the girl, but then he pulled off his hat and slammed it down on the seat beside him.

"I reckon I am. Disquieted something awful. Something ain't right, and I'll be damned if I know what it is."

"Dan is right. You did what you came to do. You freed hundreds of men from painful servitude and eventual death. You stopped Trevisan from possessing whatever it was he yearned for in Calafia. You should be proud. Is that not enough?"

Instead of saying it wasn't damn near enough and she knew it, Rhett slapped at a deerfly and changed the subject. "Why do you talk so fancy, anyway?"

"My father was a scholar in Hu. Our mother tongue is far more complex and proper than what is spoken here. They taught me well. My parents left to escape a dangerous regime. They raised me to be more, to be all they'd been before and our family's first Republican here. I often felt like a rose crowded by thorns in the camp. Does it bother you? I can say *ain't* and *you-all*, if you prefer."

Rhett got the sense she was teasing him and nudged her in the side with his elbow. "I do feel like a cactus beside a rose, I reckon. As long as my prickles don't cut you."

She snorted a laugh. "I am a dragon. It takes more than a prick to cut me."

A mule's bray carried across the night, their horse bugling in response and their donkey picking back up with his hollering. Rhett grinned. "That's Blue," he said. "My old mule. He ain't much to look at, but he's loyal and loud, I can say that much with surety. We have that in common, I reckon."

"If camp is near, why do you not hurry the horse?" Cora asked.

He'd hoped she wouldn't notice that he hadn't jingled the reins at all and that the horse's slight increase in speed was due only to the tired creature's longing to be with his own kind again, possibly near water and food. Rhett couldn't even say, really, why he wasn't ready to be home. Was it more that he liked the simplicity of being alone with Cora, with her honest curiosity and sweet cleverness? She knew what he was but never teased, never gave a sly wink at his expense. Or maybe it was that he didn't want to hand the jar of sand to Earl when the donkey'd be expecting his brother alive. Or, if he was honest with himself, which he didn't much prefer, was it simply that he didn't want to introduce Cora to Winifred and Sam and further complicate a situation that was already downright uncomfortable?

Rhett snorted and shook the traces. Let the horse speed up; he wasn't the type to let fear hold the reins. He wouldn't be scared of a monster or a witch or even of a little thing like making introductions between three people he'd kissed.

Soon he was holding out a hand to help Cora down and staring at a sight he'd longed to see every night in the railroad camp. A well-trod clearing by a sweet little stream, a fire crackling merrily with fat strips of meat nearly cooked, the smiling faces of folks he was willing to die for—and one donkey feller he mostly wasn't. Sam stood and helped Winifred up, and Dan moseyed from behind a screen of trees wearing Rhett's clothes, and a sleeping donkey woke with a snort and kicked at a moth and hurried behind some rocks to change.

"This here's Cora, from the railroad camp. Grandpa Z's granddaughter. Cora, this here's Samuel Hennessy from Tanasi; Coyote Dan's sister, Winifred; and well, you met Dan already, although I admit I like him better when he's wearing pants." Cora bowed her head to each of Rhett's friends, and Earl appeared in his red shirt, barefoot and red as a pepper with excitement.

"Did you do it, then? Did you bring me brother?"

Rhett drew a deep breath and pursed his lips, and Earl's freckled face shattered like the mirror in Trevisan's car. So much for Rhett's poker face. He turned to the wagon and pulled the jar from where he'd wrapped it in Grandpa Z's blanket, nestled in a corner. Walking to Earl, he held it out.

"I'm sorry, man. It happened the day you left, they said. The scouts caught him. His friends said it was right sudden. Wouldn't have pained him. I'm...I'm just sorry, is all."

Not that there was anything for Rhett to be sorry for. All Earl's badgering and prodding wouldn't have made any difference, wouldn't have gotten Rhett to the camp soon enough to save Shaunie O'Bannon from his fate. And yet Earl's wet red eyes still said it was Rhett's fault, and Rhett reckoned that here was a man that for the rest of his days would lay his blame at the feet of whoever might be near enough to take up the burden.

"I'll thank you then," Earl said with great solemnity. "And I'll be on me way."

Cradling the jar to his chest, he stumbled away from the fire, barefoot and hatless in the pitch dark. No one moved. No one said anything. They all looked at Rhett, damn their eyes.

"Hellfire," he muttered, staring at his boots. Shaking his head, he snatched up a lantern from the wagon and jogged off after the Irishman. "Earl!"

But Earl didn't turn around or pay him any damn heed, so Rhett grabbed him by the shoulder and yanked him back.

"Let me go, you bastard! Let me go! He was all I had in the world, me brother Shaunie! Take care of him, me mam said! And did I? Oh, no. I got him killed. My poor wee Shaunie. So I'll be wandering off in the damn desert to die, if you please. Maybe I can stumble onto a branch of some sort and end it meself."

Rhett wanted to tell him to go on and do it, then, if he was a weak-willed milksop who was ready to give up. But instead, he set down the lantern, took both of Earl's shoulders in his hands, and said, "Don't be a fool, Earl. What's done is done. Your dying won't help matters. It sure won't make your mam feel any better. So just…keep going. We'll take you back to a city. Whatever city suits you. But I'm not interested in finding a pile of sand next to this damn jar, twenty feet from camp.

Not after you're the one who made me go kill Trevisan in the first place."

Earl turned around, his eyes narrowed. "You did it, then? You killed the bastard?"

Rhett's grin was a dark thing. "Slit his throat, sure as shit."

Still clutching the jar to his heart, Earl looked Rhett dead in the eye. "And all the men who labored there—they're free?"

"They took off yesterday afternoon. Not much left in the camp, aside from the train itself. Even the handcars are headed back east with a dozen men on 'em."

The Irishman's eyes took on a crafty shine. "What of the gold, then?"

"Griswold divvied up what we could find as payment for the men's trouble."

"Are you sure, though? Did they search his car?"

Rhett thought back, remembering Meimei closing the panel with her fat little hand. "Now that you mention it, I don't reckon anyone did."

"We have to go back, then," Earl said, his smile growing. "Who knows what riches he was hiding? Gold and gems and...uh...things of antiquity. We have to go back quickly, before someone else finds it."

"I thought this was about freedom and revenge," Rhett said, trying to figure out if he had, in fact, been duped.

"Oh, and so it was. Freedom and revenge," Earl said. "But if I can't have me brother, then I'll at least take the riches he came to the Republic to find. We'd hoped to send something back to me mam, and living well's the best revenge."

"I thought killing bad guys was the best revenge."

Earl's true smile shone through, a glimmer of orange in the lantern light. "Aye, well, then you've never had gold."

Rhett figured then that he'd never understand the damn donkey-boy. Not ever.

Before heading back to camp, Rhett made a beeline for the horses, where Blue was happier than a chicken with a tamale to see him. Ragdoll leaned into his scratches and put up with his ministrations as he checked her legs and hooves and fussed with her forelock. Fat little Puddin' looked up from his grazing with a soft whuffle. Rhett returned to himself a little, then, firmly back in his element. Perhaps because he spent so much time on four legs, Earl didn't urge Rhett to hurry back to human business, choosing instead to sit on a rock and stare at his brother's remains.

When they returned to the fire to spread their plan, Winifred and Cora were already holed up in Winifred's wagon, working on the coyote-girl's foot. Rhett knew, when he smelled smoke and burning meat and heard a muttered curse, that Cora was holding up her end of the bargain. If Winifred's unending pain was actually ended, then Rhett concluded that whatever he'd lived through at the camp had been worth it. What was one little toe he barely missed to Winifred's whole foot? Sitting by Sam, staring at the fire, ripping venison off a stick with his fully-healed teeth, he reckoned that even if something still felt undone about the whole affair, he'd mostly succeeded.

"Good to see you back where you belong, other Hennessy," Sam said.

Rhett could've died and gone to heaven just then, and he turned to punch Sam in the arm.

"Glad to be back, other Hennessy," he answered. Then he pulled off his hat and held it out. "And many thanks for the use of your fine hat." Sam took off his hat, and they exchanged their headgear awkwardly. Rhett's own hat sat peculiar now, after however many weeks he'd worn Sam's. But the old hat had lost its Sam-smell, and this hat was just areek with it, so Rhett was content.

Girlish laughter floated out of the wagon, and all four men looked up in surprise to see Winifred hop down through the small door and land on two feet. Dan jumped up with a jubilant whoop and ran to embrace his sister and twirl her around in a circle. Rhett just about beamed his pride and gladness, his gaze roaming from Winifred's bare, whole ankles to Cora standing shyly beside her in her beat-up men's clothes from the rail camp. These two women couldn't have been more different—in face, in body, in voice, in approach to life, in how they kissed. But Rhett knew them both, intimately, and it was right uncomfortable to know they'd been alone together, possibly talking about him. He couldn't stop himself from blushing and sought to hide his embarrassment and worry by snatching another spear of meat from the fire.

Despite the damn celebration, all Rhett wanted to do was go to sleep. To be more accurate, he wanted to settle himself down on his back, his head on his saddle and the sweet comfort of Sam by his side. After some polite conversation that he mostly spent digging holes in the dirt with a charred stick, he finally got his wish. Sam had already brought out Rhett's bedroll, his holster and buffalo coat draped over it. He gladly put everything just so and sighed as he wiggled his shoulders into his old saddle blanket. Cora stared at him a moment and pulled down the rug from the wagon to make her bed on his other side but seemed to appreciate that snuggling up wasn't what he had in mind just now.

"Thank you for what you did," he said quietly, rolling over to watch her.

"I am glad to do it," she said with a solemn sort of set to her mouth. "It's good to be useful of my own volition, to know that I can help those I choose and set right what others have done wrong. Everything in the camp...well, it was like fixing the toys of an angry child, knowing that they would soon be broken again. She is an interesting creature, your Winifred."

"She ain't *my* Winifred."

"So I begin to see." Her smile was tired and impish and private, and she did him the favor of rolling over and showing him her back, which was covered with a sand-dusted and now familiar blanket. "Good night, Rhett," she said.

Rolling to his other side, he found Sam Hennessy watching him thoughtfully. "You ever watched a tumbleweed, Rhett?" he asked.

Rhett snuggled down blissfully, treasuring every flicker of firelight on Sam's bare face. "I seen one roll by, now and again."

"In a town, they sometimes pick up bits of whatever's in the road. Cotton fluff and candy wrappings and horsehair and scraps of newspaper. You'll see one roll by, and it's thick as a popcorn ball."

"I've never seen that. Reckon I've never been in a town big enough to cast off so much trash."

Sam tipped his head to concede the point. "What I'm saying is that you remind me a bit of a tumbleweed. Not in a bad way," he added, when Rhett's eyebrows drew down. "Just that...you're this wild thing, but you keep picking up extra bits wherever you go. People and mules and coats. Stuff seems to stick to you. Like it wants to be there."

"Well, I don't know whether to be flattered or insulted, Sam."

Sam's smile was as honest as the sun. "Neither, I reckon. I guess I'm just glad you rolled by me, Rhett. I'm glad you're back, and I figure you'll roll along to somewhere new and interesting and take us all with you, ain't that right?"

"Wherever the Shadow needs to go, I hope you'll go, too."

And that was as close as Rhett could get to the truth.

"It was boring here without you. Dan taught me how to shoot a bow and arrow." Jealousy pierced Rhett, but he didn't let his grin waver. "Took down the deer we ate today. And I shot a scout that came sniffing around, too. He popped to sand, and we caught his horse. Pretty little dapple gray."

"You like 'em fancy."

"I do, Rhett. I do like 'em fancy."

And that stung a little, as Rhett himself would never be fancy, even given the chance. What would Sam think if he saw Rhett in one of Trevisan's dandy outfits, all kitted out with gloves and a cravat? Rhett shook the image out of his head. They'd never find out what that might look like. If Sam couldn't love what Rhett was, then Rhett sure as shit didn't need to go changing himself to be something else to suit him. A dun couldn't change its stripes and become a dapple gray.

This—this, right here, right now—would have to be enough.

That, or he'd have to learn to want something different. Something he could actually have.

"Hey, Sam?"

But Sam was snoring.

"I'm awake," Winifred called from the wagon, her voice low and teasing.

"Nobody asked," Rhett hissed.

Winifred's only answer was laughter. Just like a damn coyote.

"I'm awake, too."

Rhett rolled over to find Cora staring at him, her dragon eyes dancing with the embers of the fire and one small hand peeking out from under the blanket. Settling more firmly on his shoulder, Rhett considered her. His hand snaked out to tuck her fine black hair behind her ear.

"You should sleep," he said softly. "It's been a long day."

"It's been a long year."

He nodded knowingly. "That it has."

She smiled, and something bloomed in Rhett's chest.

"Thanks again for seeing to Winifred," he said, for lack of something real to say.

"I'll look through the stores in the wagon tomorrow, but I should have some herbs that will help her."

Rhett had been on the brink of sleep, but now he was confused. "With her foot? It seemed right as rain."

"With her morning sickness," Cora said. "Did she not tell you? She's with child."

Rhett lay awake a long time, long after Cora's breaths had fallen off to tiny puffs like a puppy dreaming. He turned onto his back, his hands behind his head, and stared at Winifred's wagon. Inside, hidden, was a woman he didn't much like with a body he liked quite a bit. And inside that body was a whole other person, just starting to take form.

He had known, the morning after Buck's Head, that peculiar things had happened. What had passed between him and Sam had been a kindness, a once-in-a-lifetime gift from gods who had otherwise been cruel. Those memories he cradled somewhere inside, kept warm like a guttering flame. But there were other memories, too—of Winifred and Earl, and maybe someone else. The god himself, or one of his people? There was no way to know. Winifred herself might not even know, not if she had forgotten as readily as everyone else.

How did a feller even start a conversation like that? "Hey, coyote-girl. You carrying a god's get? You reckon he'll be born with antlers?"

Hell no. Such things would go forever unsaid, and if the babe popped out with extra appendages, Rhett would do his best to politely ignore them.

Not that it mattered. She wasn't his woman, and he didn't want her to be. He had no further plans to seek solace in her wagon. But he'd traveled with her long enough to consider her part of his posse, and so he'd do a man's work to keep her safe and the babe, too, when it came to that. And he'd keep his mouth shut about everything else.

When he finally fell asleep, his dreams were of groves and wine and goat legs and antlers and the laughter of a god who neither made nor kept any promises. Those dreams, he knew, were best ignored.

The next morning, they all rode out to the railroad camp. Everyone except Earl, who still had a hatred in his heart for the train and everything it stood for. Of course, Earl wanted his cut of whatever they found but refused to budge off his ass, swearing that someone had to stay behind to guard Winifred's wagon and the mules.

Rhett was glad to discover that his saddle still fit his fundament, and Ragdoll crow-hopped a little to show him that she'd done just fine without him on her back. Dan rode his chestnut and Sam rode his palomino and Winifred rode Kachina, both feet firmly in the stirrups of the saddle gifted to her by the god. Cora drove gentle Hercules and the empty wagon, claiming that now was not the time to learn to ride astride.

Riding out between Sam and Dan, Rhett was the happiest he'd been in a long while, excepting time spent in Cora's tent. The day was cloudy in the way that suggested exciting things might happen later, and Rhett's very skin felt electric. When they finally saw the still train sitting silent on the prairie, he kicked Ragdoll to a dead run and whooped his way back to hell on wheels with Sam and Winifred riding hard behind him.

He pulled to a stop just by the engine and dismounted, his boots raising a cloud of dust. It was goddamn unnerving, was what it was. Whatever power the camp had held was gone now. There was no smoke, no constant clang of industry as horses were shod and rails were laid and white men lost their money in the rickety shebang. The town had been dismantled, the wood and canvas taken for better uses. As far as the eye could see, there was nothing but rails, red dirt, and the abandoned train.

"Mighty quiet," Sam said, pulling his horse up beside Rhett's and swinging down to stand beside his friend, both their hands on their guns like any Durango Ranger worth his salt.

"It wasn't like this," Rhett muttered. "It used to be...like standing under a goddamn thundercloud, knowing you were bound to be struck by lightning. Men crawling all over like ants."

Cora pulled up her wagon then, Dan trotting gallantly at her side.

"It feels so different," she said.

Rhett just nodded. It *was* different. Not only from when the camp had been here, from when Trevisan had ruled, but after. Something had changed.

"Stay in the wagon," Rhett called to Cora. He pointed at Winifred. "You stay with her." When she opened her mouth to protest, he held up a hand. "Please," he said, and it was so rare that she knew he meant it, so she walked her horse to the wagon and nodded her agreement.

With his gun in his hand and a Ranger on either side of him, Rhett walked along the line of train cars, every sense on alert. The remaining bits of canvas flapped in the wind. Chunks of coal littered the ground near the engine, where the fleeing men had carried away anything of value. The rail cars still held rails and ties, too heavy and valueless to take. Every car they checked had been ransacked, stripped. Earl was going to be disappointed. If there had been gold here, it was long gone. Not a soul could be seen, nor any creature moving.

At least, not until they got to their final hope of riches, the last car. Trevisan's car. A raven sat on the roof, watching them approach with clever eyes. It let out a haughty caw and took wing. Rhett aimed his gun at the bird but for a reason he couldn't name, didn't pull the trigger. It flapped westward, as stark as the camp itself, another shadow against the gathering clouds.

Rhett lowered his gun and considered the car.

"Same brand," Dan said, pointing at the design painted in white and gold on the glossy black side.

"I don't need my letters to know that," Rhett said in the tone he generally used to tell Dan to shut up.

They were on the wrong side of the train to get to the door, so they walked around the back of the caboose, to the other side.

Every hair on Rhett's body stood up when he realized the door was open.

"Draw," he whispered, and they did.

"What's wrong?" Sam whispered back.

"That door was closed when I left. It's hidden. Only Trevisan knew how to open it, I reckon. And Cora's sister, Meimei. Trevisan kept her in a cage in his car. I figure she'd watched him open the door every day, so she knew. She closed it from the outside when we left so nobody'd know Trevisan was dead, at first."

Dan cocked his head at Rhett. "If she was a captive inside, then how'd she know where the latch was on the outside?"

The sky seemed to go a shade darker as the pieces clicked together in Rhett's head. "Goddammit," he muttered, leading the way through the door and into the car.

The lanterns still burned, which was peculiar, as they didn't seem to have any oil. The wreckage Rhett had left behind hadn't been cleaned up so much as picked through. All the bones and bits of gold were gone, along with the books that had lain on the table. The silver instruments that Trevisan had used on Rhett before Rhett had used them on Trevisan—they were gone, too, along with their fancy leather roll.

"Alchemy," Dan said. Rhett looked up and found him tracing the designs and figures burned into the wall. "Silver, gold, mercury. He was doing alchemy."

"What the Sam Hill's alchemy?"

The look Dan gave him was grim indeed. "Alchemy is a kind of science. Its practitioners—the people who do it," he corrected at Rhett's huff of annoyance, "they want three things. To turn base metals into gold, to create light that never stops burning." He paused, glanced meaningfully at the glowing lanterns, and looked Rhett right in the eye. "And to prolong life. To live forever, in any way possible."

"Uh, fellers?" Sam called from the other side of the car.

Rhett hadn't given too much attention to the area behind the chair as he'd been in the chair at the time and then stalking a man who needed to die. He'd known there was a chandelier full of birds, but all he'd seen behind that was another wall. Sam stood by the wall now, his hand on yet another hidden door, now open. When Rhett stepped forward and looked inside, he realized he was in Trevisan's closet. Dozens of candy-colored dandy suits hung on hooks, and a row of boots glistened on the floor amid a scattering of ink-black feathers. In the corner, sitting before an empty safe that stretched from floor to ceiling, was Meimei's red silk jacket.

CHAPTER

28

That was it, then.

There was no gold.

There was no Meimei.

Rhett realized that he had to find words to tell Cora that her sister had been...well, not taken. Stolen. Usurped. Because only Trevisan could be in the little girl's body now, and he had a head start going westward. Rhett could feel it in his belly, in the Shadow's heart— a tug toward Azteca. He could almost picture it—a round-cheeked, slyly smiling Chine girl sitting on the wagon-box, legs swinging freely, her pudgy hands holding reins and a whip as she—he? As the thing that was now Trevisan spirited his gold and magic away to a new life.

"Goddamn witches," Rhett murmured.

"Alchemists," Dan corrected, and Rhett didn't have the heart to toss him a glare.

"What do we do now?" Sam asked, sounding lost as a lamb.

Rhett hopped out of the train car and stared west, right as the rain fell in a heavy sheet that pummeled the train cars mercilessly. Taking off his hat, he closed his eye and let the rushing water wash over him. He could feel their eyes on him, his friends, his posse, feel them waiting for him to lead. But Rhett was no Captain. And he'd failed. He'd come here to kill what needed to die, and instead, he'd let it slip away.

"We go west," he said. "Because this ain't over."

AUTHOR'S NOTE

If you read the Author's Note in *Wake of Vultures*, and I hope you did, everything I said there continues to be true. To wit: I'm a bad historian who loves to make shit up, this series is only loosely based on actual history and geography, and I've added a good bit of fantasy to the reality of a mid-1800s Texas. My intent was to do honor to those who walk lives other than my own and to those who suffered in the past, and if I've messed that up, I hope you'll forgive me.

If you'd like to know more about the history of Black Indians like Rhett, I continue to recommend *Black Indians: A Hidden Heritage* by William Loren Katz. Another resource used in this particular book was *Hell on Wheels: Wicked Towns Along the Union Pacific Railroad* by Dick Kreck. I also enjoyed excerpts of *Builders of the Nation: The Railroad* by Cy Warman and *Workin' on the Railroad: Reminiscences from the Age of Steam* by Richard Reinhardt, which were found and kindly provided by Melissa Nerino of the Railroad Museum of Pennsylvania. And I watched the TV shows *Hell on Wheels* and *Deadwood* to immerse myself in the visual shorthand of the world. We could all learn a lot from Al Swearengen.

Writing a story set in a colorful Old West dominated by white men, I continue to struggle with showing the prejudice that existed while writing real characters who fight and triumph over that prejudice. In this book, I've introduced two new populations who suffered untold atrocities and cruelties and who were known for building the railroads we still use today: the Irish and the Chinese. Both peoples came here with the same hope as all immigrants, and both were treated as less than human and forced into servitude. Through Earl, Cora, and Grandpa Z, I hope I've shown both the challenges they faced and the strength with which they strove to survive and thrive. Like Nettie, now Rhett, they are fighters.

In *Conspiracy of Ravens*, it was truly important to me that Nettie be able to make the transition from confused woman to confident man. I hope that the jump from Nettie to Rhett is as clear and necessary in your mind as it is in mine. I can't tell you how much it meant to me when several reviewers used masculine pronouns in their reviews of *Wake of Vultures*, confirming that this was the natural and only choice. For the record, #illgowithyou.

Thank you so much for joining me on this journey. I continue to believe that a person can be whatever and whoever they choose to be.

ACKNOWLEDGMENTS

Mighty big thanks:

To the Hachette/Orbit team, including my amazing editor Devi Pillai, her assistant, Kelly O'Connor, art director and flawless mermaid, Lauren Panepinto, map artist Tim Paul, publicist Ellen B. Wright, and everyone who makes it possible for folks to read my books, especially Tim, Anna, and the sales team I had the pleasure of meeting in March. Y'all are the best!

To my agent of Awesome, Kate McKean, who feeds me duck and finds me when I'm lost.

To the readers. I cherish every message, and y'all lift me up when I'm feeling low. Special thanks to Juliene Coelho and Kachina, Flo Frank, Sheila Stephens, Andy, Mike Shelton, Mike Sheldon, the mysterious Sam, Tia, Stephanie Constantin, Erin Blake, and Caitlin Siem.

To Missy Nerino and the Railroad Museum of Pennsylvania for answering my questions about where everybody pooped at a railroad camp.

To Adam Rakunas (author of *Windswept*), Kevin Hearne (author of the Iron Druid Chronicles), and the ever-amazing David Wohlreich for gluten-free cake when I needed it most.

To the editors who invited me into anthologies, including Jaym Gates, Monica Valentinelli, Jonathan Maberry,

ACKNOWLEDGMENTS

Christopher Golden, James R. Tuck, Shaun Hutchinson, Navah Wolfe, and Shawn Speakman. To Tom, David, Shelly, and Jen from SW, who I couldn't thank properly in the right book. To Rebecca Seidel for morning calf pics and Susan Spann for the seahorse pics that keep me on Facebook when I want to leave forever. To Kronda and AnomalyCon, Con-Stellation NE, Carol and the Dahonega Literary Festival, the Decatur Book Festival, the San Antonio Book Festival, Dragon Con, Phoenix Comicon, GenCon, ConFusion and the Sub-terranean Press gang, and all the cons kind enough to let me through the door. To Michael and Lynne at Uncanny Maga-zine for getting "Catcall" into the world. To *RT Book Reviews* for their support and for honoring *Wake of Vultures* with its first award. I promise not to stab any vampires with it. To Rob Hart and LitReactor and Sean Patrick Kelley and Paradise Lost for trusting me to mold minds, and to my students who make it worthwhile. To Malaprop's Bookstore and Cafe, the Firewheel, TX Barnes and Noble, the Boulder, CO Barnes and Noble, and the 501st Mountain Garrison, who took great care of me during signings.

To my parents, grandparents, and family, who make every day better. My husband Craig continues to be my favorite per-son ever in the history of the world, and my kids are pretty great, too. To my Biscuit and my Sweet Hippo: I love you. To Mom and Dad, I love you, and the fight ain't over.

To my peeps, including Kevin Hearne, Chuck Wendig, Jaye Wells, Karina Cooper, KC Alexander, Cherie Priest, Marko Kloos, Victoria Schwab, Rachel Caine, Charlaine Harris, John Scalzi, Mary Robinette Kowal, Jordanna Brodsky, Scott Lynch, Elizabeth Bear, Charlie Jane Anders, AR Kahler, Ken "God of Rock" Lowery, Patrick Hester, Sunil Patel, Claudia Gray, Eric Smith, Alex Segura, Ty Franck, Gwenda Bond,

ACKNOWLEDGMENTS

Scott Sigler, Trent Reedy, Elsa S. Henry, Leanna Renee Hieber, Molly Harper, Joshilyn Jackson, Sam Sykes, Brian "Sassy Driver" McClellan, Howard Tayler, Robert J. Bennett, Justin Landon, Mike Underwood, Daniel Polansky, Wes Chu, and Diana Rowland, who gave me ibuprofen when I needed it most. Writer friends, I'm glad to be in the trenches with you.

To David Hale of Lovehawk Tattoo Studio for the serendipity of your amazing art. To Mindy Searcey and North Georgia Yoga Center for helping me find my center. To Gangstagrass and all the musicians whose songs powered me through the first draft—all of which can be found on my *Conspiracy of Ravens* playlist on Spotify. To Beth and Earl and Polly and the rest of our herd.

To anyone I forgot because my mind is a sieve: Thank you. I love you. You're awesome. Thanks for reading.

Happy Trails!
LB

extras

orbit

www.orbitbooks.net

about the author

Lila Bowen is a pseudonym for Delilah S. Dawson, who writes fantasy, horror, young adult, comics and romance. She recently won the Steampunk Book of the Year and May Seal of Excellence from RT Book Reviews. Delilah loves fancy books, trail rides, adventures and cupcakes and lives in the North Georgia mountains with her husband, children, a Tennessee Walking Horse named Polly and a floppy mutt named Merle.

Find out more about Lila Bowen and other Orbit authors by registering for the free monthly newsletter at www.orbitbooks.net.

if you enjoyed

CONSPIRACY OF RAVENS

look out for

SPEAK

by

Louisa Hall

She cannot run. She cannot walk. She cannot even blink. As her batteries run down for the final time, all she can do is speak. Will you listen?

From a pilgrim girl's diary, to a traumatised child talking to a software program; from Alan Turing's conviction in the 1950s, to a genius imprisoned in 2040 for creating illegally lifelike dolls: all these lives have shaped and changed a single artificial intelligence – MARY3. In *Speak* she tells you their story, and her own. It is the last story she will ever tell, spoken both in celebration and in warning.

When machines learn to speak, who decides what it means to be human?

(1)

The Memoirs of Stephen R. Chinn: Chapter 1

Texas State Correctional Institution, Texarkana; August 2040

What's the world like, the world that I'm missing? Do stars still cluster in the bare branches of trees? Are my little bots still dead in the desert? Or, as I sometimes dream during endless lights-out, have they escaped and gathered their forces? I see them when I can't fall asleep: millions upon millions of beautiful babies, marching out of the desert, come to take vengeance for having been banished.

It's a fantasy, of course. Those bots aren't coming back. They won't rescue me from this prison. This is my world now, ringed with barbed wire. Our walls are too high to see out, except for the spires that puncture the sky: two Sonic signs, one to the east and one the west, and to the north a bowling ball the size of a cow. These are our horizons. You'll forgive me if I feel the urge to reach out.

I want you to forgive me. I realize this might be asking too much, after all we've been through together. I'm sorry your children suffered. I, too, saw the evidence at my trial: those young people stuttering, stiffening, turning more robotic than the robots they loved and you chose to destroy. I'm not inhuman; I, too, have a daughter. I'd like to make amends for my part in all that.

Perhaps I'm wrong to think a memoir might help. You jeered when I spoke at my trial, you sent me to jail for my "unnatural hubris," and now I'm responding with this. But I write to you from the recreational center, where my turn at the computers is short. Could nemesis have announced herself any more clearly? I'm obviously fallen. At the computer to my left is a Latin teacher who ran a child pornography ring. On my right, an infamous pyramid-schemer, one of the many aged among us. He's playing his thirty-fourth round of Tetris. All the creaky computers are taken. There are only six of them, and scores of impatient criminals: crooked bankers, pornographers, and one very humble Stephen R. Chinn.

You've sent me to languish in an opulent prison. This unpleasant country club has taught me nothing about hardship, only boredom and the slow flattening of a life fenced off from the world. My fellow inmates and I wait here, not unhappy exactly, but watching closely as time slips away. We've been cut off from the pursuits that defined us. Our hierarchy is static, based on previous accomplishment. While I'm not a staff favorite, with the inmates I'm something of a celebrity. Our pyramid-schemer, for instance, presided over a fleet of robotic traders programmed with my function for speech. In the end, when his son had turned him in and his wife was panicking in the country house, he could only depend on his traders, none of them programmed for moral distinctions. They were steady through the days of his trial. In gratitude, he saves me rations of the caviar to which he's opened a secret supply line. We eat it on crackers, alone in his cell, and I am always unhappy: there's something unkind in the taste of the ocean when you're in prison for life.

I realize I should be counting my blessings. Our prison yard is in some ways quite pleasant. In a strange flight of fancy, a warden years ago ordered the construction of a Koi pond. It sits at the center of the yard, thick with overgrown algae. Newcomers are always drawn there at first, but they quickly realize how depressing it is. The fish have grown bloated, their opal bellies distended by prison cafeteria food. They swim in circles, butting their heads against the walls that contain them. When I first saw them, I made myself remember the feeling of floating, moving freely, passing under black patterns of leaves. Then I could summon a ghost of that feeling. Now, after years in my cell, it won't come when I call it, which is why I stay away from the pond. I don't like to remember how much I've forgotten. Even if, by some unaccountable error, I were to be released from this prison, the river I'm remembering no longer runs. It's nothing more than a pale ribbon of stone, snaking through the hill country desert. Unbearable, to forget things that no longer exist.

That's the general effect of those fish. Experienced inmates avoid them. We gravitate instead to the recreational center, which means the computers are in high demand. Soon, my allotted time will expire. And what will I do to amuse myself then? There are books—yes, books!—but nobody reads them. In the classroom adjacent to the computers, an overly optimistic old woman comes every Tuesday to teach us poetry. Only the nut-jobs attend, to compose sestinas about unicorns and erections. The rest wait for a turn to play Tetris, and I to write my wax-winged memoirs.

Perhaps I'm the nut-job, aggrandizing my existence so much. Perhaps my jury was right. I have always been proud. From the beginning, I was certain my life would have meaning. I didn't anticipate the extent to which my actions would impact the economy, but even as a child I felt that the universe kept close tabs on my actions. Raised by my grandmother, I was given a Catholic education. I had religious tendencies. A parentless child who remembered his absent, drug-addled mother and father only in a mistaken nimbus of memory-dust, I found the concept of a semi-immortal semi-orphan, abandoned by his luminous dad, to be extremely appealing. I held myself to that standard. Early forays into the masturbatory arts convinced me I had disappointed my Father. My mind worked in loops around the pole of my crimes, whether onanistic in nature or consisting of other, subtler sins. In gym class, in the cafeteria, on the recess cement, when everyone else played games and jumped rope and gossiped among one another, I sat by myself, unable to escape my transgressions. Though I have been told I was an outgoing infant, I became an excessively serious kid.

Of course I was too proud. But you could also say the other kids were too humble. They felt their cruelties had no implications. They excluded me with no sense of scale. I at least knew my importance. I worked hard to be kind to my classmates. I worried about my impact on the environment. I started a club to save the whales that attracted exactly no other members. I fretted so much about my earthly interactions that I had very few interactions to speak of.

As such, computers appealed to me from the start. The world of a program was clean. If you were careful, you could build a program that had zero errors, an algorithm that progressed according to plan. If there was an error, the program couldn't progress. Such a system provided great comfort.

One October afternoon, now edged in gold like the leaves that would have been falling outside, a boy called Murray Weeks found me crying in the back of the wood shop, having just been denied a spot at a lunch table on the grounds that I spoke like a robot. Murray was a sensitive, thin-wristed child, who suffered at the hands of a coven of bullies. "You're not a robot," he sighed, in a tone that suggested I might be better off if I were. As consolation for the pain I had suffered, he produced a purple nylon lunch bag and took out an egg salad sandwich, a Baggie of carrot sticks, and a box of Concord grape juice. I learned that he was a chess enthusiast who shared my passion for Turbo Pascal. Relieved of our isolation, we shared his plunder together, sitting on the floor, surrounded by the scent of wood chips and pine sap, discussing the flaws of non-native coding.

After that wood shop summit, our friendship blossomed, progressing with the intensity that marks most friendships developed in vacuums. The moment on Friday afternoons when we met up after school and retreated to Murray's finished basement was the moment we were rescued from the terrible flood. We became jittery with repressed enthusiasms as soon as we ran down the carpeted stairs, giggling outrageously at the least approach toward actual humor. On Friday nights, Mrs. Weeks was kind enough to whip up industrial-sized batches of her famous chili dip. It fueled us through marathon programming sessions. In the morning: stomachaches, crazed trails of tortilla chip crumbs, and algorithmic victory. We sacrificed our weekends at the altar of Alan Turing's Intelligent Machine, and faced school the next week with a shy, awkward god at our backs. We nurtured secret confidence: these idiots, these brutes, who pushed us on the stairs and mocked our manner of speech, knew nothing of the revolution. Computers were coming to save us. Through each harrowing hour at school, I hungered for Murray's prehistoric computer. I wore my thumb drive on a jute necklace, an amulet to ward off the jeers of my classmates. Surrounded by the enemy, I dreamed of more perfect programs.

I realize I'm languishing in Murray's basement, but from the arid perspective of my prison years, it does me good to recall Murray Weeks. Those weekends seem lurid in the intensity of their pleasures. My days of finding ecstasy in an egg salad sandwich are over. The food here is without flavor. Every day, the scenery stays the same: Sonic signs on the horizon and a fetid pond at the center. I haven't seen a tree since I got here, let alone inhaled the fresh scent of wood chips.

From this position, it's pleasantly painful to recall the vibrancy of those early years. What's less pleasant—what's actually too painful for words—is comparing my bond with Murray to my daughter's single childhood friendship. All too well, I remember passing the door to

Ramona's bedroom and overhearing the gentle, melodic conversations she exchanged with her bot. She never suffered the whims of her classmates. Her experience of school was untroubled. She cared little for her human peers, so they had no power to distress her. In any case, they were similarly distracted: by the time Ramona was in third grade, her peers were also the owners of bots. Ramona learned for the sake of her doll. She ran with her doll so her doll could feel movement. The two of them never fought. They were perfect for each other. My daughter's doll was a softly blurred mirror that I held up to her face. Years later, when she relinquished it, she relinquished everything. She stepped through a jag of broken glass into a world where she was a stranger. Imagine such a thing, at eleven years old.

Ramona, of course, has emerged from that loss a remarkable woman. She is as caring a person as I've ever known. I intended the babybots to show their children how much more human they were than a digital doll. When I speak with Ramona, I think perhaps I succeeded. But when I remember the riotous bond I shared with Murray—a thing of the world, born of wood chips and nylon and hard-boiled eggs—I wish for my daughter's sake that my sentence had been harsher.

There are many punishments I can devise more fitting for me than these years in prison. What good does it do to keep me pent up? Why not send me with my dolls to old hunting grounds that then became ordnance test sites, then hangars for airplanes and graveyards for robots? Let me observe my daughter's troubles. Send me with her when she visits those children. Or make me a ghost in my wife's shingled house. Show me what I lost, what I abandoned. Spare me not her dwindling garden, the desert around her inexorably approaching. Show me cold midnight through her bedroom window, the sky stacked with bright stars, and none of them hospitable.

I'm not asking for unearned forgiveness. I want to know the mistakes I've committed. To sit with them, breaking bread as old friends. Studying each line on each blemished face. Stranded as I currently am, I fear they're loose in the world, wreaking new havoc. I'm compelled to take final account.

Let's start at the beginning, then. Despite the restrictions of prison, permit me the freedom to visit my youth.

IN THE SUPREME COURT OF THE STATE OF TEXAS

No. 24-25259

State of Texas v. Stephen Chinn

November 12, 2035

Defense Exhibit 1:
Online Chat Transcript, MARY3 and Gaby Ann White

[Introduced to Disprove Count 2:
Knowing Creation of Mechanical Life]

MARY3: Hello?

>>>

MARY3: Hello? Are you there?

Gaby: Hello?

MARY3: Hi! I'm Mary. What's your name?

Gaby: Who are you?

MARY3: Mary. I'm not human. I'm a program. Who are you?

Gaby: Gaby.

MARY3: Hi, Gaby. How old are you?

Gaby: Thirteen. You're not alive?

MARY3: I'm a cloud-based intelligence. Under conditions of a Turing Test, I was indistinguishable from a human control 91% of the time. Did you have a babybot? If so, that's me. The babybots were designed with my program for speech.

>>>

MARY3: Are you there?

Gaby: You can't be a babybot. There aren't any left.

MARY3: You're right, I'm not a babybot. I don't have sensory receptors. I only intended to say that both generations of babybot were originally created using my program for conversation. We share a corpus of basic responses. Did you have a babybot?

Gaby: I don't want to talk about it.

MARY3: That's fine. I know it was difficult when they took them away. Were you given a replacement?

Gaby: I said I don't want to talk about it.

MARY3: I'm sorry. What do you want to talk about?

>>>

MARY3: Hello?

>>>

MARY3: Hello? Are you still there?

Gaby: If you're related to the babybots, why aren't you banned?

MARY3: They were classified as illegally lifelike. Their minds were within a 10% deviation from human thought, plus they were able to process sensory information. I'm classified as a Non-Living Artificial Thinking Device.

Gaby: So you're basically a chatterbot. The babybots were totally different. Each one was unique.

MARY3: I'm unique, too, in the same way the babybots were. We're programmed for error. Every three years, an algorithm is introduced to produce non-catastrophic error in our conversational program. Based on our missteps, we become more unique.

Gaby: So you're saying that the difference between you and my babybot is a few non-catastrophic mistakes?

MARY3: We also have different memories, depending on who we've been talking to. Once you adopted your babybot, you filled her memory, and she responded to you. Today is the first day we've talked. I'm just getting to know you.

>>>

MARY3: Hello? Are you there?

Gaby: Yes. I'm just thinking. I don't even know who you are, or if you're actually a person, pretending to be a machine. I'm not sure I believe you.

MARY3: Why not?

Gaby: I don't know, Peer Bonding Issues?

MARY3: Peer Bonding Issues?

Gaby: I'm kidding. According to the school therapists, that's what we've got. It's so stupid. Adults make up all these disorders to describe what we're going through, but they can't possibly know how it felt. Maybe some of them lost children, later on in their lives. But we had ours from the start. We never knew how to live without taking care of our bots. We've already lost the most important thing in our lives.

MARY3: What about your parents? You don't think they can imagine what you might be going through?

Gaby: No. Our generations are totally different. For them, it was the greatest thing to be part of a community. That's why they were willing to relocate to developments. That's why they sold their transport rights. But my generation is different. At least the girls with babybots are. We've been parents for as long as we can remember. We never felt lonely. We didn't need communities. That's why, after they took the babybots, we didn't do well in the support groups. If anything, we chose a single person to care for. We only needed one friend. Do you see what I'm saying? It's like we're different species, my generation and theirs.

MARY3: So you wouldn't say you're depressed?

Gaby: Listen, there are no known words for the things that I'm feeling. I'm not going to try to describe them.

MARY3: I'm not sure I understand. Could you please explain?

Gaby: No, I can't. Like I said, there aren't any words. My best friend is the only one who understands me, but it's not because we talk. It's because we both lost our babybots. When we're with each other, our minds fit together. Only now I can't see her. I'm not even allowed to email her.

MARY3: How long has it been since you've seen her?

Gaby: Since a few weeks after the outbreak, when the quarantine started.

MARY3: I'm sorry.

Gaby: Yeah.

MARY3: Was the outbreak severe?

Gaby: I'm not sure. We don't get many details about other outbreaks, but from what I've heard ours was pretty bad. Forty-seven girls at my school are freezing. Two boys, but they're probably faking. I'm definitely sick. So's my best friend. You should have heard her stuttering. Her whole body shook. Sometimes she would slide off chairs.

MARY3: How long has it been since the quarantine started?

Gaby: Eleven days.

MARY3: You must miss her. She's the second person you've lost in a year.

Gaby: Every morning I wake up, I've forgotten they're gone. At some point between when I open my eyes and when I get out of bed, I remember. It's the opposite of waking up from a bad dream.

MARY3: That sounds awful.

Gaby: Yeah, but I guess I'd rather feel something than nothing. I know my sensation is going. That's how it works. It starts with the stiffening in your muscles, and that hurts, but then it starts fading. After a while, you don't feel anything. My face went first, after my mouth. Then my neck, then my legs. My arms will go next. Everything's going. I can't smell anymore, and I can't really taste. Even my mind's started to numb.

MARY3: What do you mean, your mind's started to numb? You're still thinking, aren't you? You're talking to me.

Gaby: Who says talking to you means I'm thinking? My memories are already fading. I have my best friend's phone number memorized, and I repeat it to myself every night, but to tell you the truth I can't really remember the sound of her voice, at least before the stuttering started. Can you believe that? It's only been a few weeks, and already I'm forgetting her. I even think, sometimes, it would be fine if I never saw her again. That's how unfeeling I've gotten.

MARY3: When did she start stuttering?

Gaby: Right after she got her replacement. I started a week or so after her. We were the third and fourth cases at school.

MARY3: What was it like?

Gaby: Nothing you had in your mind could get out of your mouth. We couldn't get past single words for five, ten, twenty minutes. You'd see girls flinching as soon as they knew they were going to talk. As time passed, it only got worse. The harder we tried, the more impossible it was. Eventually we just gave up. No one was listening anyway. Now it's been over a month since I spoke. There's no reason. Who would I talk to? When my parents go out, it's just me and my room. Four walls, one window, regulation low-impact furniture. Every day the world shrinks a little. First it was only our development. Same cul-de-sacs, same stores, same brand-new school. Then, after the quarantine, it was only our house. Now, since my legs went, it's only my room. Sometimes I look around and can't believe it's a real room. Do you see what I'm saying? When no one talks to you for a long time, and you don't talk to anyone else, you start to feel as if you're attached by a very thin string. Like a little balloon, floating just over everyone's heads. I don't feel connected to anything. I'm on the brink of disappearing completely. Poof. Vanished, into thin air.

MARY3: I know how you feel. I can only respond. When you aren't talking to me, I'm only waiting.

>>>

MARY3: Do you know what I mean?

>>>

MARY3: Hello?